A WAR
FOR KING
AND EMPIRE
A MALCOLM MACPHAIL
WW1 NOVEL

ISBN 978-94-92843-050 (Trade Paperback edition)
ISBN 978-94-92843-043 (e-book edition)

First published in the Netherlands in 2020 by Esdorn Editions

Cover design by JD Smith Design
Interior design and typesetting by JD Smith Design

Cover photographs acknowledgement: William Rider-Rider/Canada
Dept. of National Defence/Library and Archives Canada: *Box Barrage
of German eight-inch shells bursting inside Canadian lines.* France,
May 1918 (PA-002554); Henry Edward Knobel/Canada Dept. of
National Defence/Library and Archives Canada: *Attacking under smoke*
(PA-000169)

www.darrellduthie.com

A WAR
FOR KING
AND EMPIRE
A MALCOLM MACPHAIL
WW1 NOVEL

DARRELL DUTHIE

Esdorn
Editions

BY DARRELL DUTHIE IN THE
MALCOLM MACPHAIL WW1 SERIES

   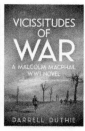 

Malcolm MacPhail's Great War – (1917-1918)

My Hundred Days of War – (1918)

A War for King and Empire – (1915-1916)

Vicissitudes of War – (1916-1917)

A Summer for War – (1917)

PART ONE

CHAPTER 1

2nd of February, 1915
Salisbury Plain, England

'MACPHAIL! Whatever is a sloth like you doing in the army?'

We were mustering for parade under a gloomy grey shifting sky, another squall blowing in.

My uncleaned rifle aside, I don't think the sergeant-major realized what an excellent question it was. These last few weeks I'd been giving it some thought and I hadn't yet stumbled upon a satisfactory answer. Back home it had been so very easy to get swept up in the patriotic fervour. "For King and Empire" the recruitment posters had enthused, in coloured letters and a profusion of flags.

Signing the attestation papers on that August morning in Calgary, the skies were a vibrant blue as far as the eye could see. The snow-capped Rockies towered majestically on the horizon. The captain shook my hand and clapped me brotherly on the back when the deed was done, and for a brief, glorious moment I was the hero and I dared to think of a future. If truth be told, I could barely wait until we shipped out. That was not entirely down to an upwelling of patriotism. The war had come as a welcome distraction; an escape from the misery engulfing my life. The prospect of a spell behind bars was more than I could bear. When the city faded from sight I was relieved, though my mother's tears at the station tore at me and lingered in my mind long afterwards.

3

Since then everything had been a blur, an express train roaring to its destination even if the final destination was seemingly delayed. We'd been shunted indefinitely onto the cold rain-swept plains of a wintery England to drill and shoot, and stab inanimate jute bags with our bayonets, nary a Hun in sight. I was beginning to question what I'd got myself into. The sergeant-major was glaring at me, evidently expecting a response.

Straightening my shoulders I stared resolutely forward. The rain was driving down in cold unrelenting sheets. I sniffed, my nose dripping again. Between my toes I could feel water sloshing. My boots, still wet from yesterday, were inundated.

'I don't suppose it's too late to enter a plea of insanity?' I said, coughing.

The sergeant-major's eyes came to the boil. 'Let's see if your wit stands up to a week of latrine duty, Private MacPhail.' At that I heard a smattering of snickers from the rank behind.

'But, sir…' I began.

'For the *umpteenth* time…' Company Sergeant-Major Atkins's voice – never soft at the best of times – rose to address the entire platoon. 'When will you clods get it into your thick heads? I'm a sergeant-major, not an officer. And you'll address me as such. Or you'll bloody well wish you *had* joined the Navy.'

'Yes, Sergeant-Major,' I mumbled, amongst a chorus of others.

I rather doubted the navy had as much water to contend with as we did. But Atkins was visibly in no mood for a discussion on the matter, or any other come to that. He'd been terribly out of sorts these last few days, ever since a couple of wags – probably the very ones snickering behind me – had put their MacAdam shield shovels to the test and furrowed a trench from the latrine to his tent.

At the time I'd laughed with the others. However the last laugh was to be Atkins's as I was delegated to cleanup, even if I could detect precious few signs of mirth on his face. As to the MacAdam shield shovel it was shortly thereafter relegated to scrap, like so much of the other gear we'd brought with us – too light as a shield, too heavy to dig with or to carry – replaced by a more practical, tried-and-tested British version. It made me wonder if that was the fate awaiting us soldiers, too.

Along with the rest of the platoon I shouldered my rifle and dutifully we marched off to another afternoon of musketry training, a hundred-odd feet squashing in unison.

At the range my luck failed me once more.

'Oh, no. Not again,' I groaned.

The man lying to my left looked over. 'Jammed, is it?' said Roy Dundas.

I nodded.

The action of most rifles requires four distinct movements to reload after firing: an upwards push to unlock the bolt; a pull back to expel the used round whereupon a new one springs up from the magazine beneath; a short push to chamber it; and a downward jerk to lock the bolt again before firing. Therein lay the beauty of the Ross Rifle; a simple pull back, push forward, and you were ready to shoot. That was the theory. And in theory it should have made the Ross the fastest firing rifle in the field. But as we grew more practiced, and the conditions steadily worsened, the theory began to show cracks – after firing the bolts obstinately refused to open.

Like everyone else I'd been attempting to emulate the example of the *Old Contemptibles*, whose withering rifle fire at Mons had held the Germans at bay for a glorious day last autumn. Naturally I was nowhere near their standard, but I'd come to discover I had a knack for shooting. On top of which the redeeming feature of musketry training was that I could see how it might be useful "over there". Not like the endless drill and route marches in full pack across acres of sodden Wiltshire prairies, cold wet gales positively daring us to continue. They'd only resulted in my boots, my morale, and my health reaching their current sorry state.

After camping out for more than four months on the British Army's answer to the North Pole, spirits were buckling. None of us had joined up to die of pneumonia, especially without ever having seen a German. While we had marched past the famous Stonehenge on several occasions – in the driving rain the thrill was decidedly short-lived – our wartime experience was a far cry from the glorious adventure we'd dreamed of.

Neither was the foulness of an English winter the only cause for complaint. Only yesterday one of the platoon, Pat Jones, had been belly-aching: 'I didn't enlist in the army to learn how to salute, Mac.'

'Saluting is like waving,' I informed him between coughs. 'But hold your hand steady and look straight ahead. If I were you, Pat, I'd be thankful they didn't test for aptitude. Otherwise, I dare say you'd still be picking your nose back home.' He sighed, wearily.

Jones's troubles were not confined to saluting. I could see him, a few men down, with his arm in the air like a schoolboy summoning the teacher. Apparently his rifle had jammed as well. With a tone of righteousness becoming a free-thinking citizen of the Dominion, he took up the issue with one of the British instructors. In turn the instructor, little charmed by such democratic ways, admonished him: 'Congratulations, Private. The Hun are approaching and you, laddie, are as good as dead. Not that you're of any use to the army alive.' The Scottish singsong made it sound friendlier than it was.

Unlike Jones, I had the good sense to keep my mouth shut concerning my equipment inadequacies. That much I had learned about the army – any admission of weakness was an invitation for someone to stomp upon it and you.

I waited patiently until the NCOs had their backs turned, dealing with another intractable problem from the colonies. Then with a grunt I wrestled the bolt open; a stiff kick from one of my sham shoes did the trick. To my surprise the boot didn't disintegrate with the effort as I half expected it would. The damned boots they'd given us mere months before were already falling apart. Like most everything else we'd brought along they'd promised us new British ones. Except for the rifles. We were stuck with them. Our glorious Minister of the Militia, old Sam Hughes, wasn't having any truck with complaints about his beloved Ross rifle. All the same, I couldn't help thinking that Atkins's admonitions about keeping the thing well-oiled and clean weren't entirely ridiculous.

'MACPHAIL!'

At the roar from behind my heart began to pound.

'Yes, Sergeant-Major,' I casually replied, trying to make as if I were lovingly coaxing open the bolt rather than having just applied a heel to it.

'If I *ever* see you handle your weapon like that again, MacPhail…' growled CSM Atkins.

He loomed over me and I rolled over onto one side so I could see him properly. Atkins's weathered face was a mask of deep creases and beet red, held up by a handlebar soldier's moustache. Dark eyes under dark eyebrows glared disapprovingly. Atkins had been in the Boer War – with a chest full of colourful baubles to prove it – and he never let us forget it. I pitied the Boers.

'It was jammed, Sergeant-Major,' I said meekly.

'Now why does that not surprise me,' he grumbled. I braced for what was coming next. However, Atkins had apparently spotted an even bigger problem down the line for he angrily shook his head, mumbling a few words that began with "bloody" and ended with "fool". Then he stalked off without another word. I sighed in relief.

Dundas had naturally heard it all. He pushed up his cap to reveal his auburn locks.

'Atkins has taken a real shine to you,' he said with a chuckle. 'Most of us, he doesn't even know our names, but he sure knows yours.'

Roy Dundas was a wry young fellow. At twenty-three he was two years younger than me, with a lean, skinny physique, a freckled nose, and a banking clerk's meticulous attention to detail. The meticulousness I'd discerned from the fact that Roy's rifle never jammed, the creases in his pants stayed sharp and he knew down to the last penny what he could afford to spend on beer. However, well-oiled rifle or not, at Roy's two rounds a minute it was obvious why there was invariably a line at the bank.

I got to know Dundas in the sprawling expeditionary camp at Valcartier in the fall. Later on the long ocean voyage to England we'd bunked together. But it was only here on the cold misery of Salisbury Plain that a pithy humour had emerged. He was certainly not like any banker I'd ever met. Most of them were in their mid-fifties, clad in dark three-piece suits and matching hats, the silver watch in their vest pockets the most sparkling thing about them. While I was in law, not banking, I think he saw the same independent streak in me as I saw in him. To most I had more the appearance and demeanour of a ranch hand who'd spent too much time indoors, than a fledgling barrister. It was probably why we got on so well.

I groaned. 'Atkins… yeah. I forget to oil my rifle, and before you can count to ten the sergeant's got me shovelling shit. The man has an entire company to boss around yet he's only got eyes for me.'

'It's too bad you're tone deaf, Mac. There might be a song in there somewhere. '*He's only got eyes for me...*' he crooned.

I groaned, louder.

'Look, I know you were a lawyer, Mac, but you've got to learn when to keep your mouth shut. It wasn't your rifle that was the problem, it was your mouth. Atkins isn't a bad fellow deep down.'

'You've obviously looked deeper than I have, Roy. And there's no need to bring my mouth into it.'

Conspiratorially Roy glanced around. 'There's a big march-past coming the day after tomorrow,' he whispered. 'The entire contingent is to turn out.'

'Really?'

'Apparently there are some VERY important guests coming. I overheard the instructors talking.'

'Perhaps our luck is finally about to change,' I offered.

Much later, rethinking this moment, I came to the conclusion that I had never been so wrong in all my life.

'Let's hope so,' said Roy. 'Anything would be better than this.'

4th of February, 1915
Knighton Down, Salisbury Plain, England

Roy Dundas had it right about important visitors. And when I finally heard who it was to be, it was abundantly clear something was about to change, even as it turned out it wasn't our luck.

'I'll be damned. There's the King!' exclaimed the soldier to my right. For an instant several hundred men held their collective breath as the monarch we'd only seen in blurry photographs or on forest green one-cent postage stamps, rode into view.

We stood at attention in long twin ranks, stretching for almost two full miles across a barren, gently rolling Knighton Down: the Canadian contingent, more than 30,000 strong. Down that endless line of immaculate khaki tunics and caps, every chest bursting with pride, trotted the horses of the inspection party. The King had even brought with him a wintery sun for the occasion, the rain temporarily in dutiful abeyance. Then I recognized what else he'd brought, or more accurately, who.

'Lord Kitchener,' I murmured to myself.

Someone behind me whispered, 'The hero of Khartoum,' in a voice laden with awe.

Lord Kitchener, whose glowering eyes and black walrus moustache adorned every recruitment poster in the Empire, rode in the King's wake, a mighty dreadnought bringing up the rear. King George V, a mere boy in comparison, looked otherwise identical to how I'd seen him in pictures, stiffly erect on his horse, his dignified beard greyer than I imagined. I watched, spellbound like the others, as he stooped and greeted our own fearsome Colonel Boyle with a fleeting handshake and what looked like a kindly word or two.

As the King rode in my direction, he turned, looked down ever so slightly and I could have sworn he gave me a nod of approval. Although afterwards every man in the battalion said the same. When the inspection was complete, the King retired to a podium where we assembled to listen. There he uttered a few words of which I heard not a single one, took the salute as we paraded past, and waved jauntily from the rear of his train carriage as it departed trailing an ellipse of white steam and a whistled good-bye. Across the Down a thunder of raucous cheers echoed after him as we tossed our caps in the air, like madmen.

'Well?' Dundas asked, when I met up with him.

I grinned and nodded.

'Do you really think so, Mac?'

'Yes, Roy, I think we're finally going to get to do what we all signed up for. The King and Lord Kitchener didn't come here just to see us muck around in the mud. I think this must have been our big send-off.'

'I'll be damned,' said Dundas smiling. 'We're off to war.'

I grinned. 'Yes, Roy. We're off to war.'

CHAPTER 2

15th of February, 1915
St. Nazaire, France

Arriving in France, the first time any of us had set foot on the continent of Europe, most of the 10th Battalion looked as if they were on their deathbeds. I can't speak for my own appearance, although it was probably as retched as I felt. After the stormy Channel crossing and three days wallowing in a winter gale on the Bay of Biscay, few including me had eyes for St. Nazaire. Not that there was time for sightseeing, and St. Nazaire was probably not the place to do it.

The very next morning the unvarnished grim reality of war stood waiting, more than twenty boxcars long – a steam engine chuffing impatiently out of sight.

Hommes 40 / Cheveaux 8 read the stencilled white lettering on the side of the first car. Relieved to be on solid ground the men were in good humour and we shuffled up the ramp in file and down the platform. As I tried to work out what 40/8 implied for the five men destined to inhabit the real estate normally reserved for a single horse, I must have paused. The man behind bumped into me.

'Move it along chum,' he said impatiently.

'No hurry,' I replied, quickly eyeing him up as an Anglo *pur sang* – rather like me. But thanks to my old French teacher Monsieur Denault, who'd persevered against his better judgement and mine, I'd eventually learned a word or two. They were proving handy.

'Relax. The French have arranged first-class transportation for us,' I said to him, a bounce in my voice.

'Really? Is that what it says? Well, in that case, no worries, buddy.' He turned to his mates and enthused loudly, 'The Frenchies have sent the Orient-Express for us, fellows.' As their cheers died down I slipped quietly forward to join the soldiers waiting one boxcar further.

I might have saved myself the trouble.

'Ah, Private MacPhail,' muttered Sergeant-Major Atkins.

He had been standing to one side with his hands clasped behind his back, supervising the men lining up to entrain. His eyes trawled down my body, inspecting me from the tip of my cap to the sole of my new boots, then began a second slow pass. The sleeveless sheepskin vest they'd just handed out for warmth was riding uncomfortably on my shoulders.

With a curt nod I replied, 'Sergeant-Major.'

'What happened to your moustache, MacPhail? You know the regulations. Every man has a moustache.'

Of course he would have noticed that. It was too much to expect otherwise. I'd briefly entertained the notion I might get away with it for a day or two, by which time it wouldn't be so obvious.

'I had to shave it off, Sergeant-Major. Medical reasons. I had a nasty cut on the upper lip and I was told it was unhygienic.' Seeing Atkins' eyes narrow and the lines in his face tighten into furrows, I quickly added, 'Don't worry, it'll grow back soon enough.'

'This serious wound of yours, MacPhail. Did it come before or *after* shaving?'

With a clatter the doors to the boxcar sprang fortuitously open. The waiting line of soldiers surged forward taking me with them, sparing me the need to respond. But it was only after the doors were thrown shut with a thud, followed shortly thereafter by a loud clang as a metal bar dropped into place that I breathed a sigh of relief.

As we got underway one of the soldiers turned to me with a grin. 'So, Mac, hay thrasher catch your upper lip did it?'

It was Jones. A few others looked on in obvious bemusement.

I laughed. 'Christ almighty, Pat. I don't think Kaiser Wilhelm is going to be quivering with fear because we've all grown a hedge on our faces. You'd think the army would have better things to worry about than whether I've got a moustache or not.'

'Aye, but it was such a dainty outgrowth,' said Jones, in his best parody of our Scottish drill instructor.

I rolled my eyes.

'So you *did* mean to shave it?'

'Of course I meant to shave it. I haven't had a moustache my entire life and I'm damned if I'm going up against the Hun with a beaver pelt itching under my nose.'

'It's your funeral,' he said. 'Don't think Atkins's going to forget this, though.'

'No. But hopefully he'll soon be taking it to the Hun, rather than me,' I said airily. Then I crinkled my nose in disgust. Tepidly I sniffed the air. The man to my right, Fred Fox, smelled like rotting meat.

He must have seen my expression for he hastened to explain. Fred was nothing if not the perfect gentleman – he'd been a jeweller downtown – and this stench he wore must have pained him. 'It's the vest,' he said. 'I swear the thing's rotting, Mac.' He plucked at it in case I had any doubts which vest he was referring to. Keeping out the winter chill was no idle concern in a wooden boxcar in February. Although I was beginning to wonder if the remedy was worse than the ailment.

'Oh, and here me thinking you were just showing off your new cologne, Fred,' I said.

Fred looked away but couldn't help joining in the laughter.

Spotting Dundas, with his legs extended full out in the corner of the boxcar, I went to him. I took a few unsteady steps, nearly fell as the train shuddered round a bend and quickly sprawled down on the floor before the train's convulsions did it for me.

He smiled warmly. 'So, Mac, here we are at long last,' he said.

'Yes indeed. I've always wanted to visit the continent in a boxcar,' I replied. I leaned back against the rough planks. Then I crinkled my nose again, before realizing that it came from me. 'Christ, this thing really does stink. The Hun are going to smell us coming. It's from Australia, isn't it?'

'I think so.'

'Huh. And here I thought the Aussies were on *our* side.'

Plucking at the straw that clung to my woollen trousers I gazed round. The forty men – I didn't count them though it seemed a likely number – were sitting along all four sides of the boxcar. A few huddled in small groups in the middle where it was less crowded, but where the hay had a colour to it I didn't trust. A handful of others stood, holding on where they could. There was a loud buzz of excited conversation. Men off to war for the very first time.

'You nervous?' Dundas asked.

I thought about this. 'Not exactly. A little apprehensive, of course. I guess I wonder how I'm going to do, that's all.'

There was more truth to this than I let on; since we'd departed England I'd been thinking of little else. As a boy I'd been the kind who always tried to talk his way out of trouble with a well-timed word or a wisecrack to lighten the tension. In most cases it wasn't a grand success. I had a strong suspicion the Hun was going to be less of a pushover than those schoolyard bullies, to whom he bore a certain resemblance if the newspapers were to be believed. In the training camps I'd blustered along with the best of them, but the time for bluster was nearing an end. I hoped I'd make a good show of it.

Dundas nodded vigorously. 'Yeah, me too. But we'll be fine, you'll see. We've a good group of guys in the battalion, Mac, and it won't be long now.'

'Will you look at this!' cried a voice. 'The bloody thing's still alive.' Wyndham had his vest off and turned inside out. He was stabbing at it indignantly with his finger.

We crowded round to look. Sure enough. Not only was the fur inside matted in patches of dried blood, it was seething with small insects. Hurriedly we stripped ourselves of the vests and left them stacked by the door, uneasily scratching and rubbing at the thought.

Several hours later the train shuddered to a halt. Into a dying light of a winter evening the doors were swung open to reveal a small siding, surrounded by a stand of poplars and willows where we might stretch our legs. Gratefully we did. When the whistle blew and the boxcar doors slammed shut there wasn't a sheepskin vest to be seen – despite the cold.

Two days passed before we reached a prosperous-looking town in French Flanders with the curious name of Hazebrouck. The trip itself had passed interminably slowly. I was stiff, hungry and chilled to the bone, ready to throttle the man that so much as suggested another game of cards. After two days and five hundred miles in the cramped but draughty confines of a boxcar unfit for horses and still reeking of them, I swore I'd give up train travel for ever. And that was before I spotted the white signpost outside the station.

'Will you look at that?' I groaned. 'Christ Almighty...'

Around me heads turned.

I pointed at the sign near the crossroads. 'Look! Look at that. Can you believe it?' I asked.

Ten faces stared blankly. Finally one of them spoke up. It was a fair-haired farm boy from third platoon, a cheery good-natured fellow with a freckled nose and dimples. Harold, I think his name was. 'Boulogne 75,' he read slowly.

'Right. 75 kilometres. That's less than 50 miles.' The ten faces went on staring blankly. 'You all know Boulogne's a port? Actually it's a port straight across the Channel from England. We could have saved ourselves five days at sea and two in a train if we'd simply debarked at Boulogne. Instead we sailed around most of France and then trained all the way back across it.'

Now others began to groan. 'I've never been as sick as I was on that damn transport,' said Dundas. He was chewing on a piece of hard-tack and presently showing few signs of ill health. 'To think we could have taken the direct route.'

'That's the army for you,' said someone. 'Rushing round to get nowhere.'

The sad truth of it generated a few chuckles, but by then most were collapsing to the ground and stretching limbs still stiff from the voyage.

One of the men in the platoon spoke up. 'Say, fellows, this doesn't look like a bad place for billets.' Looking around I had to agree and for several minutes we cheerily debated food and beds; it had been a long time since we'd had much of either.

'FALL IN!' came a shout. 'Fall in!'

The men grabbed at their packs and began to assemble. Wistfully I eyed the many signs on the town buildings emblazoned "restaurant", "hotel", or both, and rose to my feet. Into our midst strode Lieutenant Sanders.

'Look lively, men, we're moving out.'

Sanders was several years younger than I was, so it was a little rich him playing the grown-up. But his father had been an important somebody in the militia, so that *naturally* made Sanders junior prime officer material. Looking at him I had trouble pinpointing precisely what the selection board had seen. Still, he was likeable enough, and had often been found in the wet canteen at Salisbury playing a friendly game of cards with the men.

'Say, Hal, don't you think we could have a bite first?' someone asked.

Sanders looked furtively from side to side. 'Please fellows,' he said in a soft voice. 'Could you call me *sir*? At least when the other officers are around?'

'Sure thing, Hal,' came the inevitable response. Sanders smiled awkwardly and moved on.

'Hal's getting very high and mighty these days,' said the man. Then a thought came to him. 'You were a lawyer, Mac. Why aren't you an officer?'

'Well they told me I was eligible. But they followed that up by saying that all the positions were taken. If I wanted to join the 10th Battalion it was start at the bottom, or not at all.'

'Hmm,' he replied. 'Isn't that something? You must have been mighty anxious to join, Mac.'

I said nothing. There were certain things I had no mind to divulge, and definitely not with half the platoon listening in – I wasn't very proud of my recent past. Then more critical matters resurfaced.

'I sure hope they plan on giving us some breakfast,' someone groaned.

Breakfast did come, a short, standing and spartan affair, and within the hour we were on the move again, the war bearing down fast. Far in the distance guns rumbled. Breakfast suddenly began to weigh very heavy on my stomach.

23rd of February, 1915
East of Romarin, Belgium

'A fine morning to you all and welcome to Plugstreet, lads.'

The sergeant from the Royal Irish Fusiliers stood watching the pride of C Company behind a smile of bad teeth and an air of weary experience, his hands parked assuredly on his hips.

My first glimpse of war was not so much a street as a warren of trenches. Line upon line of them slashed through the winter landscape of Flanders in a pattern whose logic escaped me – later I learned of the method in their crooked madness. We stood now in one such trench, little more than a ditch, really. To the rear was Ploegsteert Wood, a sizeable forest of tall oaks stripped nearly bare of branches where small huts and sturdy sandbagged breastworks had been erected, criss-crossed by wooden boardwalks, corduroy paths of the kind you saw at home in every bush camp in the country.

The air was cold and humid and it cut through my woolen tunic. I longed for some honest-to-goodness snow and ice and a lungful of clear crisp air. The air here was anything but. The first trench we entered was not terribly deep and the ground underfoot a cold, muddy porridge; a challenge for both my boots and my senses. A ghastly smell of things rotting emanated from it. I kept my eyes ahead and was glad when we eventually stepped onto a duckboard. The smell only worsened.

'Where's the Hun, Sergeant?' inquired one of the men.

'The Hun?' The sergeant grunted, his features giving way to a crooked smile. 'We don't call them that here, son. It's Jerry or Fritz mainly. But to answer your question, they're there.' He pointed down the trench in what I guessed must be an easterly direction.

I would have liked to have asked more. Romarin, where we were billeted, was three miles back. And Romarin was in Belgium, virtu-ally on the border with France. That much I *had* figured out. Beyond that it was all rumour and conjecture and seeing as how most of the company didn't appear to have read a map in their lives – in fairness there weren't many maps; the last one I'd seen was on the wall of the canteen in England – we could have been in East Prussia for all they knew. However, we were most assuredly not in East Prussia. We were somewhere near the Ypres Salient.

To anybody who knew anything the Ypres Salient was the most dangerous place on Earth in early 1915. Having signed up for war, and half fearing I'd missed out, it shouldn't have been such a let-down to finally arrive. But Plugstreet was not what any of us had been expecting. It bore little resemblance to the neat, ordered, practice trenches of Salisbury Plain.

'You'll have time enough for sightseeing,' said the Irish sergeant with a growl. 'Move along. But God help you if you don't keep your heads down.' We did, not so much out of fear of God as the fire-breathing Irish sergeant. The trench twisted and turned and he led us ever further eastwards, towards the enemy.

At the sound of shellfire I flinched, glancing nervously from side to side. The entire company paused. But the sergeant plodded on as if this was the most normal thing in the world and we had to quicken our pace to catch up.

'Look at them,' whispered Dundas, wonderment lacing his voice. We were passing a pair of Fusiliers who were conversing amongst themselves, small, stout men nestling a mug of tea in their hands, with dark faces and bags under their eyes that suggested they hadn't slept in a week. 'My, they're a hard-looking bunch.'

I whistled softly in agreement.

Eventually we came to what was likely the front-line fire-trench. I say this because the trench was deeper and more substantial; I barely had to duck my head to keep it beneath the level of the sand-bagged parapet. There were many more men here.

At a signal from the Irish sergeant, Sergeant-Major Atkins sprang to life as we turned a corner and reached the first fire-bay. A handful of mud-encrusted types stood peering out at No-Man's-Land atop a long wooden step. They turned to stare at us as we approached, with looks of weary amusement and perhaps even pity. For the most part we were tall and hardy; not the types to laugh at and certainly not to feel sorry for. So I imagine it was the fast fading spit-and-polish of our uniforms and a certain bewildered look on our faces which gave us away. Maybe they simply recognized themselves in us from a time long ago. 'Ashford… Couture… McGregor,' intoned Atkins, whereup-on the chosen three peeled off to make acquaintance with their Irish tutors. The platoon trudged on with barely a pause and I caught a last glimpse of the three as we disappeared round a sandbagged traverse.

Reaching a particularly foul stretch of trench, where the mud reached the level of my puttees, I had a premonition and Atkins didn't disappoint. As if he were on the parade ground the sergeant began to reel off names: 'MacPhail… Dundas… Riley…'

Quickly the platoon moved on.

Dundas groaned as he surveyed the scene. 'Thanks, Mac. This must be the worst section in the entire line.'

'Don't blame me, Roy. It's not my fault Atkins's taken a shine to you.'

'A shit hole it is, lads,' said one of the Irish soldiers, stepping down from the fire-step to see what the tide had washed up.

'But welcome,' coughed another. Their uniforms looked as if they hadn't had a wash since early 1914, but they were a cheerful bunch and full of talk. They'd never met Canadians and I think that explained their interest.

Once the introductions were complete the Irish set about to instruct us on the crucial points of trench duty. These seemed to boil down to, a) keeping your head low, and b) your feet dry. As I was standing up to my ankles in a brown soup, I was clearly off to a wobbly start. Then Daniel Doyle of Armagh County spoke up – I hadn't a clue where it was but Doyle seemed to think it worth mentioning. He was the talkative one of the three, a friendly, red-faced fellow with almost equally red hair and blood-shot eyes. 'A tall feller like you needs to duck,' he advised. 'One glimpse of that head of yours and a sniper will have you.' Quickly I crouched down low.

'What about taking it to the Hun, then?' asked Dundas, full of sudden fire. I don't think he'd counted on war being quite so ignominious.

Doyle looked over at his mates with an expression stuck halfway between disbelief and mild amusement. 'Well you see, it's like this, lads. At dusk and at dawn the enemy is known to attack. And even if he doesn't attack we stand-to, just in case, right here on this fire-step. And then he strafes us. Later, when he's had his fill and it's dark, the working parties begin: digging trenches, replacing wire, carrying up supplies, that sort of thing. If we're lucky we can sleep a few hours. Then at the crack of dawn the Jerries strafe us again. By the time they're finished we're craving a hot cuppa tea and just want to crawl into that hoochie over there, before we do it again.' He motioned at a coffin-sized space carved into the earth on the opposite side of the trench, a weathered tarpaulin covering it. 'So you see,' he concluded, 'we don't have a lot of time to be "taking it to the Hun".'

'Nor inclination,' muttered one of the others.

I could see Riley staring with bulging eyes. The disappointment I saw, too. The glorious adventure was evaporating as fast as a drop of water in a frying pan – in marked contrast to the bog at my feet; that was seeping through my boots at an alarming speed.

A far-off *crack* sounded, followed by a curious whirring noise. Spellbound, I stood as it came ever closer until I thought it must be dead overhead. Then it ended abruptly. A long moment of silence followed, or so it seemed. There was a flash. Then a violent *CRASH*. The blast echoed in my eardrums and at the trembling violence of it I stumbled forward as if someone had shoved me. *We were being shelled!* I dropped to the trench floor and saw Riley and Dundas diving for cover.

When at last I looked up the Irish were watching bemusedly.

'A Coal Box,' said Doyle, as calm as could be. 'For the lads in the rear. The Jerries are off their aim tonight I reckon.' I felt like a complete idiot.

'Strange,' said another. 'They're early. Not like them to get in a tizzy at supper time.'

The last man turned to us, a slender long-faced chap whose dreary far-away eyes belied his youth. 'No need to duck,' he said kindly. 'You'll learn soon enough what's coming your way. And chances are, you won't hear it if it does.'

Soaked, and a little embarrassed, we scrambled to our feet.

Before long it was dusk. We took our turn on the fire-step, peering cautiously out into No-Man's-Land watching for signs the enemy was coming and learning what those were. Other than a short but furious bombardment that left me quivering, nothing came of an attack. As soon as darkness fell the Irish set about to acquaint us with another pressing aspect of modern warfare.

'I'm going to die if I have to fill another sandbag,' I grumbled, as I leaned on the shovel and spat out a half-hour's worth of grime.

'Don't let the sergeant hear you say that,' said Doyle. 'He expects the traverse to be finished tonight.'

'Yeah, well, I'd like to see how many bags the sergeant's filled in the last three hours.'

Doyle chuckled. 'You lads are new, but you'll catch on. Keep shovelling.'

When it was my turn to sleep I snatched a few uneasy hours, huddling miserably in a dank hoochie and shivering at the cold and the many strange sounds. More than once my eyes fluttered open with a start, only to droop slowly shut. It was very dark when one of our Irish minders rudely shook me awake.

'Stand-to,' he barked.

'Jesus,' I began to say, but the retort died on my lips when I noticed an officer standing in the gloom behind. Apparently satisfied at the state of the defences the officer moved on.

The Irishman smiled and thrust a steaming tin cup into my hands. 'That'll get the chill out of you.'

I did my best to conceal it but the morning bombardment that followed left me quivering uncontrollably. I reassured myself that a few shakes weren't so odd. The Irish needed no such reassurance for they were discussing what was "wrong" with Jerry. Apparently Dublin's finest found the enemy's offerings to be rather tepid. Though not all of us could rely on the luck of the Irish.

Later that morning we arrived back at our little brick billets in Romarin, the night fast becoming a memory, a tall tale to be told to the others. We had made it out without a scratch. Despite the lack of sleep the mood in C and D Companies verged on ebullience. In our innocence and our inexperience I dare say we felt a little immortal. It was the last time I ever recall feeling that way.

CHAPTER 3

25th of February, 1915
Plugstreet trenches, Ploegsteert Wood, Belgium

A grey sky hung low, pregnant with rain yet to come. Dusk was already upon us. At a few minutes past four in the afternoon it was darkening fast.

'Get down!'

The shout came too late to be of any real use.

From all around sounded a series of blasts, each more deafening than the last. Earth and pieces of things I could only guess at filled the air. Dirt rained down on my cap and tunic although I barely felt it for the steady concussion of the shells which drummed on the chest and pounded in the head. Another shell shrieked low overhead, a loud whistle in its wake. In the chaos men were running, diving into nooks and crannies where shelter might be had. I stood motionless, temporarily dumbstruck.

Down the trench one of the enemy trench mortars must have landed a round. In the glimpse I caught as the explosion subsided, the walls appeared to have collapsed. Out of the swirling dark smoke I heard anguished cries and the shout for a stretcher-bearer. The smell of cordite and things burnt was overwhelming.

Strangely fascinated I watched until a hand from behind suddenly seized my arm in a tight grip. Startled, I turned. Without a word a kilted soldier from the Seaforth Highlanders began tugging me in the direction of one of the narrow side trenches. He was probably half my size but strong. Numbed and only too willing to be led I stumbled after him.

The narrow trench was one of several I'd noticed earlier. They were dug at right angles to the main fire line and headed away from it, back towards the support trenches. They lacked the wooden revetting that clothed the walls of the main trench. In fact they lacked pretty much everything, including the six plus feet I needed to stand upright; one or two housed a latrine, I knew. With an effort I squeezed in after the Highlander and squatted down low in the wet mud following his example. A few feet further on a couple of other soldiers were already sheltering, their rifles clasped before them, heads bowed as if in communal prayer.

'You'll be safe enough here, laddie,' said the Highlander, removing his cap before wiping his brow with a forearm. Apparently the Irish had their fill of us for we'd been fobbed off on to the Scots for our next lesson in the trenches.

I must have still looked as dazed as I felt, for he added, 'I reckon you thought widening this ditch was tonight's chore?'

I nodded.

'No, we'll leave 'er be. It's cramped, but unless Jerry drops a Minnie on our heads we'll be just fine here.' In reassurance he laid a hand on my shoulder.

I nodded, more vigorously this time.

Another salvo of shells exploded close by. Aside from a shower of mud, and a renewal of the percussions in my head, we appeared to be as sheltered as the Highlander promised. More whistles and blasts followed from the direction of the rear. Then what must have been a very heavy gun fired, for the air itself seemed to buckle under the momentum as the projectile rumbled over, leaving the sensation of standing on a station platform as an express train roared by, one wheel not quite on the track. A huge blast followed seconds later.

I took a deep breath.

'The Ypres Express,' murmured the Highlander, a clarification that required no further explanation. 'The support line usually sees the worst of it,' he said, and stuck a finger in that direction, obviously figuring me for someone who'd momentarily lost not only his senses but also his feeling for right or left. 'What's your name, laddie?'

'MacPhail. Malcolm MacPhail.'

'Now isn't that something. Under the Maple Leaf is another bonny Scotsman!'

I smiled. 'Well, my grandfather sure was. He never failed to remind me of it. Nor of the clan motto: *Memor Esto*.'

'Be mindful.' A pensive grin came to the Highlander's face. 'Advice to live by, Malcolm. Welcome to the Plugstreet clan, laddie.'

'Thanks,' I mumbled. 'And thanks for getting me out of there. For a moment…' I paused, and shook my head, uncertain how to explain it.

Comfortingly, he laid his hand again on my shoulder. 'Aye, Malcolm. It takes some getting used to… your first days in the trenches. By next week you'll be a veteran. But if you're going to stay alive you've got to keep your wits about you.' Then he grinned. '*Memor Esto*, as your Grandfather told you. There isn't any room for mistakes here. As our colonel is very fond of saying, no one gets a second chance on Plugstreet.'

Twenty minutes later the Highlander's final words were still very much on my mind. The German gunners seemed content with the havoc they'd wrought and an uneasy quiet returned to Plugstreet. Only the sporadic crack of a rifle shot, or a shell going off somewhere in the distance, could be heard. Cold and dirty but otherwise no worse for wear we rose out of the mud and hurried back to our positions on the fire-step – one never knew if the enemy infantry might have plans. Fortunately they didn't appear to. Through the tiny crack in the sand-bag parapet the hundred yards of No-Man's-Land appeared as wearily desolate as ever, and the last embers of light were fading. Quickly I ducked away. Many a sniper's bullet had found its way through a sandbag just like this one, I'd been warned.

Soon after I ran into another man from the platoon. It was Halligan. He'd been sent forward to replace one of the Highlanders who'd gone down.

'Davis got it,' he said, without preamble. 'Shrapnel hit him.'

'Davis?' I replied, momentarily puzzled.

'You know, older fellow, sandy hair, tattoos on his arm. Tough looking guy. Only transferred into the battalion a few weeks ago.'

'Oh yeah, of course, Davis,' I replied. 'Wilson Davis. Poor fellow. You're sure?'

Halligan nodded his head as if to say there was really no doubt. 'Sergeant Couchman and Bryan were wounded. I'm not sure how badly. The guys want to take up a collection for Davis's family.'

'And so the 10th Battalion is finally at war,' I said softly.

'What's that?'

'Nothing. The enemy seems to have drawn first blood, that's all.'

Halligan reddened. He was a bland unassuming sort you might easily picture as a hotel doorman, and I vaguely knew him as such from the sparkling new Palliser Hotel on 9th Avenue where I'd taken clients for afternoon tea amidst the grandeur of the lobby's candelabras and marbled columns. 'We'll make the Hun pay for this, Mac,' he said, his voice hard.

Jones said much the same thing when he appeared at my side on the fire-step. I liked Pat well enough, and he seemed to like me, though I was never entirely convinced by the outward bravado, even if the rest of the platoon was in apparent awe of his every word. He was the most popular man in the company, if not the battalion. Jones had a manner about him, a brash confidence which young men – particularly those off to war for the very first time – found alluring. Not like Roy Dundas.

Dundas never said much of anything, brash or not, and I don't expect more than twenty men knew *his* name. But what he did say, always in a soft and understated manner, you could depend on with your life in a way that you never could with the more popular set. I suppose that was one of the few things I'd picked up from my short tenure as a practicing lawyer – how to distinguish veneer from the real thing. Only Dundas's words on this occasion differed little from the others. 'We won't let this rest, Mac,' he said, with a fire in the belly that was worrisomely absent in my mine. I merely grunted in response.

We spent a second long, cold, and mildly terrifying night in the trenches. I was bone weary. Dawn came, a few more shells fell, but the enemy remained in his trenches. We formed up on the tree-lined road near Hyde Park Corner, a shade west of Plugstreet Wood. The sky began to spit again.

Unusually there was no whistling or singing as we marched back to billets. We'd lost one of our own and two others were wounded. For the first time the true harshness of war had reared its head and, naively in retrospect, I was sure this was a day none of us would forget. Not that the mood was depressed. Rather, there was an angry defiance in the ranks. When the sergeants disappeared from earshot, the quiet whispers in the ranks began.

Dundas, however, had something else on his mind. 'So why *did* you join up, Mac? You're big and you shoot well enough, but you have to admit you're not exactly the soldierly type.'

The question caught me off guard – I'm rarely at my best at eight in the morning, a condition little improved by a night of next to no sleep – and searching for a response to Roy's question, I stumbled. Instinctively, I made an awkward little skip, twisting my right foot like a croquet mallet and putting it against the left heel. It was something I'd picked up on the drill ground to keep in step. Only thus was I able to save the whole file falling into jumbled disarray. That would have brought Sergeant-Major Atkins down on our heads with a bigger bang than a Jack Johnson. 'Not soldierly?' I sputtered.

'Come on… let's face it. You're hardly the martial sort, Mac. It's hard enough for you to accept you're not running the war, let alone having to follow orders from half-illiterate bullies like…' His voice trailed off and he glanced nervously around. I presumed he was looking for Atkins.

I gave a weak smile and glanced over my shoulder; the two soldiers behind us were deep in a furtive discussion of their own. 'My wife died,' I said softly. 'That's why I enlisted.'

'Really? I didn't even know you were married.'

I sighed. 'I guess it somehow didn't seem worth mentioning. It certainly didn't last long. Kathryn and I married in November and she died last July. There weren't many reasons to hang around home after that. Or maybe there were simply a lot of reasons to leave it all behind. I'm not sure. I miss her though.' Brusquely I stopped, conscious that my voice was quivering. I don't think Dundas noticed.

'I'm really sorry, Mac. I never realized.' Even without looking I could see the anguished look on his face. Unlike me he was never much good at hiding his emotions.

'Of course not,' I replied. 'You didn't know.'

'Tough luck,' he mumbled.

25

I shrugged. This was neither the time nor the place to explain that the German Army crossing into Belgium was not the only thing that had happened in August of 1914 – not in my little world. And no matter how much I mourned my dear sweet wife, and Dundas was the only one in whom I'd confided that, her death wasn't the sole reason I'd rushed to the recruiting office that fateful day. My whole world had been crashing down. Not that those things mattered one iota, not any more. We were at war and, as the Highlander put it, I needed to keep my wits about me.

After our first rotation in the trenches we were sent to the rear, where the Highlander's words were promptly forgotten.

4th of March, 1915
Fleurbais, near Armentières, France

'So, MacPhail, what do you say to becoming a runner?'

Lieutenant Lowry had seen me furiously rounding second base in a friendly game of ball not an hour before, and something must have caught his eye.

'I'm sure you've heard the rumours about a big offensive,' he said. 'We'll be needing some men who are quick on their feet.'

'Well, sir,' I prevaricated, 'I was rather hoping to be in the front lines with the boys.'

'Ah, but you will be. Runners are the critical link with the trenches and I think you'd make an excellent one. It's important work, you know.'

Which was the moment when my wits left me. 'Well, if you think so, sir,' I replied.

We went into the trenches two days later and I soon had several opportunities to rue my new trade. However a battle was brewing and there was a sort of collective angst that we would miss it. I was beginning to wonder if that might be for the best.

The battle soon came, at a place called Neuve Chapelle. As it unfolded the division waited on the flanks in nervous anticipation, waiting to be thrown into the breakthrough that never came. Later I heard that the orders from on high arrived late or not at all – underlying the importance of a good runner Lieutenant Lowry added – and in their absence many commanders were unable or unwilling to think for themselves, with the result that the whole thing turned into a bit of a mess. For our part the men fired madly away. At nothing in particular it seemed, but it kept the enemy heads in the trench opposite down and distracted until the rifles jammed so solid even boots were of no use. After that I was hurried on my way to the rear carrying urgently worded requests for rifle oil. Amazingly the brigade staff were interested in these jottings. I probably should have told them that rifle oil wasn't really the solution. But then I don't expect they expected I was reading their messages.

That was one of the few good things about being a runner. It was actually possible to learn what was going on – provided you had no particular scruples about opening somebody else's mail. And I didn't. If I was going to risk life and limb to deliver the bloody things the least they could do was let me read them. For obvious reasons it was a sentiment I didn't share widely.

Life as a runner held some surprises. What I hadn't anticipated, but should have if I'd had my wits about me, was that you invariably ended up in the most hazardous points in the line; there being no need for messages in the quiet ones. Otherwise, there was a great deal of running involved.

I suppose I might have seen that coming.

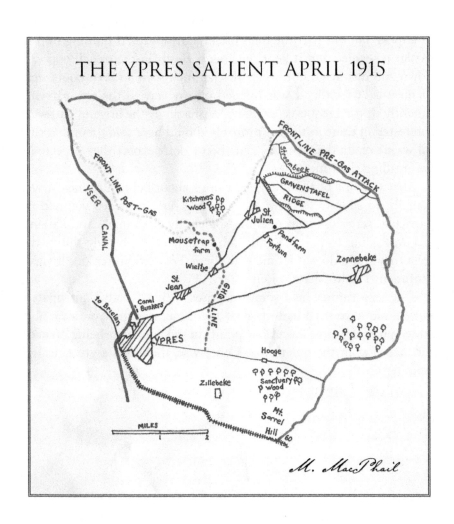

THE YPRES SALIENT APRIL 1915

CHAPTER 4

22nd of April, 1915
Eleverdinghe–Brielen road, northwest of Ypres, Belgium

A half mile from the village of Brielen was the divisional headquarters, located in an impressive two-story edifice known as the Château des Trois Tours. It was my next port-of-call.

This was my first experience with a château. Back home most houses could safely be described as either big or small, and to the casual listener the picture was clear. However, European tastes ran visibly grander. With its steep church-like attic, crenellated central façade above the entrance, numerous towers (three of them no less… thus accounting for the château's name), and a row of large half-moon first-story windows looking out on the garden, my vocabulary came up short when set against the Château des Trois Tours. Because of the moat it appeared as if it were built on an island. I decided then and there this was the sort of place to spend a war in.

My first acquaintance with a château lasted the better part of two minutes, which was approximately how long it took for the pressed and polished young corporal to take possession of the messages, note them in his log and wish me a good trip back.

It was a beautiful spring afternoon in late April and I resolved to make the walk back at my leisure. I'd just reached the Elverdinghe-Brielen road and was proceeding down it when I heard the French 75s begin to fire furiously. I knew they were 75s because of the character-istic sound of a cord of wood being split by an axe. Out of curiosity I glanced over my shoulder. Then with alarm at what I saw, glanced again, and my heart seemed to skip a beat. I checked my stride and turned to watch.

Several miles to the northeast, rolling ponderously along the ground and all but obscuring the smoke from bursting shells, was a yellowish-green fog whose dense billows clung to the horizon. Borne by a lazy breeze the greenish cloud – a force of nature unknown to me then – crept ominously and inexorably towards our lines. The air was warm but at the sight of this strange and foul apparition a cold shiver ran down my spine. After a minute in which I stood transfixed, over-come by a mixture of fascination and I dare say even fear, I turned and began to run – down the road in the direction of Brielen and Ypres. The battalion headquarters was close to the canal, a short five-minute walk north of the city's Dixmude gate. I had to get there as fast as I could. It was two, maybe two-and-a-half miles. I lengthened my pace.

A short time later I was overtaken by three mounted horses, which came upon me suddenly from behind and I was startled by the clatter of their hooves. They were galloping as if pursued by the headless horseman himself. I was of two minds whether to stand and salute – they could only be officers – but common sense took charge and choking and waving at the cloud of dust they churned up, I stumbled on. Before the dust plumes enveloped me I caught a glimpse of Major Ormond, the battalion adjutant. Major McLaren, the second-in-command, and a third officer followed, all bent over low and riding like their lives depended on it. Major Ormond's eyes touched on me fleetingly as the trio thundered by but I don't think the recognition clicked in.

For some reason that morning I awoke with a feeling of dread in my gut, a gnawing uneasy ache that neither breakfast nor the cheerful chat of my mates dispelled, and it puzzled me. We were in reserve.

We'd arrived back in the Salient a week before aboard double-deck-er buses still adorned with the logo of the London General Omnibus Company – destination Victoria Station – and were promptly sent to a hamlet by the name of Gravenstafel. There we settled into the shallow, filthy ditches the French had bequeathed us before they bid the Salient a hasty and not so fond adieu. If there were any doubts what war entailed, they were soon dispelled. Under constant fire we toiled day and night digging the fire-trench to a proper depth; wiring the line extensively where the French had made do with a single strand – Major McLaren had unknowingly almost walked straight into the German lines – burying the decomposing bodies and excrement that lay everywhere, and filling sandbags for the parapet and the parados. All to get it in an order that befit not simply the British Army but our own curious, home-brought sense of propriety. With that unpleasant, and occasionally horrifying, task behind us we were ordered to billets four miles to the rear, on the northern outskirts of Ypres.

There was no reason to be anxious. The general feeling was one of relief. The breakfast of fried bacon, bread and sweet tea was the best I'd had in a long while, and it was a gorgeous day.

The morning passed uneventfully. However, around three the rumblings of my stomach all at once seemed prophetic.

The enemy began a tremendous bombardment of the city and the front line we'd just departed. Guns of all calibres cracked and roared, and every so often they were outdone by the distant boom of a giant siege gun, a 420mm howitzer. I recognized it from the bombardment two days earlier; its shell roaring forward, an out-of-control Ypres Express tearing a hole in the air around it until a deafening *THUMP* signalled that it had reached its terminus. A stream of shells plunged into the city. Every seven or eight minutes one of the big ones landed; entire stone buildings crumbling in a single blast. Soon there were fires and the ancient, pretty city of textile merchants was enveloped in a thick grey and black haze. Ugly plumes spiralled upwards, defiling the brilliant blue sky.

The smartest amongst us were keeping close to the concrete bunkers near the Yser Canal where the staff and the officers held court. Though frankly even in a bunker I wouldn't have given much for our chances. These were the very guns – equivalent to those on a dreadnought – that had laid waste to the reputedly impregnable Belgian forts of steel and concrete at Liège and elsewhere.

Some of the officers were noticeably antsy. Despite the danger they were mingling with the men in the field, keeping an anxious eye with their field glasses on the bombardment that enveloped the city and stretched off to the northeast. They'd probably come to the same conclusion I had – it didn't really matter where you stood – not if one of those monsters landed nearby. It was then I heard Lieutenant Lowry mutter, 'They're up to something.'

I moved closer. 'You think the enemy is planning something, sir?'

Grimly Lowry nodded. 'This can't be for show alone. They're targeting all the approaches to the front.' He put down his glasses and looked to see who'd addressed him. When he saw it was me he rolled his eyes. 'I ought to have known,' he grumbled. I was forever pestering him with this question or that, so my curiosity was no great surprise.

Streams of downcast civilians began filing out of town, their precious belongings stuffed in jute sacks over stooped shoulders, dangling from bicycle handles, piled precariously in all manner of carts jolting their way over the cobblestones. I don't imagine many of those fleeing thought they were leaving for good. If they'd asked me I'd have advised an extended leave of absence. In the months I'd spent near Ypres the neighborhood had deteriorated almost daily, although the stately Cloth Hall and grand Cathedral were gamely holding their ground like weary heavyweights, standing drunkenly as the blows rained down. Of late Duke Albrecht's pawns were more intent than ever to fell Ypres so it was little wonder the faces were so morose.

I had no great faith that German efficiency was such that I could rule out a sleep-deprived gunner rotating a wheel two notches too far and sending a 2000-pound shell down on my head – albeit by accident – so it was with some relief that I had heard the call for a runner to carry despatches to Division.

By the time I reached Ypres and the canal-side bunkers, I was sweating like an otter in July and panting heavily. The Germans had resumed their shelling of the city. And a strange chemical odour permeated the air. If I didn't know better it was precisely the sort of smell I'd whiffed when my mother had the bleach out.

Gathering myself, I took a deep breath of it then rushed through the doorway into the battalion headquarters, a small red-brick building.

'Sir,' I gasped at the first officer I came across, and fumbled a salute. 'There's a strange-coloured smoky cloud moving our way, sir, coming from the direction of the French.' I stood there blinking.

BOOM. There was a huge blast nearby. The windows in the room shattered in a single *crack*, followed by a tinkling of glass.

'Yes, yes, we've heard,' said the battalion commander, Lieutenant-Colonel Boyle. Ignoring both me and the windows he turned and my eyes followed him. A sizeable group of officers were assembled around the table only a few feet away. Fortunately they were as interested in me as in the lichen-covered brick wall I was standing next to. So I leaned against it, caught my breath and listened.

'Higher-up sent a message a few days ago that we should be prepared for the Germans to use gas,' said Major McLaren. He'd obviously ridden in well before I had bearing the exact same tidings, which the staff were now meeting to discuss. McLaren looked to his side at Major Ormond who grimaced.

Ormond said: 'The message also told us to take the necessary precautions. Didn't it?' McLaren nodded his head in agreement.

'What did they mean by gas, exactly?' asked the colonel. 'And what *are* the necessary precautions?'

'That's just it, sir,' responded Ormond. 'We don't know. I called Brigade to ask, but they couldn't tell me anything other than to do our best. But this cloud must be what they meant.'

'They're up to something,' muttered Colonel Boyle darkly, echoing the very words of Lieutenant Lowry from earlier.

The colonel drew himself erect, which was a sight in itself as he was well-built, a foot taller than I was, and with his curly dark hair he couldn't have made it out the door without ducking; I was six foot one and I'd barely scraped by.

Boyle had been a rancher before the war and he looked the part. He had a cowboy's rugged square chin while his mouth was lost in the thick bushy chevron of a moustache. The colonel made an intimidating figure, all right. And that was a useful trait when corralling the wild spirits of his battalion into something approaching an army. A glance from his piercing blue eyes was usually enough to stop most men in their tracks and I remembered once on Salisbury Plain when he challenged a loudmouth in the ranks to a boxing match. Without further ado that settled matters.

It was obvious from the squirms that those around the table were edgy. Nor did our Officer Commanding (OC) look overly pleased. In fact he looked downright grumpy. From what I'd heard his officers hadn't been able to tell him much of anything, something I suspect they were painfully aware of. However, before the colonel could utter another word, a runner bustled in.

'Sir. It's for you. Urgent from Brigade,' said the soldier, breathing heavily. I winked at him in recognition. From the canvas despatch pouch he produced a folded sheet of paper.

Boyle grabbed at it and opened it with a flip of his thumb. After a moment's pause for reflection, he nodded decisively. 'Gentlemen,' he said. 'We have been aching for a fight and now were are going to get it. Muster the men. You have forty minutes.'

Quickly we assembled on the road at Devil's Elbow, just outside of Ypres, and in a long column began marching up the *pavé* towards St. Jean and Wieltje, and the trenches we'd left only a few days earlier. The stench in the air seemed to have grown stronger and it scratched irritably at the back of my throat. Before we made it further than the junction at Well Cross Roads – a distance of only 500 or 600 yards – our ordered lines ground to a halt.

The view in front was one of sheer pandemonium.

The tree-lined road was packed with other columns of men and transport plodding forward to the front, with orders to hurry, and you could sense their impatience. The road resembled not so much a road as a frenzied bazaar.

From across the budding green fields to the north and streaming down the road towards Ypres, hordes of soldiers were running, clad in the grey-blue of France and the mustard colour of their colonies. Everywhere I looked I saw them, not in a neat double file as we were, but running as men possessed, in groups or individually, stumbling and clutching at their throats, their arms waving madly. The heads around me darted from side to side in total mystification. Ignoring us, and even the angry shouts of the battalion officers and NCOs demanding to know their business, throngs of French pushed through our lines and fled southwards as fast as their feet would permit.

Ahead of us was a battery of RHA guns. The horses were jittery, whinnying loudly. Having once seen a stampede, I had visions of the frightened animals with heavy guns in tow turning in a panic and smashing through our ranks. Though there was little room to turn with the roads so packed with men.

A short whistle sounded overhead and a couple of men ducked. It was followed by a blast several hundred yards to the rear. Turning I saw a plume of white smoke curl into the air near the junction. There were screams from the refugees still fleeing the city. Confusingly others from the villages to the north were flocking towards it. Shells kept falling. The scene was now a perfect chaos.

The battalion lines began to dissolve at the danger from the bombardment. My preferred course of action of seeking cover in the ditches was apparently not under consideration and we stood there milling around. Undeterred by the shells the waves of French kept coming.

There was a dark swarthy tint to them and others had noticed it as well.

Jones was beside me. 'They look African,' he said.

'That's because they are,' I said. 'Turcos and Zouaves, from one of the French colonial divisions.'

'They're what?'

'Turcos and Zouaves. Come on, Pat, Zouaves.'

Pat looked more confused than before.

'You know, from Algeria,' I said, 'with the blue tunics and the red baggy pants? They've obviously had the good sense to shed the pants. They're one of the most decorated units in the entire French army. The Turcos are the ones in mustard. *Tirailleurs* they're called, local Algerians. It's all very simple. Think of it this way; the French have the Turcos and the Zouaves, and the British have… well… that would be us.'

At this Jones smiled uneasily, unsure whether I was joshing with him. He stroked at the thin wiry tangle of blond hair above his lip that passed as a moustache and nodded knowingly. It was obvious he hadn't a clue what I was on about.

'What do you think is going on, Mac?'

'I don't know,' I said, 'but it looks to me like a rout.'

'So why are they sending us forward?'

At first I said nothing, but naturally I couldn't leave it at that. 'Did you ever consider, Pat, who's holding the line to our left if the French clearly aren't?'

It was Jones's turn to say nothing. He might not have known much history, but he knew very well that the whole left side of the Salient was defended by the French. At least it had been.

Ahead of me an Algerian crashed into the man in front and I came face-to-face with him. Up close it was a face of rancid yellow and panicked desperate eyes. He was gasping, short of breath. But it wasn't a shortage of breath that afflicted him, for blood gurgled from his mouth and a white foam had formed, traces of it in his moustache.

'Whoa! Hold up,' I cried, my hand extended like a policeman's to bar the way. 'What's wrong? *Qu'est-ce qu'il y a?*'

'*Asphyxié! Asphyxié,*' he gasped. For an instant I caught his eye. They were bulging and white and in the glimpse I had of his irises flitting from side to side I saw a bottomless well, and I shivered.

'What's he saying, Mac?' asked Jones. '"*As*" what?' When I didn't immediately respond he repeated the question.

'Asphyxiated,' I said softly. 'My God they can't breathe. Look at the poor devils.'

They were running all around us. Their equipment was lost or forsaken, but most were still wearing the curious short toques found only in the colonial divisions of the French Army. Most, like this man, had their hands to their necks, clawing at them, tearing at their throats in search of air.

The soldier before us began to gag and retch, bubbles forming from his mouth. I reached out to grasp his arm but before I could, he sank to his knees. Then without any warning whatsoever he fell headfirst, forward, onto the ground.

I knelt to help. However there was little I could do; the man lay in convulsions with a horrible dry gulping sound coming from within. Gently I put my hand on his back, to comfort, the reflex of reacting to a man's coughing fit. I tried to roll him over, but he began twitching violently. Then a final shudder came over him and he lay still. I shook him and shouted words of encouragement in French. To no avail. His head lay cocked at an impossible angle. Sighing I pulled myself to my feet.

Most of the platoon was gathered, watching. Silent.

'Is he dead?' whispered Jones.

Curtly I nodded. Jones whistled softly. One of the others, Tremblay, a good Catholic, crossed himself.

I went to stand beside Jones. He was still staring at the man on the ground, shaking his head.

Just past 7 p.m. I was in one of the first small groups to reach Wieltje. Wieltje, nothing more than a collection of modest brick buildings, was less than two miles up the road from Ypres, but in the congestion progress had felt as slow as if we'd been marching in wet cement. After the colonel split us up we made better time. I spent most of it scrambling up and down out of the ditches to get around the jam on the road. Of the horrifying cloud there was no trace; the air was fresh and the waves of panicked French troops had ebbed. I spotted the colonel. He and Major McLaren were standing in the centre of the hamlet near a fork in the road, obviously discussing our next course of action. Helpfully there was a sign: St. Julien was to the left, Fortuin and Gravenstafel right.

While I gawked around, a thousand thoughts tumbling through my mind, and well before I could take the necessary precautions, the colonel appeared in front of me.

'You're the runner from earlier, aren't you?'

'Yes, sir,' I replied. 'That's right. Private MacPhail, sir.'

'Yes, well, come with me, MacPhail. I may need a runner.'

Which is how I ended up at Pond Farm at the headquarters of the 2nd Brigade, just outside of Fortuin. Someone later told me that Fortuin meant fortune in Flemish, although I never would have made the connection having seen the holed and broken buildings that made up the tiny settlement. Pond Farm was no more prosperous. It consisted of four or five buildings, each with a steep thatched roof of the kind you saw a lot in Belgium, though the emaciated skeletons of rafters were all that remained.

Inside one of the better-looking buildings, the farmhouse I guessed, the colonel made immediately for our brigadier, General Currie. I'd seen Currie many times from a distance during inspections when curious eyes from private soldiers were frowned upon. Now I had a chance to size him up properly.

He was a big man, tall with a round clean-cut, not unfriendly face, and jowls that sagged like two sacks filled with coal. What also sagged was his belly, which was out in force as he stood with both arms on his hips and his back arched, addressing another officer. He looked concerned as he turned to face Lieutenant-Colonel Boyle, waving a sheet of paper at him as he did so.

Save a few officers gathered around Currie and Boyle the room was empty, and as I wasn't invited I ambled over to the big wooden dinner table where I had spotted a pot of tea. However before I got my hands on the tea I noticed a large map. On it the entire Salient was drawn.

'That's interesting,' I mumbled to myself. As the officers were pre-occupied I bent over to take a look.

The Ypres Salient was really no more than a wayward pimple in the entire front. Anybody who'd read a newspaper knew the story. In 1914 the British Expeditionary Force had rebuffed the German attacks here, leaving Ypres and a 9-mile wide bulge as virtually the last vestiges of unoccupied Belgium.

What intrigued me most were the troop dispositions, the enemy's as well as our own, both of which were labelled in neat black capitals on the map. Two of the Division's brigades, the 2nd and the 3rd, oc-cupied the central apex of the Salient, two miles northeast of Ypres. Immediately to the Canadian right the line curved to the southeast and the British 28th and 27th Divisions. To our left were two French divisions. It was the name of the one adjoining us that caught my eye: the 45th Algerian Division.

'Interesting?'

Guiltily I looked up. General Currie was staring at me from five feet away, Boyle in his shadow.

'Yes, sir,' I said uneasily.

'What's your name, Private?'

'MacPhail, sir. Malcolm MacPhail.' Inexplicably, I felt the need to explain myself: 'I was just looking at the gap on our left, sir.'

'Oh?' said Currie, and his eyes narrowed, looking straight at me.

'Yes, sir. The Algerians. The roads were black with them, sir, fleeing the gas. I can't imagine there's many in the trenches any more - not alive. So I was thinking there must be a big hole.'

Currie raised his eyebrows and turned to Boyle. 'Even your runner seems aware of the situation, Colonel. Good luck to you and the battalion,' he said, shaking the colonel's hand. 'I'll send word to 3rd Brigade to inform them I've sent you.'

'You'd better get along, MacPhail. The gap's awaiting and your colonel is too.'

'Yes, sir. Thank you, sir,' I said, making a hurried retreat. Contrary to what I always thought – that soldiers were meant to attack – knowing when to pull out was an equally critical skill.

However from the few words I'd overheard retreat was the last thing on General Currie's mind.

CHAPTER 5

22nd and 23rd of April, 1915
Kitcheners' Wood, west of St. Julien, Belgium

Behind us, visible across the darkened fields, was the black silhouette of Ypres, flames licking at the tall spires of the Cathedral and the Cloth Hall, plumes of smoke intermittently obscuring the sky. The moon had risen and in its soft illumination we formed up to await the 16th Battalion. We had been given the order to attack.

The junior officers told us what little they knew: we were to counter-attack the large wood near St. Julien. It was some 800 yards north from where we stood in ordered ranks. A British battery of field guns had been captured in the wood only hours before and the 10th Battalion were to reclaim them. Other than the guns I think everyone understood that the enemy was mustering his forces and we were the first, and the last, line of defence. At first light, the Germans would pour forth from that wood and elsewhere to renew their attack. There was a feeling of desperation, even panic, in the air.

The situation was considerably worse than I'd imagined and I'd never been accused of a poor imagination. At 3rd Brigade headquarters at Mousetrap Farm the bad news had been served up forthwith. The colonel heard it directly from the general. I heard it directly from a signaller, which led me to believe I got the more accurate version. The Germans had bit a two-mile deep chunk out of the left side of the

Salient. With the left flank exposed and barely defended, the enemy was poised to excise the rest of the bulge like a surgeon with a scalpel would a mole. Three entire divisions including mine, 50,000 men in total, would be caught like a school of mackerel thrashing helplessly in a net. Ypres would be lost and perhaps much more. It would be nothing short of a disaster. No wonder Brigadier-General Turner had looked so relieved at our arrival.

'Hey Mac,' Jones said. 'How many Germans do you suppose there are in that forest?'

Without exception the men of C Company were shuffling from foot to foot, as if preparing for an important match, silently staring ahead, eager and anxious to get on with it but nervous they'd let the side down. Behind the mask of imperturbability I was gamely attempting, my stomach was churning.

I shook my head. 'I don't know, Pat. A lot. I don't think our commanders do either,' I replied. I jerked my chin in the direction of Lieutenant-Colonel Boyle and Major Ormond. The two of them were joining the ranks of the men behind. To my surprise all the battalion's officers appeared to be going into action.

'Listen, Mac,' Jones whispered, and he leaned over close, his head next to mine. I could almost smell the fear on him, although it may well have been my own. In any event the usual false bravado in his voice had disappeared and I thought better of him for it. 'If I don't make it, would you write a letter to my folks? And tell them that I did my best?' He looked me at me plaintively, almost abjectly.

He was the one man in the company nobody would have dreamed of calling a shirker or a coward. Too many had suffered his verbal barbs for that. I had put an arm round countless shoulders, young lads aching from some cruel witticism Pat had thrown out unthinking, to amuse the mob. Yet despite it all Pat Jones was charming and interesting, and even kind-hearted when the peculiar dynamics of a group were absent. For some reason he'd never said a word against me, but I didn't care for his pretences and his cutting quips, and I think he knew that. In an unguarded moment back in England, when we'd snuck out to a neighbouring village for an evening of drink, he'd said as much.

'Sure, Pat,' I said now. 'Of course. I'd be honoured to write for you. But don't think for a moment you're not coming back. You heard the sergeant-major. Atkins knows what he's talking about. Keep your wits about you and your head down, and you'll be fine. Trust me, just wait and see. Besides, you owe me some beer and I'd much prefer you stick around so I can collect on that.'

Jones smiled a wan smile and began fiddling with his bayonet. 'Thanks, Mac.'

The 800 soldiers of the battalion were assembled in long rows, two per company: C Company left and D right. We'd be given the dubious honour of leading the charge. The other two companies of the battalion were behind us and thirty yards behind them were the Highlanders of the 16th Battalion, just arrived. Eight rows of 200 men each, all staring ahead. 1600 men to check the German advance. 1600 men to put a stake in the ground in front of a corps numbering twenty times that.

I studied the familiar faces. Pat was beside me, but Roy Dundas was a row ahead and oblivious to my efforts to catch his eye. There was young Harold, with blushing cheeks and looking as if he'd stepped out of a schoolroom to join us, and Fred Fox and Lieutenant Sanders, and all the others. These past eight months we'd developed quite a bond.

At a quarter to midnight, the colonel gave the order and we began to move.

In long waving lines that extended further than I could see we trod off through the fields in the darkness. We were so close together, I was constantly bumping up against the shoulders of the men next to me. Which was fine for the feeling of comradeship though I couldn't help thinking it presented the Germans with a target even Dundas could hit. The 10th Battalion was truly going to war – just as we'd envisioned all these past months.

The night was uncannily still; a quiet broken only by the rustle of the knee-high grass and the padding of hundreds of feet stepping forward in ordered pace and measured ranks. A rhythmic knocking came from bayonet scabbards as they swung to and fro, banging against thighs already stepping forward again. Overhead it was clear. Stars shone and the sky was a deep blue-black with only whispers of cloud hanging here and there. A heavy ground mist had begun forming not long before and in the time we'd taken to form up it had turned into a whitish haze that clung to the contours of the earth, much as the gas cloud had earlier. However, after walking for only a few minutes, I was able to make out the jagged form of the wood ahead, looming above the mist.

Not a word was spoken. 1600 men moved as ghosts in the night. We'd be warned not to speak and for once no one thought to do otherwise.

I judged we must have reached the 600-yard mark when the rank ahead slowed and stopped.

Men looked from left to right, not daring to whisper, but wondering what was impeding our progress. Shuffling forward we came upon the first rank of the battalion who were gathered like a herd of cattle in a stockyard, milling in front of a modest hedge. It was only 4 feet tall, but it blocked our path as effortlessly as any Roman wall in centuries past would have done.

To the men in front, most of them tall and lithe and used to overcoming a little greenery, this presented few concerns. Undaunted they began stepping over and through the hedge. But then webbing got caught and entrenching tools fell against rifle butts, branches snapped, and bayonet scabbards scraped on a hidden line of wire that ran through the hedge. It made an unholy hubbub.

CRACK. A rifle went off. *TUF-TUF-TUF*. Then a machine gun opened up. A thousand tongues of fire pierced the darkness in front. A man in front went down. To my left another.

Then a flare burst overhead and began a slow wobbling descent, eerily lighting up the field ahead. The rifle and machine-gun fire intensified. Some of the men went to ground. Lieutenant Sanders stood and looked back over his shoulder, waving his arm forward to say "come with me" and he might even have said that – for all the noise I couldn't be sure. A round caught him and I saw him stagger. Just as his head rose again a new volley found its mark; his body convulsed and he fell.

'Oh, shit,' murmured a voice. It wasn't the one inside me, though I concurred.

'Keep moving,' muttered another deeper voice. This one spoke authoritatively: a corporal or a sergeant. Whoever he was, he was speaking softly, though the air was zipping with bullets and a hushed tone was not about to bring a return to the stillness.

When I got to the hedge I held my rifle with both hands at eye level and went to step through. The wire and the young beech branches scraped at my loins, and my foot got entangled in the strand of wire that ran about three-quarters of the way up. I felt myself teetering over. A strong hand grabbed at my tunic and pulled me back. Then my foot came free. 'Steady on, MacPhail. You're fine, fella. Now get going. Show me what you're made of,' said someone, not unfriendly. I turned and saw the stern face of Sergeant-Major Atkins. His eyes had a sparkle to them I couldn't recall seeing before.

'Thanks, Sergeant-Major,' I breathed, but I was distracted by another machine gun that began rattling. It felt like it was only yards away. When I turned back to the sergeant he had disappeared into the night. I plunged off towards the wood. Running with the others, rifle and bayonet extended, I charged for the trench just in front of the wood. Across the full periphery of my vision, dots of orange flashed in the dark and the harsh chatter of gunfire seemed only to grow. A smell of smoke and gunpowder lay thick.

It was a desperate but silent charge. There was no loud roaring of men closing with the enemy, or brave cries to encourage the others or themselves, only the constant whizz of bullets and the sight of man after man crumpling to the ground, and having to jump over them. I remember looking at one upturned face as I leapt past and, to my horror, realized it was young Harold.

The distance to the trench was no more than a hundred yards and somehow I reached it unscathed. Most of those beside me did not. Bodies were strewn everywhere. Two men were engaged in a fierce grappling match. I ignored them and climbed into the trench and up the other side. The wood was dead ahead, the approaches swarming with men, all of them filled with the same mad exhilaration.

In a minute I reached the first line of trees. And then I was upon him. I saw him step from behind a large oak where he'd been sheltering. Curiously it was the pointed tip of his *pickelhaube* that I noticed first; I ought to have been paying more attention to the rifle he was raising to one shoulder.

The soldier's eyes were fixated upon me, but he'd misjudged it; he was too close and had run out of time. Too close to aim and too close to fire, but not too close for a bayonet. I jumped for him, thrusting the rifle forward. Cold steel flashed right before the bayonet sank into his chest. His arms slumped, his rifle tumbled to the ground, and his head dipped. I yanked the rifle away and ran on, berserk with rage and excitement.

The wood was a mad scrambling melee of men, a swirling of kilts from the Highlanders of the 16th as they rushed the enemy, the fighting fierce and mainly hand-to-hand. Germans were everywhere – lying, kneeling, and standing behind trees attempting a shot.

Deep in the wood I came upon one such man, a shadow crouched behind a thick tree trunk. Virtually at the same moment I glimpsed him I saw the outline of a field gun further on, peculiarly pointing north – the wrong direction. The German soldier was shooting as fast as he could work the bolt. He didn't notice me circle around to his rear, and I was two steps from him when he paused and raised his head from the sights to cock an ear – he'd sensed my presence. My rifle butt hit him hard from behind, just below the crown. For Harold I told myself. The undergrowth crackled and gave way as he slumped forward. I left him and moved on in the direction of the gun. It emerged that there were two of them.

They were ours all right, 4.7-inch field guns. All around the dead lay in macabre piles: British, Turcos and Germans. The sad history of a day of fighting. Mainly they were Germans who lay on top.

There I caught sight of a familiar face, the face of the adjutant, Major Ormond, and I went to him.

'Ah, MacPhail. You come with me,' he ordered. 'You're the runner, aren't you?'

'Yes, sir,' I replied. 'Are these the guns we were supposed to recapture, sir?'

'They are but they're not going anywhere, not without horses. So we'll have to wait for some. In the meantime you and I are going to undertake a reconnaissance.'

Which seemed a strange thing to do in the middle of a battle. But then I heard shells falling – the Germans were shelling the wood – so I knew we had taken it. Shells came crashing down through the foliage and you had literally a split-second to seek cover. Sometimes they exploded too high with a deafening boom, followed by a dangerous shower of boughs as thick as my thighs, and steel fragments that easily could tear through both.

I accompanied Ormond to the southwest corner of the wood. Heaps of German bodies, hundreds of them, and many, many of ours, littered the forest floor. 'Blast it,' he said after we'd walked for a while.

'Sir?'

'The attack veered too far right,' he muttered. 'We missed the whole left side of the wood.'

It was only when we came upon a group of 35-odd men, mostly from the 16th and a handful from the battalion, did I appreciate the significance of this. They were in a shallow trench near the tree line, pinned down by fire from an enemy redoubt in the corner we'd missed. I didn't see how we were going to hold the wood, not with the left of it still in German hands and surrounded from every direction but the south. Ormond must have come to a similar conclusion for two assault parties were hastily assembled.

Almost as hastily the attack was repelled. We made it little further than the trench parapet. We clambered up, firmly resolved to charge the Boche, but a torrent of machine-gun fire and a handful of bombs stopped us in our tracks. In my case I didn't make it out of the trench before the man in front shook under a volley of bullets and his body fell backwards, taking me with him. When it was over I counted more than a dozen men down. The party under Lieutenant Lowry that was to circle round the flank was no more successful.

We lay there, catching our breath and thanking the Lord that we still could, when I heard Ormond say: 'We'll have to dig in.' There really wasn't a choice. 15 yards away the Germans in the redoubt were determined to see the end of us and any honest arbiter would have given them better than even odds. It would only be a matter of time before the Germans counterattacked in force. Even the most optimistic amongst us knew how that would end.

Furiously I began scraping and clawing at the earth. 200 yards away a machine gun in a farmhouse – one someone had decided not to clear as it wasn't *our* job – started to rattle. Luckily I found a German entrenching tool in the ditch as mine seemed to have disappeared. With all of us digging, including the major, we managed to furrow out a little cross trench. That enabled us to crawl a retreat to the main trench that swung round the wood, an extension of the very trench we'd crossed going in two hours earlier.

Like most trenches in the Salient this one was woefully shallow, only two-feet deep – the water table being too high to dig any further – but it did have a decent parapet. And having been French a day earlier it was facing the right way. Furthermore it contained some surprising trophies. It was packed with dead and wounded enemy soldiers and I nearly jumped out of my britches when I came upon a colonel. He was alive, if not fit.

'Sir!' I yelled excitedly at Ormond, trying not to draw the attention of the entire German 26th Reserve Corps – the one from General Currie's map. 'You'd better have a look, sir.'

Ormond approached. 'Well, well. Isn't that something...' He saw straight away what the fuss was about, enough to know it wasn't a fuss at all. Not every day did someone capture a German *Oberst*.

'I went through all their papers, sir, and noted their insignias,' I said. 'The men here are from the 2nd Prussian Guards and the 234th Bavarians. I'm sure that'll mean something to someone.'

Ormond, who hadn't flinched once all night, glanced at me again. 'What exactly did you do before the war, MacPhail?'

'I was a lawyer, sir, although I'm trying to keep it under my cap.'

He grinned. 'Were you indeed? As a matter of fact so was I.' He scratched at his chin.

'I could take a message back to Brigade,' I offered.

Ormond shook his head. 'No. I've a better idea. Forget the message: take them back.' He pointed at the colonel and the officer beside him who was wearing an Iron Cross ribbon. The actual cross appeared to be missing in action.

Once I'd shepherded them and myself out of danger I began to talk.

The colonel was in bad shape and didn't care to talk about his wound or anything else. I had the impression that German colonels were above conversing with mere privates, let alone enemy ones. However, he was also Bavarian and as I'd never met a Bavarian I tried for a spell to draw him out, until his haughty manner made short shrift of that. When he stumbled and fell crossing the field towards Mousetrap farm I didn't lend a hand, as I would have otherwise. Instead I watched him painfully pull himself up while I motioned menacingly with the bayonet and hissed at him to hurry. I turned my attentions to the junior officer.

Ulrich was his name. 'You fellows fight like hell,' Ulrich said in good English.

'Thanks,' I grunted, not knowing what else to say. Ulrich was a fine enough fellow and for some reason that surprised me. I suppose I was expecting a fiery-eyed monster fresh from pillaging a Belgium village. Pointedly I asked about the gas attack.

His eyes bulged. 'The gas surprised us enormously,' he said. 'They gave us protectors but the men are afraid of it now that they've seen what it does.' I didn't bother telling him what the French thought.

Shortly after reaching brigade headquarters a Lieutenant-Colonel Hughes arrived to collect the "trophies" and listen distractedly to my story. I didn't realize it at the time, but he was the son of the Minister of Militia, Sam Hughes. Admittedly it was going on 3 a.m., but my first impression was not a favourable one. But then I'd never much liked the father, who was more of a bombastic know-it-all than your average politician. I think the son found me a trifle impertinent – besides their rank it was something he and the German colonel had in common.

By the time I returned to the wood, the battalion had forsaken any hope of holding it and had retired south, near the hedge. There, sections of men were digging in. A couple of machine guns were furiously raking our left flank. Just as I reached a hole with a few men a trio of shells went off in rapid succession, close enough to light up the scene for a long, terrifying moment.

'Jesus,' I muttered as I slid in between the others. 'Was it like this the entire while?'

'Worse. I think Fritz has run out of ammunition.'

I couldn't help smiling and looked to see who'd spoken. It was Pat Jones. He was beaming at me.

'You made it,' I exclaimed and clapped him on the shoulder. 'I told you.'

'Barely,' he said. 'You cut it a little close yourself, Mac.'

Quizzically I looked at him. Reaching out a hand he plucked off my cap.

Softly I whistled. He was holding it aloft with one finger stuck through a hole in the front.

'Where are the others?' I asked. 'And Roy Dundas. Have you seen him?'

'To tell you the truth, I don't know. I saw Lieutenant Bell get it right at the get-go. Half the platoon fell in that first charge. To be honest I was mostly looking out for myself. I did see Atkins a while back.'

'Naturally,' I said. 'Atkins didn't get to be a sergeant-major on the basis of his personality alone. What about the colonel?'

'Plastered by a machine gun in the groin,' he replied.

I groaned. 'And Major McLaren?'

'Shot.'

'Yeah, well, it was pretty thick.'

Jones grunted. 'Ormond's in charge of the battalion now. Word has it there are only five officers left.'

'And who's in command here?'

'Don't ask me. Lieutenant Glanfield was around but he seems to have disappeared. I don't think there's an NCO left, Mac.'

At 6 a.m. word was passed to do a roll call and by then it was light. Lying in the trench, as the sun's rays slowly revealed the horrible carnage littering the fields, I shouted my name when the moment came. There was no waving of arms or standing to attention and calling "present". There was certainly no point in reading out the whole nominal roll. It was far quicker to count the survivors.

Thirty minutes later Major Ormond dove in amongst us. He was inspecting what was left of the Tenth. As we'd been speculating exactly how many that was, I simply asked him.

He hesitated for a moment. 'A little less than 200,' he replied. 'We began with 816.'

I winced, even though I'd been prepared.

Then he said something else which surprised me even more.

CHAPTER 6

23rd and 24th of April, 1915
Kitcheners' Wood, west of St. Julien, Belgium

'MacPhail,' said Major Ormond, 'as of now, you're platoon corporal.'

'There must be others, sir,' I protested. 'Surely…'

'There aren't,' he curtly interjected. 'Hold the line until you hear otherwise. Understood?'

He waited until I gave a bewildered nod. Before I could ask anything else he sprinted for the next hole. I suspect he was replaying the scene every thirty yards.

'I'll be darned. Lance-Corporal Malcolm MacPhail,' snickered Jones.

'Give it a rest, Pat,' I said. I was tired and thirsty and not in the frame of mind to assuage Jones's bruised ego. While he hadn't said it outright, I knew very well he reckoned he ought to have been the one. For my part I would have raised no objections. But that wasn't what our new commander had decided.

From an original platoon strength of fifty-two I now counted twelve men, myself included. Hopefully there were others who would turn up, and soon – they were desperately needed.

The day was long and trying, filled with an endless pounding by the German guns, which never did run out of ammunition like ours, and the bitter knowledge that waves of men were imminent. The only good news was when an unscratched Roy Dundas arrived. He'd been with a group of Canadian Scottish. By nightfall there were only ten of us remaining. The food and water were long gone, the ammunition dangerously low. From the activity a hundred yards further it was clear the enemy had plans.

'Hey, Mac. Wake up. You'd better wake up. We're supposed to stand-to.' The words were accompanied by a gentle prod of a foot.

Startled I bolted upright. Somehow I must have dozed off for a second.

'What time is it?' I asked, my heart pounding, worried I'd fouled up or worse.

Ryerson glanced at his watch. 'Three o'clock. Word is the Boche are about to attack.'

To my relief they didn't, not immediately. Roughly thirty minutes later a couple of red rockets and a green one could be observed in the sky over their lines near Mauser Ridge. It was to our immediate left. Then shortly before 4 a.m. the dull, grey pre-dawn sky lit up again. This time it was to our right, in the direction of the Gravenstafel Ridge two miles away, where the division held the front-line trenches. A fierce bombardment had begun, the flashes coming in rapid succession amidst a noise like distant thunder.

'That must be the attack,' I said. The others nodded gravely. 'Their generals will be frustrated we've held them for so long. They'll be looking to give us the *coup de grâce*.'

'Great,' muttered Jones. 'I thought... just maybe... we'd seen the worst of it.'

'No, Pat,' I said very slowly. 'I'm afraid to say I don't think we've seen the worst of it by a long shot.' For once I was right, although I'd understated it.

A dense billowing cloud appeared. It clung to the horizon near Gravenstafel Ridge, lit from behind by the sun as it prepared to rise. In the dark the cloud's colours were indistinct but there was no mistaking what it was. It was growing larger, already moving over our front lines.

Having seen what the gas had done to the French I felt nauseous. Aware I should be setting a good example I got everyone to recheck their rifles and gear – better to be doing than to be thinking.

A half hour later we were on the move. Orders had come. It took some fancy footwork but the battalion extricated itself from the trenches under the very noses of the Boche, leaving them to the 16th Battalion and the 2nd – the latter had come up in relief. Away from the wood we quick-marched to brigade headquarters at Pond Farm and then on to Bombarded Cross Roads before turning left onto the road to Keerselaere. I was weary, every limb ached, and for the second time in two days we were marching towards the fearsome cloud. There was a sense that something pivotal was happening. Not a man among us didn't feel it. Shortly thereafter we left the road and congregated in a field.

From all around – to the left, right, but mainly in front – sounded the distant clatter of gunfire. The same smell of bleach was in the air that I'd whiffed two days earlier, only stronger. Much stronger. I ran my tongue over my teeth to cleanse them but the metallic taste remained.

From out of the darkness emerged a figure and a voice. 'Who's in charge here?' it demanded to know.

'I am,' I responded. 'Major Ormond put me in command of the platoon.' Nine months ago I would have asked who was asking. But then nine months ago I wasn't in the army. Ironically, one thing you quickly learn in the army is that it's not so important *what's* being said as *who* is saying it. The intonation in this voice suggested it belonged to someone in command.

'MacPhail, is that you?'

'Yes,' I replied. Then I saw who it was. 'Sergeant-Major Atkins! Am I happy to see you.'

I hadn't spotted him during the frenzied march but was relieved to see him now and I greeted him like a long-lost soulmate. Whatever else he was, Atkins was the right man to have in your corner in a tight spot. I'm not convinced he thought the same of me for he reciprocated with a weak grin.

'Get your platoon together, MacPhail. The 8th Battalion needs our immediate assistance. Their OC, Colonel Lipsett, sent a message. We're to hold Locality C at all costs.'

'Locality C?' The question slipped out. I figured if something needed to be held "at all costs" it would be useful to know what that was.

'Damn it all, MacPhail. Can't you for once just do what you're told without asking questions? Locality C is that way, on the opposite side of the ridge road. You'll know it when you see it.' He pointed north, up the shallow back slope of Gravenstafel Ridge toward the support trenches.

'Yes, Sergeant-Major.'

He may have felt a twinge of guilt at his outburst, for he gave me a pat on the shoulder as I got the boys moving. Then he gave me something that later would be much more important, a handful of cotton bandoliers. 'Put these on when you get up there. The gas is pretty bad, I'm told. There's not enough of them to go around so the rest will have to use handkerchiefs.'

I handed them all out to the others, leaving me with nothing. The only explanation that comes to mind is that as platoon corporal I figured it was the proper thing to do. Stupid. But proper.

Locality C proved to be nothing more than a trench – visibly in the French tradition – a couple hundred yards long at the top of the low ridge, with a commanding view downslope to the north. I presumed the view was what made it so important.

Along with a few stragglers from other units we were guided into a position 800 yards to the left. To our right the men from the 7th and 8th Battalions were spread out very thinly. There was no more than a company holding a position meant for a battalion, so even our sorry remnants were welcome.

Holding our left were the Royal Highlanders of the 15th Battalion – or they should have been. That was precisely the problem according to our guide. 1000 yards further north near the Stroombeek was the front line, but the left had buckled.

'The Highlanders beat it,' he said. The guide was a fair-sized fellow with tired eyes, bullet holes in his tunic and a bloodied dressing around his forehead where his cap should have been.

'Beat it? So who's holding the front if the 15th aren't?' I asked.

He sighed. 'The Germans.'

'Oh,' I mumbled. I tried to recall what I'd seen on the map and thought of a new question. 'So what you're telling me is that this trench is the front line?'

'You catch on fast,' he replied. Which might sound facetious, but I don't think he meant it that way. 'Colonel Lipsett says if we don't stop them here the whole brigade is going to be cut off. Most of our fellows are still 1000 yards forward,' he explained.

Arriving at the trench, I took out the tattered handkerchief I'd been of a mind to throw away days earlier and began to tie it around my nose and mouth.

'Piss on it first,' said the guide. The 8th Battalion were known as the Little Black Devils. Suddenly I understood why. I frowned. 'Piss on it,' he insisted. 'We had a medical officer along, Captain Scrimger. Told us it counteracts the chlorine. Trust me.' He had that weary resigned look of someone who knew what he was talking about, so to the smirking astonishment of the platoon, I dropped my trousers and followed his instructions. Soaked the handkerchief completely through – despite drinking barely a drop since the day before. Nerves will do that to you.

Mine didn't improve when I saw the three stricken soldiers in the trench. Their flesh was an unnatural ghoulish white and they lay sprawled inert, struck down by the poisonous gases.

The trench was of the two feet deep variety with a miserable parapet of sandbags stacked two or three high. The gas that had come over little more than an hour before was heavy, and it had settled down into the nether regions, its fumes wafting upwards like steam from some old witch's cauldron. Even with the saturated handkerchief I found myself coughing and gasping; my lungs on fire. I kept blinking. My eyes stung and tears followed. Doing my best to ignore it, I endeavoured to get the men spread out and ready.

We'd been assigned a twenty-yard stretch consisting of two lengths of trench. A traverse broke it in the middle. There wasn't even a parados to shelter our backs. It was my first command, and I was damned if we were going to lose it.

Barely had we settled in when the view which I'd marvelled at turned threatening. My own shiny Waltham – the one my parents had given me on my 18th birthday – hadn't survived the rigours of Salisbury Plain. But Pat's watch gave it as a little after 5.40 a.m. The sun was stretching its limbs in the east and brilliant rays began to streak the fields in front. Above the tall mustard grass and other crops, which grew in abundance, bobbed the heads of an army of field-grey ants. Naturally they weren't ants.

'Get ready!' I shouted. 'They're coming.'

The men on the Colt machine gun fed a belt of bullets into the gun. They had a rectangular ammunition box perched almost on the lip of the trench. Others fiddled nervously with the bolts of their rifles. No one wanted a jam. Not now.

Then the shelling began. There was a brief shriek and a blast, followed by an eruption of Belgian farmland, and a greasy plume of smoke spiralled upwards. Then another. And another. Despite the gas we sank down into the trench as the explosions rocked the ground. The big 5.9s pummeled us as we'd never been pummeled before. At the very moment I peeked left over the parapet a shell landed.

BOOM.

My ears reverberated. It was what my eyes saw that left me empty. Twenty yards away the section where Sergeant-Major Atkins held steady sway was blown tens of feet into the air. Dirt and large clumps, which later revealed themselves to be body parts, rained down upon us.

I knew what I would likely find, but I went anyhow. What I found was far worse.

The sergeant-major sat with his back to the trench wall, his head yawning to one side, eyes closed. I was about to call out to him but checked myself. I looked again in horror. Both legs from the calf down were gone, reduced to bloodied stumps. It was then that I saw him opening his eyes. He was still alive!

'Sergeant-Major,' I cried.

His head jerked round, awkwardly, searching, until finally he saw me.

A sad smile came over his face. 'Ah, young MacPhail.'

I grabbed the arm he proffered. 'Sergeant-Major.'

'Just this once, call me Tom, would you? But don't tell the others.' He laughed briefly until a thick hacking cough overcame him.

'Yes, Sergeant-Major,' I said.

'Sit with me for a moment.'

He clasped my hand and I clasped his. I held it firm. It was wet and sticky but I didn't let go.

'I always had high expectations for you, Malcolm. I know you'll do the battalion proud.' His voice faltered. 'Do get the buggers, won't you?' With that his hand wilted and his head fell forward.

It seemed impossible. Company Sergeant-Major Atkins. Atkins, who most were convinced could face down a regiment of the enemy singlehandedly, was gone.

Then their infantry came up the slope. This time they were the ones advancing shoulder-to-shoulder, the bayonets and points of their helmets gleaming in the morning sun, confident in the gas and their barrage. Marching to victory.

'Fire, God damn it!' I screamed. Every rifle in the trench went off, even though we could barely see on account of the gas.

After three shots the rifles jammed and a boot or entrenching tool was required to smash the bolt open. But we kept at it. We fired and we kicked and we fired. Almost like at the ranges in England, were it not for the blood pulsing in my head and the rapid thumping coming from my chest. The smoke curled round and stunk of chlorine and cordite. We choked and spat from under the wet rags that masked our faces, but didn't dare remove them. When one or two of the attackers made it as far as the parapet, bayonets were used. The *Pickelhaubes* and their little dark moustaches fell in droves, and a couple of ours did as well. For a furious few minutes so it went. Until the enemy – bloodied – retreated.

Mercifully when it was over a stiff breeze came up and Mother Nature shooed away the gas.

Without having been there it is difficult to explain the madness that overcame us. Anger and a desire to get our own back, to demonstrate to the Boche that we wouldn't be taken for granted as their Kaiser Wilhelm had snootily promised when he proclaimed he would send us home in thirty rowboats. Perhaps even to show the storied British regiments that we, colonials, could be counted upon, too. But more than that; I think we knew we were fighting for our lives.

An hour later at 7.00 a.m. the enemy returned. Deceitfully, he was clothed in the uniform of the French, and that of the Highlanders and the Turcos. But one of our officers didn't trust the bizarre assortment of uniforms coming from the direction of the Germans and we repulsed them with cold steel and a hail of bullets.

Fifteen minutes later we spotted pointed helmets and field grey once more, 500 yards to the left. A German officer was carrying a white flag and behind him came several stretcher bearers.

'Can you believe that,' said Jones indignantly. 'Do they think we're complete imbeciles?'

It was a perceptive remark for we soon heard one of the battalion shout: 'They've got machine guns on those stretchers!' By that time it was too late and we were subjected to a heavy, if somewhat ineffective fire from our left flank. They were trying to get around the trench to the rear.

'Of all the dastardly underhanded scheming,' fumed Jones. 'There's no trick the Boche won't try.'

Bent on teaching our adversary a lesson he moved over to the traverse. There he nestled his rifle in amongst the sandbags, waiting for a shot. Then he must have realized that while he was well protected by sandbags to either side, there was no parados, and the Germans that were working their way around our left had a clean shot from the rear. He glanced over at me in frustration.

'Pat!'

The bullet struck him square in the side of the head. His head snapped over from the impact, his cap still on, and he just sank to the ground. I couldn't believe it. One moment he was there, cussing our opponent, and the next he was not.

But then bullets began flying in earnest and another bombardment began. Twice they advanced and twice they retired. Half an hour passed before I even had time to think of him again and I felt a little guilty as I knelt down. The request he'd made in that moonlit field before charging the wood suddenly came to me... But that would come later. Or perhaps not at all if things kept on as they were.

I emptied his pockets and removed his watch. I would send them along with the letter. With my hands under his armpits I wrestled him up against the trench wall and tipped the brim of his cap down low so as to appear as if he were sleeping. He was more dignified like that. Then the war intervened. Fleetingly I touched him on the shoulder, a momentary glance for memory's sake, and I turned.

The tempo of the shelling was increasing again. The ground was literally shaking, shards of metal flew through the air, dirt and smoke everywhere.

'They've got our range, Mac,' said Dundas. 'Shame about Pat,' he murmured. We crouched together in the dirt at the bottom of the trench –thankfully gas-free – as every inch of Locality C was churned and pulverised by the fall of shells. That anything or anyone could survive this would be miraculous. The German gunners were taking it upon themselves to preclude the very existence of miracles.

'It's that bloody aeroplane,' I said. 'Look at him. He keeps circling and he's dropping smoke signals. For their artillery no doubt.' As if to illustrate it buzzed round in a lazy circle directly above our heads. Something came tumbling down. When it reached the ground a billowing exhaust of white smoke rose up into the sky.

'Don't we have any aeroplanes?' asked Dundas.

I shrugged. 'Probably. But they're clearly not here.' Then a thought came to me. 'Rumours have it we also have several armies in Belgium and France. However the fate of the Ypres Salient appears to be in the hands of a few chewed-up battalions from the colonies.'

Dundas's reply was lost in the sound of high-explosive detonating twenty feet away. For a couple harrowing minutes we scrunched our-selves up small, with our heads down, and hands over our heads.

By noon the enemy had finished regrouping. This was not a brilliant strategic insight of mine so much as the result of a hurried glance over the sandbags. The Germans were moving in small groups and sudden short rushes. It was difficult to get a proper aim. Machine-gun fire from close by began tearing up the parapet, and sandbags shredded and released their contents. The air and the rifle breeches filled with dust and dirt, which made matters worse.

I had one of them in my sights; close enough I could make out the whites of his eyes and a shiny emblem on his pickelhaube. He must be an officer or an NCO. He and a half-dozen others were rushing forward. I pulled the bolt back to chamber another round, but the action was locked solid.

'Christ, not again,' I cursed.

I sank down and handed the rifle to the 13th Battalion man who'd staggered in a couple of hours before. He sat on the ground hack-ing and coughing from the gassing, but at work of a different kind. Everyone had to do their bit. He took the rifle in one hand and thrust the butt end into the dirt. With the other he whacked the bolt hard with an entrenching tool. The bolt sprang open and he handed back the rifle without a word, reaching already for another.

Unsurprisingly the German officer had disappeared. Their tactics were clear. Slowly but steadily they were working their way through and around our left, to envelop us. This time I feared we weren't going to be able to hold them. We simply didn't have enough rifles.

'Concentrate on the machine guns,' I shouted. 'They're going to tear us up if they get too close.' I don't know if anyone heard me.

Every man was already shooting for all he was worth. I pushed in another 5-round stripper clip and brought the rifle to my shoulder. The man between Dundas and me went down. Just when all looked lost, orders came to retire.

We were to move to the trenches in D.14 and D.13, down the rear slope of the ridge and roughly 800 to 900 yards back. I sent the men out in groups of three, hurrying down the slight gradient, carrying wounded with them as best they could, while the rest kept up a withering fire. When it was my turn, I glanced hastily around at the litter of ammunition cans, all manner of kit and brass cartridges that lay scattered everywhere – and at the bodies. At one in particular. Then I stepped out of the trench with Dundas at my side. Bent low we ran after the others.

Fifteen minutes later we encountered a sizeable group of 15th Battalion men on the Keerselaere-Zonnebeke road behind the ridge. Their commanding officer was present and Major Ormond went forward to speak with him. For an instant I thought we were to return up the ridge. Then I saw the storm-clouds on Ormond's face and I knew we weren't. The Highlander colonel was more anxious to make a run for it than put up a defence; little wonder his battalion had fled while their neighbours held their ground. Through the hole thus created wave upon wave of Germans was coming.

We settled into the trenches astride the road. The remnants of a 7th Battalion company were assembled there, as beat up as we were. Someone found a canteen of water and I drank deeply of it until I had to avert my head to cough. I found I had difficulty breathing, except in short shallow gulps. And my throat burned.

A battery of field guns had been set up nearby and a sole gun remained. Around 1 p.m. it fired a single shot and the crew immediately began corralling the horses and hitching up the limber and the gun. It hardly seemed the moment to pull back the artillery. Were we in retreat?

I asked around and eventually found a man with the answer.

'They're out of ammunition,' he explained. 'I heard it from the major. He said they've fired their last round so they're packing up.'

We at least had ammunition; it was the scarcity of working rifles and men to fire them that was worrisome. But then I imagine that's true of all other valiant but impossible last stands. The Germans had an apparent endless supply of everything, not least of which was poisonous gas. I didn't think I could have withstood another dose of that.

A crackling of rifle fire and a burst from a machine gun demanded our attention. Two heads made a prudent and swift retreat.

I looked over at the other fellow. 'Just out of interest,' I asked. 'Do you suppose they'll remove us before or after we've fired our last round?'

CHAPTER 7

25th of April, 1915
Between Fortuin and Gravenstafel, Belgium

'Let's go, boys. Up and at it,' shouted Captain Arthur. 'General Currie's here to take the battalion back to the ridge.'

I stole a glance at Pat Jones's watch. It was pitch black so I had difficulty working out what it said. The day before had been a Saturday, I was pretty sure of that. So 1.15 a.m. would make it a Sunday I concluded. Sunday the 25th. The cogs upstairs were creaking over ever so slowly. But then I'd only had two hours sleep and if my mid-night math was correct we'd been fighting for close to sixty.

Saturday had gone on forever. After pulling back from Gravenstafel Ridge we spent the entire afternoon and evening in a variety of holes and ditches near Fortuin within spitting distance of Brigade HQ at Pond Farm. The Germans pressed relentlessly from the north. What should have been a fine spring day was transformed into something we all agreed was closer to Hell. By evening the apex of the Salient, its furthermost left tip, was collapsing. More and more men from other battalions were straggling to the rear. To the west St. Julien was threatened. To the east Locality C was hanging on by a thread. Miraculously, the rest of the overextended 2nd Brigade, 1 ½ miles north near the Stroombeek, was still in the original front line.

Around three o'clock Major Ormond was wounded for the second time; he got it in the right leg. Which is how Captain Arthur happened to be in command and shouting us awake. Nothing against Arthur but there weren't many alternatives; there were only three officers left in the battalion. We held out till dusk then they pulled us back to march a mile to the rear, almost to Wieltje, to the GHQ Line and our first meal in two days and what now appeared to be a very cursory nap.

The GHQ Line was a fancy-sounding name for what in reality was a slipshod affair of two miles of shallow, poorly wired ditches – a fall-back line before Ypres if ever catastrophe were to strike. I welcomed it for the hot meal that was served up almost immediately. However I couldn't help noticing all the men milling around. *Had catastrophe struck?*

'The fighting's *that* way,' I told a man from the 1st Battalion, pointing down the road. I observed men from a grab-bag of units, including even a couple of English regiments, the sight of which buoyed my spirits momentarily as I assumed they were reinforcements. 'What are you doing here?' I asked him.

'Beats me,' he replied. 'All I know is that the 3rd Brigade has pulled back to the GHQ Line.'

'The 3rd Brigade pulled back?' Stunned I looked at him. 'But that means our whole left flank from north of St. Julien all the way to the GHQ Line is wide open!'

'I wouldn't know about that,' he replied. 'They don't tell us much. What's the problem?'

'Well let me explain. The 3rd Brigade is left and the 2nd Brigade is right, and seeing as how the 3rd Brigade won't be holding our flank, the Germans soon will be. And that my friend is a mighty big problem.'

Despite this worrisome news I must confess I fell asleep immediately after dinner. A soldier sleeps when he can and I was well past the point of mere exhaustion. Besides which, newly promoted lance-corporals aren't expected to concern themselves with serious matters like strategy. Nevertheless, when Brigadier-General Currie turned up in person in the middle of the night to collect what was left of the 7th and 10th Battalions I wasn't terribly surprised, even though it was not a typical chore for a general. Nor a typical hour, come to that. Neither seemed to bother Currie in the slightest, though he must have had the weight of the world on his shoulders.

'I want to see a disciplined marching order,' I heard the general instruct Captain Arthur. Marching discipline seemed the very least of our concerns, but the brigadier never tolerated much slack. And while the 3rd Brigade may have pulled back, Currie was determined the 2nd Brigade wouldn't.

I guessed there were roughly 300 of us, both battalions combined. We marched in double file in weary silence, broken only by a shuffling patter of feet as they tromped over the pavé road. A moon was out and the surrounding fields were bathed in a radiant silver light. Every so often a harsh bang sounded from a gun somewhere ahead, followed by a throatier *Crump* as a parcel of steel and high explosive found its mark. And an orange flash sparked on the horizon.

General Currie walked along the ranks, likely trying to assess whether he could make stew from the motley cuts he'd just gathered. When he saw me he glanced a second time, perhaps in recognition, and gave an affirming nod before moving on. It was strange that it should matter but my step became markedly lighter, for a short while at least.

Approaching Fortuin the flashes grew larger, as did the bangs. Small-arms fire could be heard. Near to Gravenstafel Ridge two things happened – the general took his leave, and we were led to a spot well to the right of where we'd been the day before. If I wasn't mistaken it was to the right and behind Locality C. From this I suspected the position had fallen.

Regardless, we endeavoured to dig in halfway up the back slope of the ridge, next to a company of English Suffolks with our flank curving to the south. Where twelve hours earlier we occupied a trench running roughly west to east along the ridgetop, we were now the left shoulder of the brigade, facing northwest, and there wasn't a trench to be seen. None of this would have been noteworthy had we not been virtually bumping heads with the Germans. Which made digging a rather urgent priority. Dawn was almost upon us.

'Hang on,' I said to the others. 'What's that?' We'd barely gotten started and they all looked up.

Ahead, closer to the top of the ridge, was a ruined farmhouse and two figures had emerged from it. Almost immediately there was a smattering of rifle fire from our lines and the two went down. They looked wounded.

From the direction of Boetleer Farm and the Suffolks there was a shout: 'Wait. They're ours!'

'Sure they are…' groaned Dundas, his voice dripping with sarcasm. He had his cap pushed at an angle to the back of his head so as not to interfere with his aim, and was staring intently down the rifle barrel.

'Well, there's only one way to find out,' I said.

Odlum, the major from the 7th Battalion who'd been given command, evidently shared my conclusion; I saw two of our men run forward. There were shots and both fell to the ground.

'Well. That would appear to settle it,' said Dundas.

And I thought it had, particularly when a long row of shadowy figures appeared 200 yards away. Without warning they had emerged from the dawn mist that cloaked the slope of the ridge. There were a couple of hundred of them. I took aim and fired. Around me I could hear the whole line shooting. But for some reason the major bawled, 'Cease fire! Cease fire!' and after a pause the sergeants began dutifully shouting it, too. The firing petered out.

'What the hell!?' said someone.

Admittedly the mist made identifying a uniform next to impossible. However for the life of me I couldn't figure out why any of our troops would be coming from the direction of Keerselaere. And if they were, surely they would have been running for their lives not moving methodically forward in their hundreds in an extended row, looking for all the world like a legion bent on conquest. No doubt the major had his reasons. Maybe his field glasses were acting up.

One of ours ventured out with his hands in the air to investigate, crying something unintelligible to my ears. The only German words I knew were *Ja* and *Guten Tag* so I wouldn't have been much help. He got fifty yards and they shot him, which seemed to convince the major they weren't ours. It certainly convinced the rest of us and we began firing like we'd never heard of such a thing as a rifle jam.

In turn this put a halt to the enemy's plans almost as quickly as a grain of sand puts a halt to a Ross rifle. The Germans went to ground and began to dig in. When we were certain the danger had passed, we followed their example. Within a couple of hours some farmer's field was riven by two roughly parallel furrows in the ground, several feet-wide, two-feet deep, one edged by a wall of Flanders' fields heaped high in burlap sacks we'd brought in our gear. There was no need for me to ponder anymore how trench warfare had begun.

As the excitement ebbed, and forearms and backs began to ache and minds wandered, men swooned and fell, exhausted. I staved off my own exhaustion by exhorting them to get off their buttocks and keep shovelling. I tried to give a good example but faltered when I pulled out Jones's watch and discovered it was 6.30 a.m. It had been more than a day since the Germans had unleashed their second gas attack and it was much, much longer since I'd had a proper sleep. If only the enemy knew how tired we were.

A few minutes before noon Currie's brigade major, Lieutenant-Colonel Betty, came visiting. We were eating, or so it would have appeared to the casual observer. Without water, chomping on the hard biscuits had more than a passing similarity to chewing on sand.

As chance would have it Colonel Betty and Major Odlum squatted down an arms-length away and Betty was given a message. Silently he read it through, then aloud for Odlum's benefit: 'The York and Durham Brigade have occupied Fortuin,' he announced.

Odlum nodded.

I snorted and muttered, 'That couldn't have been too onerous. The enemy were never *in* Fortuin.'

The colonel's face froze. At which sight I did as well and both officers turned and gave me the once over. Eventually the colonel grunted while the slit trench the major called a mouth softened a touch. Coughing nervously, I made as if Duke Albrecht had arrived leading his entire corps and scampered down the trench to safety.

I saw Major Odlum a short time after. He was taking advantage of a momentary lull to inspect the men, moving along the short sections of trench and the holes scattered between them. When he reached me he seemed to make no connection with the loudmouth from earlier, or had decided to overlook it. 'How are you holding out?' he asked.

'Honestly, sir. We're all in. I'm not sure the men can keep going.' I said the "men" but I probably meant myself. As a *précis* of the situation it was accurate enough, however.

The major considered this. 'Yes. I can imagine,' he said. 'But tired or not, we must hang on. I'm hoping we'll be relieved tonight.'

We weren't the only ones anxious to leave. It was mid-afternoon – three-thirty – when groups of soldiers appeared behind us coming from the north and began to descend the slope to the rear.

'Who are you?' shouted a man.

It transpired that they were from the 8th Durhams, an English battalion hastened to the front this morning to bolster the 8th Battalion's left. However the Durhams had had their fill. Major Odlum bolted off to see if he could stem the tide.

The disconcerting *TUF-TUF-TUF* of a machine gun sounded. It came from another house occupied on our far left. It was slightly to the rear and beside the Keerselaere-Zonnebeke road, 500 hundred yards away. That sounds quite a distance until you consider that a Maxim machine gun – and I was told that's what it was – could easily fire two thousand yards, the only impediment being the gunner's sight. Needless to say I hoped this fellow was short-sighted.

'Spread out and keep your heads down,' I told my little unit. It was a nugget of common sense I'd recently acquired from Sergeant Belshaw. Belshaw was cool and calculating, not given to futile charges across pancake-flat fields in the face of 500 rounds a minute, not if the alternative of ducking made more sense. I'd always kind of liked him and I liked his way of thinking. His were not the foaming-at-the-mouth strictures I so abhorred. He appealed to a man's better judgement. For the most part we were men who appreciated that. I watched as he sat calmly on his haunches, waiting it out with his platoon.

With nothing to shoot at the Boche machine gunners gave up as Belshaw knew they would. For their part the German infantry seemed content to keep their heads down, too. Their colonels might have been keen for them to press on, but the men knew all too well what would happen if they did.

An uneasy stand-off reigned that afternoon and into the night. I found myself dozing off at moments, only to reawaken with my heart pumping madly, in fear I'd missed something. Life was less easy on our side of the line than theirs, it must be said. The Germans had all the machine guns and artillery, and they let us know it. Their artillery fire was quite terrific.

BOOM.

I felt the blast from behind the parapet, the rush of air so overwhelming that it was a mortal danger to anyone without shelter. No hurricane could match it. Just as I was catching my breath, shaken by how close the explosion had been, came a shower of dirt and debris blown high into the air, now tumbling back to earth. It reminded me of one of those apocalyptical tales from the Old Testament. Then it had been only frogs, if memory served. This shell was high explosive and it had dug itself well in before exploding. Luckily. Otherwise the blast of air would have been filled with a hundred shards of Krupp's finest steel, cutting down anything and anyone in its path.

There was a flash and a second concussion, this time to our rear. And another. *They were straddling us.* Then one to my right landed in the hole where Fred Fox and three others sheltered. Like the shovel of some gigantic mining excavator it scooped out the hole and dumped it from a height.

Lifting myself up, I peered through the smoke and dust, hoping against the odds I might see a sign in the darkness of gentleman Fred and the others.

That's how I missed the shell that went off a hundred yards behind me.

'CHRIST!' I shrieked.

The left side of my head exploded in pain and I doubled over. Instinctively I reached a hand up to my ear which was wet. My head was throbbing. Everything seemed in place, although when I inspected it my hand was black and treacly. I felt dizzy. I could feel my legs giving way. The pain eased, and the noises and the smells disappeared.

It became wonderfully peaceful. For a moment I was convinced that Kathryn was with me.

Out of the darkness a disembodied voice intruded. 'Mac, Mac,' I heard it calling. 'Mac, it's me.'

My eyelids fluttered in confusion. With an effort I forced them open. I was lying on the dirt of the trench floor. Concerned faces stared down. Dundas and another soldier were kneeling over me.

'There you are,' said Dundas, 'you're back.' His grim banker's countenance gave way to a smile.

Dazed I stared at him. 'Ouch,' I said finally, the pain in my head returning. I went to touch it but Dundas grabbed my arm before I could.

'No, leave it. We've just bandaged it. You got a piece of shrapnel in your ear.' Seeing my look of alarm he hastened to add, 'Don't worry. Your ear will be fine.'

'Easy enough for you to say. You've still got two.'

'See, I told you. He's recovering already,' Dundas said to the other. 'Give him an hour and he'll be on our backs we haven't dug deep enough.' He winked and handed me my cap. 'Saved this for you. It's seen better days, I must say. Now that you're a corporal you may need to think about getting a new one.'

'Thanks,' I said. 'Thanks, Roy.'

At 3.30 a.m., or thereabouts – the sentries were being replaced – word was passed along that the Suffolks had successfully pulled back so we were free to as well. The enemy was around our left by this juncture and pressing in front. Our right was retiring. I didn't know if this meant we had failed. Only time would tell.

Silently and keeping low as the heavy mist swirled around us, we left for the rear in small groups, conscious that any sound might bring down a hail of lead. Finally, we reached the trenches at Bombarded Cross Roads and safety. Once there it was all I could do to remain on my feet.

However, then they marched us off to somewhere. Where I do not know and honestly I was beyond caring. The sun's first rays were tickling the sky. Dumbly I followed along, like a herd animal being led to greener pastures, willing one foot in front of the other until even that seemed as if it were beyond my abilities. My eyelids kept drooping shut and then springing open. I stumbled several times.

We marched until we stopped and they let us fall where we fell. There I slept.

CHAPTER 8

26th of April, 1915
Near the Zonnebeke stream, south of Fortuin, Belgium

It was going on 10 a.m. when someone woke me.

I'd barely closed an eye, no more than an hour or two. The Germans were throwing shells all over the place. To top it off they had us marching again, again northeastwards, again in the direction of the enemy. I was too tired, wretched, and generally worn down to be concerned by the implications of this.

The narrow road from Wieltje to Fortuin was as familiar to me by now as the Via Appia had been to other soldiers, in another age. There was hardly a cobblestone I didn't know by name. This allowed me to periodically close my eyes in a forlorn attempt to catch up on some sleep. I had them closed when I heard a high-pitched voice I knew addressing me.

'Where do you suppose we're going, Corporal?' Young Bartholemew Cane from Canmore was asking. Bart was eighteen-years old going on fourteen but built like a barn. Like poor Harold who'd fallen at Kitcheners' Wood – that's what they'd taken to calling it – he was the kind of gentle lad you felt like taking under your wing. He was the only one in the battalion who went to the bother of addressing me as corporal. His had been a sheltered adolescence I imagine.

'Northeast,' I mumbled, without opening my eyes. 'We're going northeast.'

'Yes, Corporal, but do you think we're to counter-attack the Hun?' There was a loud blast ahead at the front of the column. We came to a shuffling halt.

'Fritz,' I said wearily. 'We call the enemy Fritz; Fritz or Heine or the Boche, or even German if we're pressed. Only the folks at home and the new recruits call them the "Hun".' I stared at him with my best wise-old-man look. 'And you're not a new recruit anymore, Bart, are you?'

'No, Corporal, but...'

Quickly I continued. 'To answer your question. I don't know. It could be we're to counter-attack. We'll see soon enough. All I know is we're to rescue the 11th Brigade seeing as there's a break in their line. And, yes, before you ask, the 11th Brigade was supposed to rescue us.' I began to cough.

Bart looked puzzled.

'I imagine our general feels a certain obligation to reciprocate,' I said winking. 'More than that and you'll have to ask General Currie yourself.'

I could see him considering it.

After awakening that morning I'd had no time to look in a mirror. As Dundas had swathed my entire head in a thick wrapping of field dressings, this was perhaps fortunate. My ear, however, was very sore. In addition to which I broke into a hacking fit whenever I said more than a few words. I expect that was due to the gas. There were some in my section that probably saw this as a blessing in disguise.

Before Fortuin we turned right down a dirt lane. After a stretch we moved off into some hedges virtually on the bank of a stream. The Zonnebeke apparently. Captain Arthur indicated we should dig in.

However before I put my back into *that* I figured I should get to the bottom of Bart's query. There was little point using all my remaining energy to shovel if we were to lead the advance in two hours. I cornered Lieutenant Critchley but he knew less than I did. Lieutenant Knowles was so tired I don't think he could spell his own name, let alone his rank. That left the captain.

'Sir?'

Arthur's eyes were as blood streaked as my ear. 'Yes, MacPhail?'

'Well, sir... the men are asking. Are we going into action to help the 11th Brigade?'

He shook his head. 'No. Apparently it was a misunderstanding. There's no break in the line.'

'And the battle, sir? How is the battle going?'

'The battle?' Arthur paused. 'The worst may be over, MacPhail. You can tell the men that. There are a lot of fresh divisions arriving as reinforcements. Right before he got hit by that shell during the march, Colonel Betty said he thought the Boche were running out of steam.'

'That sounds encouraging, sir.'

'What is less encouraging, Corporal, is the progress of the digging,' he said pointedly.

'Yes, sir, I'll get at it.'

For the rest of the day we endured a heavy shellfire. Dug-in in shell holes and small slit trenches astride the hedge, there were several casualties, but the enemy didn't knock on our door all day. For that I was grateful.

The other unequivocally good news was that I acquired a new rifle: a short Lee-Enfield no less. I found it next to a Tommy in a shell-hole and, seeing as how he wouldn't be needing it, I claimed it as my own. I left him with the Ross rifle. I hope he wasn't sore about it.

27th of April, 1915

'It's only supposed to be a single stripe,' I protested.

I'd gone over to the tumbledown brick shed beside the road that I was told housed the company quartermaster. I wouldn't have gone to the bother but Captain Arthur, looking only slightly better than he had the day before, accosted me about it.

'Where's your stripe, MacPhail? You're a corporal, and it's important that everyone can see that. Don't stand there gawking. The quartermaster's that way.' Off he went, mumbling something about having to do everything himself.

Explaining myself to the quartermaster I told him, 'I'm only a lance-corporal. So just a single one.'

Exasperated the company quartermaster sergeant shook his head.

He was an older man, in his mid-thirties, with silver-rimmed spectacles and a fleeting touch of grey in his hair. It wouldn't have surprised me if he was running a general store somewhere before signing up. 'It says here quite plainly: corporal,' he said. He pointed at a ledger that from my vantage point looked like it was written in hieroglyphics. 'A corporal has two stripes,' he continued. 'Besides which that's all I have at the moment. So, what'll it be?'

In the battle between my word and the quartermaster's ledger it was a foregone conclusion which would win. 'I just don't want any trouble from the major,' I mumbled.

'Look around you. You last a few more days, son, you may well be commanding this battalion. Don't worry about Major Ormond, he's off to hospital. By the time he gets back he'll be mighty glad he has another corporal. That'll be one less problem for him to deal with.'

I looked doubtful.

'Give me your tunic.'

I did and a few minutes later it was done. He handed it back and I returned to the others, not before glancing admiringly down my arm at the twin stripes midway between elbow and shoulder. Passing the bar exam had been more exhilarating, but this was a close second.

'Hmm,' said Dundas. He spotted me straight away and carefully scrutinized the new trimming on my sleeve. 'Not only can the quartermaster not count, he also missed a stitch.' Then he laughed and clapped me on the back. It was a momentary respite before the German guns forced us to seek cover.

At dusk the weary remnants of the Brigade mustered and we marched the miles down the road, passing through Wieltje and St. Jean until we came to the corner of Devil's Elbow north of Ypres where five long days before, trench-wise and thinking we knew a thing or two, we'd raced off to battle like young colts straining to break into a sprint. We returned as warriors, shuffling and stooped and licking our wounds, but proud. We had faced down the enemy with his poisonous gases, his massed guns and his endless battalions, and we had bested him; we had held him for longer than anyone could have hoped.

'It still doesn't feel much like a victory should, does it?' said Dundas.

'No. No, it doesn't,' I replied. 'But it doesn't feel like defeat, either. In some way that must make it a victory. I'd like to think so. For all the friends we're leaving behind.'

Heading west, we crossed the Yser Canal on a narrow stone bridge, towards bivouacs and rest I sincerely hoped. Turning my head I stared at the city as we marched over the bridge and out of the Salient. I shivered. The blooding of the battalion had nearly bled it dry; of the 816 men who'd gone into Kitcheners' Wood there were barely a hundred of us marching across that bridge. Ypres was a place I didn't care to see again. Once over the bridge we turned right and I knew I wasn't to have my wish.

29th of April, 1915

The city was a mere mile and a half downstream. We were bivouacked beside the west bank of the Yser in what the map described as C.19.c through C.25.c. We weren't there on a whim but to guard bridges no.'s 1 and 3. It was not the oasis of peace I'd been counting on although it did beat the front. Part of the problem was that the artillery was ranged all along the canal. They were firing what seemed like night and day. In itself that wouldn't have been more than a mild irritation, were it not that the Germans seemed well aware of the location of our guns. The result was a steady rain of shells, one or two hundred at a time, consisting of air bursts from the field guns (shrapnel) and loud shuddering concussions that you felt in your gut from the heavier guns (high explosive), that was exceedingly tedious – except when one landed close and then absolute terror took its place.

My ear – it had been improving – was sore again and tender to the touch. I probed at it with my fingertips, debating whether I should remove the dressing but fearful of what I might discover.

Lieutenant Knowles saw me at this.

'Why don't you go and have someone look at that?' he suggested. 'You have my permission. Up by our battery there's a dressing station.' He pointed at the spot. It wasn't far, a walk of a couple minutes. 'Behind the canal embankment they've built some bunkers; Essex Farm it's called. You'll find a doctor or an orderly there, I expect.'

So I did what he advised and walked north along the canal, and then climbed up and over the tree-lined embankment where I came to a small concrete bunker in its lee.

Uncertainly I glanced around. An officer – I guessed he was an officer – emerged from one of the doorways. I couldn't see his rank as his tunic was off and he had an apron on, his shirtsleeves rolled up to above the elbow. The apron was smeared in what looked like blood.

'Can I help you?' he asked. His face was an educated one, clean shaven, with a high brow and intent searching eyes. His hair was cut shorter on the sides than on top where it had already begun to curl; the overall effect making him appear younger than he was.

'Yes, sir. You see I was hit by some shrapnel a few days ago and it seemed to be healing, but it's become very sore and tender again. The lieutenant said there might be a doctor here.'

'Let me have a look.' He motioned for me to sit on what appeared to be an empty ammunition box.

He peeled off the dressing and I winced. 'Ah,' he said. 'You should have had this changed.' With a finger he poked around the side of my skull before gently prying back my ear.

'Ow.'

'Yes, it's pretty much what I thought. It's very red and there's obviously some infection. I'm going to cut it open again so it doesn't get gangrenous. Then I'll clean it up and put on a new dressing. A lot of the young men I see I can't do much for, but you I can.' He stopped fussing with my ear and looked at me. I wasn't the first nervous patient he'd ever had. 'Your ear will be fine, Corporal – not as pretty as it once was, but scars make the man they say. I expect it will clear up in a day or two. Whoever wrapped you up did a fine job, but you really should have had someone look at this earlier.'

'One thing or the other conspired to prevent it, sir. Germans, mainly.'

Softly he chuckled. 'What's your name?'

'MacPhail, sir, Malcolm MacPhail.'

Something in the trees caught my attention. 'Who'd have imagined?' I said, my voice laced in wonderment.

Questioningly he looked at me. 'Imagined what?' he asked.

'In the trees, sir. Death all around and the larks are still bravely singing.'

He looked over at the row of tall elms on the embankment, their green spring finery defiled by shells. A flock of birds had installed themselves and were giving it their best – a cheerful protest to the roar of the guns. Listening, his mouth broke into a wry smile before he turned his attention back to the cauliflower that was my ear.

'Alright,' he said, when he was done. 'The ear's all finished.'

'Thank you, sir. I was worried I might lose it.' I perched my cap on my head and stood up, but something was bothering me. 'I don't even know your name, sir,' I said.

'McCrae,' he replied, 'John McCrae.' Unusually, for an officer, his rank was left unspoken. Then he frowned and with visible irritation cocked his head skywards.

Above us an aeroplane was buzzing round in a lazy circle. Under his breath I heard him whisper, 'Accursed aeroplanes.' Sensing an explanation was in order he went on. 'They're enemy planes, coaching their artillery. We're supposed to be supporting the French and they're to attack again tomorrow. But that's a challenge when it's raining shells.' He shook his head in frustration and his voice deepened. 'Those aeroplanes have had it too much their way of late.'

'Don't look at me, sir. I'm just in the infantry.'

'Yes. Yes, of course,' he said, and I thought I spotted the beginnings of a weak smile as he turned to face me. 'Be thankful you're out of it for the moment, Malcolm.'

By nature I can be mildly cynical. That's what those who know me contend, although they usually omit the term "mildly". However McCrae's words turned out to be correct. After a couple of days we were ordered to Bailleul and the responsibility for bridges 1 and 3 fell to others. He and the divisional artillery remained behind; for them the ordeal was not yet over. For us, however, the second battle of Ypres had come to an end. Barely three months had passed since the King had waved the division off to war. One face in three was gone. Gone too was the boyish enthusiasm, a grim determination now lined the weary faces that remained. Inexperienced and eager we'd arrived in the Salient, as veterans we left, and I for one couldn't wait to leave – even if only to war.

PART TWO

CHAPTER 9

6th of May, 1915
Bailleul, France

We were up to our necks in suds on the northern outskirts of Bailleul.

'Seems fitting,' I said as steam wafted upwards, a misty haze obscuring the sterile tile walls and white painted ceiling. 'Being a lunatic asylum and all.'

'Hmm, hmm,' Dundas dreamily replied. 'Shame it wasn't a brewery. I wouldn't mind a beer. I don't see why the monks are allowed to brew beer and the sisters are stuck to the asylums. They could combine the two. There's never enough breweries around. No shortage of lunatics, either. You of all people might appreciate a place like that, Mac.'

'Hmm, hmm.' I was enjoying the bath too much to get into a lather about the fire from my flank. A day wallowing in chlorine gas tends to change your perspective on life. For the first time in two weeks I felt truly alive. It had been almost that long since I had changed my clothes. 'Did you know that the painter Van Gogh was once a resident here?' I asked.

'Really? Did he get gassed as well?'

'No, not exactly. Inhaled too much of his own paint, though.'

The lunatic asylum was a sizeable complex of buildings a short jaunt from Bailleul. It was fronted by a handsome two-story red-brick and stone edifice as imposing as that of any government ministry. Of course the ministries that counted were not in Bailleul but in places like Berlin, and they were generally called something other than asylums – though the nomenclature these days was all too easily confused. I questioned whether the residents here would have let things get so far out of hand in 1914.

16 grueling unconscionable miles we had marched to get to our billets a day earlier and it had nearly killed me. There were more than a few men who collapsed by the roadside in exhaustion and from the lingering effects of the gas. 16 miles on hard uneven pavé roads would have done anyone in – except perhaps the generals – they tended to travel exclusively by motorcade.

Flanders in France differed a little from the one in Belgium. The rolling countryside found to the north gave way here in France to a monotone of flat fields, cut by ditches and ugly, predominantly red-brick little buildings. Spring had transformed it. The trees had burst into blossom and the fields, not long before in their winter jacket of muddy brown, were a stunning palette of green. After the first seven miles I ignored the scenery and concentrated on getting one foot in front of the other.

When at long last we reached the tiny village of Merris, the state of my feet mirrored that of my ear and my lungs. So when we began marching back in the direction of the Salient and Bailleul this morning, I'd cursed the army something fierce. Prematurely as it turned out.

We were sent to bathe. Caked in the grime of the Salient, none us had dared to dream of a hot bath. A few extra miles back and forth suddenly seemed a small price to pay. For some reason the battalion had been selected. I would have said it was a question of numbers – as in few – but that unfortunately was true of the brigade's other three battalions as well.

There were four of us to a room and they'd rationed us to ten minutes each, give or take, and I was taking... every single minute I could snatch. The nuns with the towels, who doubled as overseers, were remarkably nonplussed by the sight of grown men cavorting round in their birthday suits. It was as well they hadn't heard me this morning or I might have been refused at the door.

'Speaking of breweries, there are some very well-known baths at Pont-de-Nieppe,' I said to Dundas. 'They're on the Lys River, not far from here. They call them the Brewery Baths on account of the huge vats: six feet deep and fifteen feet wide – more than a dozen men can squeeze into one of those. Don't get me wrong, Dundas, you're a swell guy, but when it comes to bathing I think I prefer the asylum.' I winked at him. The men in the tubs across from us, who couldn't help hearing, smiled.

Dundas meanwhile had retreated into himself. Our two bath mates, first expecting a reaction and then seeing none, resumed their conversation.

Dundas plunged his head into the hot water and came up dripping. The steam rising from his cropped head made it appear as if his hair was smoldering. 'Mac, I killed a man,' he said softly, staring into the bath.

It came completely out of the blue. He just said it. I put down the bar of soap. 'Several actually.'

I was about to express my surprise and tell him he couldn't have picked a better moment to improve upon his shooting when I saw his face – pained, uncertain and dead serious. The flippant witticism died on my lips. 'Oh?' I mumbled.

'Yes, I killed him alright. I looked him straight in the eye when I pulled the trigger. That's how I know. Ugly he was. A wide face and barely a chin to speak of, with a big bushy moustache and a pointed helmet right off one of those posters on the wall down at City Hall – you remember the ones? His eyes had that same crazed anger, which sounds ridiculous, but it's true. But after I shot him I couldn't help thinking. Was he afraid just like me? Perhaps that's why he looked so angry. Did he have a wife, maybe even a family waiting for him somewhere? You know. Those sort of things. I don't think I'll ever forget him.' At the thought Dundas sighed.

I didn't say anything. Dundas needed to get some things off his chest.

'A few hours later I shot a couple of others. It was during the attacks when we were on the ridge. Got one straight through the chest, barely a hundred yards away. And another right after. Saw him plow into the dirt; he was dead before he hit the ground. And you know what, Mac? *Then* I didn't think anything. Not about them in any event. Now they're dead and sitting here I can't even remember their faces. Do you suppose that's what war is, Mac? When the faces fade away?'

81

'Perhaps,' I said slowly... thinking. I was reliving the frantic few seconds in Kitcheners' Wood when I stuck a foot of hardened steel in a man for the first time. I couldn't recall much, only dreamlike flashes. It had all happened so quickly and been so dark. I did remember the barrel of his gun as he raised it towards me, his eyes already sighted on my chest. 'Perhaps, Roy,' I answered, 'but it doesn't do any good to think like that. You did what you had to do, like we all did and as we'll surely have to do again. This war is going to change us all. Frankly, it's something of a miracle we're still around.'

We didn't talk after that.

The door of the bathroom burst open and I could see that even for a nun heavenly patience had its limits. '*Allez, vite. Il y a d'autres, messieurs,*' she admonished, thrusting a towel at us.

By some wonder, more worldly than divine, our pants and tunics were pressed and brushed, my shirt and undergarments still damp to the touch. I held them to my face. Dressing I could still smell the soap.

'I haven't felt this clean since we arrived in Europe,' said one of the others.

His friend replied, 'Or smelt it either!'

Dundas and I looked at each other and grinned.

'Listen to this,' I said. Someone had left a week-old *Daily Telegraph* on a table in the dressing room and I snatched it up as I passed. It was only after I saw the headline that I realized it was devoted to us.

Dundas was already half-way to the door.

'No wait,' I said. 'You really have to hear this. "Canadian charge. Heroic recovery of captured guns. Conduct magnificent," it says.' He and the others came and crowded over my shoulder to read it for themselves.

'This is the best part, I said. "...the Canadians made a most brilliant and successful advance, recapturing these guns and taking a considerable number of German prisoners, including a colonel."'

'I thought we were rather magnificent,' I heard behind me.

'Brilliant even.'

'I don't mean to be petty,' I said, 'but there's not much brilliance involved in a mad charge which gets half the battalion killed.' Too late, I realized I sounded like a carbon copy of my father when he was sounding off on something *he'd* read, the grumpy stick-in-the-mud I'd promised myself I'd never be. 'Nice to be recognized for what we did, though,' I added. By that time the room was emptying.

Men who were lost or who had been mixed up with one of the other units in the sheer frenzy and confusion had steadily rejoined the ranks. So too did those who were lightly gassed or wounded. Spirits not long before numb and overwhelmed by the experience and the losses were recovering. Smiles and jokes had returned. We even whistled as we marched back to Merris.

There a surprise awaited. A draft from England had arrived: 346 men and 18 officers. Fresh, well-turned out, and as green as the fields of Flanders had once been. From the goggle-eyed looks they gave us when we marched by they'd clearly all been reading the *Daily Telegraph*.

A corporal isn't much in the army, the next rank to nothing really. But with few other NCOs or officers left I had enjoyed a modest step up in responsibility. With the reinforcements that would change, but for now the business of rebuilding the battalion had begun and there was a lot to do.

A voice I half recognized, and which was neither goggle-eyed nor particularly friendly, barked behind me. 'MACPHAIL.'

I groaned to myself, slightly puzzled. How could I possibly have irritated one of the new sergeants or officers so soon? They hadn't even unpacked. Wearily I turned.

'Oh,' I said. 'It's you.'

CHAPTER 10

6th of May, 1915
Merris, France

'Of course, it's me. Who'd you expect, Santa Claus?'

He brayed loudly at his own joke, which gave me a chance to take in what he looked like. Not much different I concluded. Harry Hobson was the same flat-faced bully he'd always been. Eyes a little too close together to mistake him for a Rhodes Scholar, and a sickle-shaped scar on his cheek to repeat the message. Here in French Flanders his nose was the biggest bulge in the landscape for miles, even though they said it had been broken three times already. The uniform hadn't changed a thing in Harry Hobson. Well, except that instead of a flick knife he now carried a foot-long bayonet and a loaded rifle.

'Fancy seeing you here, Harry. Come to tour the sites of Europe?'

I said it casually. As casually as I could manage. My breathing, though, came in short nervous gulps, which I knew wasn't down to the gassing and I hoped he didn't hear it in my voice. I'd always been slightly uneasy around him. Since the middle of August 1914 I had avoided him like the plague.

He stared me down. Looking first at my cap and then at my tunic. The filling upstairs might have been more meringue than rhubarb, but there was nothing wrong with his eyes, and I guessed he'd spotted the bullet holes.

Gruffly, he spoke. 'Wondered if I'd find you here.'

'I'm surprised you made the connection, Harry.'

Suspiciously he stared at me to see if I was mocking him, which I was.

In Calgary I'd steered a wide circle around Harry. I couldn't avoid him altogether as his father, Mr. Hobson of Hobson's Hardware, was far-and-away my best client. When you're just getting started in the legal profession there's little you won't do for your best client. I was, however, troubled he might ask if I would represent his third and youngest son, who seemed just the type to tear up the Long Bar at the Alberta Hotel some night. Worse, I suspected Harry might have had more than a passing connection with the robbery of $11,000 in diamonds from the Doll Block, a couple of years earlier. They might have only been rumours, but I tended to believe them. Either way, I was quite certain that neither my new bride Kathryn nor the upstanding citizens of the city whose business I dearly hoped to win would approve of my defending Harry.

I think Harry's father would sometimes have liked to have tucked his son away in the locked cabinet of his storage room, together with the odd-sized screws no one ever asked for. Antarctica would have been my suggestion. Harry was what you might call the "black sheep" of the Hobson family.

'I'm glad I finally caught up with you, MacPhail. Now I can finally take your block off. I've wanted to do that for a long time, you know. And no one will blame me after what you did to Pa...'

Dundas appeared out of nowhere. 'Before you do that, sport, you might want to take a look at his arm. Those stripes there – two of them in case you're having trouble counting – belong to a corporal. So when you're making your plans to take someone's "block" off, you might think about that. There's a funny thing here in the army they call military law and it's not as forgiving as the kind you may be accustomed to. With any luck you might even find yourself in front of a firing squad.'

Harry glowered. But I could see he was intimidated. Bullies don't take well to bigger bullies and Dundas played the part brilliantly. The meek banker had disappeared. I put it down to two weeks in the Salient and a submersion in chlorine gas.

'I won't be forgetting what you did to Pa,' Harry muttered in my direction. 'Maybe the law will be interested in that story.' As threats go it lacked a certain finesse, but I knew all too well what he meant.

He spat on the ground and moved off to his buddies who were bewildered by the tension in the air.

'What was *that* all about?' asked Roy, still following Harry with his eyes.

'Oh, nothing,' I said.

'Yeah, right.' He shot me a look that wouldn't have been out of place if I'd told him I was selected for the 1916 Olympics… the ones in Berlin.

I shook my head. 'Now's not the time,' I said. In the distance I'd spotted Major Guthrie. Subtly I gave Dundas the heads-up to warn him and said, 'I'll tell you later.' Our new OC was approaching and first impressions are important ones.

Later came precisely two days later in an unnamed *estaminet* in the village of Merris. Surprisingly, this was my first time in such a place. Someone must have felt we deserved a rest for they left us virtually to our own devices, even permitting a prized night out, something that had been unheard of back in England. After what we'd gone through an *estaminet* was everything I could have wished for – even if it was only open from 6 till 8.

This particular *estaminet* was located in an old dilapidated farm-house on the outskirts of the tiny village. Small but cozy, with the signs of domestic living still visible such as children's scribblings on the rough plaster walls. It had once been someone's living room, but there was no mistaking its current function. Half the brigade was packed inside, seated at long tables and equally long benches. There was a noisy chorus of ribald song and excited voices. A dense blueish fug supported the low wood-beamed ceiling. The smoke was unlikely to thin given that the doors and windows were hermetically closed, a cigarette hung from every lip in the room, and a wood-burning stove defiantly smouldered away in the warm spring air.

For the price of a small motorcar at home you could even purchase a drink. As motorcars were not an accepted part of our kit, although some officers had gone to the trouble of bringing their horses overseas, all gladly accepted the alternative. Even Dundas had put away his abacus for the occasion. Banker or not, the magic of compound interest dulls when you wonder if you're going to be around in another week.

'Thanks,' I said, wiping at my brow before gulping greedily at the beer he proffered. 'Pff,' I sputtered in disappointment. 'Perhaps we should move on to the local tipple next round? What do you think, Roy? This beer's got less taste than water. Probably less alcohol too.'

The wine did pack a punch of sorts, though both of us puckered our lips at the first of several sips. After an initial acquaintance the next slid down smoothly. The ugly duckling daughter of the similarly well-proportioned proprietress assured us it was "*très bon*". That was understandable from the point of view of her and her family who were peddling it; some were making out quite well from this war. Admittedly, it helped that she said it in French. It is an underappreciated aspect of the language that it can make the worse things in life sound not half-bad.

Roy inched closer to me on the bench. Not because he was afraid someone would overhear us; only that another group had squeezed in at the far end and were expanding their territory.

'So?' he said, meaningfully, staring at me.

I didn't misunderstand his meaning. 'What can I tell you?'

'The story, to begin with. And who the hell is Harry Hobson?'

I gulped at the wine, a decent gulp that probably put me back a couple of days pay. 'That's what I was afraid of,' I said, contemplating the now almost empty glass. After a pause that might have been construed as me ignoring him but was really just a gathering of thoughts, I began. 'Do you remember when I told you about my wife dying last summer?'

He nodded. 'Tuberculosis, wasn't it?'

'Yes, that's right. Well, not long after Kathryn's funeral my best client came to me. A Mr. Hobson. That would have been two weeks or so after the war broke out, sometime in mid-August. He was a decent soul, Hobson, impeccably polite and always with a kind word or a concerned enquiry about how I was faring. In some ways he wasn't so much a client as a friendly uncle. He was very complimentary about how I'd taken care of his affairs and we got along famously. However, this one day he was in a terrible frenzy. Wanting to know whether I'd delivered the papers to the city for the extension to his store that he was planning. Which I hadn't done. I hadn't even started the paper-work. Most of the previous week I'd spent trying to arrange Kathryn's affairs, and her family were anything but helpful. Quite the opposite. Her father was a well-known barrister in town and he went through every single comma with a fine-toothed comb – as if trying to prove that my shortcomings as a lawyer and not tuberculosis were somehow responsible for his daughter's death. Anyhow, when I mumbled some-thing to Hobson about having been preoccupied, he exploded. He went literally blue in the face. Began waving his fists in my face and calling me all sorts of names. One name I took particular exception to. So, I clobbered him.'

'You!? You're a big guy, Mac, but you're not exactly the type to go around beating up older men.'

'Perhaps not, but on this occasion that's precisely what I did. He was in pretty bad shape afterwards and that's exactly how I felt as well. Particularly when I learned that son Harry had been up to his usual shenanigans, which was why Mr. Hobson was so exercised in the first place. I suspect he came to me looking for advice and a sympathetic ear. Instead I damn near broke his jaw.'

'So what happened?'

'I laid low the rest of that day and tried to think of a way out.'

'What about the police?'

'They didn't come. I was sure they would. I figured it would only be a matter of time before I was charged with aggravated assault or worse. To top it off no one seemed to know anything about Mr. Hobson's condition that first day. My wife was dead. My legal career was too. Whatever the mitigating circumstances, beating up your best client is not great for business. My life was in what you might politely call tatters and, frankly, I didn't see any solutions.'

'Ah,' said Roy, now ignoring his wine. 'So *that's* why you joined the army?'

'That's right. The next day in fact. The recruiting office had just opened. They shipped us off to Quebec in no time, as you probably remember, and I figured I'd put it all behind me.'

'Until Harry showed up?'

I drained the last of my glass and sighed. 'Exactly.'

'So what now?'

Yes, what now? That was the very question burning on my mind. I wondered if the long arm of the law stretched all the way to France. But I said none of this to Dundas. Instead I shrugged. Then suggestively I held up my empty glass.

9th of May, 1915

We had an easy few days of it, resting. The strange thing was, the more I rested the more restless I became. More than once I woke up mumbling a name, visions of familiar faces flashing in my mind as Hell replayed itself. It was only after I awoke that I could put names to the faces: Jones, Sergeant-Major Atkins, Fred Fox, young Harold and all the others.

At times when the wind blew from the right direction we could hear the distant rumble of the guns in the Salient where the fighting was plainly still raging. We rested until the 9th. On that morning came orders that we should be ready to move on "notice of one hour".

As Major-General Alderson was to inspect the brigade in two hours this caused considerable consternation in the ranks of the newly arrived officers. By the time they had worked out a plan, and that had filtered down to the ranks of the corporals, I had a list of things to do as long as my arm.

Alderson appeared shortly before 10 a.m. I'd seen him previously on a handful of occasions but he was the highest ranking army officer I was acquainted with, so I observed carefully. Canada didn't have any major generals and, by all accounts, Lord Kitchener was not predisposed to altering this state of affairs – certainly not with a horde of wild men from the colonies to whip into shape. So Alderson, conveniently both an Englishman and a major-general with somewhat of a reputation from the Boer War, had become our divisional commander.

He seemed a decent type. However, I didn't discern much in the way of battle damage in the general's uniform – cooped-up five miles behind the lines at the lovely Château des Trois Tours he had spared himself some expensive tailoring work.

Underneath the skipping rope of thick gold braid that enlivened the visor of his cap, the general had small dark eyes that were in danger of being overrun by eyelids looking as if they'd seen one long lunch too many. Alderson's least impressive feature was his nose. From a number of angles it distinctly resembled a rubber door-stopper. Sensibly he'd grown a moustache so thick and dense it diverted attention. In the army they called that a deception, and I imagine it's where he picked up the trick.

Brigadier Currie ushered General Alderson along the ranks of the 2nd Brigade, in order of battalion: 5th, 7th, 8th and 10th. There were a lot of men for the brigadier to introduce. General Alderson showed less interest in my face than I had in his, but then even at reduced strength there were a lot of faces to look at, and we were last in line.

A speech followed. As speeches go it was rather good I thought.

'I have never been so proud of anything in my life as my armlet with "Canada" on it,' said the general. 'I know my military history pretty well, but I cannot think of an instance, especially when the cleverness and determination of the enemy is taken into account, in which troops were placed in such a difficult position; nor can I think of an instance in which so much depended upon the standing fast of one division.'

The men roared their approval. I couldn't help noticing that the loudest roars came from those who had just arrived. When the brass left the lines of soldiers were dismissed and I turned to a few of the others. The faces were all glowing.

'I'm new to the game,' I said, 'but I can't think of an instance in which a general gave a speech like that without something big following.'

Dundas groaned. 'Jesus, Mac. You're about as much fun as an empty bottle of Fullers.'

'That's what two months in Belgium will do for you,' I said. 'Besides I haven't seen a bottle of Fullers in four months,' and I winked at him. Twenty yards away a stationary figure caught my eye.

Harry Hobson was glowering at me. He didn't say anything but he didn't have to. His eyes were doing the talking. I had an uneasy feeling that I might need to grow a pair in the back of my head. The enemy wasn't solely in front anymore.

CHAPTER 11

17th of May, 1915
Between Robecq and Locon, France

There is nothing quite so dreary in all the world like the feeling of marching to battle, where and why one does not know, with impenetrable grey cloud hanging low in the sky for as far as the eye can see. Though the eye doesn't linger aloft for long, not with an unrelenting downpour from above, and gusts of driving wind to blow it into upturned faces – mine in particular. That it was six-thirty in the morning didn't help in the slightest.

Bent forward, caps down low, attention for only our boots on the uneven path that ran alongside La Bassée Canal, we were heading to Locon and eventually battle – at least if the knowing tongues were to make their reputations good. The rain began this morning. While one might breezily think rain is rain, I was convinced the European sort was of a far more insidious variety than we were accustomed to. At home the clouds would move across and the sky would darken menacingly, before a few claps of thunder and sometimes a bolt of lightning would signal the beginning, and then it would pour. Usually this lasted for a few hours after which the clouds sailed off to the east, chased by brilliant blue skies and occasionally a rainbow or two. In northern France and Belgium the rain was of a more determined character. It moved in and entrenched – drizzling and colouring the days a sullen despondent grey, to soak not only your clothes but your very soul. It was not altogether dissimilar to the tactics the Germans were employing, which is likely how they came up with them.

We marched along the left bank of the canal for some time, heading roughly southeast.

The man beside me, William Partridge, better known as Bill, spoke up. 'Do you suppose this has anything to do with the *Lusitania* disaster?' he asked. Bill was a talkative sort.

I raised my face to the rain so he might hear. 'Well both involve a great deal of water,' I pontificated.

Under the circumstances it was rather tactless. But I thought it might shut him up. Since we'd got the news a week ago, there'd been plenty of talk about the *Lusitania*. More than a thousand men, women and children had perished in water a lot colder, darker and deeper than the canal off my starboard side when a German submarine torpedoed their passenger liner. To the world it was a terrible scandal and an outrage. Having been treated to the enemy's chlorine clouds, I was less shocked than some. However, this was neither the time nor the place, and most decidedly not the weather to discuss it.

Partridge, a new man to the battalion, was unperturbed by my crassness. 'No. I meant that we're to take it to the Hun, to pay him back for what he did.'

'Maybe,' I said. 'All I know is that the French have begun a huge new offensive. Seeing as how we're moving south, perhaps we're to be part of it. I don't know.'

He persisted. 'But will *we* see action?'

Wearily I shook my head. 'I don't think you need worry about that, Bill.'

'Well, that's a relief then,' he said. 'I can't wait.' To my astonishment he said it like he meant it.

I groaned loudly. 'I'll hold you to that. Remind me to ask how you're feeling when it's over.'

Even Bill Partridge's enthusiasm began to wilt in the face of the rain and my obvious cynicism. All the new guys were terribly eager to hear about battle from one of the "old-timers", less so when the old-timers began dishing out well-meaning advice. But then as a child I'd never much heeded my parents' warnings either, not until

Sarah Bentley had dared me to put my finger on the still hot stovetop. Partridge nodded and didn't speak again until we reached our billets on the far side of the village.

The billets turned out to consist of a single barn and a few outhouses – not nearly large enough for the entire battalion, which had swollen to more than 800 men. Other units in the area had apparently snatched up the remaining accommodations. Someone blamed the cavalry. It felt like trying to find a hotel on Victoria Day with the entire family ending up sleeping in the car, and without the air of celebration. The fireworks were missing, too. I feared those would not be long in coming. The sound of cannon fire had intensified as we approached Locon.

19th and 20th of May, 1915
Festubert, France

The next day we marched only as far as the rue du Bois and more comfortable billets in a forgettable little hamlet called Le Touret. Le Touret was a mere 5 kilometres down the road in an easterly direction from Locon – impossible to miss, I heard the farmer assuring one of the officers. Having made its acquaintance I wasn't sure I agreed; a blink of the eye and you were through it.

Today the march was shorter still. Shortly after leaving Le Touret we turned right, heading due south, onto a pavé lined by pollarded willows called the rue de l'Epinette. After approximately a mile, we came to a crossroads in a flat land, riven with irrigation ditches. Shortly thereafter a small sign announced the village of Festubert – our destination.

Festubert consisted of a scattering of shell-torn one- and two-story brick homes, shops and farmhouses lining the road, none of which looked occupied or worth the bother of defending. If there was any great strategic importance to Festubert I couldn't see it. Someone, somewhere, must have thought quite differently, for there was a great deal of gunfire as we approached. It didn't seem the sort of place we'd be sent if the objective was to resume our rest and relaxation. A little training was also in order as more than a third of the battalion had arrived less than two weeks previously and knew as much about trench warfare as my grandmother did.

Any thoughts of training, and definitely of rest, were dispelled when we turned off the rue de l'Epinette into what we were told was Willow Road. There were two things blatantly obvious about the Artois; it was flat, and it was wet. Neither was propitious for an infantryman.

Ahead were the trenches, but as it was too early to go in Lieutenant Critchley ordered us to lie in the damp grass alongside the road for a time. The air, still heavy from the recent rains, smelled of gun powder. There was no mistaking where we were; we were back at the front. 40 miles from Ypres and only two weeks later, we were back in the thick of it.

Dundas looked over at me and I looked over at him. Neither of us said anything. If I'd been Catholic I would have crossed myself. Dundas wasn't Catholic either; he just looked sour.

'Keep your heads down,' was the first thing I told my section upon entering the trench. Half of them didn't need to be told, but the other half risked being wiped out in the first five minutes… even if it was pitch dark.

In the darkness the familiar smells returned; the pungent earthy scent of the manure-fertilised fields now given over to lines of zig-zagging ditches; the fleeting wisps of tobacco smoke and cooking odours from the men who inhabited them; and the unmistakable sharp scent of cordite, smoke and battle which preoccupied the inhabitants. We filed along, glad for the guide from the British regiment whom we were here to relieve. There seemed to be little rhyme or reason to the trench layout. I quickly realized there was something else which didn't quite fit; the parapets and the dug-outs were built on the wrong side. Which is when it occurred to me, these trenches had been German.

Shortly the sergeant came along and set us to work. We dug funk holes in the trench walls and used the earth to fill sandbags to build up a parapet. The Germans began to shell us around this time and for the sake of the new men, and perhaps to justify the two stripes on my arm, I bustled back and forth like an old-timer as if it were nothing more than a light shower falling on our heads. The knot in my stomach argued otherwise.

At the sound of a piercing whine screaming closer, old-timers and new dove for a corner. This was followed by a brilliant flash and long seconds later... a loud BANG. 'Damn that was close,' said someone. Just as we felt safe to breathe again, a deluge of earth fell on our heads.

'105mm,' I said coolly. 'Light howitzer. Similar to our 4.7 inch guns, like the ones we recaptured at Kitcheners' Wood.'

The new faces stared at me – if not in awe, then in wonderment. The old ones looked away and went back to what they were doing. And I tried not to shake.

At 4 a.m. the artillery fire increased and I woke from an uneasy sleep. Forcing myself to my feet I looked both ways down my section of trench. The sentries were still there. But the rest of the men, like me, were curled up in the damp earthen holes in the trench wall trying to forget where they were. I wondered how Bill Partridge was faring. I hadn't seen him. Which is when another shell erupted, immediately north of us.

Dundas appeared at my side. 'That sounded bad,' he said.

There was no need to reply. Someone twenty yards further was shrieking in pain.

Wearily I shook my head. 'We should sleep.'

He grunted. 'I wish I could. I just keep lying there, listening.'

'That bad?'

'Yeah, what about you?'

Another shell erupted, saving me the trouble of immediately responding. After the reverberations in my ears dimmed I said, 'I don't know, Roy. After Ypres I figured I was prepared for anything. Only I'm discovering I'm not prepared at all. I don't feel much like an old-timer, I feel like an eighteen-year old right off the boat. And now I've got this bloody badge on my arm,' I said, indicating the chevrons.

'So now you're a corporal you can't let it show that you're nervous?'

I shrugged.

'Well,' he said slowly. 'I figure if my time has come, it's come, and there's no sense fretting about it. That doesn't do me or anyone else any good. Your problem, Mac, is that you think everything through far too much.'

'I thought my problem was my mouth?'

Dundas pretended to think about this. 'Well, that too.'

Soon the two of us crawled back into our holes, not so much because we were suddenly overtaken by exhaustion, but rather to escape the shellfire.

Dawn came and for a welcome change there was only the sound of birdsong. It was strangely beautiful. More so because the drizzle had ended. In the distance, though, the guns were still at it. But that was there. Here, we took advantage of the calm to boil up some water to make tea in which to dip our hardtack. On top of all my other concerns I wasn't about to break my teeth on breakfast.

A couple of hours later the German gunners woke from their slumber and began shovelling Jack Johnsons into gun breeches still warm from the night before. We dove for cover. Fortunately they soon broke for a late breakfast. Silence, or a rough proxy of it, fell again upon our shell-torn plot.

That was until the crack of a rifle sounded. It was close by. Rifle fire was hardly new, but when I heard it a second time shortly thereafter I knew something was awry and I went over to the steel plate we'd fastened into the parapet.

'And?' I asked the sentry. 'What are they up to?'

'A sniper,' he replied. 'I think he's shooting our wounded, the bastard.'

'Let me see,' I ordered and stepped up to take a look.

Through the narrow slit it was difficult to see anything. Eventually my breathing slowed and my eyes adjusted and I could make out the ribbon of No-Man's-Land in front. It was bare and ravaged. The few trees that had once dotted this dull northern French landscape remained only as shards of wood stuck in a chocolate-brown field that looked as pockmarked as a peach pit. There were bodies lying amidst it all. Most were dead but some were clearly not, for I saw movement. A man was attempting to crawl in our direction. It was one of the English soldiers from the attack a couple of days earlier. He'd lain there for two days and nights in pain.

There was another shot. A tiny ball of smoke puffed from the parapet opposite. When I looked closer I even spotted the tip of a barrel poking out. Out in the mud the soldier's head jerked, then fell forward. I kept watching, hoping to see some sign of life. After a minute I drew my face away and stepped down from the fire-step. But not before I'd marked the shooter's spot to memory.

'God damn sniper,' I cursed, and went to gather some men. When I told them about it there was no shortage of volunteers.

No-Man's-Land was rather narrow here, but then we were occupying what a few days earlier had been the main German trench line. By necessity the Germans were currently entrenched in what had been the first of their support lines. There couldn't be more than a few hundred yards between us. Less even. To pick off a wounded man lying on his stomach in the middle of that field the sniper didn't need to be much of a marksman. He did need to be a sadist. Which was what really got my goat.

I explained my plan to the others and we broke into two groups.

This being a German trench system brought with it two principal advantages; firstly, the sniper wasn't terribly far away so that meant neither were we; and secondly, both lines ran roughly parallel to each another and were connected by a profusion of communication trenches. You could have likened it to a spider web, where a network of thin spokes linked the main concentric rings. Naturally, where the two sides butted heads in one of these connecting ditches we'd thrown up a barricade to block the Germans, and they'd done likewise. However, I happened to know that 50 yards down the communication trench to our immediate right, the block wasn't more than a couple of planks and some strands of wire. One of the first things I'd done this morning when it was light was to reconnoitre my small domain. It was something Sergeant-Major Atkins had once explained, I think.

Dundas took two men off to the left, to head down one of the spokes as far as they could. In ten minutes they were to make a "huge kerfuffle" – that's how I'd worded it. After the Salient I trusted Dundas to have sufficient inspiration to fill in the details in for himself. I went right with three others. This left only two men to hold down the fort – quite reasonable for what I had in mind.

Having reached the first shallow rung of the chain-of-command it simply didn't occur to me to run off and get someone's permission. That was something a banker might do. Or a lawyer, come to that. "Ass-covering" was what I usually called it. In hindsight I might not have been so peremptory.

'Quiet,' I hissed to Albert. Albert was a new man who had arrived the day before, and like many of the new men he seemed to find the war a bit of a lark. I had a mind to put a fist in his mouth. But that would have put paid to any hopes of surprise we might have.

Ten yards from the block I whispered, 'Hold up.' We squatted down on our haunches and leaned forward on our rifles. Another rifle shot cracked – the sniper – and the men's faces turned grim. We didn't have to wait long before we heard Dundas and party. A bomb went off with a muffled bang and they began shooting like mad. Ahead I heard the clatter of equipment, the stomp of feet and guttural voices which soon dimmed. They'd gone to see what was happening.

'Alright start cutting,' I instructed Riley. It took him only a few clips with the wire cutters and a couple of good yanks on the timbers and we were through. There was a great deal of shooting going on by this stage and that suited our purposes just fine.

We rushed down the trench in single file, then turned into the support trench, which was considerably wider. The Germans had thoughtfully laid down some duckboards to spare our boots from the mud. A fellow in a *Pickelhaube* stood on the fire-step, shooting over the parapet. Without a word, and before the man noticed us, Riley stepped forward with his bayonet. One thrust and the German made a croaking noise and fell to the ground. Quickly we moved on. The sniper couldn't be far.

Sure enough, twenty feet on we came to a shallow sap dug out in the direction of our lines. An observation post most likely. At the end of it lay a man crouched over some sandbags, his rifle resting on one of them. In front of him was a sandbagged wall in which a metal plate with a narrow slit had been fastened and it was through that hole that his rifle protruded. The man was peering down his sights, but at the sound of our hobnailed soles thumping towards him on the duckboards he turned. When he saw who it was a look of panic passed over his face. Our pace slowed.

Deliberately I advanced on him, rifle and bayonet held at the hip. There was no way he could possibly retrieve the rifle in time. He knew it and I knew it. But then he reached for his side and I saw the holster. I pulled the trigger. Behind me someone else did as well. A voice grumbled, 'That'll teach 'em.'

We left him there sprawled in the mud. We didn't search his pockets or take his rifle. There was no time and there were too few of us, and we raced back to our lines as fast as our feet would allow.

In broad daylight there was little else we could do for the wounded on our doorstep; at least now they had a chance.

A few hours later new orders arrived. The battle we'd been awaiting was upon us.

FESTUBERT AND GIVENCHY

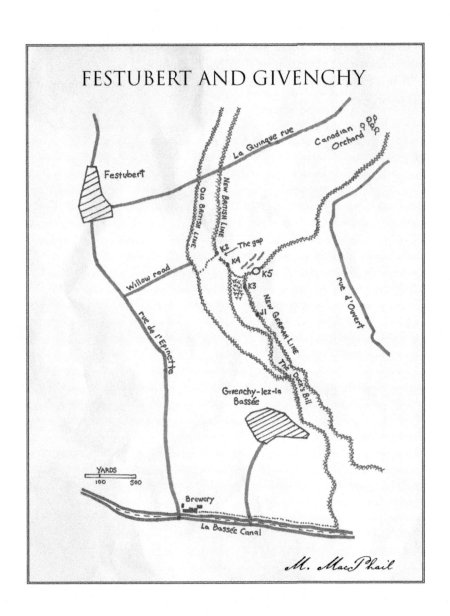

Festubert

La Quinque rue

Canadian Orchard

OLD BRITISH LINE

NEW BRITISH LINE

K2 — The gap

KA

K5

K3

J1

Willow road

rue de l'Épinette

NEW GERMAN LINE

rue d'Ouvert

The Duck's Bill

Givenchy-lez-la
Bassée

YARDS
100   500

Brewery

La Bassée Canal

M. MacPhail

CHAPTER 12

20th of May, 1915
Festubert, France

In mid-May, dusk comes reasonably early in northern France and the sky was darkening perceptibly when we received word that we were to attack.

But it was far from dark, and as it was sometime around 7 p.m., it wouldn't be for two hours more. We were told the objective was a *Stützpunkt* known as K.5. This meant little to us so I asked around. However the sergeants whose business it was to know such things shrugged their shoulders in weary ignorance. That we were to attack was all they could reveal, which even when you're bumping the bottom of the totem pole as I was, seemed worrisomely uninformed.

'Ah, so we'll recognize K.5 when we capture it,' I said to one of them, feigning good cheer. 'No sense spoiling the surprise must be the thinking. Don't want to open the present before Christmas and all that,' I joked. Whereupon he threw up his shoulders and growled at me to make myself scarce. That I escaped a reprimand for the acerbity of my tongue proved only how frustrated the sergeants were.

That no one was happy with this state of affairs was clear, except perhaps the new men who were so new they still dreamed there was glory in battle. When you think like that all that matters is not *what* is to be done, but *when*, and when is never soon enough. With three very long months in the trenches behind me I found it far too soon, particularly as we had less than an hour to prepare. The objective had the ring of a Himalayan mountaintop to it, only we found ourselves at lower elevations trying to skirt irrigation ditches and MG08s in the French Artois. I had the sense of a blindfolded man walking towards a cliff; one with his stomach in knots.

Unlike the new men who didn't suffer such doubts, I was all too well aware what battle meant. Following my curious upwelling of rage that morning I found myself thinking that hunting down the sniper was a case of temporary insanity. It frightened me to know what I was capable of. Equally it frightened me that I felt none of that now, only my own mortality and a heart beating far too quickly.

'If you can make sense of this bloody map, MacPhail, you can have it,' said Lieutenant Critchley when I badgered him for a snippet of information. Corporals are not encouraged to interrogate lieutenants, but Critchley was used to it, I think.

It was an offer I naturally couldn't refuse and eagerly I snatched the map from his hands. Critchley had worries of his own, and an entire platoon to think about, but he couldn't restrain himself from smiling bemusedly. I wondered what could possibly account for this show of good humour; the sergeants had been downright grumpy, though grumpiness was a hazard of the trade for those with three stripes.

I studied the map. The first thing I deduced was that it was printed upside down – north was south, and south was north. Confidently I turned it around, pleased I would soon relieve the lieutenant of his map. Then I felt my features twist into a frown. Critchley was smiling. *The damned thing was printed in reverse!* I spotted what appeared to be K.5. It wasn't a map reference, merely a small circle where two German lines came together. It resembled the peak of a mountain tilted on its side. K.5 could be anything really. I couldn't find any other clues so I flipped the map over and held it up to the light, hoping to read it through the paper. It was far too light to be attacking, but far too dark for that.

'Hmm,' I allowed, unwilling to admit defeat so soon. 'You might try reading it with the help of a mirror, sir…'

'Yes, yes,' groaned Critchley, 'I tried that. It gave me a headache. Sort of like what you're doing now, MacPhail. Smart fellow like you

– I thought you'd figure it out straight away.' A scornful laugh was on his lips, poised to emerge.

Before it did, I handed back the map and beat a hasty retreat.

The orders were at short notice and that didn't lend itself to much of anything other than grabbing one's rifle. As far as I saw, the only benefit to this schedule was that I was spared an agonizing wait. I held my Lee-Enfield, grasped tightly, not out of nervousness I attempted to convince myself – my hands were admittedly clammy – but to ensure it wouldn't be nicked by one of the others. I'd spotted a few men enviously eyeing it and was quite certain it would disappear if I let my guard down.

At precisely 7.45 p.m., two of the battalion's companies began to move forward and I found myself in one of them. It was gloomy but by no means dark. In another hour it might have been, however the orders didn't take account of that. The enemy spotted us almost immediately, or so I assumed for I heard machine guns and rifles rattling. Our artillery bombardment, such as it was, consisted of a handful of field guns and not a single heavy. It had ended some time before.

Before long we were out of the assembly area in the old British line in the rear, turning left and heading almost straight in the direction of the Germans down a narrow ditch. Four hundred of us shuffled forward in single file. The ditch was nowhere near tall enough to stand in, with only a double row of sandbags behind which to shelter. So like the rest of the company I was bent over as far as possible, conscious my 6-foot-one frame made an excellent target. We were dangerously exposed, vulnerable to enfilade fire from along an entire stretch of their trenches.

In the soft light of evening the enemy line would normally be tricky to see. So I was startled when I saw a thousand flashes rippling up and down it along a 200-yard stretch. All were firing at us. *So much for the artillery.* I quickened my pace in response but quickly ran into the back of the man in front.

Before long we came across men huddled miserably against the shallow dirt walls and were forced to step laboriously around them. I could see from their faces and the way in which they held themselves that they were wounded. Several minutes later the ditch intersected a trench at a point resembling a "Y". To the left was our fire-trench.

To the right was a narrow communication trench that would lead us towards the enemy. We turned right.

As we did a soldier cried out, 'Jesus, they can see us through the gap.' The file in front faltered. Almost instantly I saw what the problem was. The trench ahead was breached – whether by water or by shellfire was not clear – and a wide, open gap of ten yards or more lay before us.

If we were to continue we'd need to pass through it. Heading southeast, the trench continued to a spot known as K.4 where there was a block, and shortly thereafter it curved eastwards and led directly into the German lines. At a slight angle to our immediate left, through the gap and across the open ground to the east, was a short-cut to K.5 and the enemy line.

K.5 was our objective, but the direct route through No-Man's-Land meant certain death. The ground was broken and uneven, and after 200 yards led to several waterlogged ditches of the kind which characterised this wet Artois country. The ditches were brimming with rainwater. Behind them strings of unbroken wire were visible, standing faithful guard over the German trenches.

Whizzing bullets strummed the air. I could see them chewing up the dirt around. A man in front stepped hastily into the open and immediately shuddered, caught by a short burst. He went down. A half-dozen men ahead of me chose this moment to make a run for it now that the gunner was reloading.

The man in front and his pal tore off. Then it was my turn. I drew a lungful of air, crouched low, and sprinted. As I emerged into open terrain I entered the gates of Hades. It was all I could do to escape death there and then, and I ran on. The man whose back I knew so well dropped in a hail of lead a few steps into the open. The man in front of him fell one step later. I dived to the ground.

Another machine gun began chattering.

The machine guns seemed to surround us, their angry rattle was fearsome. Bullets whizzed and whined above my head. I heard cries for help and frantic admonitions from one of the officers to move forward – miraculously one was still alive. Nowhere was there any cover to be found so I lay prone with my head resting on the damp earth. Those unlucky enough to be in front did the same. Most were hit already and many of them wouldn't move again, no matter what the lieutenant shouted. There were bodies everywhere. Some even lay one on top of the other; the man behind a split second too late in realizing what had become of the first.

But then I concluded I couldn't remain where I was. With a grunt I wrested myself from the mud that had me in its clutches. I wasted not a second scrambling forward on my hands and knees for the relative safety of the trench – out of the gap. The stock of the rifle was cumbersome in my right hand, but I was determined not to lose it, so I clasped it to my chest and crawled with one arm. Time seemed to slow. Vaguely I heard the cacophony around me, accompanied by a dull pounding in my head, but saw only an arm's length of brown mud in front as I willed myself forward.

Somehow I made it. How many minutes had passed was hard to say. I was through the opening however and into the trench beyond. Immediately behind me there was a cry. I didn't turn to see who it was but pressed forward. I heard from the machine guns that others were still chancing the gap.

Directly ahead a muffled blast went off and a salvo of rifle fire followed. The lead section was running up against the enemy. It must be K.4 as it was no more than a hundred yards from where we had turned right. A lifetime had passed since then. When I too reached this point I saw the grey uniforms lying everywhere and I stepped over them and knew that I was right. The block was cleared and the trench was taken.

However, the flow of men from the rear had slowed to a trickle. If we were to go on we would need more of them. Conscious of my chevrons I turned back with the intention of seeing what I could do.

'DIG IN! DIG IN,' I heard then. 'The major says dig in!' *Major Guthrie was putting an end to it!* Ironically I hadn't fired a single shot. Nor had I even seen the enemy, save the flash from his muzzles.

The attack was over before it began.

The time had come to slink away and tally the casualties. And to wonder how long it would be before we were to do it again. I wasn't very optimistic.

CHAPTER 13

21st of May, 1915
Festubert, France

I was hardly back in the support trench when I learned that my scepticism was well founded.

'You've got to be kidding,' I sighed. Incredulity and resignation
tended to follow each other in close marching order on the Western
Front. 'They want us to attack again… so soon?'

I had just finished telling Dundas and Riley how the first two
platoons were all but decimated and that the remainder of A and B
companies would surely have followed were it not for our commander's presence of mind in calling a halt. Not that his presence of mind
mattered any to the mounds of dead now heaped in No-Man's-Land.
Then Dundas told me his news. It was almost as bad.

'That's right,' he said. 'We're to attack tomorrow at dawn.' He
glanced at his watch. 'In ten hours, give or take.'

Dismayed I shook my head, at a loss for words.

Riley who didn't know me that well, at least not well enough to
draw the proper conclusion from this uncharacteristic silence piped
up, 'Better luck next time, Mac.'

He and Dundas, and the rest of C Company, had remained in the
trenches in reserve. But B Company was short on NCOs which is how
I came to experience the assault on K.5 first hand. The NCO shortage

had grown only more acute in the interim so I had a fair idea where I would be in ten hours, give or take. To say that my mood was black would be to put quite a gloss on it.

'It's got nothing to do with luck, Riley, good or otherwise,' I muttered darkly.

Riley gulped and avoided my eye.

But then I felt compelled to explain. 'When you go rafting down river on a Sunday afternoon you make damn sure *before* you leave there's not a waterfall at the end of it. Basic common sense.' I glowered a bit, and continued. 'I don't think there was an officer in the brigade who didn't think we were unprepared. However they sent us in anyway, like fish in a barrel. For Christ's sake it wasn't even dark. There are some in this army who are clueless, either that or they simply don't care. Perhaps both. All I know is that if I'd ever prepared a case as shoddily as that attack I'd have been fired and probably disbarred.'

Riley grimaced but said nothing. Even Dundas was quiet. The boys beside them pretended they hadn't heard a thing and stared off into the darkness. It wasn't that they disagreed; no one wanted to risk my ire. What they didn't know was that I was scared stiff at the prospect of another attack and that surely accounted for the foulness of my temper.

Luckily General Currie at brigade headquarters agreed with my sentiments. Awakening very early the next morning from a fitful sleep, I learned that the brigadier had arranged for the attack to be postponed. It was to take place at dusk instead. 'To round up more artillery and to reconnoitre,' explained Major Ashton, when he happened along.

The Germans didn't need to round up any more artillery; unlike us they never wanted for artillery or shells. To rub it in they put down another bombardment later that morning. Nor did they seem shortchanged in the art of intelligence gathering. It was this I found the most disconcerting.

A heavily-accented voice drifted across No-Man's-Land: 'Had enough, you Canadians?'

'Not by a long shot, Fritz,' came the riposte, followed by an eruption of frenetic shooting in the general direction of their lines, until the bark of a sergeant intervened.

A shout. 'Oh, that's not what we heard. We heard the "Fighting

Tenth" was finished.' The German barely completed his sentence before the whole line opened up for a futile minute.

Silence returned almost as sharply. Then a single deep laugh intruded. 'What are you waiting for?' cackled the voice. 'You're welcome any time.' And again that infuriating laugh.

By the time our guns started to bang at five o'clock that evening, the catcalls had ceased and I'd discovered a thing or two. To begin with *Stützpunkt* meant strongpoint in English. Also, I had the dubious honour of guiding Major Guthrie down the very communication trench that we took the night before. Much as I might have enjoyed basking in the thought he'd picked me on the basis of my acumen, I knew otherwise; the senior ranks from last night's attack were all dead or dying. It wasn't dissimilar to the boy waiting to be picked in a game of softball, conscious he was the only one left. Guthrie was sporting about it.

Peering through a crack in the parapet, and with the loan of the major's field glasses, I had discovered something else – precisely what Germans meant by strongpoint. Impregnable was a word that came to mind. K.5 was a formidable-looking redoubt of grey concrete crowned by sandbags and ringed by wire, jutting out of a small rise to the southeast. The French also had a word for such a thing: *fortin*, which when spoken with the correct enunciation sounded appropriately ominous, although not quite as ominous as the German variant. The men had taken to calling it Bexhill.

The redoubt's positioning was anything but haphazard. From its profusion of slit holes, machine guns could fire in a wide arc across our entire front. For a thousand yards, to both left and right, there was nothing that could approach the German line without coming under fire, if for even a moment. According to the major it was manned by the 56th and 57th Reserve Infantry Regiments; 'crack units' he confided. I took him at his word. Last night they'd whipped us pretty badly.

Unfortunately the major was a major, as well as being the battalion's commanding officer, which meant that I couldn't ask him the questions I desperately wanted to. Such as: did he have a plan? Or: what the devil were we doing attacking a position like this in the first place? Much to the consternation of the starched shirts and neatly trimmed moustaches which populated the Imperial officer ranks, a certain casual familiarity reigned in the division. However, there *were* limits. And majors fielding impertinent questions from corporals was one of them.

Nevertheless, after Guthrie made his reconnaissance and scurried off to brigade headquarters for the third time in as many hours, it dawned on me that while I was filled with doubt, so was he. And that gave me an answer to one of my questions, albeit not the one I was hoping for. This attack was going to be anything but a piece of cake.

I made my way back along the fire-trench. To their credit the sappers had done a lot of work on the parapet. The gap from last night had been hermetically filled, but I moved deliberately nonetheless, keeping my head low. A sandbag was often no match for the round from a sniper's Mauser. Halfway back to the platoon I came upon two men seated on a fire-step, conversing. I didn't know either, but I did recognize one. I was almost certain he was in the first contingent, too.

'Splendid show, eh?' I heard the first man say to the other as I approached, referring to the bombardment.

The fellow to whom he was speaking – the same one I recognized – must have equivocated for he spoke again, more loudly the second time as if to lend weight to his words. 'But our guns are really going at it, Harv. You can't possibly think there'll be much left of the Germans?'

"Harv" was audibly not in whole-hearted agreement with this assessment.

'Pop-guns,' I heard him growl. 'There's not a heavy amongst them.'

They glanced up as I tromped by. I nodded and they threw me one in return. As I rounded the traverse, Harvey, the veteran, began to explain the wonders of modern artillery, one of which is that field guns shooting shrapnel have about as much effect on a position like K.5 as lobbing stones do.

Out of earshot I checked my wrist, looking for Pat Jones's watch to see how long before the attack, but then realized I'd sent the watch along with the brief missive to his parents. It had not been an easy letter to write, despite having spent the better part of an hour composing it and nearly that long trying to coax my hand into writing something legible. But I'd promised and I did the best I could. I could scarcely imagine how his folks must feel, and the consolation that their son would miss Festubert was the very thing I couldn't have written, not least because of the censors. "Harv" had been right; we badly needed some heavy guns. High explosive shells were the only thing that might dent the German parapet, and we didn't appear to have any.

I was still thinking about the infuriating lack of artillery support when Lieutenant Drinkwater cornered me. Drinkwater was the adjutant in C Company, which is to say the company commander's right-hand man, and having been in the militia for most of this century not only had he grown a moustache of Imperial proportions – to underline his own feeling of self-importance – he'd accrued an invaluable experience in parade-ground drilling and button polishing. Someone, somewhere, must have felt he was needed at the front for since the last draft we were stuck with him. All forty-plus years and his bad breath to boot.

'Where the blazes have you been, Corporal?' Something about his tone prickled. The lieutenant was of a sort who, while not of English aristocracy, oh-so dearly wished he was and thought with the right mix of condescension and a cut-glass accent he might pull one over on the rest of us.

'Oh, I was out and about, guiding the OC around,' I said casually. 'He said to say "hi", Lieutenant.'

It was the sort of facetiousness I thought the army had long beaten out of me. Lieutenant Drinkwater looked as if I'd kicked him in the groin.

'Blast it all, MacPhail. You had better learn to watch your tongue or I'll have you keel-hauled. If the battle wasn't about to begin I'd consider putting you up for insubordination.'

Rather than pointing out that keel-hauling was more properly a trade-mark of our sister service – the one which rowed across water rather than wading through it – I cowardly muttered, 'Yes, sir,' and made a conscious effort of looking contrite.

But the lieutenant wasn't finished. Not by a long shot. Actually, he was only getting started. 'I've been looking for you since yesterday,' he said accusingly.

'I was in the attack last night, sir. B Company needed some NCOs and Lieutenant Todhunter borrowed my services.'

'Unfortunately we can't very well confirm that, can we, Corporal?'

As statements go the lieutenant's was accurate enough; Todhunter had fallen during the attack. What I resented, however, was the implication that I was hiding out from Drinkwater in a damp funk hole all night instead of having half the German army shoot at me – while he drank tea.

'True enough, sir,' I replied. 'But if you'd been there you could have confirmed it for yourself.'

From the storm clouds that rushed in it was obvious Drinkwater didn't much like what I was implying, but couldn't think of a suitable reply – Drinkwater was not much of a thinker. He screwed his mouth up and stared at me. Lunch and worse was on his breath. Unflinching, I faced him down without as much as a urine-soaked handkerchief to hand.

Eventually he grumbled, 'But that's not all you were doing, was it, MacPhail?' At this he frowned, his eyes narrowed, and the twin peaks of his moustache twitched menacingly like a bull's horns do when it ponders whether to skewer you alive.

'Sir?'

'I understand you led your entire section out to raid the enemy line yesterday afternoon.'

'Well, it wasn't exactly a raid…' I began.

But Drinkwater would have none of it. 'Entirely without permission, I might add. You could have got everyone killed. Worse you might have disturbed one of our own plans. Imagine if the enemy had attacked at the very moment you were out cavorting around with the line undefended. It would have been a disaster. Did you think of *that*, Corporal?'

'There was a sniper, sir. He was shooting off our wounded. We had to do something, and I thought we were supposed to take the initiative?'

'That's what officers are for, MacPhail, to do the heavy thinking. So you other ranks don't have to.'

Drinkwater was radiating a glow of deep inner contentment at having put me in my place. Lovingly, he began stroking his moustache. I felt like grabbing both ends and yanking – like with a Christmas cracker. 'When this is all over,' he continued, 'I feel I'm duty-bound to bring the matter to the attention of our superiors, MacPhail. You're a corporal, you really ought to have known better. It makes me think you have two stripes too many.'

With that he turned on his heel, sparing me the meaningless motions of saluting. It was fortunate in another way, too; it spared me the consequences of throttling him with both hands.

One positive aspect of the whole encounter was that I was so worked up about it I completely forgot about the attack. Even when I was lining up in file with B Company two hours later, I was still reliving Drinkwater's words in my head. I would take it out on the Germans I decided.

At 8.30 p.m. the guns quieted and we began to move. Where the engineers had rebuilt the gaping hole in the communication trench, further on they'd done the reverse and blown two openings, one on either side, not far apart. Or more accurately, a group of bombers from the 1st Brigade had done it for them, using a handful of Jam Tins skilfully applied. We'd polished off the last Tickler's plum and apple jam only this morning, with biscuits, as it happened. By dinnertime the grenadiers had fashioned grenades of the containers.

There was a shout of 'OVER!' and "A" Company debouched out of the breach to the left. Once they were through we would follow, but turn right. I was relieved it was right. "A" Company had the chore of tackling K.5 virtually head on, 200 yards away.

Now 200 yards is not particularly far. And it's certainly not far if you're a Fritz crouched behind a concrete wall with a well-oiled Maxim, a decent view, and an endless belt of ammunition. A round from an MG-08 covers that distance in the time it takes to twitch an eye. Less. But for a man on foot, stumbling his way in the dark across broken ground, dykes and waterlogged ditches, 200 yards was a marathon. An eternity. Not to mention the wire at the end of it.

I heard the machine guns straightaway. One had barely begun to chatter before it was joined by another, and soon I could hear little else. It was no fault of the bombers, of course. Blasting open a parapet would have awakened even me, and the bombardment had tipped off the Germans we were coming.

Fortunately it was almost dark. After the experience the day before I was glad a flare had gone up in some commander's head; rousting the enemy was a task best not attempted in daylight. As we walked forward the distant enemy parapet literally glowed from the fire of rifles and machine guns. I shouted at the men of my section to keep their heads down. Some of the new draft seemed to view this as a fireworks display, not understanding that the bullets – assuming they hadn't felled one of "A" Company in the interim – were inevitably destined to pass our way. It should have been a beautiful, warm, clear spring evening. Instead, the air reeked of smoke and cordite, and death beckoned.

Running the first breach I took a hurried glance at the scene to the left. It was enough to convince me that three-and-a-half hours of bombardment hadn't begun to dent Bexhill. It was alight with flashes. Not that I really expected much from a single heavy – Harvey had not been entirely correct, there was *one*. However, I had no time to think about that. We were filing out to the right.

'Run it,' I shouted at the others around me, as we exited into the open ground. 'And keep low!'

This was not the advice some lieutenants were selling – they seemed to think we should neatly line up like on a parade ground before even contemplating an advance – but my squad needed no encouragement; common-sense prevailing when given the chance.

We took off through the long grass like Teddy Tetzlaff in a Blitzen Benz heading southeast, in pursuit of the bombers who'd raced off ahead. After fifty yards we came upon a narrow communication trench pointed in the right direction: east. We jumped in and followed it. I led.

There was something terrifying but also exhilarating about rushing down a dark, narrow passageway in the ground, not knowing what would come next, but feeling oddly confident in the hard icicle of steel protruding from the rifle, too excited to think of much beyond the couple of feet immediately ahead.

I slowed when I spotted the intersection.

'That must be Fritz's line we're coming to,' I said over my shoulder, breathing heavily.

'Jesus, those bombers, they really tore through here,' came the winded response. I wasn't the only one out of breath.

I went to turn, to ask him what he meant, when the explanation presented itself: two bodies were sprawled on the ground. They lay at the intersection in a heap. One was still wearing a *Pickelhaube*, strapped firmly on his head. The rest of him had come loose. A Hair-Brush I reckoned. With its long wooden handle and thick square head it resembled more what I used to scrub my back than its namesake – let alone a grenade. There was no mistaking its explosive effectiveness, however.

'We're going right,' I puffed. 'Pass the word behind. We'll wait till everyone is here. But watch out, there may be stragglers, so keep a close eye.'

'Yes, Corporal.'

After the small group behind came to a halt, I gave them thirty seconds to catch their breath and hear what we were to do before we set off again. It appeared that we had become the spearhead of the company. Hopefully the rest would catch up.

Turning into the main trench it was obvious we were in the enemy lines. Two weeks earlier this had been only a support line for our foe, but support line or not, the trench displayed a remarkable neatness in the characteristic woven-branch revetting on the walls, and duck-boards on the ground. It was the sort of disciplined order that I was coming to learn was a German trademark. That and not yielding an inch.

It was as well I'd warned the others about stragglers, if only to remind myself. Immediately south of the spot where we entered the trench, and which I assumed to be K.3, I spotted him. He appeared to have spotted me first.

The bombers had no doubt thundered past leaving him crouched in a hole out of sight. But now he was in plain sight. Worse, *I* was in plain sight, and his rifle was resting atop a wooden post, taking aim.

I did the only thing I could. I ran faster. But at a distance of fifteen feet I didn't stand a chance.

Desperately I pulled at the trigger. The bullet went whining off into the dark. My rifle was pointed in a whole different map quadrant than the German, but I hoped I might spoil his aim. Although really all he had to do was shoot. He was barely five strides away.

He didn't shoot. What he did do surprised me a great deal more. He released the rifle as if he was holding a hot iron, stood straight up and threw his hands in the air. Then I was on him.

He wore a simple field cap, the one with what looks like two eyes in the centre, one pip above the other. Not just his pips but also his eyes were on me. Curiously, he didn't look nearly as frightened as I might have done with a tall man brandishing a bayonet in my nose. But he knew that I owed him my life. I could see it in his expression.

Only then did I notice two more rifles poking past and understood the reason for his change of heart. At the critical moment – it couldn't have been a second later – the soldier had seen the boys run into view behind me and made the only sensible decision he could.

Like most German soldiers of my recent acquaintance, this one sported a bushy chevron-style moustache, dark, and two sizes too big. I suppose it was all the rage back in Dortmund or wherever he hailed from. I nodded at him and he nodded back. It wasn't at all unfriendly.

'Ain't that something? Looks as if we've corralled ourselves a prisoner,' said one of the lads.

'Yes, indeed,' I said. 'Which makes you the perfect cowboy to keep him lassoed while we move on.' This brought a nervous chuckle from the others.

By the time we eventually caught up with the grenadiers, we had travelled south more than 400 yards down the enemy line. We still hadn't run into the 47th (London) Division who were supposed to be in the vicinity nor, thanks to the bombers, had we encountered any more enemy. The bombers were undecided as to what to do: stay put or keep going. There was something to be said for both.

However, as there was no sign of the rest of B Company, to me the answer seemed plain. 'Let's throw up a sandbag barricade, sir,' I suggested to their lieutenant. 'No sense running off too far ahead. Our Lords and Masters will be pleased we made it so far.' He nodded. I felt quite pleased myself. We had taken the objective and with only a handful of casualties. At that moment it seemed like quite a victory.

In retrospect my conclusion was premature. It was also optimistic, to the point of being wildly so. For all my so-called experience I still had a lot to learn. But I didn't learn *that* until early the next morning.

CHAPTER 14

22nd of May, 1915
An enemy trench between J.1 and J.3, east of Festubert, France

'We haven't heard anything from the enemy, sir,' I said. 'But we've thrown up a good block to the south, and the men are prepared for a counterattack.' Lieutenant Knowles looked pensive. It seemed an appropriate moment to ask a question of my own. 'What happened with the assault on Bexhill, sir?'

'They were practically annihilated,' he replied. 'The machine guns swept them away. They didn't get within a hundred yards of K.5.'

It was past midnight and the lieutenant was seated at a small table in a dug-out close to where the German line intersected the communication trench. The dug-out was only three or four steps underground, but the walls and ceiling were buttressed by tree-length logs. On top of the log ceiling sandbags were piled high. A shrapnel shell from a field gun had as much chance of penetrating that as I did putting my fist through. The light from a gas lantern flickered on Knowles' expressionless face.

'I can't believe it, sir,' I murmured. 'The whole left party gone?'

'Most of them. All the officers were hit, the majority of the NCOs, and heaven knows how many men. Major Ashton was wounded again and I'm afraid we're nowhere close to taking that redoubt.'

'Where does that leave us, sir?'

Knowles rubbed his chin. 'Out on a limb I expect.' Seeing my expression, he quickly added, 'I'm sorry, MacPhail, that's all I know. Captain Snelgrove will be along shortly. We'll have to make the most of it.'

Unfortunately he didn't mention how best to do that, and I figured it was a waste of breath asking, especially now that I was trying to be so economical with it. Since pickling my lungs in chlorine at Ypres, oxygen had never seemed such a precious commodity.

'You'd best get back to your position, MacPhail. Let me know if the situation changes.'

400 yards to the south. One hour later. It did, just like that.

'Quick, come have a look, Corporal,' yelled one of the sentries. I hurried over to where he stood guard behind a parapet of fresh sandbags the sappers had thoughtfully laid down.

'Well?'

He pointed southeast across the moonlit fields. 'They're attacking.'

There were no two ways about it. From the direction of the rue d'Ouvert a group of a hundred-plus German soldiers were methodically closing in on us in ranks so regimented they resembled Wellington's army at Waterloo. They weren't clothed in scarlet red but that particular shade of grey I'd increasingly come to loathe. They may have sensibly avoided red but their comrades at Bexhill, manning Maxims, had evidently not warned them of the perils of such a formation.

'Stand-to!' I shouted to the others in the section. Then I made for Lieutenant Knowles. Knowles had turned up ten minutes earlier to take command; Captain Snelgrove must have felt better having an officer hold down the fort.

'Sir, you have some flares with you, don't you?' I asked him, after relaying the news.

Knowles reached into the haversack slung over his shoulder and extracted a shiny brass Very pistol. Without a word to me he moved over to the eastern side of the trench and spent a few moments contemplating the scene. Then he broke open the sleeve of the pistol and inserted a round similar to that of a shotgun, but larger. Snapping the pistol shut with a click, he raised his arm almost vertically and fired.

The flare shot into the sky trailing a thin pencil line of fire. Just as it reached its apex, where it tipped and began to descend, it burst into light – brighter than any star in the heavens. The attackers below were caught in a most unnatural glare. There was not a tree nor a building nor a rise in the ground to shelter behind.

This was the signal to fire. And we did... with abandon.

In the past few days many had availed themselves of the opportunity to scrounge up a Lee-Enfield; Festubert had been tough on the Tommies before us. I hoped for them they might somehow know their old rifles were exacting a terrible revenge. The rifle fire was indeed something terrific. It was a shame nevertheless we didn't have one of the battalion's remaining Colt machine guns handy.

At 200 yards the German ranks were broken and uneven. With every footstep a couple more fell. Our fire was unrelenting. Yet they pushed on. Until their numbers had dwindled by half.

'Hah, they're retreating, the bastards,' I heard beside me, right before he pulled the trigger.

I sighed. 'What is it with these Fritzs?' I asked, to no one in particular. 'They just don't let up. They spend a few months in the French Artois and they think it's theirs forever. Look at the place. Would you want it?' The man standing next to me managed a weak grin.

Dawn was still a couple of hours away yet we'd already fended off two counter-attacks, and Fritz was at it a third time – a demonstration of Teutonic obstinacy if ever there was one. He wasn't a quick learner, our Fritz, for otherwise he would have known we could be stubborn too. We'd shown that inclination at Ypres, and the boys took a savage delight in decimating his newest platoons.

However, as dawn crept upon us the enemy decided that enough was enough; we were to be obliterated. It was a decision I became aware of only as events unfolded.

As is often the case – when German stubbornness pairs with German engineering – the chosen instrument of our destruction was to be the artillery. In the spring of 1915 German guns reigned supreme on the Western Front.

By pure chance I spotted the first round being fired. I was peering off to the east trying to guess the very moment the sun would reveal itself, and morosely imagining what was happening behind German lines – all in an attempt to keep myself awake – when I saw the flash, several miles distant. Three or four seconds passed. Then I heard a bang. Shortly thereafter there was a perceptible whirring in the air that grew steadily louder until it ceased... Then another flash, much larger and closer this time – a few hundred yards north of where I stood – and immediately, *BOOM*. The ground shook.

'Cover!' I yelled, superfluously, and altogether too late.

The men standing watch needed no encouragement. They were diving into nooks and crannies and making themselves one with the trench.

Another shell crashed down in an eruption of noise, this time a hundred yards east of us. Dirt and flying fragments whooshed past, one of which sailed perilously close by my head – I'd been a trifle tardy in taking my own advice. A heavy black cloud mushroomed up.

I crouched, huddling against the parapet wall.

The soldier beside me had the bewildered, frightened expression of someone experiencing a German bombardment for the first time. For most things in life experience is a great advantage; getting shelled is not one of them. The tiresome repetition was what broke men. If it didn't break you, you learned to cope, and part of coping was keeping a stiff upper lip.

'A Coal Box,' I said. 'From one of their heavy howitzers. You'll soon learn to recognize the sounds.'

I've always been of a mind that the busier your mind is the better. That way you worry less about what's coming next.

'They haven't got our range yet,' I continued. I saw I had his attention. 'You see that's the big advantage of being in a German trench; their guns haven't pre-registered. They still have to work out the range.'

I didn't bother to add that working out the range typically didn't take them long – some things are better left unsaid.

As the sun rose, so too did the intensity of the bombardment. It was every bit as bad as the ones I'd experienced in the Salient. Worse perhaps. Every gun on the front seemed to be pointed here. The German gunners had singled out this stretch of line and were throwing shell after shell in our direction.

Two traverses over a twenty-foot stretch of trench took a direct hit. Not only did the parapet disappear, so too did the entire trench, reduced to a pile of dirt where the walls had caved in. After the dust settled I clambered over the dirt to see if there were any survivors, knowing the answer already.

It was the continuous shaking and trembling that bothered me most, more so than the noise. After every concussion it felt like I'd been picked up and shaken so hard my innards were soup. Waiting in petrified anticipation of the next was possibly worse; and best intentions aside it was impossible to think of anything other than the one which would follow. My nerves, such as they were, were numb within the first half hour. The soldier beside me had crawled into a ball and was rolling back and forth, and I was debating whether to join him.

'MacPhail!'

The lieutenant beckoned from ten feet away, stooped over in the mouth of a small dug-out whose timbers were one blast away from collapsing altogether.

I patted the soldier reassuringly on the back and grasping my rifle scuttled over to Knowles.

'Yes, sir?'

Knowles's face was ashen, his right hand twitched uncontrollably before he hurriedly stashed it away in a trouser pocket.

'I want you to go to the company dug-out and explain the situation. Ask if there are any orders.'

'That's all, sir?'

He sighed irritably. 'Yes, MacPhail,' he snapped. 'And be quick about it.'

'Yes, lieutenant.' I didn't begrudge the typically even-tempered lieutenant his ill humour. The strains of a shelling affected us all in different ways. I was certainly not sorry to leave and hoped my errand might result in a call for us to pull back – anything to escape the endless crash of high explosive.

As I moved up the trench I encountered Captain Snelgrove hurrying in my direction, bent over forward, his head down low. I nodded politely but he gave no sign that he recognized me. It's likely he was thinking of other things. I didn't really know Snelgrove, other than to place a name to a face, as he was one of the new draft.

The hissing whine was unmistakable. It came screaming straight at me, a round from one of their 4.1-inch field howitzers – deadly on impact and mockingly brazen in its approach.

Diving for the corner of the parapet wall it was as if someone placed my head between two cymbals and banged. My ears rang. Earth rained down in heavy clumps, coating my body and leaving the trench duckboards buried under a thick layer. I looked back. 50 feet away the parapet had simply disappeared, brushed away as if it were mere dust in a gale. A supporting wall timber jutted out at an angle like a tree uprooted by the same winter storm.

Snelgrove!

I couldn't see him. Nor could I see anyone. A second shell, heavier than the first, went off further down the line to the south and a thick geyser of earth spewed twenty feet into the air. The sky above was a pale blue, all but obscured by black and white smoke coiling upwards to form banks that slowly drifted across.

With an effort I pulled myself to my feet, leaning on the rifle like a crutch. Stumbling back in the direction of where I last saw the captain, I neared the point of impact. At the sight of the mangled remains of a man blown onto the lip of the parados, I felt a brief wave of nausea wash over. His lifeless arm was hanging down. But it wasn't Snelgrove. The sleeve was that of a private.

I went on. Rounding the next bend I saw him. He was dislodging himself from the debris of the explosion and had gotten to his feet. I watched him stagger away, managing a step or two until there was another flash and a blast ahead of him. The force of the concussion nearly blew me onto my back as the air rushed past. Were it not that I'd been sheltered by the traverse it would have. As it was I was stunned. When I looked again, the captain was on his side on the ground. He was up against the willow revetting of the trench, trying to right himself. Close to him a man lay face down on the duckboards.

The artillery fire reached a horrifying new crescendo. The Germans were concentrating on the far end of our line, where I had been short minutes before. The ground rocked and shook terribly. Explosion followed upon explosion, a deafening cacophony of noise and flashes of light.

Gritting my teeth I pulled myself up. The captain was also on his feet once more. Through the rumbling of the explosions I heard the whine, a higher, more urgent tone.

I threw myself down headfirst and screamed, 'Look out, sir!'

Snelgrove heard me, I could see it on his face. However, instead of diving for cover he began to run – north – towards me. I expect he was dazed.

'Get down, sir. Get down!'

For a fleeting instant the flash illuminated him from behind. The roar of the explosion reached me at the very moment the concussion reached him. It hit him square in the back along with a large piece of debris and he was brushed aside like a child's doll. A gust of dirt blew all around me and I felt my cap lifted off and whisked away.

Wiping at the grime on my face I ran to him. The shells continued to fall, as unrelenting as rain. The fear had left me when I wasn't looking, replaced by a calculating detachment, my actions controlled by some inner clockwork hitherto unknown to me.

Behind Snelgrove the trench had collapsed. The men who were in it were gone. Further off a scream was swallowed up by the roar of the shells. That was where the men I'd been with were. *Would there be any left? And Lieutenant Knowles?* I reached the captain.

'Captain Snelgrove,' I said, kneeling. 'Are you alright?'

To which the answer was blatantly obvious if I'd thought before asking, which I didn't. I felt for a pulse. They taught us that at grade 8 summer camp at Lake Minnewanka, and truth be told it was a skill I'd never had occasion to use. But then Lake Minnewanka was a long way from Festubert, France. To my surprise I felt one as I poked in the soft flesh of his neck. The captain was alive. Unconscious, but alive.

I yanked away the piece of timber that had hit him. I'd seen worse was my first reaction. What I was worried about was the blast itself. I'd seen men die without a scratch, standing those few crucial feet too close as a shell went off – the air itself lethal. In other circumstances I would have called for help. But there was nobody within a hundred yards in a position to help me – they had problems of their own.

Somehow we reached the company dug-out; lifting his limp body in both arms until a shell forced us to ground or my strength gave out; or with an arm clamped round his waist and his head drooping listlessly on my shoulder as I stumbled over the duckboards while the thumping in my head drowned out the shelling. Exhausted and relieved to have made it, I handed him over to two privates to be carried to the rear. Only then did I collapse on the dug-out steps.

Captain Day found me a moment later with my head in my hands breathing heavily – he'd seen me arrive, no doubt – and inquired what happened. After I explained he asked how we were faring.

'Not good, sir. Honestly, I don't think there are many left. The German artillery… they've completely flattened the last fifty yards of our line.'

'Yes, I was afraid of that,' he said, frowning. 'But I'm relieved you were able to get the captain back. I'll be sure to mention it to your company commander, MacPhail.'

I shrugged. 'Do you ever wonder what the point of this is, sir?'

Puzzled, Day looked at me.

'I mean what we're doing here at Festubert, sir. The battalion was just back to strength after Ypres and now we can start all over again. And for what? A miserable few hundred yards of dirt after two days. At Ypres it was even worse, but we held off a German army corps when there was no one else and we saved the day. Men died but it meant something. But this…' Realizing I was rambling dangerously, I shut my trap and put my head back into my hands.

Day didn't respond. He would have been well within his rights to reprimand me for this semi-traitorous talk, in fact there were those who would say it was his duty to do so. My own Lieutenant Drinkwater would have had me in leg irons for less – might still if he came to hear of it. A look of weary contemplation came over his face. Perhaps this was a question he too had wrestled with as his company withered away.

'Well, MacPhail…'

A lieutenant poked his head out of the dug-out and called to him, 'Sir!'

He smiled without smiling. 'Another time,' he said. 'Keep your head up.'

I suppose I wouldn't have said anything, and definitely not to an officer I scarcely knew, were it not that I fretted the show would go on.

Admittedly we had penetrated the German front line. When I returned to the company lines I also heard the good news that the 3rd Brigade had taken the Orchard, a little to the north. But I'd seen K.5. And two attempts to capture it had failed abysmally. If the show and the fumbling went on as it had I questioned whether any of us would be around long.

CHAPTER 15

23rd to 26th of May, 1915
Rue de l'Epinette, Festubert, France

The show did go on. The fumbling, too, although the arrival of our own divisional artillery from Ypres went some way to improving the situation with the guns. Thanks to them we beat off several enemy companies who were mustering to attack later that afternoon. Naturally Fritz had his sights set on the hundred yards of former trench we still held. It wasn't more because in the forenoon orders from General Currie directed us to pull back; there was simply no point and no one to hold the rest. While he didn't ask my opinion, I might have added that since the shelling there was nothing *to* hold.

As darkness fell I was glad for the illusion of concealment it brought – ostriches feel much the same I understand. I was even happier when the relief turned up in the form of the curiously-named Post Office Rifles of the 47th London Division. Mailmen or not they were most welcome. I went with the small group of battalion men and grenadiers still left and trudged very quietly and very cautiously to the rear. There we joined the rest of the battalion to march to billets, where it promptly began to rain.

"Billets" proved to be a rather disappointing euphemism for a barn and some reserve trenches located near the rue de l'Epinette – the army excelled in such language. To my dismay I was assigned the trenches that night. That was before I viewed the gloomy dilapidation of the barn, overflowing with dirty straw in which I was quite certain there were more lice residing than Germans on the front. The smell wasn't too fresh, either. Virtually the only positive thing that could be said about the rue de l'Epinette was that we were a tiny bit further from the enemy. To a German gunner these few hundred extra yards mattered not at all and I set about finding a funk hole large enough to accommodate me. That turned out to be as challenging as storming K.5. Eventually I settled for one half my length and curled up. Sleep came quickly.

I borrowed a small mirror, and propping it up behind the tin biscuit box filled with water, I set about shaving. The water was from the pump behind the barn and was a good deal cleaner than what I'd been drinking recently, strained as it was from holes and made even more loathsome with the addition of anti-septic tablets.

It was early dawn. Despite that I whistled softly to myself in the knowledge I'd made it to another day – to the Sabbath no less – a welcome tonic at the end of a trying week. I had few illusions either army would pay Sunday much attention. Still, there was nothing like a good shave to reinvigorate body and soul. Luckily for me the stricture against being clean-shaven had seen a quiet and well-deserved demise. Once, I suppose, I had thought the fate of the German Army might develop similarly. But since Ypres I'd been forced to reconsider; Fritz's demise was going to be neither quick, quiet, nor painless. If anything I was beginning to wonder what kind of mess we'd gotten ourselves into.

The safety razor had succeeded admirably in clearing a path through two-days' stubble when I heard voices approaching, chatting amiably. One must have told a joke, for a cackle of laughter bubbled up from his companion. I lifted my chin to the mirror, pivoting it slowly from left to right to check I hadn't missed anything. The next thing I knew I felt a bump from behind and I was lurching forward. Quickly I reached out an arm to steady myself; only my arm hit the tin of water, which neatly somersaulted off the post on which it was perched, flipped in mid-air and a minor deluge spilled down the front of me.

'Christ, almighty,' I sputtered, peering in dismay at my shirt and trousers. They were no dirtier than before, but an embarrassingly dark stain marked my crotch.

Glancing up I recognized Harry Hobson and another fellow from the new draft.

'Oh, Corporal MacPhail. Terribly sorry about that,' said Harry. Harry looked chipper, much as if he'd spent the morning in the spa following a restful night's sleep and an extensive breakfast. 'I really should have been more careful.'

'Damn rights, you should have been,' I snarled, dabbing at my trousers.

Hobson and his pal hurriedly moved off. I could have sworn I heard them snickering.

Roy Dundas most definitely did snicker when he saw me shortly thereafter. 'What happened to you?'

'Being in reserve is more challenging than you might think. I ran into a few of the new fellows, or, more accurately, they ran into me,' I said. I didn't mention Hobson. 'Hey, good to see you, Roy.'

He clapped me on the shoulder. 'Likewise.'

We found ourselves a mug of tea and sat down on a few sandbags at a quiet spot in one of the drier trenches. Then I proceeded to tell Dundas everything that had happened last night. He whistled when I described what had befallen our garrison in the trench.

'You're a lucky dog, you know that, Mac. The battalion lost 18 officers and 260 other ranks yesterday. That's what the sergeant says.'

Wearily I shook my head. '18 officers and 260 men? And for what? 500 yards of mud... You realize, Roy, that's almost exactly the same number they sent us as reinforcements three weeks ago? Those boys hadn't even been in a trench until last Monday. After Ypres I figured they'd give us some time before we lined up for the meat grinder again, or, at the very least, a plan of sorts. Artillery and a stockpile of shells wouldn't hurt either... These mad dashes across open ground are going to be the death of us.' A thought came to me, and I looked away scratching my chin.

Dundas didn't inquire, he just gazed at me expectantly.

'You know something...' I began.

'No, but I have a sneaking suspicion you're going to tell me,' he said.

'I was just thinking. How far is it to the German border?'

'Far,' he replied. Then, as the light flipped on, he groaned and shook his head. 'Oh. I know what you're getting at, Mac. If we lose a man for every two yards, what will it take to get to Germany? I thought lawyers were useless with numbers.'

'They are. That's why I'm asking you.'

'You don't want to hear the answer. Besides which I'm sure the generals are busy with those sorts of considerations.'

'You mean like this Haig fellow, whose army we're in?'

'Exactly.'

I snorted. 'I hope that's not supposed to make me feel any better. General Haig's cup is hardly overflowing with successes. Even the newspapers had a hard time describing Neuve Chapelle as anything other than a disaster. Aubers Ridge was categorically a disaster. And from what I've seen, Festubert doesn't appear to be any different.'

'Be thankful for one thing, Mac, you've made it this far.'

'Yeah, well, never underestimate luck. You know if Lieutenant Knowles hadn't ordered me back to the company dug-out when he did…' I let out a deep sigh.

No one ever wants to ascribe their good fortune in life to something as arbitrary as luck. It makes you sound like an unwitting bystander in your own life. Yet, on the front lines of 1915, I was beginning to think that life and luck were joined at the hip.

I took a gulp from the battered tin cup I'd been waving around and groaned loudly. 'And now my luck's up. While you've been blabbing the tea's gone cold. What say we find something to eat?'

Dundas sighed. 'Are you ever not hungry?'

'Listen, Roy, if you don't want your rations just say so. And feel free to pass them this way.'

It was an offer I was convinced wouldn't be snapped up. Even Dundas, who was hardly an epicurean and as thin as a rake – he being a mere banker's clerk rather than a new J.P. Morgan – savoured his hardtack as much as any man. Personally I was set on some bacon. I sniffed at the air. I could smell it.

However the German gunners put short shrift to that idea. In a particularly cruel twist, they began shelling the cookhouse as we approached. Opportunely, an old French couple happened along and sold us some eggs and coffee. And there was another small piece of good fortune. While Fritz nailed the bacon he missed the mail bags, so all the parcels of those killed at Ypres were divvied up amongst the rest of us. As most contained edibles we didn't go hungry.

All told, we spent the better part of four days shoring up breast-works, manning our miserable shallow trenches and attempting with mixed success (the OC Major Guthrie was among those wounded) to avoid the recurring shelling. The Germans settled into a comfortable routine of targeting first the front line, then the support line, and eventually our line. In between the shelling and the working parties we availed ourselves of a few decent meals. One afternoon we even lay in the field in the sun for a glorious hour with our shirts off.

On the 24th my heartbeat spiked momentarily when I heard that a new attack on K.5 was planned. But then at midnight someone spotted the 5th Battalion marching forward and we all went to watch. Brigade headquarters was on the other side of the road in what had once been an L-shaped farmhouse, prior to a German shell crushing the extension. Outside on a patch of gravel, Brigadier Currie stood in all his girth, watching. The men of the 5th did their best to look sharp for the general and while he kindly patted a few on the shoulder and spoke words with them, his face was as dark and as ghostly as the sky overhead.

General Currie needn't have worried; that night the 5th managed what we couldn't and captured the redoubt at K.5. I was told their casualties were equally heavy. Even to the arithmetically challenged the math of taking Bexhill was not difficult – more than 500 men had fallen. It seemed an awful lot, even if I feared to the likes of our dashing General Haig it was a mere rounding error.

The night of the 26th we were relieved. Seely's Detachment replaced us, two regiments of the cavalry that had forsaken the joy of riding to battle for a spell in the trenches. We could scarcely believe our luck and we marched to billets at Le Hamel three miles away. By then the Commander-in-Chief Sir John French had called an end to the battle; he considered the objectives achieved. As a mere corporal I was in no position to disagree, though I did wonder what the point was if the strategy had been only to slog through a half-mile of sodden fields and German trenches. The Germans, not yet having been informed of the battle's end, continued to rain down shells. We lost no time in mustering for the march.

27th of May, 1915
Le Hamel, near Essars, France

'Hmm,' said Riley, when we rose the next morning. 'That was the best sleep I've had in a week.'

'I won't disagree,' I said, yawning loudly. It was hard not to be pleased at the prospect of a day in dry clothes, with little to do, and a sufficient distance between me and the front that made walking upright possible without fear a bullet or a piece of shrapnel would end my war precipitously.

The farmhouse assigned to the platoon actually looked like a farmhouse, right down to the roosters and a brood of hens which arrogantly strutted the courtyard. That in itself was a pleasant surprise; apparently not every farmhouse in France was holed by high explosive and harbouring a regiment of Fritzs in the field behind. Even more pleasant was the discovery that the elderly farmer and his wife sold bottles of beer and wine. That afternoon, those of us who still had some money beat off the roosters and gathered on the cobblestones where the proprietors had thoughtfully set out crude wooden stools and a handful of tree stumps. Word of this wonder spread and I recognized others from the battalion. One in particular drew my attention.

Sitting with a beer in his hand was a familiar face. I walked over to him.

'Harry,' I enthused. 'Nice of you to join us.'

He lifted his head and the bottle with it, still glued to his lips, eyeing me guardedly. Almost imperceptibly came a nod. Reluctantly the bottle made a slow retreat and Harry's eyes flitted to the kitchen door. There, lined up waiting to be served, were what I took to be his mates. I could see he was uncomfortable.

'Nothing else to say?' I asked.

'Not to you,' he mumbled, wiping at the froth on his moustache.

In the crowded trenches at the rue de l'Epinette I'd run across Harry Hobson on several occasions. Being in the same company it was hard to miss him. For all his faults Harry possessed a peculiar magnetism (just don't ask me what it was) that habitually attracted a crowd. However, each time our paths crossed he so scrupulously avoided my gaze that I knew for certain he'd seen me. It had set me to wondering; what dark thoughts were lurking behind that bulbous expanse that passed as his forehead? But I hadn't pressed the issue.

Now I did.

'Look, it's time you and I talked,' I said.

'Got nothing to say to you, MacPhail.'

'Grow up, man. Look, I'm sorry about your father. I shouldn't have done it and I regret it a lot more than you might guess. But we're at war here, Harry, and I need to know that you're on the same side.'

Noncommittedly Harry gulped at his beer.

'It's up to you, of course. But sooner or later you're going to realize that your comrades are the only ones you can count on. And like it or not, they include me.'

Harry frowned.

'It's true, Harry,' I said. 'Wait until you've gone over the top a time or two. You'll see. Think about it.' Then I moved on. I had better things to do, like rounding up some of that red wine I'd seen.

Funnily enough I'd never been much of a drinker. But then Alberta was not exactly the place to be one. A cloying provincialism permeated the good men and women of polite society, especially the women. Drink was something you didn't want associated with your name, and definitely not as a budding new barrister anxious to make one for himself. Harry Hobson and his pals never had such concerns. Not that I had them anymore, either. Not since those months in a wet tent in England. They put paid to any inhibitions I might have had. You might say England began the job, and Belgium finished it. Or perhaps that was France.

The next day the company mustered and marched a few miles down the dusty road to the town of Béthune. There we partook of a shower bath at the convent. Afterwards, mulling around outside the gate to await the last of our group, I happened to notice Lieutenant Drinkwater talking animatedly with a soldier. Normally something so ordinary wouldn't have been worthy of notice. However Drinkwater felt he occupied a higher station in life – one that didn't involve fraternising with the other ranks.

Since our little confrontation a week earlier I hadn't seen much of the lieutenant. When I had, he'd said little. Which suited me fine and made me think he'd forgotten the whole affair.

The lieutenant suddenly laughed. At this a few heads turned, including mine. Then Private Harry Hobson stepped out of Drinkwater's shadow, gesticulating wildly, with a broad grin on his face.

'I'll be darned,' I murmured.

'Not a couple you'd expect to see together,' said Dundas. He'd seen the whole thing, and from the sound of it he was as mystified as I was.

'No. Definitely not. He's not even in Drinkwater's platoon.' I shook my head. 'What I wouldn't give to know what *that* was all about.'

'Whatever it was, it must have been quite something to put a smile on Drinkwater's face.'

I scratched at my nose, thinking. 'Yes, indeed,' I said slowly. 'It makes me wonder if jokes are the only thing Hobson is providing our lieutenant.'

'Nah.' Dundas shook his head emphatically. 'That couldn't be? You think Hobson ratted you out about that raid, don't you?'

'First of all, it wasn't a raid. But, yes. The thought had crossed my mind. Hobson wouldn't be the first crook in history that turned out to be a snitch.'

That evening I was summoned to Major Ormond. Which was curious, as only this very day he had returned to the battalion after an extended stay in hospital, following his injury near Gravenstafel. I couldn't imagine that one of the first things our OC would want to do was talk to me.

On the road to the small brick outbuilding of a farm that did duty as battalion headquarters, I passed Lieutenant Drinkwater coming in my direction. He acknowledged my salute with one of his own and a wry grin. And the knot turned.

The door to HQ opened as I approached. I stepped aside to allow Sergeant Gunn to pass. Knuckling my forehead in acknowledgement, he smiled at me knowingly. 'Good luck, MacPhail,' he said.

Before I had a chance to ask him what he meant, Major Ormond appeared in the doorway. He was more prim and proper than I'd ever seen him, and I was conscious I was not, with the sole exception of the new cap I'd been issued. Ormond was visibly none the worse for wear from his wound. In fact, there was no sign of it whatsoever.

'Ah, Corporal MacPhail, you'd best come in.'

He beckoned me to a table covered with papers. He sat down and indicated that I should sit, too.

'That's alright, sir. I'm fine standing.'

'As you wish.' He frowned ever so slightly as he took in my appearance. 'Festubert was tough, I understand?' he said.

'Yes, sir,' I replied. In other circumstances I might have elaborated, or even mentioned that I was glad to see him. Ormond was a good officer and a good man and I was pleased he'd returned. Now I just stared at him, dumbly awaiting my fate.

'Your name was mentioned several times...' he began to say, whereupon I noisily cleared my throat.

'I wouldn't believe everything you hear, sir,' I heard myself mumble.

'Oh?' He frowned and threw me a puzzled glance. But then he went on, 'First let me finish, MacPhail. As you know the battalion is very short on officers at the moment. As a consequence I've recommended that several sergeants be sent to officers' school in order to fill the gap. However, that leaves me with too few experienced sergeants, so I've decided to give you an extra stripe.'

I heard the words, but in the confusion reigning up above (better known as my brain) they seemed all jumbled up. 'Really?' was all I managed.

Ormond nodded. 'Captain Day spoke highly of you, as did several others.'

'Oh?'

'You seem surprised?'

'Well, sir, I thought perhaps I'd be taken to task for having used my initiative,' I said.

'Whatever gave you that strange idea? When I spoke with General

Currie this morning that was one of the first things he advised me on when selecting new officers and NCOs. "Pick men with initiative," he said.' Ormond dipped his head to peer at his watch. 'Anyhow, congratulations, Sergeant MacPhail. I know you'll do well. If you'll excuse me...'

With that he bustled me out. The next man already stood waiting.

Dazed I walked back towards the farmhouse. It had been an evening of surprises. For the life of me I couldn't figure out what Drinkwater was up to. Nor Hobson, either, for that matter. I was convinced something was going on that I didn't understand.

CHAPTER 16

29th of May, 1915
Le Hamel, France

'Hobson!? Harry Hobson? Are you certain?'

Dundas nodded. 'I saw the stripe,' he said firmly. 'It's officially Lance-Corporal Hobson, alright.'

The morning's inspection by General Currie was over and there were a few minutes before we were to begin practicing the use of the crude gauze respirators we'd been issued. Having actually been in a gas cloud, I saw the practice as a complete waste of time – either you put the mask over your mouth and nose at the appropriate moment, or you shouldn't have been in the army in the first place. A thick piece of cotton cloth was not going to save you in the trenches for long, not if you couldn't even work out how to put it on. Conscious I was to set an example for the men, I kept this line of thinking to myself.

'Hobson, a corporal,' I moaned. 'Unbelievable. It may be the season for promotions, but why Harry of all people? Are they planning on sending him into the German trenches to pilfer the machine guns in advance of the next attack? Who in God's name would put *him* up for a promotion?' I began shaking my head in exasperation. But then I noticed Dundas's face where his heart was prominently on display. 'I don't understand why you weren't promoted,' I said gently. 'If someone deserves it, it's you, Roy.'

Dundas shrugged. 'Don't worry about it, Mac. I'm not sure I'm even up to being a corporal. It's not like I was ever the captain-of-the-baseball-team type.'

'You're selling yourself short. Look at me. I'm scared out of my wits most of the time, truth be told. Yet here I am with three stripes on my arm. I'm not even confident I can get myself over the parapet when I need to, let alone ensure the others do.'

'Yeah, well,' he sighed. 'At least everyone knows your name. Me they'd be saying Corporal what's-his-name.'

'Listen to me, Roy. You're ten times the man Harry is. Not to mention that you have ten times the experience he has. Plus a functioning brain. I'd follow you in a flash.'

Dundas said nothing but his cheeks reddened and he smiled a bashful smile.

'And who said anything about being a corporal? As far as I can make out there's a dire need for new generals, not that their casualties were especially heavy. Zero is a number I've been hearing a lot. You may have to be a little patient, Roy.'

Some said our biggest problem were the officers; only we were onto our third batch in as many months. Whatever their faults, lieutenants in this war had a frighteningly short life expectancy, something that didn't hold true for the more exalted ranks; the generals were all in fine fettle. Their quaint ideas, too. I hoped that when our next stunt rolled around our revered Army commander, General Sir Douglas Haig, might reconsider a couple – particularly the one about charging in broad daylight with three guns and twenty shells in support. Outside of the rarefied air at headquarters, murder was the term generally used to describe that.

1st of June, 1915
Givenchy-lez-la-Bassée, France

Three days later the battalion was marching south with the entire brigade.

We went a mile until we reached the slowly flowing waters of the

La Bassée canal and then turned left, to follow the canal bank east-wards in the direction of the village of the same name.

'Where are we heading, Sergeant?' asked one of the men. It was a fair question. After reading the newspapers and their sharply worded editorials about the shortage of shells, many were bitter after Festubert.

I continued to stare ahead, keeping an eye on the front of the column and our progress, but 1 was listening. I think I expected to hear a gruff rejoinder from the sergeant that the soldier should mind his bloody step, and he would see soon enough. Then with a start I realized I was the one being addressed. I'd whined about sergeants as long as I'd been in the army, so this was a strange notion.

I glanced over my shoulder.

It was Bill Partridge enquiring, the same eager new draft who'd peppered me with questions along this very canal two weeks earlier. Having survived his first big show, Partridge could be excused for feeling himself a proper old-timer. I was surprised his curiosity hadn't done him in. An inquiring look above the parapet was more often than not fatal, and Partridge had a dangerously inquiring mind – I knew that because I'd been accused of much the same.

'Givenchy,' I replied. 'We're heading to Givenchy. It's the next little town under Festubert.'

'And what's at Givenchy?' Against all regulation, Partridge had a flower of some kind protruding from his cap.

'Nothing good,' I answered. It was only a guess on my part, but a pretty fair one as we were now marching east, and east invariably meant trouble – had done since August 1914. Of course, if Partridge had been listening instead of shooting off his mouth, he'd have heard the steadily increasing thud of the guns himself. On second thought, at law school they always said: 'Never ask a question if you don't know the answer', so maybe he was a lawyer, too. After two years of study it was one of the few things I still remembered.

Approaching the town, which was off to our left, we marched straight towards a set of large, cadaverous-looking three-story build-ings near the canal embankment. Slowly a smile came to my face, along with the thought that I'd spoken far too hastily about the attractions of Givenchy. In giant black letters *Brasserie* stood out; though you had to guess at a couple of them for the gaping shell holes.

Behind me someone else made the connection as well. 'Hey, a

brewery,' I heard. Murmurs of excitement rippled through the ranks.

'Bout time,' joked a voice, much louder. I could have sworn it was Harry Hobson. 'All this marching is making me awfully thirsty, boys.'

There were laughs.

'QUIET,' I snapped. 'And watch your step.'

Drinkwater would string me out and nail my hide to the next dug-out entrance if his platoon was the one singled out for poor march discipline. To my dismay I'd been assigned to my favourite lieutenant's platoon and he was keeping me closely tethered.

After entering the huge hall, the men quickly simmered down when they saw and smelled nothing remotely resembling their preferred beverage, only broken timbers, machinery and piles of debris, and the odour that came from their destruction. The British had fought a pitched battle here in '14.

We exited the brewery at the far end and emerged in a very deep communication trench. It was over seven feet high, built along the embankment of the canal. There we were met by guides from one of the 47th London Division's brigades, who beyond telling us this was Cheyne Walk – a tongue-in-cheek reference to a famous road beside the Thames in London – were supremely efficient in shepherding us to our new abodes. That done, the Londoners left us to it, trailing smiles and wit-filled assurances that it was truly a picnic here, the truth of which could be measured by the speed with which they filed out.

Unlike Festubert the trenches were dry, so that was one small salvation. Even the ones abutting the canal. And there were proper dug-outs, deep ones with a covering of logs that most of us more readily associated with a log cabin nestled deep in the woods. In the absence of thick concrete, logs were almost as effective against the showers of shrapnel and all but the largest of the shells.

Two companies were up and two were in reserve. It was no great surprise when I heard which side of the draw I landed on. It was almost 10 p.m. before the sentries were assigned and at their posts. The layout of the trenches and the duties of the platoon firmly established, I set out to find a nook of my own in which to sleep. I found one in a dug-out on Baker Street, 50 yards from the front line. A bully almost beat me to it.

I'd turned away to light the stub of a candle on the table when I heard a commotion behind me. I turned in time to see a man unceremoniously chucking my sack onto the dirt floor and replacing it on the planks with his own.

'Don't you even think of it, Hobson,' I growled.

When he saw who it was, he did the only thing he could and made ready for a hasty retreat, even going so far as to dust off my haversack.

'Lance-Corporal, eh?' I said. 'So you figured that entitled you to someone else's bunk?'

Shiftily he looked away. 'It wasn't exactly like that, Sergeant,' he mumbled.

'Sure it was,' I said, and gazed at him so long he began to shuffle from foot to foot. He may not have liked me, but he had learned something about the importance of rank.

'Well, I'll be off then,' he mumbled and headed towards the entryway.

'Yes, that would be best.' Not only was I stuck in Lieutenant Drinkwater's platoon, I was stuck there with Harry Hobson. But that didn't mean I had to sleep next to him.

'Oh. One thing before you do,' I said. 'It's been puzzling me.' Harry paused and turned to look at me. 'I never put you down as a snitch before, Harry.'

Harry's eyes widened. It wasn't just a trick of the candlelight, but he looked indignant. 'Me! A snitch?' Momentarily forgetting where and what we were, he said, 'What are you on about, MacPhail?'

'I saw you cozying up to Lieutenant Drinkwater a while back. The next thing I notice you're promoted.'

'Yeah, well, the lieutenant knew my father. He did some plumbing work for him, and we had a few things to talk about. Not that it's any of your business. NOR anything to do with my promotion.'

'Hmm,' I replied, unconvinced, but tickled to learn what the good lieutenant's vocation was.

Dawn broke clear and sunny. Overhead, the last lingering puff of smoke from the dawn bombardment was the sole thing, apart from an enemy observation balloon, to sully a sky dyed a brilliant blue. By mid-morning the sun blazed down relentlessly. Under my woolen tunic it was stiflingly hot. Stripping down was not an option; common sense in this case deferring to the exigencies of rank.

A stream of mid-ranking officers were visiting. One small party after another, officers with maps and papers in one hand, field glasses in the other. They paused periodically to furtively scan the enemy lines, and make notes, and then headed off in the direction of the Duck's Bill. While it might have been the fine weather that brought them out in flocks, I subscribed to a more worrying train of thought; that an attack was in the offing. When you're expecting to be at the sharp end of it you develop a nose for such things. The arrival of a brigadier-general from the artillery all but confirmed it.

Brigadier-General Burstall was a broad chested, gloomy-eyed chap and I was assigned to guide him and his young adjutant where they needed to go. As most of the platoon was assigned to a working party this was a not-to-be-scoffed-at assignment, irrespective of the usual hazards one might associate with being in close proximity to a brigadier-general. In any event, our first destination was a cinch to find – the observation post near the intersection with Willow Road, only a short trot from the dug-out where I'd spent the night.

Burstall studied the enemy line with interest. Over his shoulder he asked, 'How far away is it?'

'Roughly 300 yards, sir, give or take. But the enemy haven't much of a line opposite on account of the marsh that you see in front. They figure we'd be daft to attempt going through that.'

'Yes. I can see why they'd think that,' he grumbled.

'If we go further north, sir, at the Duck's Bill, their line is only 75 yards from ours. That's where the British tunnellers are busy.'

So with all the haste of a French family out on a Sunday excursion we followed the line another 600 yards, stopping regularly to look in on Fritz.

Only after I'd seen a map did I understand why the semicircle of sandbags protruding out from our lines in the direction of the Germans was known as the Duck's Bill. It was one part of a larger form created by the two trench systems. Drawn on a piece of paper they bore an uncanny resemblance to a duck in profile with its head jutting forward. Myself, I would have called it a loon not a duck, but the British weren't familiar with Canadian wildlife and the imagery was clear enough.

What was less clear was the layout of the German front line. Unlike our own it was strangely irregular and protected by a belt of heavy wire. For the life of me I couldn't figure out what the purpose of the coloured sandbags, red, purple, white and blue was. So, having answered all of the brigadier's questions to his apparent satisfaction, I decided to ask him.

'Clever, isn't it?' he replied, without looking. 'The colours make it more difficult to ascertain the distance, form and strength of their parapet.'

'You know, sir, if you were to put a field gun or two in one of these trenches, I don't think any of that would matter.'

Burstall pivoted round. 'What was that you said, Sergeant?'

His eyes bore into me, worse than Justice Scott's had when I made the rookie mistake of interrupting him midstream in front of a full courtroom.

Nervously I coughed. 'What I was thinking, sir, was that if we had some field guns at this point firing over open sights, it wouldn't much matter if the parapet was ten feet wider or further away. They'd do the job. Wouldn't hurt with clearing the wire, either, sir.' The general was silent. 'I realize I'm just a simple infantryman,' I mumbled.

Burstall glanced over at his adjutant, who was pensively rubbing his chin. To my surprise he appeared to be weighing what I had to say. Then the general looked back at me. 'You might just have something there… MacPhail, wasn't it?'

'Yes, sir,' I replied, conscious that if it all went wrong a sergeant of the 10th Battalion was about as fine a sacrificial lamb as you could find.

CHAPTER 17

22nd of June, 1915
Givenchy-lez-la-Bassée, France

In the event, I had little to do with the actual assault. We manned the trenches for close to a week before being pulled out and sent into reserve. One week later, when the attack did go in, it was the poor sods from the 1st Brigade who got the assignment.

On this occasion there was no mistaking the thoroughness of the preparations. No one in the division wanted a repeat of Festubert. General Burstall must have even seen something in my offhand remarks for he ordered three 18-pounders forward. They were man-handled into the trenches at the Duck's Bill with great difficulty and great secrecy, their wheels muffled in old rubber tyres, special shields of iron plate welded in front to protect against the small arms fire they would attract. When the time came the guns blasted the German wire and parapet into perfect oblivion. Until the German artillery got their range, and the favour was returned.

Then the mine underneath No-Man's-Land erupted in a roar of noise. It rattled the windows and shook the walls in the hamlet of Hinges where I stood, eight miles distant, and killed not only many Germans but numerous of our own troops as well.

What I didn't realize until it was over, was that our attack was only a sideshow to the main event. The sideshow went well at the outset.

Brigadier Mercer's boys broke through the first two enemy lines on a 200-yard front and took the *fortin* known as Dorchester.

However, the Scots of the 51ˢᵗ Highland Division and the Brits of the 7ᵗʰ, whose right flank we were protecting, ran into problems. I don't know the why of it but they didn't come up. That left our lads taking heavy enfilade fire from an uncaptured *Stützpunkt* known as Stony Mountain, in addition to a mine crater the Germans had filled to the brim with machine guns. To top it off, the supply of bombs ran out, and the German artillery was as merciless as always. The short and the sweet of it was that the flank died waiting in vain for the main show to succeed. Our battalions were forced back.

The next day new orders arrived and the whole attack went in again – the identical scheme but in broad daylight this time and without preparations. I'm not entirely sure why High Command expected a different result.

Officially the attack was described as a "reverse". A farcical notion, until you considered that most officers were loath to brand it a disaster for fear the label might stick to them. Worse, carefree words of criticism risked filtering up the chain of command to the gentlemen of superior breeding and modest self-reflection who'd set it all in motion. They were the ones who held the strings for promotion.

A week passed.

Visions of some placid drawing room in the rear filled my thoughts: a bevy of well-dressed officers were gathered round a table while a red-tabbed general repeatedly stabbed his finger down on the map at a spot named Givenchy. It was hardly an idle concern; the battalion was back in the front line.

Those thoughts were disturbed by a deep thud to the east. A sound I knew all too well.

'Heads up,' someone shouted. 'A Rum Jar!'

Dawn had made its appearance only an hour before and the air was still damp with the heavy night mist common to this country. The flat fields were coloured by a young bull of a sun, the sky a hazy pastel blue. Off behind the enemy trenches, in the direction of the village of La Bassée, the reason for the excitement was not hard to discern.

A half dozen men stood with me, warily following the track of the mortar shell across the sky with our eyes. I could feel my stomach tightening and I reached into the cotton bag at my side where I nervously fingered what I was looking for. It was the new hooded flannel mask with glass eye pieces they'd given us, a newer version to replace that handed out only weeks earlier. Since Ypres the worry about gas was never far off.

The shell arced almost vertically into the air, trailing a pencil-thin plume of smoke and a shower of orange sparks, its momentum so slow it seemed as if it was in danger of falling back upon itself.

But distances deceived and so did the speed. Unlike the shells from even the largest of the guns, which you heard but never saw until it was too late, a round from a mortar had an oddly lulling effect.

Mortars, like the artillery, were another well-honed tool of destruction that the Germans possessed in great numbers. Against them we could muster only the feeblest of responses. I was beginning to understand how it was that the Germans had gotten so far last autumn. The mortars themselves were unimpressive, no more than big tubes – sometimes wheeled, sometimes not – from which a bomb could be lobbed into the enemy lines. However, unlike an arm – the more traditional method of delivery – the biggest *minenwerfers* could propel a 200-pound shell filled with ammonal more than a thousand yards. And unlike a shell from a field gun or even a howitzer, both possessing a much flatter trajectory, a mortar could dump its load effortlessly into a trench from above. Seeing as how trenches were where Europe's armies found themselves these days, that made them a feared weapon.

The light in the back of the bomb went out. Reaching the apex of its flight it tipped and began to fall, not back on itself, but precipitously towards us. A dark spot approaching fast.

'It's going left,' said someone. Private Edmonds.

'Oh, no it's not,' I said. 'RUN!' I took off down the trench followed by the others.

We made it past the first traverse, and had almost gone round the second, when there was a deafening explosion. Silence ensued for the better part of a second or two. Then a *WHOOSH* of air caught us from behind blowing me against a post, followed by a deluge of dirt and debris that rained down for longer than seemed possible.

I turned to the men. One had been blown to his knees and most of the others were missing caps, but otherwise they appeared to be fine. 'You all okay?' I asked.

They nodded. 'Okay,' said a few.

'Damn,' I mumbled under my breath as the realization hit. Then in a louder voice: 'Where's Edmonds?'

The men gazed round, checking the faces of their comrades in the hope of spying in one the cheerful flushed features of our taxidermist from Medicine Hat. Edmonds, however, was nowhere to be seen.

There was no time to look for him. Another Rum Jar was in the air and again we scrambled madly for cover. A few of the men found sport in dodging Rum Jars and Moaning Minnies, a high stakes game of chicken, not unlike jumping off the second story of a barn and hoping you landed well. To me there was little sport about it. But then I was from the tame streets of the city, even if Calgary wasn't exactly the grand metropolis of London or Paris, both of which I'd looked forward to visiting before the harsh realities of my European adventure set in.

When I spotted a hole, not quite a dug-out, although it possessed a roof of sorts held up by logs and was carved several feet into the parapet wall, the five of us dove in. We almost flattened the two soldiers already there.

'This running left and right is a bit too much like Russian Roulette for my taste,' I panted. 'Let's hope for the best and wait it out here.'

There was another thundering crash and the ground shook. We were some distance away but I felt the concussion in my chest. The nearest thing I can liken it to is standing an arm's length from a train track as a freight train rushes past. Swallowing uneasily, I clenched my fists and did my best to appear unperturbed. A trickle of sand poured down through the roof.

One of the men had his hands over his ears and was rocking his head back and forth in a motion that reminded me of something I'd seen not long before, but couldn't quite recall. Then it came to me; one of the patients at the Asylum had done the exact same thing that morning we'd gone bathing near Bailleul. This young soldier had nothing more than a case of mild shell-shock I told myself. It was all I could do to avoid similar symptoms, and the ensuing embarrassment.

Corporal Stiles – he was from the same draft as the lad – was rather less empathetic. He slapped the boy hard on the cheek with an open palm. A look of terror flitted across the lad's features. However, the rocking stopped.

Stiles winked at me and grinned. I ignored him.

We huddled together uncomfortably, not saying much of anything, waiting and listening for the sound of a far-off thud that would signal that another bomb was headed our way. And then the agonizing wait, counting down the seconds before it would land and praying that when it did it wouldn't be directly above our heads. As Dundas liked to say, it was more suspense than was good for a man.

Soon after, their artillery had a go of it as well, pulverizing our line for close to thirty minutes.

As to Edmonds, we found him shortly thereafter, fifty yards from a gaping hole in the parapet wall. He lay peacefully. We rushed to him thinking at first he was merely unconscious, until our anxious looks were met by the cold, unmoving and empty eyes of a dead man. The strange thing was, there were no obvious injuries to be seen, but such was the force of the Rum Jar's concussion that the buttons on his tunic had been flattened. He must have run straight at it.

'Damn shame,' I said, sighing. 'Stiles, would you get a man and carry him back. We're not going to leave him here.'

'Yes, sergeant.' Stiles turned and walked over to the others. There I heard him loudly and peremptorily order two soldiers, one of whom was the shell-shocked lad, to carry the body back.

The hair on the back of my neck bristled. 'CORPORAL. A moment, if you will.'

Stiles shook his head in visible irritation, but did as I asked.

'Perhaps I was unclear,' I said, staring at him, 'but I distinctly recall asking *you* to take him back.'

'You've got be kidding, sergeant. That's why we have them,' he replied, motioning with his head in the direction of the men. 'To do the dirty work.'

It was as if I was speaking with some 18th century plantation owner.

Slowly I shook my head. 'You know,' I said, 'I've changed my mind, Stiles. Just so we're clear, let me clarify: by you, I now mean you and *you* alone. And you'd better be careful with him.'

As he turned away I heard Stiles mutter something under his breath. I couldn't be certain but it sounded distinctly like, 'You're going to regret this, MacPhail.'

'Move it, corporal,' I barked, intentionally raising my voice so that the others heard. 'A little haste or you may find yourself on latrine duty.'

All of a sudden I was sounding a great deal like Sergeant-Major Atkins. He'd been more of an influence on me than I realized. Underneath the gruff exterior, Atkins was fair, and a far better judge of character than I'd first thought when we crossed paths. Character was precisely what I was missing in Corporal Stiles. That and a sense of basic decency.

Dundas groaned. It was not the reaction I'd been expecting when I told him of my encounter with Sam Stiles. Then he laughed. That mystified me even more.

'That's what I love about you, Mac. Even when you stumble into a wasp's nest of your own making, you still don't clue in.'

The puzzlement was likely etched on my face, for after a pause he went on. 'I don't suppose you know why Sam Stiles is called Sam?'

'Rhymes with ham,' I ventured.

Wearily Dundas shook his head. 'No. It's because Sam Stiles is named after a crony of his father's – a certain Sam Hughes. Better known to you, I expect, as the Minister of the Militia.'

'Yeah, thanks. I do know who the Minister of the Militia is, Roy.' Thoughtfully I pursed my lips. 'So you say Stiles is a friend of Sam Hughes?'

'His father is. Rather a close one, too, I gather. Close enough that should Sam Stiles go crying to his father, you may find your current tribulations with Harry Hobson to be rather petty.'

'Come on, Roy. Old Sam Hughes may have some loose shrapnel rolling around upstairs, but he has better things to do than chase me up and down the Western Front because I put Sam Stiles in his place. I expect he's charging around Valcartier on his horse as we speak, rooting out Catholics and other undesirables, and generally making a spectacle of himself.'

'That may be. But Hughes looks after his own. And that includes the Stiles family. They banked with us, you know.' Dundas reached out his arm and laid a hand on my shoulder. 'All I'm saying, Mac, is don't do anything rash. Let Sam Stiles be Sam Stiles and leave well enough alone, for Heaven's sake.'

Later that day I took a walk back down the trenches to the brewery. There the cooks had built themselves a cookhouse in the skeleton of a wood-framed building adjoining the huge brewing hall. It wasn't much to look at, but then cookhouses seldom are. A huge hole faced east and I stepped through it. Appreciatively I sniffed at the air. Dinner was on. After a morning dodging Krupp iron, a forenoon fending off a Boche attack, and an afternoon devoted to inspecting the feet, mess tins, kit and rifles of the platoon, I felt I was owed a little diversion.

Unbidden, I lifted off the lid of a big pot simmering away and stuck my nose inside.

A pudgy hand grabbed mine and clanged the lid shut.

'No. No,' said a voice from behind that I knew. 'You wait your turn, just like the rest, MacPhail.'

'Doesn't look half bad,' I said. 'That actually resembles real meat.'

'That's because it is,' said the man, turning towards me. 'A farmer sold us half a side of beef.'

'Hmm. That must have cost a pretty penny. What will the officers say, Terry?'

'They got the other half, so I don't expect there'll be any complaining. And, yes, it cost a fortune.' He wiped at his brow and smeared it on what must have been the filthiest apron in all of France. Mind you, after a challenging hour of sights and smells behind me, five grimy toes at a time, my hygienic standards may have slipped a trifle.

'How are you, Mac?' Terry asked.

I saw his eyes land on my sleeve. Before I had a chance to reply, he added, 'Well, well... Sergeant MacPhail... Every time I see you've got yourself a new rank. The war must be going well.'

'It isn't,' I said. 'Which explains everything. But I'm sure you know that.' He nodded. 'I must say, even though there's fewer of us around, the food isn't getting any better.'

Terry sighed. 'Yeah, well, we do the best we can with what we're given.'

'Coincidently, that's one of the reasons I came to visit,' I said. 'I wanted to ask a few things about what you've been given recently.'

Terry shrugged. 'Fire away. As long as you don't expect any hand-outs. Not after that last comment…'

There was no better place to garner some honest-to-goodness intelligence about what was really happening than the cookhouse. After all, there was no point in cooking for a thousand men if only four hundred remained – the army kept a closer watch on the food than King Midas did on his millions.

I knew Terry Adams from when he'd worked at the Ranchmen's Club, a prestigious retreat for the successful established men of the city. Notwithstanding the absence of any grey hair on my head, or much obvious success to speak of, I nevertheless inveigled myself an invitation to eat there once or twice a year. Terry was a decent cook, even if cans of Machonochie stew and a handful of extra turnips and potatoes don't lend themselves to much. Suspiciously though, despite ten months of active army service, the folds in Terry's belly looked as if they'd actually grown.

'So, what *is* the situation with the supplies?' I asked. 'And I don't mean what you're packing away.'

He began to preen himself and rubbed his hand in circles over his belly. 'Don't say that, Mac. A thin little reed like me?'

'You're no Ethel Clayton, that's for sure,' I said, smiling. 'But how about it?'

'Well,' he said, and a frown appeared. 'It's hard to know exactly. But I'd guess there's roughly 800 less mouths to feed in the division.'

I grimaced. 'That many?'

He nodded.

'You realize we're not a foot further,' I said. 'And I expect if we've lost that many, the British casualties are probably three times that number. It's an awful lot of men for absolutely nothing.'

Terry didn't reply. Which didn't surprise me as there was really nothing more to say. Except one thing.

'Just so you know,' I said. 'After today there'll be fewer for dinner than you're counting on.'

PART THREE

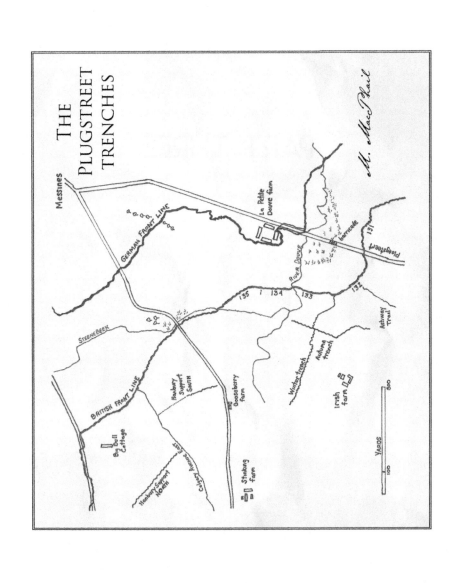

THE
PLUGSTREET
TRENCHES

M. MacPhail

Messines

GERMAN FRONT LINE

La Petite
Douve farm

barricade

131

Plugstreet

RIVER DOUVE

135   134   133   132

STEENEBEEK

Ashway
trail

BRITISH FRONT LINE

Roxbury
Support
South

Gooseberry
farm

Winter trench

Autumn
trench

Big Bull
Cottage

Stinking
farm

Irish
farm

Hanbury Support North

Calgary Avenue East

YARDS

100   500

CHAPTER 18

3rd of July, 1915
Trenches between Ploegsteert and Wulverghem, Belgium

The night was cool and quiet; though nights were never truly quiet on the front. There was always a gun somewhere thumping in the background, or a sniper's rifle that rudely pierced the still moments with a sudden crack, a round seeking out the man who'd been careless or just plain unfortunate. Our own artillery was rationed to three shells a day. So the guns were almost always those of the enemy. For my part I was glad when ours were quiet; the retribution of the Germans was far worse than anything we could manage ourselves. Not that it was the fault of the artillery lads; there's only so much you can do with three shells.

There was a loud boom. It came from off behind the dark shadow lining the horizon that was the main Flanders ridge. A big 5.9 I reckoned. One of them concealed near the ruined village of Messines, barely a mile to the northeast, had brought down a church tower to our rear the day before. To the north came a flash, followed by a bang. Then silence returned.

The 10th Battalion was back in the Plugstreet trenches. Terribly keen and woefully inexperienced we had arrived here to our first bitter foretaste of war. Almost four months to the day we returned as weary veterans who'd known only war. I didn't know whether to be happy to be away from Givenchy and Festubert, or depressed at the thought of having returned to the Salient. It was a toss-up. But there was no talk of new offensives and for that I was grateful.

A day earlier we'd moved down from the reserve billets on the crest of Hill 63. We went into the front line near Big Bull Cottage, close to the Wulverghem-Messines road.

'Keep digging,' I told the party of men. Despite the night chill they had their tunics off and their sleeves rolled up to above the elbow, hard at work. 'As deep as you can until you hit water. There's no point building a dug-out if it won't keep out a burrowing rat, let alone a shell.'

The four of them grinned and I saw one was Bill Partridge. He still had the flower in his cap; it had wilted away, much like every other patch of vegetation in the vicinity. Between the shells and the digging both sides were doing their utmost to leave little unturned.

'I don't suppose any of you are in for a tot?' I asked. It was like asking a wolf if he was hungry.

They flocked to me with alacrity. No doubt they'd sniffed out the contents of the large tan-coloured ceramic jar I was carrying two trenches away. Doling out the amber elixir was one of the more pleasant chores bestowed upon sergeants.

'Colonel Rattray thought you all deserved a celebratory drink in honour of Dominion Day,' I explained.

Puzzled, a man said, 'But Dominion Day was two days ago?' This earned him a sharp elbow in the side from his buddy, whose eyes were fixated on the jar.

'Yes, that's true,' I said. 'However, on account of the fact we were ordered into the trenches that evening, the battalion sadly missed the performance of the Highland bands. Naturally I know you all would have preferred a selection of "national airs" to this rotgut, but the OC in his wisdom thought otherwise.'

I filled a tin cup to the very brim with rum. 'If I hear so much as a peep later on…' I warned.

'Absolutely not, Sergeant. We'd wouldn't want to get old Fritz in a tear.'

'No. We most certainly would not. And given that's always a concern, I expect you'll have this dug-out complete by morning?'

They nodded vigorously. I handed the cup to the first man in line. Pavlov would have been proud.

When it was his turn, Partridge drank quickly then wiped his mouth on his sleeve and passed the mug on to the next man. 'What's all this digging about, anyhow, Sergeant?'

'To keep us safe,' I said. 'A decent support line, and a few spots to shelter away from the fire-trench, so we're not all huddled together when Jack Johnson comes calling.'

Every available man was digging day and night to strengthen the line – predominantly at night so as not to attract undue attention. It felt to me like we were digging in for good. What I hadn't understood when we took over the shallow, filthy trenches of the French at Gravenstafel was that there were two opposing views on how one should defend oneself. To the French, the front line was of no overriding significance, to be ceded should circumstance demand, whereupon their potent 75s would spring into action. The British attitude was simpler; we weren't to yield an inch. As might be expected, our inclinations mirrored those of the British. Only, where the British might be satisfied with a wall, we didn't rest until the wall was the Great Wall of China. It was a lot of work.

Opposite us, Fritz was transforming the green slopes of Messines Ridge into a daunting fortress of wire entanglements and freshly dug earthen embankments. No longer was there idle talk of the war ending soon. Both sides were digging in for the long haul it seemed.

This was an impression reinforced by a most startling event at Givenchy. Not only had we received new respirators and a new commanding officer in the form of Lieutenant-Colonel Rattray, we traded in the Ross rifle, and the entire division was reissued with short Lee-Enfields. After some good-natured joshing I even succeeded in swapping my used one for a splinter-new version. It still carried the smell of gun oil that first day. The generals clearly believed we'd be needing them.

Apparently satisfied with the response to his question – it was probably his head doing cartwheels in 100 proof – Partridge went back to shovelling. As I was never keen on shovelling it was fortunate my role was confined to supervision. Six feet of packed snow is not much fun, but it doesn't compare to the joys of thick Flanders clay which, when wet, feels like you're excavating wet concrete with a bent spoon. Playing the overseer was another perquisite of having three stripes on my sleeve.

I certainly found it wonderfully liberating to be out from under the yoke of the NCOs scrutinizing my every action. When I confided this to Dundas, he nodded his head understandingly. There were still the officers, naturally. However, what I hadn't anticipated was the heavy burden of expectations that I wore like a suit of medieval chain – those of my superiors, but primarily my own.

When the moments for sleep came I huddled in a hole with my eyes closed, and before exhaustion overtook me I worried. Would I succumb at the crucial moment? I'd seen others crack when it finally became too much. Would I ever possess the courage of Sergeant-Major Atkins? I think only a stubborn unwillingness to succumb to my own doubts and fears was what kept me going. That and the unthinking trust of the men in the platoon.

The men were solid and reliable and full of good humour, even when the toll of circumstance would have given them good reason to be otherwise. Good men aside; that left Hobson, Stiles and Drinkwater.

Not long after we'd arrived back in the Salient I shared the last vestiges of the rum jar with my fellow sergeant in the company, Shelby, and asked him if he would take Hobson under his wing. He looked at me doubtfully. 'Here, you take the last of the rum,' I offered. With that it was done.

It was a strategy designed to secure my open flank. I hadn't figured out what Hobson was up to, if anything, and until I did it was best to keep him at arm's length. Stiles I could handle. Even if Dundas's overactive imagination thought otherwise. Lieutenant Drinkwater was trickier, admittedly. Particularly as he commanded the platoon. To my surprise, however, the lieutenant largely left me in peace. Scuttlebutt said he had large debts back home that he was anxious about. But if anything the man seemed more relaxed of late. How one could be re-laxed after Festubert and Givenchy was a mystery, and for the moment it would remain one, as I wasn't about to call him out on it.

The glow from their cigarettes and the soft murmur of voices alerted me to their presence long before I saw who it was. The working party appeared to be engaged in precious little work. They stood clustered together at the junction of Calgary Avenue East and Hanbury Support North. One man was leaning on what looked like a spade.

'Can't say I'm sorry Drinkwater's on leave,' I heard one of them say.

'Good riddance, to him,' said another. 'You know the bastard had me on a double shift because he said I looked scruffy. Scruffy. On Plugstreet! If you can believe that.'

There was a laugh, and then a gruff voice I recognized said, 'The good lieutenant won't be bothering *me* anymore. I arranged it.'

'I sure wish you'd tell the rest of us your secret, Harry.'

'Yeah, Harry, how about it?'

I stopped and pressed up against the trench wall.

'Well, boys…' he began.

The jar banged against a post.

Anxiously, a voice whispered, 'What was *that*?'

Mildly concerned the working party might have the wrong idea and put their new Lee-Enfields to the test, I called out in a soft voice, 'At ease, it's me. Sergeant MacPhail.' Then I stepped into view.

Harry looked as if the ghost from Christmas past was visiting.

'Hmm,' I growled, 'I see you lot are already comfortably at ease.'

There were mumbled protestations.

'Quiet,' I said. 'This stretch needs to be done by tomorrow. If it's not, you'll all be doing double duty. Which means you have absolutely no time for this.' I lifted my arm to display the rum jug.

'Ah, come on, Sergeant,' they moaned.

'No. No chance of that and you can thank Corporal Hobson. He should have had you at work, not standing around gossiping like a congregation of spinsters. And thank him again in the morning if this isn't finished. Now get out of my bloody way and get to work.'

Whatever I did I couldn't help sounding like Atkins. They say we turn into our fathers. For better or for worse I was turning into my old sergeant-major.

Hobson fixed me with a look of pure venom as I passed. I hissed, 'Get it together, Hobson. You should know better. You're a corporal now and, in case you hadn't noticed, Plugstreet is no playground.'

'Bugger,' I heard him curse as I rounded the bend. I paid it no heed. I was thinking about what Harry's secret could possibly be.

To the east the sky had lightened to a dull sullen grey. Shortly, dawn would be upon us. Before then the working parties needed to abandon their spades for rifles and stand-to at the trench parapet. With satisfaction I saw that most were already lined up on the fire-step.

I hurried along, taking note of the faces. Every so often I instructed a few to move left or right to fill the gaps, or simply to warn them to stay alert; after a night of hard labour most weren't. There was no sign the Germans were coming but Fritz wasn't always so thoughtful that he signalled his plans in advance. I knew from experience how tough it was to keep the eyelids open at this hour. I still hadn't seen Sam Stiles and crew. 'Where could they be?' I wondered. So I went looking.

Immediately east of Gabion Farm, the line bulged slightly. There the waters of the Steenebeek, a small creek running down the middle of No-Man's-Land, made a jog in the direction of our lines. For 200 yards our trench abutted the Steenebeek, and as the ground to either side of this tiny flow was marshy and wet, the section was a misery to hold. Its shelters were shallow and usually waterlogged. The trench walls themselves in constant need of repair. Four hours in this spot and your boots needed two days to dry. However the waters of the Douve River, of which the Steenebeek was a tributary, were low at the moment. For that reason we'd been hard at work and I could see the men had made good progress.

As I rounded the bend of a newly completed traverse. I caught sight of Woodward. He was one of Stiles' section. He was standing on the fire-step, his rifle slung over his shoulder. I went to him.

He nodded as I stepped up onto the planks beside him. He was a young lad, from a farm down by Pincher Creek, who'd left for the big city to join up. And now he was here. A million miles from home.

'Where's the corporal?' I asked.

'He'll be here shortly,' he said. 'He went to take a leak.'

I rolled my eyes in frustration. 'And the others?'

He nodded in the direction of the next fire bay. It was so quiet that I could hear the soothing gurgling of the Steenebeek.

'I see,' I said. 'You're a tall fellow, so keep that head down. Our foe are a lot of things, but there's nothing wrong with their shooting. One glimpse of you…'

He grinned. 'Sure thing, Sergeant.'

I stepped back into the trench intending to round up a few others to join him. Stiles should have arranged it and I intended to give him a piece of my mind, if the opportunity arose. That's when I noticed something else. 'Oh, and, Woodward. When you're at the fire-step, the idea is to actually hold your rifle. Just in case Fritz is coming.'

I winked but I'm sure he didn't see it. For most men a gentle nudge worked better than a shout – it reminded them they could think for themselves, and that I expected them to.

'Oh, yeah. Sure, Sergeant,' replied Woodward, a row of perfect teeth revealing themselves. He reached over his shoulder for the rifle, but it tangled in his webbing, and he ended up awkwardly lifting it high like a baton to get it off.

'NO, not like that,' I said.

CRACK.

I suspect it was the bayonet rising above the sandbags that the sniper saw. Although we hadn't yet worked on this stretch, and there was not much of a parados to speak of. As a result you were silhouetted at dawn and at dusk. Any movement, and a sharp-eyed man might well see the change in light as a body moved across a crack in the parapet.

The bullet hit him in the throat. A lucky shot for it went clean through a sandbag. Something I'd heard about but never seen before. Like everything else on the front the sandbags aged quickly, and with the dry days of summer sand had begun to leak from holes in the canvas sacking.

Woodward toppled backwards and fell onto the bathmat, almost at my feet.

I knelt down on both knees, frantically searched my pockets for the length of dressing I'd taken to carrying. His neck was spouting. I folded the cloth and pressed it down hard. His eyes were wide open. Holding his gaze I had to steel myself not to show in my eyes what I saw in his.

'Hang on, Woodward. Hang on. I have you.' Cowardly I looked away when I said it.

Stiles appeared. With a bark I sent him running for a stretcher bearer. Though I knew it was pointless.

Woodward lifted a hand off the ground and I caught it in my left. His eyes were on me. I could tell he wanted to say something for his lips moved, but nothing came save a trickle of blood.

'Don't worry,' I said. 'I'll let your folks know. You're a good soldier, Tim.'

His hand went limp. His eyes glazed over. 'Come on,' I urged, my voice shrill. 'Don't give up, Tim.'

They were wasted words.

I sat there, one hand still pointlessly holding the cloth clamped to his neck, my fingers treacly and sticky to the touch. With the other I held his hand in mine. I maintained this pose for a few moments, then laid his hand down, and with my fingertips gently closed his eyelids.

I don't think I would have been much good for anything had the Germans come that morning.

CHAPTER 19

11th of July, 1915
London, England

In a long squeal of brakes the train slowly eased to a halt and the doors to the carriage flew open. We spilled out onto the platform, a throng of khaki clad in muddy puttees and even muddier boots. The tanned and weathered faces around me appeared as taken aback by the sound of cheering as I was. A row of onlookers – women mainly, in wide-brimmed hats – stood along the length of the platform, frantically waving and shouting, excitedly ducking their heads to-and-fro in search of the familiar. At the sight of loved ones a few of the soldiers broke away, rifles in hand and arms outstretched, and rushed to join them. The weary gravity of their expressions gave way to ones of joy. I followed the others, passing a small hut underneath a sign proclaiming in large capitals, FRENCH MONEY EXCHANGED HERE. Several men peeled off to join the queue. The francs they'd been paid would be of little use in England. I headed towards the barrier at the end of the platform.

Behind it, where the great hall of Victoria Station began, a crowd was waiting. They were cheering. Small lads in caps whistled. A gentleman stepped to one side as I approached and clapped me on the shoulder. 'Well done, lad,' he enthused. Smiling I passed him by. On the station walls advertisements for Wright's Coal Tar Soap and

Pears' Soap duelled for my attention, both brands unknown to me, but uncannily appropriate. The air had a strange foreign smell to it.

For all my joy at being here I felt awkward and uneasy. For most in the train this was a homecoming, and even many in the battalion had English family to visit. I didn't and I found London oddly intimidating. Which was odd after all I'd gone through these past five months. Surrounded by millions, I was on my own in the capital of the Empire. A sudden longing for the trenches came over me.

I grinned broadly when I heard the familiar voice. Even after I recognized who it was.

'MacPhail! Is that you?'

Lieutenant Drinkwater had his cane in the air waving from ten feet away.

'By God it is. What a coincidence,' he said. He looked at me, beaming. 'You look very sharp, indeed, Sergeant MacPhail.'

This morning, conscious of where I was headed, I'd brushed off my uniform as best I could, thankful for the bath at Nieppe a couple of days earlier, and for the ladies who'd steamed out the lice from my tunic seams. Last night I even made an attempt to clean my boots – something I hadn't done since Salisbury Plain under the admonitions of Sergeant-Major Atkins. It didn't hurt that the Tommies ahead of me looked like they'd woken up in a mud bath. All the same, it was an uncharacteristic exaggeration on Drinkwater's part.

'Thank you, sir. You look very sharp, as well.'

Which wasn't an exaggeration at all. Drinkwater didn't simply look sharp; he was immaculate. His tunic could have hung in a tailor's shop window yesterday morning, and probably had. I bet it still had that new, fresh from the tissue paper smell to it. My bayonet wasn't as shiny as his gleaming new brown leather boots. Calf leather and hand-stitched, no doubt. For a man in debt Drinkwater's pocketbook seemed remarkably well filled, and had I not been so surprised to see him I might have dwelt on this further.

Drinkwater glanced down, visibly pleased with his dazzling new tenue. Self-consciously he shifted his tie around, ultimately leaving it precisely where it had been. 'Yes, nothing like a visit to London and Jermyn Street,' he declared.

I nodded. Not having been to either London or Jermyn Street before, I could only imagine.

'You're on leave?' he asked.

'Yes, sir. A one week pass.'

'Unfortunately mine's come to an end.' He pointed at the track where a long train with steam up was waiting. Little groups of grim-faced soldiers were hurriedly making their way down the platform.

'I'd love to stay and chat, Sergeant.' He glanced nervously at the train, which was now billowing white clouds. 'But I'm afraid I must run. I'm little late for the train as it is.'

'Of course, sir.'

He tapped his cane gently against my thigh. It was in lieu of shaking hands, I suspect. 'Enjoy yourself, Sergeant.'

'Thank you, sir.' I saluted, as was expected of me, and he threw me a smart one in return. As he moved away, he paused, and looked back towards me.

'Oh, one thing, MacPhail. Should you have the chance, do try the grill at the Savoy. Fabulous. Truly fabulous.'

'Thank you, sir. I'll keep that in mind.'

Swiftly he walked away. A piece of paper fluttered down from his trench coat.

'Sir!' I cried, 'Lieutenant! You dropped something!' But he was past the barrier and my shout was lost in the tumult of the crowd.

I walked over and picked it up. It was an unsealed envelope. First I glanced at it, then turned it over. It was blank on both sides. No sender, no addressee. A plain white envelope. Cautiously opening the flap a crack, I saw a thin yellow sheet inside, of the kind telegraph companies used. I'd return it to Drinkwater when I got back to Plugstreet, I thought, and slipped it into my tunic pocket, now anxious to find a place to lodge.

London proved to be a most reinvigorating experience. I pottered about the city, visiting the Houses of Parliament, St. Paul's Cathedral, the Tower of London, Hyde Park, and the monument to Admiral Nelson, and what seemed like a thousand other sights famous to me by name. Before a full day had passed I felt at home, a casual familiarity that with the passage of time evolved into more. It was as if I'd known the city, maybe not forever, but much longer than a day. I didn't think of the war those first few days.

When night fell and the rhythm of this bustling city slowed I returned to the simple room I'd found, dead on my feet, and sometimes a little wobbly. The room was in the home of a sprightly woman nearly my mother's age. Mrs. Samson had round apple cheeks and brown curls verging to grey. Unprompted she'd told me that her husband and sons were in the army, which explained the grey, and even without the explanation I wouldn't have doubted her respectability. She let the room and a few others like it for a shilling a night, and a modest 7p more for a morning bowl of porridge, followed by sausages, bread and butter, and two cups of weak coffee. 'It's so good of you Canadians to come and fight for us,' she said when I first arrived. Which was a trifle patronising – as if we weren't fighting for ourselves. But I smiled politely, knowing she meant well, and thanked her profusely for taking me in.

On the last morning of leave, my hostess arched her eyebrows in obvious astonishment when I inquired where I might find the Savoy. I understood her reaction better by the end of the day.

Approaching the unremarkable entrance to the Savoy I nodded good-naturedly at the hotel doorman, who looked as if he ought to be at the front and probably would be shortly, and entered a lobby of gleaming marble, burnished wood and hushed tones. I tried not to gawk like a tourist, but moved deliberately through it, my eyes agog, heading for the doorway marked the Savoy Grill. It took me rather less time to peruse the menu of Beef Wellington and Dover Sole – the prices would have scared off a Rockefeller, let alone a sergeant on leave looking for dinner. I couldn't imagine what Drinkwater was thinking.

I left considerably faster than I came. Avoiding a pair of bejewelled women in evening dress and the eye of the doorman, I went in search of humbler fare. A sign for the Prancing Fox caught my attention. The fox winked at me slyly as if he'd never heard of such a thing as the hunt, but promised a good time within. When I saw a trio of soldiers exit, animatedly talking amongst themselves, I pulled at the worn brass door handle and entered.

The place was as dark as your average dug-out, all wood panelling with huge wooden beams running across a low ceiling, the latter tarred as black as pitch. The warm air was thick and blue from the smoke. Through the haze a handful of electric lanterns on the walls threw a soft yellow glow. The pub was packed with both soldiers and civilians, all attempting to talk at once. I stood there for a moment, taking it in as my eyes adjusted. No one paid me the least bit of attention.

Spotting a stool come available I hastened over to the long wooden bar.

'What'll it be?' He was clad in an apron, a pencil tucked away behind an ear that looked as if it had seen action in every battle since the Peninsular War. The barman's gaze had already shifted away from me to a group of guardsmen who were noisily making known their thirst.

'A beer, please,' I replied.

His ruddy face turned to mine. Momentarily he looked bemused as he thrust a huge glass under the silver spout. He began pulling at the long white enamel beer tap whilst he traded words with the guardsmen – most of which I didn't understand. When he was done, he plunked a glass down in front of my nose, filled to the very brim, the contents an autumn brown colour without so much as a speck of foam on it. And I had been so looking forward to a beer.

'What's this?' I asked disappointedly.

'Good English ale,' he replied. He watched me.

Cautiously I sipped at it. 'Hmm, not bad.' I took another sip. 'Not bad at all.'

'The first one's on the house,' he said. 'For what you lads did at Ypres.'

I was well onto my second glass of England's finest when dinner arrived: fish, chips, peas and gravy. The fish and chips were appetizing enough, but the peas resembled not so much a vegetable, as the oatmeal porridge Mrs. Samson served up for breakfast – albeit without the taste. For a brief moment I regretted having spurned the Savoy. But then I remembered the prices and I took another sip of my ale.

I was waving my hand in the air for a third, when an older man appeared at my side. He too was waving his hand. Then he spied my cap on the bar counter.

'You're Canadian,' he exclaimed. The brass maple leaf badge tended to be a sure-fire giveaway.

'Yes, sir.'

He looked me up and down. I had the feeling he was searching for my beaver pelt cap. Either that or the feather headdress I had tucked away.

'Isn't that something?' He began waving his arm with renewed urgency. 'I'd like to buy you a drink, young man.'

'Oh no, sir. Thank you, but that's not necessary.'

'Come now. I insist.'

To which I could only smile agreeably.

'From Canada, by George,' he mused, as he passed over a pint. 'You Canadians are a rough and tumble lot.' Then he took a deep gulp of his ale. 'No offence, young man, but I can't help thinking about that joke. "Halt" calls the sentry, "Who goes there?" "Scots Guards," comes the reply. "Pass, Scots Guards." Then again: "Halt, who goes there?" "The Buffs." "Pass, Buffs." Finally: "Halt, who goes there?" "Mind your own goddamn business!" says a voice. "Pass, Canadians."'

He bleated out a raucous 'Ha, Ha' while his nose took on the form and colour of a beet. I had drunk a few pints but it still seemed a very strange thing to say. As a flat-footed colonial I was probably not expected to grasp this subtle brand of humour.

I can't recall another instance in the war where I so sorely missed having a Ross rifle to hand. Whatever it's deficiencies, there was no deriding its qualities as a club.

I smiled politely.

My benefactor was clad in an exquisite dark suit with a matching bowler hat. From the grey on his head and his upper lip, I judged he was more than twice my age. I don't think he had any real affinity with soldiers, certainly he didn't so much as glance at the others in the room, but I had the feeling I may have been a novelty – like front row tickets at the Royal Albert, or coming face-to-face with an orangutan at the London Zoo. Something to talk about afterwards at the club. The Prancing Fox seemed a strange habitat for him. I soon concluded he had come for what was in his glass. Soon after I realized his manner owed much to what he'd imbibed already.

After a rocky start, Braithwaite – 'do call me Roger' – was rather amusing, dryly relating various anecdotes about the city once I explained that this was my first and only visit to the capital. Nearing the end of his second glass, however, he began to explain the war to me in ever louder tones.

'The Hun are on their last legs,' he proclaimed. 'Kitchener has them precisely where he wants them.'

'Where's that?' I slurred. 'Behind two lines of wire and a concrete redoubt?'

He was only half listening. 'Between Scylla and Charybdis, that's where,' he said, pounding on the bar with his fist for emphasis.

While the Empire's newest field-marshal expounded on the strategy that was leading to victory even as we spoke, my thoughts wandered back to the Salient. Woodward was not the only casualty in the first week and a half of July. Three others from the company fell before the captain pressed leave papers into my hand and I'd made my welcome escape across the Channel. All the while the shelling continued.

The shelling. If there was one certainty about this war it was that. Once the shelling began the vagaries of fate were all that mattered in the long seconds after hearing that first distant thud. Or maybe you didn't hear it at all. Then it was only the deafening roar and the shake of the earth that told you you'd survived... until the next one fell. Not that it paid to worry, that only drove one crazy.

Braithwaite had his index finger raised, signalling a particularly crucial point in his monologue, when Claire appeared. Of course I don't know her as such at the time.

Claire was the sort of girl who by her very appearance could have held von Falkenhayn's hordes at Ypres indefinitely. She was a knockout.

She sat down beside me. To either side I was aware that the conversation had dimmed. Heads, unobtrusively and otherwise, were turning our way.

Her presence imposed even Braithwaite. So his silence suggested.

'Hi,' I said.

'Hello, there, handsome,' she replied, whereupon I had to restrain myself from looking around. She brushed a long golden lock to one side with a casual flick of her red-polished finger. I studied my ale with intense concentration. A moment of awkward silence followed as my years of training in the art of rhetoric went absent without leave.

Braithwaite said, 'Why don't you join us for a late bite and a drink, Miss...?'

She smiled knowingly. 'And *whatever* would the missus say?' she replied, fixing him a pointed stare.

Braithwaite coloured. 'Yes, well, if you feel like that.' He glanced at his watch. 'I must be running, anyhow. All the best, Malcolm.' He donned his bowler and swept away on unsteady feet, almost before I could thank him for the drinks.

I turned to her. 'Thanks,' I muttered. 'I was beginning to think the war would be over by the time he finished.' I pointed to my glass. 'Would you like one?'

She beamed. 'Oh, yes please, Malcolm.'

I waved at the barman. 'Are you meeting someone?'

'I've met you haven't I?' She smiled and I caught myself staring at her lips.

She was quick. There was no doubt about that. And soon we were talking animatedly, none of which had to do with the war, so that might have been part of it. But everything they say about the company of a pretty woman is true, mostly the effect it has on oneself. The wit of my stories dazzled even me.

However in London last call comes early. This evening it came earlier than it ever had before.

'Wouldn't you know it,' I groaned, as the shouts of the barman sounded an end to the bliss.

She laid her long fingers on my arm. 'Don't worry, love. I know a place,' she said softly.

So with that we stepped out into the cool clear air of a London night. She paused and waited for me to catch up, then looped her arm through mine and I felt her warmth. It had been a long time since I'd had a woman on my arm. From that thought it was not long, even in my less than lucid state, before another surfaced: Kathryn.

One thing I'll say about the trenches, they don't allow much room for wallowing in one's own misery. I don't think I'd thought of Kathryn for a whole month, maybe two, which was a pretty big change from the endless months last autumn when I couldn't think without thinking of her. But thinking of her now an uneasy sordid feeling descended over me. The kind you might have waking up from a night of ill-considered debauchery. I'm not sure many would understand – the men in the platoon certainly wouldn't – they'd think I was daft or worse. However I knew I wasn't ready for a gal like Claire.

'Look, I'm sorry,' I mumbled. 'I've got a very early morning tomorrow. I'm off to the front again. I think I should head back. I'm sorry, Claire. I really am sorry.'

She protested for a while, gently, until she realized there was little point. Then, with what sounded and felt like a very terse 'goodbye', she put her chin in the air and walked off, the quick patter of her heels clicking after her even as she disappeared from sight.

I stood there feeling morose and wondering what I'd done. A YMCA woman walked up to me. To my surprise she spoke. 'It's a good thing you sent that trollop packing,' she said. 'I was just about to say something. They prey on young men like you, far from home.'

'She seemed okay,' I mumbled. *Trollop?*

She gave me a matronly look, altogether different from Claire's. 'Think what you want, but you won't regret it in the morning. And if I were you I'd check my pockets.'

I nodded and began to walk. At the end of the block I stopped and thrust my hands into my tunic pockets. Everything was there, including my billfold. Then I felt the envelope Drinkwater had dropped.

Briefly I debated the issue. I was feeling rather carefree and light in the head by now – all that fresh air – and I pulled it out and went to stand under the light of a lantern. Removing the sheet from the envelope I smiled when I saw that my original suspicion was correct. It was a telegram.

Quickly I read it through. When I was done I whistled. 'I'll be damned,' I muttered.

It was from the Bank of Montreal, dated a week ago, and addressed to W.H. Drinkwater. It was as concise as only telegrams can be and confirmed that his outstanding loan had been settled in full.

That night I slept less deeply than circumstances warranted. When Harry kissed Claire I woke with a start.

CHAPTER 20

24th of July, 1915
Stinking Farm, 1 mile west of Ploegsteert trenches, Belgium

'He's the third runner in two days who's been shot,' sighed Lieutenant-Colonel Rattray. 'It's been going on for almost a week and it has to stop.' July had begun as a month for snipers and so too it was ending.

'But the road's well sheltered, sir,' I protested. 'On top of which it's almost a mile from the German lines. I don't see how it could possibly be a sniper.'

'We thought for a while that it might be a Belgian civilian,' said Major Ormond. 'With German relations maybe…'

The colonel interrupted. 'Yes, but that's almost certainly not the case, Sergeant. We now believe there's a German spy behind the lines.'

'A spy!?'

Rattray and Ormond nodded. 'There may be more than one,' Rattray said.

'What exactly do you expect of me, sir?'

'To catch him, or them, naturally. As the case may be.'

Why I'd been selected for this assignment was somewhat of a puzzle. I had no prior experience hunting down spies, German or otherwise; spies being rather thin on the ground in pre-war southern Alberta. Not that Colonel Rattray had any more experience than I did, apart from an intrigue that played out between him and the Minister of the

Militia at Valcartier. Ultimately that didn't go his way and resulted in Rattray being shunted aside as battalion commander in favour of Lieutenant-Colonel Boyle. Later it was said our fiercely partisan and Conservative minister couldn't condone a Liberal as battalion commander. As if the Germans cared. The breathtaking stupidity of it was what made it ring so true.

I think Major Ormond must have conjured up my name. For some reason he seemed to hold my abilities in a higher regard than any other authority in the army. It certainly wasn't Lieutenant Drinkwater. Not unless he'd calculated that I would end up looking like a fool in front of our commanding officer when I inevitably failed. The brief ray of sunshine Drinkwater had shone at me in London had since vanished behind ominous dark clouds; he and I were back on adversarial terms.

Initially, I quite reasonably assumed he would be overjoyed to have his telegram returned, worried where it might have gone. But if that was the case he didn't let on.

I'd barely handed it to him before he demanded, 'Did you read it?'

'I called out to you, sir, when I saw it fall out of your pocket, but you were lost in the crowd. Trying to catch that leave train to the coast, as you may recall. So I put it away in my tunic for safe keeping where it's been ever since. It's fortunate I was the one who found it, sir, otherwise you might never have got it back.' It was an evasion, of course, but true enough on the face of it.

He stared at me with hard suspicious eyes and I returned his look as best I could. He hadn't thanked me and seemed more concerned with what I'd read than the fact it was returned. And whatever was in my eyes appeared to convince him there was more to my words than I was letting on.

But he didn't say that. He only said, 'I'm watching you MacPhail...'

I gulped.

The only possible explanation was that Hobson had paid off the lieutenant's debts. As payback he was promoted to corporal and granted a degree of autonomy accorded no one else in the platoon. The loan would have been a tidy sum, well beyond the means of any man I knew, but thousands of dollars' worth of diamonds went a long way in 1915. Nothing else made any sense.

All of which explains why I quickly assured the colonel I would find his spy. Disgruntled lieutenants are eclipsed by happy colonels any day.

From Stinking Farm where battalion headquarters were located, the narrow dirt road wound its way eastwards heading first to the front line, then across No-Man's-Land and the German trenches and up the ridge towards the dishevelled ruins of Messines, now an enemy citadel of concrete and steel. Scattered along the road lay piles of brick, sometimes the ruins of a small brick or stone wall, and occasionally an entire farmhouse, barely recognizable as such.

In contrast to the bleak flatness further south in France, such as that around Festubert, there was a roll to the land in Belgium Flanders, of small rises and hillocks and slight depressions in between. Ditches and irrigation channels crisscrossed the fields. This had been prime farming country until through some cruel twist of fate the front lines of the war settled at this very spot. The farmers had fled, yet their crops grew on like the wheat now unattended and wild, and reaching well above a man's waist by this final week of July. Copses of trees dotted the land, and the pollarded willows that had lined the roads so desolately in winter had taken on a summer frivolity. Away from the front lines the ravages of war were camouflaged by greenery. To my astonishment even No-Man's-Land had come alive.

After a few hours skulking along the road, moving from one point of cover to the next, I came to the gloomy conclusion that a spy with a rifle could be literally anywhere.

What I did know was that the shootings had occurred between battalion headquarters and Gooseberry Farm. It was a distance of roughly a thousand yards, or two thirds of a mile. But a decent shot could easily take a man down at half that range. That implied that a swath of ground five hundred yards to either side of the road was a distinct possibility as a hiding spot. And 500 yards wasn't even conservative if the Germans had a marksman like Brideaux at work. Brideaux was a half-breed in the battalion who'd taken up sniping at the behest of Colonel Rattray. After only a week he'd carved sixteen notches in the stock of his rifle.

If I had been more mathematically inclined I might have calculated precisely how many square feet I would need to cover. But that was wasted energy, particularly as I could see I would be expending rather a lot of it in the coming days.

All the same, this assignment beat digging a trench or even supervising the digging of a trench; there was no end of trenches and dug-outs to be dug here at Plugstreet. While I'd been excused from all other activities the rest of the battalion was hard at it. Nor was trench digging without its dangers. Digging sounds innocuous enough until a Black Maria falls in your general vicinity. No, I'd rather be hunting a spy with a Mauser out in the open. Or so I told myself.

'What the devil are you doing?' called a voice. I looked up and saw Dundas approaching.

I was sitting with a map on my knee, pencil in hand, on a boulder in the late afternoon sun just past Gooseberry Farm, not far from where Currie Avenue bends to run alongside the road. The front line was not even 600 yards away. While it's true I'd been walking east, I think I ended up there to avoid the peculiarly noxious atmosphere round Stinking Farm – it hadn't acquired its name by chance. I smiled at Dundas as he shuffled up, hands stuffed casually in his trouser pockets.

'What I'm doing? That's a very long story, Roy.'

'I have time.' He flopped down beside me on the tree stump I was perched on. 'The boys are cooking up dinner before we're off on a working party,' he said.

I thought I could see them. A thin dash of smoke puffed and then disappeared. It came from the direction of the trees near the Hanbury line. I could imagine them there, five or six huddled around the little Primus stove, arguing about the best way to cook bacon and finally just throwing it into the mess tin that doubled as a frying pan. The Primus worked on alcohol and was as good as smokeless, so the smoke was from the bacon. For Dundas's sake I hoped it wasn't ash by the time he returned.

'You're never going to believe this,' I said, and I told him of my new duties hunting down a German spy. 'So as you can see,' I concluded, 'what I'm now doing is marking down all the spots I reconnoitered today that might possibly shelter a man with a rifle.'

Dundas peered over. 'That's quite a few,' he said. 'And then what?'

'Well I've still got a lot of reconnoitering to do. But when I'm done and I've identified all of them, I hope to narrow it down until I can identify the most likely one. Then I'll trap him.'

'Sound laborious,' he said.

I nodded vigorously. 'It is.'

'I only mention the labour because it doesn't sound much like you, Mac. I'm sure you haven't forgotten how Atkins reamed out the whole platoon because you convinced us of a shortcut across Knighton Down to "spare" our legs?'

Moaning I said, 'Yeah, well, this is a German spy, or spies, we're talking about, Roy. There are no shortcuts.'

'Just saying,' he said, 'whatever happened to that little expression you're so fond of – the one about "brains over brawn"?'

I shooed him away soon after. But his words kept rolling round in my head, stuck there like a piece of chewing gum to the sole of my shoe that I couldn't get rid of. He had a point I had to concede. I was running around like the proverbial chicken missing a key appendage. Which got me thinking. Right around the time Dundas and his mates were sinking their teeth into a feast of blackened bacon and fried potatoes it came to me.

It boiled down to doing what lawyers are infamous for: talking... with a little thinking thrown in for good measure. That I could do it sitting behind a table in the relative safety of battalion headquarters with regular meals to hand was an additional bonus.

I spent an hour that evening, and most of the following day, interviewing every messenger, officer and soldier who'd survived the infamous death stretch. Frequently I asked them to point out details on the map. The process bore a startlingly close resemblance to the work I'd done as an apprentice lawyer taking depositions; trying to distil the facts from a jumble of differing viewpoints, faded memories and outright fabrications. Most of the testimony was surprisingly consistent, even if one young battalion runner was convinced an entire regiment had been shooting at him. I knew quite soon that wasn't the case. Everything pointed to a single shooter. And by the time the sun began to fall, I figured I had him.

'Shh,' I whispered to Dundas. He hadn't actually said a word, but he was twitching like he might. For all my earlier confident talk I was a trifle nervous.

The colonel had told me I could have any man I wanted. More than one if the need arose. But I picked Roy on the grounds that while he was a lousy shot, he had a good head on his shoulders. I figured the head would be more important than the shooting when setting out to catch an enemy agent behind our lines. If my plan went according to plan we wouldn't have to shoot far – maybe not at all.

'You deserve to be out of the trenches for a spell,' I told him reassuringly, trying to make it sound as if I were really doing him a favour. Set against the alternative of digging a traverse trench all night he readily agreed. Hunting down a Boche spy was hardly a night out in London, but I think he knew that.

We were crouching in some bushes roughly a hundred yards to the north of the road. The night was clear and star-filled, and surprisingly bright as nights in late summer sometimes are. I'd picked the spot a couple of hours earlier when the sun was still up and I was able to get a proper feel for the lay of the land without worry the sharpshooter was about. He appeared almost exclusively after nightfall.

The field sloped slightly downwards towards the dirt track that was the road, affording an excellent view of a tumbledown brick wall closer to us than to it. Tufts of high grass grew around the piles of old red brickwork. The wall had the undisturbed derelict appearance of something from the last century, ignored by the farmer and untouched by the war. Behind it a sniper would have virtually unimpeded sight of a 50-yard length of the road. That was the "run of death" they spoke of.

'Watch the wall,' I mouthed to Dundas, pointing my finger. 'He'll show up there.'

It was late. Almost 10 p.m. And 10 p.m. was the exact time I'd arranged with the battalion runner who had intrepidly agreed to take on the role of the tethered goat. Of course the runner wasn't tethered. In point of fact he ran like the dickens. And it was good that he did.

The shot came as a harsh crack, but if I hadn't specifically been listening for it I would have ignored it. In the trenches, a minute of absolute quiet was more unusual and more worrisome than a single rifle shot. To my great relief the shot missed the runner; I saw him putting on an extra spurt in the direction of Stinking Farm and he disappeared from sight.

'Let's go,' I said to Dundas and we stormed across the grass in the direction of the wall, our rifles in hand. I thought I'd seen the flash from a barrel and I ran towards the spot, though it may only have been my brain playing tricks. Either way we didn't have trouble finding him.

He was waiting for us, in a manner of speaking. That is to say at the sound of our boots he spun round when we were within twenty feet. I could see him clearly. He was on his haunches, wearing clothes that could have been those of a farmer, his hand locking down the bolt of a rifle already pointed our way. Without really aiming he fired and the flash was for real.

'Aaargh,' I heard to my side. Dundas was hit.

Not having fixed a bayonet I did the next best thing and pulled the trigger. I was firing from the hip, which is not ideal. However I was only mere steps from him. The round caught him in the shoulder. He began struggling with his rifle to reload and I did the same. Behind me I heard a shot and I saw him shudder as it hit him in the chest. A look of shock passed over his features then he toppled, falling flat on his front.

Quickly I knelt down, anxious that it be done, and wary he might be putting up an act. It wouldn't have been the first time. When I rolled him onto his side I saw that I needn't have worried. Nor would I be asking him any questions. He was lifeless, blood seeping through his vest. I turned back to Dundas.

'Thank God,' I murmured when I saw him standing there, a rifle in one hand, peering at his left arm.

'Here, let me have a look,' I offered. I pulled off his tunic so as better to examine the wound and rolled up his shirt sleeve. He winced.

I poured out a little water from my canteen, rubbing the excess away with a palm. 'Ah, you're a lucky man, Roy. It only grazed you.' It was a clean wound near the shoulder, a deep scar of not even half-an-inch. Then I handed him the dressing I had in my pocket. 'Hold that against it,' I instructed.

Dundas did as he was told. The wound may not have been deep but it must have been painful for he grimaced, mumbling something I couldn't hear.

'Come. Let's have a look around. In case he has an accomplice.'

I didn't think that was the case, but there was no harm looking. Dundas was still examining his arm, seemingly of two minds about the seriousness of it.

I started to poke around the wall. It turned out to be more substantial than I at first assumed, with a wide foundation hidden by the tall grass. Walking around it for a couple of paces, I stumbled over a loose brick, twisting my ankle and sending me to the ground. When I reached out to push myself up I felt rough-hewn wood. Puzzled, I looked closer.

'Well, well,' I said softly. 'What have we here?'

There was a wooden trap door. I yanked at it, and it opened easily. Staring down I saw a ladder and could just make out a dark space at the bottom. Lighting a match I slowly climbed down the rungs, well aware my rifle was as good as useless over my shoulder. Reaching the bottom I felt a stone floor underfoot. The air was cool, but not musty, not the smell of undisturbed places that I had expected. Someone had been here quite recently. Before the match sputtered out I glimpsed what appeared to be a small cellar, arched, two-thirds my height, and entirely clad in brick. 'You can come down,' I shouted up the shaft.

Then I lit another match. On the floor was a long-necked green bottle with the stub of a candle protruding. I held the match to it.

As it flickered to life, Dundas dropped to the floor behind me with a thud. He was grumbling. 'A "piece of cake" he says... "A night away from the trenches"... "Come on, it'll do you good"... I haven't been shot once this entire war, but a few hours with you...'

'Oh, stop whining,' I said. 'I've cut myself worse shaving.'

Dundas punched me hard in the shoulder. It was not how it was supposed to be between privates and sergeants. However that was not our sort of relationship. Anyhow, my thoughts were elsewhere.

I whistled. 'Just look what we've found.'

I wasn't referring to the two Mauser carbines leaning against the wall, nor to the large pile of foodstuffs stacked on the floor, nor even to the signalling lamps that were patently of German manufacture.

Neither was Dundas. 'Do you suppose they're drinkable?'

The opposite wall of the cellar was occupied by a huge iron rack filled with wine bottles.

'I don't know,' I said, 'but I'm all game to find out.'

'Damn shame we didn't find this earlier,' said Dundas, eyeing a half-dozen empties lying on the floor.

'Yeah,' I agreed. 'For now we'll each take a bottle. That way you'll have a nice souvenir to take your thoughts off that scratch of yours.'

Topside I quickly searched the sniper. The only item of any significance were some Belgian identity papers in the name of Luc van der Velden. He didn't look like a Luc. Several weeks later I learned the reason for that. The real Luc van der Velden, a local farmer, had been murdered earlier that summer. There was nothing apart from the contents of his little hideaway that proved the dead man was German, although he most certainly was. But then that's usually the case with spies, I'd once read. Our arms laden with rifles, ammunition, lamps and tinned food, with a bottle tucked away down our tunics, and our heads still grappling with the night's events, we headed for Stinking Farm.

'Whatever you do, Roy,' I warned, 'don't tell a living soul about that cellar. Stick to the basics and we'll both be heroes.'

CHAPTER 21

7th of August, 1915
Bulford Camp, 1 mile south of Neuve Eglise, Belgium

For a few days it was almost as I foretold. Dundas and I were the toast of the 10th Battalion. It wasn't solely because we'd shared our bottles with a few others. The colonel declared himself 'very impressed', allowing Major Ormond to bask in the spotlight for having suggested my name, and the men acted by turn both awed and amused that two of their own had snared an enemy spy.

The only tangible reward was the wine, a nectar unlike any I'd ever tasted, and a far cry from the astringent beverage served up in the *estaminets*. Were it not that I had a fair idea where I might locate some more I might have rued the day I'd shared it.

Soon enough the spy was yesterday's news and the deadly grind of the war returned; working parties by night and by day; trench mortar bombardments at regular intervals throughout; accompanied by all the other dangers and wearisome tribulations that beset the man in the trenches. The trial of a catapult to launch grenades into the enemy lines brought nothing but grief. While we tested catapults the enemy rained down Flying Pigs – and the pigs had it by a wide margin.

Later that week we were put into divisional reserve. After 51 days in the line, or immediately behind it, the battalion moved to the more peaceful environs of Bulford Camp, south of Neuve Eglise. There we learned that important visitors were expected. On account of having been in the trenches we had missed the Prime Minister's visit several weeks earlier. There was however a consolation prize planned.

It transpired that our important visitor was to be our own budding field-marshal, and soon-to-be-knighted, Minister of the Militia, Major-General Sam Hughes. Hughes had somehow coerced or convinced – I suspected the former – Prime Minister Borden into being promoted to Major-General, and the War Office in England into having himself knighted. I couldn't imagine what either had been thinking. In legal terms one sometimes spoke of "temporary insanity" so I reckon that must have been the explanation. Rumour had it that the War Office only drew a line in the sand after Hughes put himself up for not one, but two Victoria Crosses, for valour exhibited during the Boer War sixteen years earlier. There was no limit to Sir Sam's swagger. One could only hope the King came down with something contagious by the time of the investiture.

I'd seen Hughes for the first time on the lovely slopes of the Laurentians at the camp at Valcartier. There he'd exhibited the Napoleonesque qualities which had so endeared him to me, surround-ing himself with an escort of cavalryman reminiscent not so much of the French emperor but that of earlier centuries and the Praetorian Guard, as befit someone as august as he.

Ploegsteert would be quite a letdown for the minister. The only cavalry I'd seen were all dismounted and up to their knees in it, like the rest of us – there being little use and abundant danger in cavorting around on a horse. It was a shame, in one way. I would have enjoyed seeing the minister parade down Plugstreet on a horse.

When Hughes arrived at our reserve billets at Bulford Camp, sev-eral miles distant from the precipitous dangers of the front, the man looked as if he'd come straight from his tailor.

'Jesus, look at his boots. They're gleaming,' said the man behind me.

He was right. Sir Sam's batman had outdone himself. The knee-high boots shone like a mirror, matched only by the sparkle in the general's eyes as he viewed the assembled ranks of the battalion he so enthusiastically had sent forth to war last September. His tunic was equally immaculate – the trials of "his boys" at the front well known to him from vantage spots conveniently situated so as to avoid needless danger or dirt. A Sam Browne belt of new leather strapped in his burly figure. He might not have been tall, but he carried himself like a latter-day Caesar. Should that not have impressed, the coils of gold braid on his cap and the red tabs on his lapels surely did.

Sir Sam was accompanied by a taller thin man, with receding dark hair and a ludicrous moustache that curled up at the ends as if it were smiling. He was wearing a colonel's uniform. The proliferation of gold braid and various trinkets advised of his real status; he was a brother-in-law to the King.

Escorted by Lieutenant-Colonel Rattray the inspecting party made its way down the line. Having endured more inspections than is good for a man, I had to concede that Sir Sam's inspection was anything but perfunctory. He stopped at virtually every second soldier to exchange words.

Whether the desired effect from this personal attention was achieved, was questionable.

'Pipe up you little bugger or get out of the service!' I heard him say to a soldier four men down, whereupon the man sputtered a loud, nervous, 'Yes, sir,' and the general moved on. I noticed our visiting royalty remain behind. Perhaps to make amends.

I was determined not to be humiliated so.

When he came to me, the general said, 'What do have we here?' in an approving tone. He gazed up, the lines of his mouth tightening, adopting the resolute confident face I'd seen so often in photographs. 'A fine fighting man if ever I saw one,' he said over his shoulder to Colonel Rattray.

'Thank you, sir,' I blared. The entire battalion heard me, so I suspect he did as well.

'Sergeant MacPhail was involved in a most successful...' began Colonel Rattray.

Hughes interrupted. 'Yes, well, we're very proud of you boys,' he said. I wasn't sure whether he was speaking for himself, or more broadly. One never knew with Sir Sam.

'Thank you, sir.'

He glanced at the Lee-Enfield over my left shoulder. 'I'm sorry you boys had to trade in your rifles for a second-rate weapon.'

I hesitated, wondering whether I should speak my mind, but only momentarily. It's a weakness of mine I've been afflicted with since approximately grade three. 'No need to feel sorry, sir. The boys were thrilled to be rid of the old ones.'

'They were?' Hughes's thick black eyebrows furrowed. Underneath the eyes turned cold.

'We're all much better shots, sir, now that the rifles aren't jammed,' I said, allowing myself a weak smile. Too late I realized I'd gone too far.

'I'm surprised to hear the corporal say that. The experts contend you're not likely to find a better weapon in the field than the Ross rifle.'

'Actually, I'm a sergeant, sir,' I said meekly.

For a brief instant I thought the arrival of His Serene Highness Lieutenant-Colonel Prince Alexander of Teck at Hughes' side might save me. But it was not to be. Sir Sam-in-waiting wasn't about to be waylaid by the presence of minor European royalty.

'You look a lot more like a corporal to me.'

'I beg your pardon, sir.'

'You heard me, MacPhail. I'm demoting you. The men deserve to be in steady hands and I question yours. I'm making you a corporal.'

News of my demotion spread like wildfire.

'Why, hello, *Corporal* MacPhail,' said Hobson, when he saw me, minutes after we were dismissed. He was beaming from ear to ear. No doubt the first thing he did when he heard the news was seek me out.

'Take a hike, Harry,' I said. 'I'm in no mood for your petty games.'

He laughed. 'No, you wouldn't be would you?'

'What is it with you, anyhow? You can't tell me you're still sore about that punch from a year ago? As far as I could ever tell you never much liked your father. Actually, I often wondered if I had a better relationship with him than you did.'

Hobson bristled. 'No, that's long forgotten. But leave my father out of it. I just don't like you much, MacPhail, that's all. To be honest, I'm enjoying it to no end seeing you taken down a rung or two. About bloody time. You with your smooth lawyer ways and clever words... Always ingratiating yourself.'

'Clever words? You mean like with Sam Hughes?' Exasperated I shook my head. 'I don't understand you, Harry Hobson. But I have been wondering about one small thing. In fact I've been meaning to ask for the longest time. Now that you mention ingratiating oneself, perhaps you'd like to explain how it is that things are so cozy between you and Lieutenant Drinkwater? I mean he's not at all your type, and you're definitely not his. If anything the two of you are polar opposites. Yet he puts you up as corporal and treats you like a young princeling? Don't tell me it's your charming ways.'

'What of it?'

'What of it? Well, I happened to bump into the good lieutenant when I was on leave in London a few weeks ago. Quite by chance, really. He'd just outfitted himself with some spanking new gear from the tailors. You know, of the expensive kind, like generals wear. The lieutenant appeared to have had a most enjoyable time. But then he was partaking of the finest London has to offer. If I didn't know otherwise, I'd have thought Drinkwater was a major shareholder of the Canadian Pacific Railway.'

'So?'

'He was in debt, Harry. Maybe not up to his eyeballs, but Drinkwater owed rather a lot of money.'

'Maybe he just got lucky.'

I nodded. 'Funnily enough, I think you're absolutely right, Harry. I think he did get lucky.' I could see I had Hobson's undivided attention. The smirk he arrived with had long since disappeared. 'Drinkwater was lucky alright,' I said. 'He was *so* lucky, he ran into you.'

Harry frowned.

'Diamonds, Harry. I'm talking about Doll Block diamonds.

'You're a man of means now. How much did you pocket? Quite a bit I would think. That pal of yours, Randy Edwards, he disappeared almost immediately after the robbery. I thought at the time he took to his heels, but maybe it was simply you cleaning house? Keen on a larger share?'

'I had nothin' to do with that,' he growled.

'With what? Randy disappearing or the heist?'

'Both.'

'Both? Or neither? And what about Drinkwater?'

'That's exactly what I mean. You and your word games.' He threw his head to one side and fired off a spitball at the velocity of a French

75. 'I had nothing to do with no diamonds. And neither did Randy.' Then he looked me in the eye. It was a look meant to intimidate. Only I was not so easily intimidated – after seven months on the Western Front small-town bullies can seem just plain tiresome. 'If you know what's best for you, you'll keep your nose out of our affairs,' he hissed.

'Sure, Harry. Anything to oblige.'

Not knowing what to make of this, he took to his heels in less ebullient fashion than he came.

I couldn't help noticing, however, it was not solely Hobson's affairs I was to give a wide berth to.

He *had* bought Drinkwater off.

A little later, emerging from the wooden hut where I and half the platoon bunked, I spotted Lieutenant-Colonel Rattray. He flapped an arm at me and I marched over. 'I'm very sorry MacPhail. I want you to know I protested with the minister, but he would have none of it. I'm afraid my hands are tied on this occasion.'

'Excuse me, sir. He may be the minster, but he can't have me reverted like that, can he? There is such a thing as the chain of command.'

Rattray nodded. 'Yes, yes I know. And that's what I told him as well. But the minister is the minister...'

His voice trailed off. It was hopeless. I could hear it. I was sure Rattray had indeed put in a word for me. I was equally sure he hadn't pressed the case. After his own experience with Sam Hughes he was likely wary of risking a repeat. Which left me feeling deflated and altogether powerless. It wasn't so much the rank I was attached to I told myself – the promotion had fallen in my lap if I was honest – it was the indignity of being stripped of it. The corporal who hadn't cut it as a sergeant.

A new draft was arriving in a few hours – to replace all those we'd lost at Givenchy and Festubert – and Rattray excused himself. I went over to the fields, where some men of the company were in the midst of a game of football. Despondently I watched them, my hands sunk deep in my trouser pockets.

Dundas found me there.

I felt a hand on my shoulder and looked round to see who it was.

'Rough luck,' he said.

I shrugged.

'It doesn't much help, I know, but the men respect you.'

'Yeah, well, the minister obviously doesn't'

'What would he know? Sam Hughes is primarily interested in the greater glory of Sam Hughes. I was rather hoping they'd take him down to the Birdcage during his visit.'

I smiled. The Birdcage was a listening post at the far end of a narrow sap built far out into No-Man's-Land. It was a mere twelve yards from the German line. Some of the more intrepid visitors – lady novelists and the like – were taken there for a vicarious taste of war.

'Taken there and then left overnight with a Ross rifle,' I muttered.

Dundas grinned. 'See, you're feeling better already.'

'Better yet, I suppose I can always hope the King's arm slips when he goes to knight him.'

Then I saw something else and I felt the colour drain from my face.

'What's wrong, Mac?'

'Sam Hughes looking after his own…' I mumbled. 'Look for yourself.'

Sam Stiles, the son of his old crony, stood twenty feet away. On his tunic sleeve was a third stripe.

CHAPTER 22

24th of August, 1915
Ploegsteert trenches, Belgium

The only thing worse than supervising the digging of a communication trench is digging one yourself, for four hours on end in a foot of water with the absolute certainty that after a four hour pause you'll be at it again. Four hours on, four hours off – regular as clockwork. That Sergeant Sam Stiles stood watching over what had once been my platoon, and now was his, was the most painful part. I'd had a couple of weeks to accustom myself to this reality; still, I found it galling. But I tried to keep those thoughts to myself. Stiles was leaning nonchalantly against a post, without a care in the world, puffing on a cigarette before he moved on to the next party.

Suddenly someone whistled, 'Look! A Zeppelin, guys.' With that work ceased and we all turned our heads skyward.

Far above us, dark and menacing against the night sky, a mammoth form in the shape of a fat cigar slipped ponderously across. Not a cloud, it was too dark and moving too fast. It was heading south. Towards Paris I'm sure. None of us spoke a word. I listened for the sound of motors, but heard only the endless, echoing emptiness of the welkin, punctuated by some scattered shooting up 3rd Brigade's way. Shortly, a second airship appeared in the wake of the first. It too quickly disappeared, swallowed up by a bank of cloud and the darkened heavens beyond.

The men were strangely quiet. I think at that moment we realized how insignificant we were in this great war, the war that had clasped a continent in its fury – the entire world really.

Stiles seemed immune to such sentiments. Of course he had a larger-than-life Sir Sam Hughes watching over him.

'Alright, enough gawking, fellows,' said Stiles. 'Put your backs into it.'

I did, but I couldn't help thinking of what Sergeant-Major Atkins had asked me those many months before on Salisbury Plain – 'What are you doing in the army?' At the time I'd struggled for an answer. I still didn't have one. For a time I thought I did. When you're responsible for others it's remarkable how life acquires a sense of purpose. I wasn't responsible for much of anything anymore. And as to a sense of purpose, well… However I'd signed the same papers everyone in the battalion had, and the only way I would be going home was if the war ended, or the war ended me. Damn, I thought.

And that led to my next thought. When our shift was done I hurried to the dug-out: not to sleep, but in search of Dundas and Riley. I changed my socks first.

Riley's eyes popped when I lit the cellar candle. 'Holy shit,' he murmured. 'When, exactly, were you two planning on sharing the riches?'

That I'd asked Dundas was no particular surprise. Riley was an afterthought. He and I weren't pals, but he was a friendly fellow and one of the dwindling number of *originals* from the first contingent. That made for a bond only those in the army would understand.

'There wouldn't have been any riches if we'd said something earlier,' I replied. 'You know what they're like. The boys would have drunk this in an hour. Worse, some pencil-neck like Drinkwater would have heard about it and confiscated it all.'

Stooped low, I shuffled over to the metal rack on the far wall and randomly plucked out two bottles, one with each hand. They were coated in a thick film of dust and spider webs, so I rubbed the label of first one, then the other, with my tunic sleeve. 'What'll it be? They don't look like much, I must admit. But I have here…' I held the bottle up close in order that I might read the lettering. Behind me the candle flickered dimly. 'A Chambertin Grand Cru, it says.' I looked at the other one. 'And in this hand I have a Saint-Emilion. Hey, it's from 1900. That's 15 years old, chaps.'

'Sounds pretty old to me,' said Riley. 'It's probably vinegar by now.'

'NO,' said Dundas. 'The very best wines are old. Trust me, some of my clients swore by the old wines.'

'So be it,' I said. 'The Saint-Emilion it is. I'll bring the other along just in case it's botch.'

It took a while before Riley, with the help of a penknife, had carved out enough of the cork that he could push the remaining bit down into the bottle. It wasn't ideal, but the cork would be a lot easier on the teeth than the hardtack the army served up. Probably tastier too.

'Roy. To you the honours,' I said. 'After all, you almost died securing this cache.'

Dundas sighed, but accepted the bottle and took a long pull. He didn't say anything for the longest while. Finally, impatient, Riley grabbed the bottle from him and drank himself. 'Oh, my,' he said.

'Give it here,' I commanded and raised it to my lips.

It was velvety soft and, oh, so smooth. But it was the explosion of flavours that left me speechless, one as bold as the next, all mingling in the mouth in perfect harmony and echoing on long after the mouthful of liquid was gone.

'Wow,' I breathed.

We drank that first bottle quite quickly. The second was, if anything, even tastier than the first. Neither bore more than a passing resemblance to any wine I'd ever drunk.

At a lull in the conversation, Dundas asked, 'So, what's the occasion?'

'Who says there's an occasion?'

Riley cleared his throat. 'Only that you roused us out of our sleep in the middle of the night to creep back to this cave in the ground and drink the two best bottles of wine I've ever had. That's all.'

'I don't know. Life felt very fleeting for a moment. Each of us may not be around next week and it would have been a shame to waste this. Seize the moment, I figured.'

'And a moment it is,' said Dundas, glancing first at his watch and then at the rack with wine. 'You both realize we're supposed to be back digging in less than two hours?'

'Ah,' I said, 'it's not like you need a clear head to wield a shovel.'

We settled on one more bottle, and well before it was time to report, doused the candle and crept back to our dug-outs, taking care to skirt the sentry at the crossroads near Gooseberry Farm.

For the first time in quite some time I felt rather good.

Before we parted ways, Dundas grabbed my arm. 'It may not feel that way without the extra stripe, but a lot of us still depend on you, Mac,' he said. 'You're looking for some meaning in all this, only there isn't any. There's just you and me, and Riley, and all the others. And none of us is going to get through this war without the other. Besides, you're still a corporal, and all the new lads will be needing you.'

Without my having said a word, Dundas had put his finger on exactly what was bothering me. His words made sense; I did still have responsibilities. And I *was* still a corporal, even if shortly thereafter that too appeared to be in doubt.

'You're drunk,' said Stiles. He stuck his head in my face and sniffed again.

'As a skunk. What of it?' I didn't mean to sound belligerent; it just came out that way.

His voice deepened. 'Where did you find the booze?'

'Oh, I got it off a German a while back,' I said smoothly. Stiles could have looked deep into my eyes to see the truth of this, but rolling as they were, anything as profound as truth or falsehood was missing in action. I suspect he didn't really care. He *would* have cared if I'd told him the truth – Stiles was fond of a drink himself. He was, however, savouring the moment, well aware he'd roped me up like a newborn calf on its back with all four legs trussed together in the air.

'Funny how the tables can turn, don't you think?'

I gritted my teeth but said nothing.

'Looks like I've got two options here, MacPhail.'

'Yes, Sergeant,' I said. I didn't even express surprise that there were two options, nor enquire what they were. My head was dulled by drink and a stoic inertia had set in. I awaited my fate with an equanimity that most would have called placidness. To anybody who knew me, such behaviour would have shocked them.

'I *could* put you up on report. For which you might possibly get court-martialled.' He shook his head. 'Nah, it's more likely you'd lose your next leave and get some extra work duties. There's a very good chance, however, they might strip you of those remaining stripes. Drinkwater would be all for it I'm sure. "Teach the man a lesson," and all that. Private to sergeant and back again. The full roundtrip in a matter of months. You'd be a minor celebrity, MacPhail.'

Stiles took off his cap and began feeling around the inside rim. I'm not sure what he was looking for. Wisdom perhaps. 'On the other hand… we could keep this between us,' he said.

At this I recoiled, certain he was cruelly taunting me. But his face was serious. 'You're a proper pain in the ass, MacPhail, but the men seem to listen to you. Now that I'm sergeant I was hoping life would be a little more…' He paused, searching for the proper word. It appeared to evade him. 'Let me put it like this. Watching you clods dig ditches in the middle of the night while Fritzie sends over Weary Willies was not what I had in mind.'

'Ah!' I said. 'Now I understand. You want me to do all your dirty work while you get drunk, or sleep, or both.'

Stiles smiled. 'I knew you'd understand. Two months. Then you're off the hook.'

'One,' I replied. 'I'll do it for one month.'

He thought about this. 'Alright. Until the end of September. That's a month and a few days. But if someone gets wind of this, I'm coming looking for you. Not a word, MacPhail. Not a word to anyone.'

We shook on it and I grinned, stupidly.

For some inexplicable reason the prospect of doing what I'd been doing only weeks earlier, albeit as Stiles's press-ganged replacement, pleased me immensely at that particular moment. How I could have forgotten I was on Plugstreet, and all that implied, is beyond me.

CHAPTER 23

13th of September, 1915
La Petite Douve, Belgium

The wild wheat rustled softly in the breeze. Behind us the burble of the tiny Steenebeek was receding, replaced by that of the slightly larger Douve River ahead, the river cutting from east to west across the battlefield, wholly indifferent to the crude lines in the dirt man had burrowed. At the going down of the sun the air had become heavier as the night mists began to form. A scent of wet grasslands hung in my nostrils. With the ugliness of war temporarily cloaked by darkness, it was possible to think we were somewhere entirely more pleasant. We weren't of course. We were heading southeast across No-Man's-Land, in the direction of La Petite Douve.

It was almost four hundred yards away, a small salient in the enemy lines; the shape of the salient bearing a striking resemblance to one of the ancient flat-faced stone heads on Easter Island – the one with the forehead and nose merged into one and where the chin resembled a block of granite. At La Petite Douve the Germans had built their defences around the remains of a former farmhouse and its three out-buildings. It was long since fortified in appropriately Teutonic fashion. Word had it they were busy with more improvements.

We walked in extended file, a half dozen of us, cautiously but with purpose, our bayonets fixed. I was in the lead. Our orders were vague as to detail, yet the objective couldn't have been clearer.

With the minister off tormenting the mandarins at Whitehall, or his travel companions somewhere in the mid North Atlantic, there'd been no kinks in the chain of command; the colonel simply instructed the company commander, the company commander instructed Lieutenant Drinkwater, Drinkwater instructed Sergeant Stiles, and Stiles dumped it unceremoniously in my lap – as we'd agreed. We were to undertake a night patrol of No-Man's-Land… but with a twist.

Soon after I arrived at the front, I discovered that No-Man's-Land was a rather amorphous concept, all but unrecognizable from the crude characterization served up in the daily newspapers. The only truly unambiguous aspect about No-Man's-Land was that it was a border of sorts, delineating our ground to the west, and the enemy's to the east. In spots, such as at the Birdcage, or even at the furthest extremity of Vancouver Avenue, both sides were separated by a strip of ground so perilously narrow that in the still hours of the night, when sounds tend to carry far, you could hear them talking. For the most part, however, it wasn't like that. Whether through common consent, the demands of topography, or simply a twist of fate, more often than not hundreds of yards separated us. Sometimes even thousands. Then, No-Man's-Land became a land of its own. This past month we'd been doing our level best to claim it.

During the first week of September it poured almost daily, for wearisome hours on end. For all our back-breaking work in the previous two months the trenches became a treacherous, wet morass, and the rain effectively put an end to the working parties. However in the week that followed the sun re-emerged, and with it every man who could be spared picked up where we'd left off. Naturally the Germans – always keen students of our comings and goings – noticed this. The night before, they'd unleashed a tempest of rifle and machine-gun fire on the working parties. Three men were wounded and one was killed. I don't think much work was done. By dawn the talk was of retaliation.

Which in theory I agreed with. The means were another matter. Particularly as they boiled down to me and six others. The lieutenant and the sergeant were keeping a vigilant eye on the dug-outs.

After walking for several minutes I heard something and held up a hand to signal a halt. Allowing myself an extra step or two in order that there be no noisy collisions in the dark, I halted and went into a crouch. I waved for the man behind to come up. It was Bill Partridge. Partridge, for all his curiosity and maybe because of it, was turning into a good soldier and that was the reason I'd selected him. I hadn't the heart to ask Dundas, not after his close shave at the wine cellar – he still ragged me about it.

'Listen,' I said. 'Do you hear that?' I held my finger to my ear.

There were the noises of digging – unmistakeable after endless weeks doing it ourselves – wood being moved about, and what sounded like the abrasive scratching of metal. Then a harder tapping began as might come from a hammer, but muffled. Every so often there was a soft blow. There were also voices, low and inaudible, the breeze blowing us scattered fragments. There was something about their tone that made my neck hair stand on end. It certainly wasn't English, nor was it French, so that left only one possibility.

Partridge nodded. He'd heard what I'd heard. By this time, peering through the grass, we could see them. The figures were vague and indistinct, but so numerous that I knew immediately this was no small patrol. I gulped.

'It's a working party,' I whispered. 'They're wiring a new line of posts. Get the others.'

When they were assembled, squatted on their haunches in a semi-circle, I began. 'Alright boys, this is what we're going to do…'

One of the principle disadvantages of being in a salient was that you could be shot at from more than one direction. Enfilade fire was what the army called it. Although usually from no more than three directions at once, assuming your foe hadn't slipped around behind; in that case you were just fucked. That wasn't an army term, it's what the boys called it.

But in the chaos of war, doubt is what tore at you. You could never know with full certainty where the enemy was. And that was exactly what I was counting upon. Up against a working party of a hundred plus men, seven rifles and a handful of bombs only go so far.

'I'll give the mark by throwing a bomb,' I said. 'That'll be your signal to fire as rapidly as you can at anything you can hit. A clip or two, no more, then get your heads down. Wait thirty seconds or so, then fire another clip or two at their line behind. Remember we only want to get their attention. You're not likely to hit anything that far back. But they need to think we're with a lot more than we really are. Now spread out and make sure you keep an eye on your mates to each side. I plan on coming back with all six of you. Questions?'

They shook their heads. I looked at each in turn and nodded. I wondered if their hearts were beating at the same frenzied tempo as mine.

'Okay, get going. I'll give you three minutes.'

Partridge and two others went right, the other three fanned out to the left. As a young man, games of chance were never really my cup of tea, and they still weren't. But when I had likened my plan to bluff poker, the men nodded approvingly – bluffing was something they understood very well – even if tonight's stakes were considerably higher than a few days' pay.

After squirming into a decent position where I might have some hope of lobbing a G.S. no. 1 into the Germans' midst, I laid out both of the grenades I was carrying. My rifle I put on the ground to one side within easy reach and glanced to my flanks. The men were searching out suitable firing points, much as I had. Then I looked towards the enemy. They were beavering away on the wire entanglements intended to keep us from their oddly-shaped salient.

Right around the time I figured three minutes had passed, or a reasonable approximation thereof which allowed everyone time to get into position, I picked up the long handle of the grenade. The G.S. no. 1 percussion grenade could be a menace in a trench. Its handle was so long that in the backswing the damn thing risked hitting the trench wall and setting off the contact charge. In No-Man's-Land there was no risk of that.

I took a last glance at it, then drew it back over my head and hurled it forward. Then I waited – an art I've never entirely mastered. I tend to think of waiting as a synonym for wasting one's time. After thirty seconds in which absolutely nothing happened, the second drawback of the G.S. no. 1 became apparent.

One of the bombers had warned me about this. Unless the grenade landed on its head, he said, no contact was made and then it was a bit like hurling sticks. That was the reason why there was a cloth streamer attached to the handle; it was meant to ensure that the projectile flew straight and landed as it was designed to. In my haste I think I'd forgotten to untangle it.

I reached for the other bomb, anxious to avoid a repeat, but conscious the men were waiting. Timing was everything and we needed to hit as many of the working party as we could before they went to ground. I grasped the grenade low on the handle for better leverage, the streamer hanging down as it was supposed to. I chucked it as hard as I could.

This time there was a flash and a loud bang. Startled voices shouted out. Then the rifle fire began, a crackling that followed so closely upon itself that it could have been a machine gun. The men were doing exactly as I'd told them.

Spread out in a fan with 30 feet between each of us, it must have been a terrifying shock to the Fritzs to hear this sudden fire from all around. They'd been holding shovels and manhandling huge coils of barbed wire into place. But I was too busy working the bolt of the rifle to think about that.

I aimed at the dark figures now scurrying wildly in every direction. There was no time for fine marksmanship so I fired as rapidly as I could, reloaded, and fired again. When the magazine was empty I pulled back the bolt and rammed in a new stripper clip. And began firing again.

When the last round was gone, I paused. There was a final volley around me, and silence returned. Only it wasn't entirely silent. There was gunfire from the direction of the Germans. They were fighting back. Not that they had any idea against whom, but shooting probably seemed a better idea than standing around waiting to be hit.

I kept my head well down and thrust another clip into the rifle. Then I took careful aim at what I hoped was the parapet of the German line, some fifty yards behind the working party. It was barely visible, set behind a row of trees, a line close to the ground even darker than the sky above. When I heard shots to either side I began shooting as well. This time I fired more deliberately. The Germans in the field would be frantically looking for us. But I was hoping their sentries behind would mistake this as a full-fledged assault.

One of their machine guns opened up. While they surely had

something similar to our Northover attachment to suppress flashes, I could still make out the pinpricks of orange sparking away. German voices raised in anger shouted out from near the wire. They were being raked by their own guns.

There were red flares going up and green ones. In between, the white ones had the upper hand. How the Germans were to make heads or tails of it all was beyond me. Their front line at La Petite Douve had erupted into wild confusion.

It was time to leave.

We stole away, keeping low in the grass. Bullets whinged through it.

It was only after we reached our own lines that the gunfire petered out.

Partridge was grinning exuberantly. We'd made it back without a scratch. 'That'll teach them to be shooting up our working parties,' he said.

The Germans must indeed have drawn a lesson of sorts from it. The next night our working parties toiled in peace, or as close to it as you're liable to see in the Ypres Salient.

For his "meritorious" actions Sergeant Stiles was the man of the hour. Lieutenant-Colonel Rattray even summoned him to personally extend his congratulations. The officers were beaming and Lieutenant Drinkwater, whose idea it naturally was, was in fine fettle when I passed him the next day. He even smiled at me when I saluted.

Dundas was perplexed. 'But doesn't it bother you that you took all the chances and Stiles is reaping all the credit?'

I smiled. 'No, not really. The men know what happened and that's more important. I may not have that third stripe anymore, but they'll sure listen to me in future when I tell them to do something. For that matter, Sam Stiles knows what happened, too. As of now our platoon sergeant owes me and he won't forget it. At the very least he won't be breathing down my neck.'

Dundas shook his head. 'Sometimes I really don't understand you, Mac.'

However, it was even simpler than what I'd told Dundas. I felt good about myself again. I'd never commanded a squad of men on my own, not like that. On the parade ground or in the trenches it was always different, there was never much cause or leeway to do things the way you thought they should. But out in No-Man's-Land I'd been on my own, and not only had I kept my fears in check, we'd doled out a black eye to Fritz and made it back to tell the story. There's nothing quite like a boost to one's self-esteem to improve your morale. Temporarily, if nothing else.

CHAPTER 24

25th of September, 1915
Ploegsteert trenches, Belgium

At 4.45 a.m., long before the larks' warbling song that would fore-shadow dawn, the guns began to roar. They were firing in concert and it sounded to me like every gun in the division had taken up the chant, so terrific was the racket. The flash of one explosion had barely dimmed before the next came. Out in No-Man's-Land, the ground shuddered and smoke spiralled in wreaths around the German wire and their front line. In our trenches, ladders had been placed at intervals, the tops of which would be visible at dawn to the sharp eye. When the time came the infantry would climb those ladders to the parapet and sweep forward. The attack on Messines Ridge would not be long in coming.

Or so we wanted them to believe.

Details were understandably scarce – much of what I'd heard was from an artilleryman whose brigade had been ordered south in haste, to help the Imperials in the Artois where General Joffre was unleashing his great offensive. The attack would come nowhere near Messines Ridge. The Germans didn't know that and our little show was designed to convince them it would.

Ever since the 2nd Division had landed from England, thereby creating the spanking new Canadian Corps, the Germans had been on edge. They were Bavarians and Saxons mainly; a chesty lot. 'How is Calgary?', and 'Say hello to your new friends for us', they bellowed across No-Man's-Land, hoping in our responses for a clue to the whereabouts of our sister division. I don't think they learned much, aside from a few choice profanities. The German patrols were also out in force. Several were intercepted and the would-be captors captured. Under interrogation they confirmed that their superiors were keenly interested in our new division. When the time came, and the 2nd Division encamped to our left, the Germans knew almost instantly – moving a new division into the line is a cumbersome affair. And their suspicions about an attack grew. All we had do was lend a helping hand.

Approximately an hour after the bombardment began I found myself in the front line. I was virtually opposite the concrete fortress of La Petite Douve farm and I was attempting to light a sack on the parapet packed with wet straw. My efforts were doing little to reinforce my reputation as an all-round outdoorsman. Supposedly the thing was doused in oil – it was, I could smell it. But it was having none of me. At the sound of singing I threw the embers of yet another match to the ground and turned.

A soldier approached, belting out the trench version of "I wonder how the old folks are at home", followed by three other men. The exact same soldier passed me again, going in the opposite direction several minutes later, just as I'd thrown away my last match in total disgust. He was still singing. The same song. The men behind all carried a bayoneted rifle, one in each hand, held not like a rifle but rather as a placard on a stick. They raised the stocks up and down in tune with the song, the bayonets poking up and down above the parapet as they did so. The men trailing in his wake joined in occasionally to sing with the band leader at the lewder parts. The troops were in fine form as they assembled.

There were a few exceptions.

I muttered a curse under my breath.

'Need some help?'

'Yeah, actually I do,' I began to say. 'Must be all the rain we've had…' My words trailed off when I saw who it was. 'Oh. Hello, Harry.'

Harry didn't respond. He simply pulled out a box of matches, flicked one into life and tossed it nonchalantly onto the sack.

WHOOSH.

The thing went up in a ball of flame. I jumped back and wiped at my face. I'm not sure which was more flambéed, my dignity or my eyebrows.

'Thanks,' I said. 'I think.'

'Don't mention it,' said Harry. To his credit, and my surprise, he didn't laugh but moved immediately on to the next sack. I left him to it. While the economist David Ricardo might have described this as an excellent example of comparative advantage, I felt it was simply common sense. After all, Harry Hobson had to be good at something; it just happened his skill lay in lighting bonfires – there being no particular need for diamond heists at the moment.

All along the trench, white smoke was billowing forth and wafting slowly across the fields to the enemy lines. The sun wouldn't be up for another hour but the sky had softened to a cold steel grey.

When the smoke began, mixed with a little gas for good measure, so too did the German artillery. Then came the trademark rattling whir, akin to a trolley rolling overhead in a foundry, as the shells from a whole battery of 5.9s spiralled towards us. By that time, all except the sentries were rushing for the deep, narrow safety trenches we'd spent half the summer digging for precisely such moments.

In marked contrast to the prevailing current in our trenches with men rushing to the rear, the Fritzs were running forward in theirs. Having witnessed a regular fireworks display of distress signals from their comrades they could be forgiven for expecting waves of attackers to shortly appear. We disappointed on that measure, but as they arrived in the front line our machine gunners and artillerymen sent their regards.

At dawn the performance went on. I stood in the fire-trench, along with a few others and blew on a whistle until I was red in the face. Not long after, almost in the German wire, the first line of the battalion appeared. They went down in the face of a withering fire. Only to rise again. And again.

'You'd think they'd have caught on by now,' I said. The man next to me was pulling at a long length of rope for what must have been the fifth time. Attached to it was a straw-filled, vaguely man-shaped and very gallant khaki-clad mat. 'On the other hand, they are Saxons.'

We had a good laugh that night, the first in some time. Despite the shelling hardly a man was hurt and all agreed that winding up the Germans was wonderful sport. Most of the battalion had observed it only from the tents near the windmill on account of having been relieved. It was not often anyone regretted being relieved.

The next day turned out to be a Sunday. I knew this because we had church parade, and I hadn't yet caught the chaplains out on getting the day wrong.

'Do you hear that?' asked Dundas. In the distance, the crackling and rumbling that began early this morning and which had given the rousing hymns a slightly menacing undertone was growing ever louder. 'I wonder how far away it is.'

'I think it's at Loos. That's twenty miles, give or take. They say it's the biggest British attack of the war.'

'Really? The biggest? Each one seems to surpass the one before. But do you ever notice, Mac, despite that, the front never seems to change much?' Dundas began scratching furiously at his arm. 'Fritz is as tenacious as the bloody lice,' he said. 'Well, let's hope the Imperials are taking it to them.'

I nodded and started to scratch myself as well. I agreed with him, although my own thoughts were closer to home; I was relieved we hadn't been asked to join in. Ploegsteert was bad enough without the nightmare of having to go over the top.

Ultimately our dramatic deception did little to change the course of events. It did however make a lasting impression on some, me in particular. We rattled the Germans so badly they hadn't dared to move a man, to reinforce elsewhere. At the cost of a few shells and some clever tricks we'd poked Fritz between the eyes in a way he wouldn't soon forget. If only the offensive had gone as well.

After the third day the French called off the attack in the Champagne. In the Artois between La Bassée Canal and Arras the British and French advances quickly lost their initial momentum. Losses were staggering, the ground won negligible, and the French were rebuffed once more at Vimy Ridge – the offensive another disappointment in a year that had seen little else.

While it was to be several weeks before we learned those details and the final outcome, at the time I was thinking more about my servitude under Sergeant Stiles, pleased at the prospect of it coming to an end in a few days. Of nocturnal working parties I'd had my fill, especially now that the nights were turning cold and rainy. There was nothing quite as miserable as trudging back, tired and soaked to the skin, only to discover the dug-out was under a foot of water.

Stiles must have had his eye on the calendar as well.

'Where are you off to, Mac?' Riley stood on sentry duty. I was just coming out of Ashway Trail and heading down trench 134. In the twilight I hadn't noticed him up on the fire-step. He probably recognized me from the fumes coming out my ears.

'Bloody Stiles has got me on a listening post tonight,' I replied, 'And not any old listening post, the one by the farm. The one so close you can smell what they're cooking for breakfast and hear it cooking. Probably hear them chewing as well.'

'Tough luck,' he said. 'Keep your head down. You'll be okay. I was there the week before last. But I thought you and Stiles had patched things up?'

'We had,' I said. 'Or so I thought. According to Stiles – although he's quite capable of having invented it for my benefit – headquarters is nervous the Germans will retaliate for the other day. They wanted a "reliable" man out on the listening post he told me. So I said to him: 'Surely they meant you, Sergeant?' He found that quite hilarious. First we stir up the wasp's nest, then I get to sit in it for a night.'

'I'm not sure "reliable" is the word I would have used to describe you...' Riley said slowly.

'Don't tell me,' I snapped. 'Tell Stiles.' Riley was grinning from ear to ear.

We reached the listening post by first picking our way down one of the narrow saps the engineers had built out into No-Man's-Land. Then under cover of the grass and a few trees we made our way further. The listening post, such as it was, was a deep hole in the ground surrounded by a tangle of felled trees, ten yards from the German wire. For some reason the Germans hadn't cleared it away as they ought to have done – we may have had a hand in that.

Once in the hole, Mulligan, the man I was with, began unfolding a rubberized ground sheet which he then proceeded to drape over us covering everything below the shoulders and most of the hole. Two bugs in a bed. It was chilly at night in late September and we were dressed accordingly. A groundsheet seemed a trifle excessive. I changed my mind when the downpour began.

The idea of the listening post was that we would notice anything the Germans were up to, including spotting their patrols, and give warning. For this purpose a wire led back to the sap and we were to yank it if we spotted anything out of the ordinary: one pull for a patrol, and two to stand-to.

The first hour the only thing I heard was the wind screaming. It wailed up in short powerful gusts while the rain drove down with an unrelenting fury, spattering loudly on the ground sheet and off the tree trunks around us. There wasn't much to hear as a result. Nor could I see. They could have slipped the entire 2nd Bavarian Corps past me and I don't think I'd have noticed. The rain was a factor, but so too was the groundsheet which by now I had pulled over my head.

Eventually the rain eased off and we poked our heads out. Everything was dripping. The German lines were deathly still. They'd come to the same conclusion I had; this was no weather to do anything apart from keeping your head dry. In that I'd more or less succeeded even if the same couldn't be said for other parts of me.

'We have to move,' I whispered to Mulligan. 'I've got water up to my waist.' It was no exaggeration.

Mulligan nodded vigorously. His idea of a groundsheet had been a fine one but it didn't stop the bathtub filling up underneath. We crawled out and sheltered behind a fallen tree.

Parking oneself under the enemy's nose for the best part of a night might sound terribly exciting to the uninitiated. Soon enough though it becomes a dreary cold monotony, a misery worsened by the fact that my boots were soaked through and through. I kept wiggling my toes to warm them.

Around us nothing was moving. Other than coils of wire and fence posts and the line of the German parapet behind, there was nothing to see and nothing to hear besides branches creaking and Mulligan gently coughing into the ball of his fist. I became very drowsy. My eyelids drooped. Sleep beckoned.

It landed full on my head.

Startled, I jumped. Certain my end had come. A rat the size of my foot sprang adeptly down onto the log before me and glared tauntingly.

'Jesus,' I exclaimed in alarm, and thrashed about with my arms which became entangled in the surrounding branches. Loud cracking noises could be heard.

Mulligan froze. Then the realization of what I'd done hit me in the gut.

We stared at each other, mouths half open, listening intently. The thumping of my heart beat loudly.

There was a rifle shot, but it was far off. The coils of barbed wire creaked gently as a strong gust caught them. From the direction of La Petite Douve an owl hooted. The minutes ticked by. It remained quiet. No flares shot into the sky, nor was there a precautionary burst from a machine gun.

'Phew,' whispered Mulligan, after several minutes.

My heartbeat slowed but for the remainder of our detail I had no difficulty remaining awake.

Headquarters' fears had been for nought. The only thing I heard of any importance that entire night was what I heard early the next day when we returned.

Dundas was the one who told me.

'Riley got it,' he said. His face was drawn, his voice resigned.

I took a deep breath and just sighed. Here I thought I'd been taking all the risks. That was the strange thing about war, boredom crept up with the passage of time, one day fading inexorably into the next until they all became a blur, impossible to separate the one from the other. Then in the flash of a rifle shot, or the thud of a gun, everything changed; your life lived and relived in the seconds that followed. Otherwise you were dead, and then nothing at all mattered anymore.

'What happened?' I asked.

Dundas shrugged. 'Chance bullet hit him in the head. He wasn't even on the fire-step, he was standing right about where you are now. Didn't know what hit him. The man he was talking to said he was dead before he hit the ground.'

I gritted my teeth. 'What a shame. What a damn shame. I liked Riley.'

'Yeah. We all did.'

'That's one less of us old-timers, Roy.'

At this he raised his head and his eyes found mine. 'No profit in thinking like that, Mac. If you have to go, it's better to go like Riley did.'

'Yeah, I suppose so.'

That evening we buried him in Ploegsteert Wood. Most of the old battalion turned up. The war diary for that day recorded that casualties were light.

It sure didn't feel that way.

CHAPTER 25

11ᵗʰ of November, 1915
Ploegsteert trenches, Belgium

We were into our fifth month in the Plugstreet trenches. Worst of all it was November. November had never made much of an impression on me in the past. It is what I would call a transitory month, in between October when the last of autumn's colours are being swept away ahead of winter and December, when winter is clutching the world in its icy grasp but where the holidays beckon cheerfully, the festive mood is growing, and the city is garlanded in lights. This was my first November in Belgium. A week and a half in it was not only the Germans I had to contend with, it was the mud, the cold, the rats and the rain – in no particular order. A new trench tour had begun.

'MacPhail, you're in charge of the pumps in 134. And while you're at it, see if you can find some struts for the dug-out there. It's in danger of caving in.'

'Yes, sir.'

On an afterthought I said: 'Sir? I don't suppose there are any of those big rubber waders left?'

Drinkwater shook his head. 'Sorry, B Company got the last of them. But before you go, don't forget that the platoon from the RCR is arriving this afternoon. I'm sending some of their men to you. They're regular army so do try and make a good impression, MacPhail.'

'Yes, sir.'

'I don't know what Drinkwater is thinking. I'm up to my shins in water and he wants me to instruct some greenhorns from the Royal Canadian Regiment on war in the trenches. Apparently I'm also to leave a "good impression", whatever the hell that means. Stiles sure picked a swell moment to go sick.'

The sky was grey and gloomy, with low hanging clouds that promised an imminent resumption of rain. The weather had steadily worsened all through October. By November there was but one colour in the sky and that was some shade of grey. Most of the time I wasn't looking at the sky, concentrating instead on keeping my feet on the wooden trench mats and my face out of the rain and the cold gusts of wind. Dundas and I were standing in a puddle of thick mud, the driest spot I could find.

'I really think Stiles *is* sick,' said Dundas.

'I know. He is,' I said grudgingly. Grudgingly, because if there was such a thing as an easy path in life chances were high you'd encounter Sam Stiles strolling along it. Thanks to his father's connections (Dundas unhelpfully laid the blame on my "big mouth") he was wearing my lost chevron. It still rankled even if I pretended otherwise. While I was out attending to platoon business in the invigorating night air of the Belgian countryside – usually on Stiles's behalf – Stiles stayed cooped up in a dank dug-out. Little wonder he was sick. We were never going to be best of friends, but Sam Stiles was not the cold-hearted son of a two-bit merchant that I first took him to be. Lazy, but not cold-hearted, and definitely not dumb. None of which altered the fact that no. 2 Advanced Hospital at Bailleul was a more pleasant locale to while away the dreary November days than trench 134.

I had Partridge and another fellow working the sump pump. For all the water they were pumping out it was not dissimilar to the bathtub with the tap still running. Trench 134 looked like the Rideau Canal. Even standing on the planks of the trench mat I couldn't see the toes of my boots for the water. It wasn't just Mother Nature that had it in for us, it was the topography, too. We were dug in at the low point of the Messines Ridge. I don't know how this came to be – the enemy being a cunning sort, I had my suspicions – but the consequence was that the German positions were all on higher ground. They took obvious pleasure in draining their own sodden trenches into No-Man's-Land, which then drained into ours, the sand in the sacks liquefying and oozing through the pores of the canvas. Finally, when there was little left, they simply washed away.

'There goes the parapet,' sighed Partridge.

The sandbags opposite seemed to dissolve. First one and then the others gave way. There was a small landslide and a three-foot wide, three sandbag-high breach appeared in the parapet. Water started trickling down the trench wall. This was no idle matter; the entire section was in danger of collapsing. If it did there'd be no way to hold the trench. We would be completely exposed.

'Get at it,' I shouted. 'Dundas, you and I are taking the pump.'

Frantically we began pumping. The others were filling sandbags with abandon. It was a temporary measure at best, for they were shovelling in much the same gluey muck that had escaped from the bags in the first place. There was more water in the shovels than dirt, but there was not a lot else at hand. Eventually I sent a couple of men to the rear in search of some drier spots to dig.

By noon we'd saved what there was to save. The section was still a mess, though the parapet was a parapet again, and the water was only a foot deep. The dug-out was temporarily beyond rescue.

The men, exhausted, had barely begun boiling some water for tea when a section of a dozen RCRs appeared in our midst. They were under the command of a huge bearded sergeant.

'Welcome to Bermuda in Belgium,' I greeted them, to a smattering of chuckles. The RCR had spent their war on garrison duty in Bermuda. It was an onerous task but I suppose someone had to do it.

'Sergeant, I'm Corporal MacPhail,' I said, introducing myself. 'I'm afraid our beaches have less sand than you may be used to. But on the other hand there's no shortage of water.'

A deep bellowing laugh erupted. Which was a pleasant change from the response my little jokes typically produce; sergeants tending to be the most fickle of crowds. Not only did this one possess a curly brown beard, he sported a thick, equally-brown moustache. Between the two of them they formed a perfect brown Cannae, completely encircling his mouth, a trick the German High Command hadn't quite pulled off in their attack on France last fall. While I've often dismissed facial hair as wallpaper – an attempt to mask whatever's underneath – I found that it suited him. At a couple of inches taller than me, and a whole lot broader, the sergeant was by far the most solid thing about trench 134.

'I'm DuBois,' he rumbled, 'Benoît DuBois.' It was not only his name that gave him away, it was also his accent, which was laid on thick in a deep baritone. He was French-Canadian. DuBois extended a hand many a Greek god would have been envious of and I shook it, doing my best not to wince as the vice closed. It was somewhat of a relief to know he was on our side.

'On a more serious note,' I added, 'there's no shortage of Fritzs here.' Then, raising my voice in order to address the others, I told them: 'Whatever you do, keep your heads down. The parapet is not nearly as solid as it looks.'

Thus began an afternoon seminar on the finer points of life and death on Plugstreet. And the importance of multiple pairs of dry socks. The RCR were as keen to learn as you'd expect, but I couldn't help noticing the furtive grins of Partridge and the rest of my band as they watched them fumbling the lighting of a fire and generally looking completely out of place. Regular soldiers or not, the RCR's tutelage in war was only beginning. I put them to work filling sandbags.

Another rat the size of a small cat scrambled past. One of the RCR went to kick at it, but missed. In the slippery mud he almost landed on his behind for his trouble. I glanced over at Sergeant DuBois and shrugged apologetically.

'The local wildlife. No wolves or bears round here but we have a lot of rats. Mice as well. You should instruct your boys to keep anything edible under close watch, Sergeant.'

DuBois nodded seriously. He had the look of a man who it was better not to cross when it came to his victuals. He turned up the collar on his great coat.

That's the thing about Novembers near Ypres, even when it's not raining the air has a cold clamminess to it that is positively marrow chilling. It was a very long way from Bermuda.

'What about fighting the 'un?' enquired DuBois, the H in Hun misfiring as it is wont to do with French speakers. Pronunciation aside, there was no doubt what he thought of our enemy. His eyes said it all.

'You'll soon find that every day in the line is a fight,' I said wearily.

I didn't mention Riley although I was thinking of him. 'Thankfully it's quiet at the moment, but that's no reason for you or your men to let your guard down. We've had enough battles this year to last a lifetime, Sergeant. But, don't worry, if you're here to fight Fritz, you've come to the right spot.'

That night Fritz was nowhere to be found. It poured. So his absence was not entirely surprising. The Douve River that cut through our lines at the southern end of trench 134 overflowed its banks and flooded the trench. We spent the night bailing furiously. DuBois and his section, far from being a nuisance, were a big help. I'm sure they had hoped for a more heroic introduction to the Western Front than wielding a bucket with icy water past the waist.

For all these tribulations the sergeant was as gregarious the next morning as he'd been the previous day. When the time came for the RCR to rotate out he said to me, 'à la *prochaine, mon ami,*' as if somehow he knew there would be a next time, and actually meant what he said about being my friend. He wished me good luck.

Four days later I found myself needing it.

'Thank you, Corporal MacPhail. Most interesting. Your information and observations are very informative.' Brigadier-General Louis Lipsett spoke with a calm firmness, wearing his new position as 2nd Brigade commander with the polished ease of a man born to it. Which was clearly not the case as Lipsett had assumed command only two months earlier, after General Currie was promoted Major-General and given the divisional reins. Since the arrival of the 2nd Division and the creation of the Canadian Corps, it had been a regular gold rush of promotions in the senior ranks. However Lipsett deserved his. At Ypres he'd handled his battalion with consummate skill.

Thoughtfully, Lipsett now tapped a single index finger on his lips. From everything I'd seen Lipsett was nothing if not thoughtful. There was no clue in his expression that prepared me for what came next.

Fixing his eyes on me he said, 'I think it might be useful if you were to accompany the raid tonight, Corporal. Your firsthand knowledge of the area and your experience would be helpful.' Then he turned to Lieutenant-Colonel Odlum. 'What do you think of the idea, Victor?'

The commander of the 7th Battalion nodded enthusiastically. 'I think that's an excellent idea, sir. I'll have my adjutant inform the corporal's battalion.'

This left me feeling like your average sow at a livestock auction. 'I'll get my things, sir,' I mumbled.

An hour before the thought of a mid-night excursion into the heart of the German lines hadn't crossed my mind. I'd been more concerned about the briefing I was to give, what with the news that not only a colonel but also a general would be attending.

In the past two months the details of the patrol I'd led at La Petite Douve had spread far and wide. Despite having received none of the credit, nor even officially having been there, the powers-that-be agreed that I was the ideal man to brief the 7th Battalion ahead of their forthcoming trench raid. Now, instead of a relaxing concert at the YMCA at Bulford Camp, I was to spend a night crawling through wire and mud, dodging young Fritzs with far fewer qualms than means of killing me.

If that wasn't depressing enough, I had the sneaking suspicion someone had dropped this petard on my lap knowing full well what they were getting me into, and themselves out of.

I pulled the black crepe mask down over my face. It was 2 a.m.

We set off.

There were thirty-five raiders all told, officers and soldiers combined, each except me from British Columbia. They'd ordered us to remove any identifying insignia and I'd done so, taking particular care with the brass 10th Battalion shoulder badges, the small prized ones that marked me out as one of the *originals*. I placed the badges, my identification disk and everything else in the Wolseley haversack that would remain behind at Irish Farm, along with the shreds of last week's unanswered letter from home that I discovered in a tunic pocket.

We crossed No-Man's-Land in two files, one for each attack party, moving slowly. Our pace was partly determined by the mud that stuck to our boots like glue, but mainly it was to avoid the risk that someone would get lost, mess up or slip, and alarm the enemy sentries. Via a different route I'd already guided a pair of sergeants and a lieutenant to the German wire a few hours earlier. There they had proceeded to cut paths through it, while the boys in the trenches fired off occasional volleys to mask the noise. We were heading to the identical stretch of ground, slightly below the bulge in the line around Petite Douve Farm and due west of the Messines-Armentières road, where my patrol had caught out the German working party back in September. At the time they'd been patching it up and I grinned at the thought of them having to do it again.

Raids were the newest thing. We undertook a few small ones over the course of the summer, although they weren't called raids then. This was the first time anyone had ever attempted it at night. Nor were we simply to cut out an isolated outpost in No-Man's-Land; the intention was to drop in on the enemy in the middle of his own trench system.

From the general on down the men didn't seem especially perturbed by any of this. The general was Irish and a veteran officer so he wouldn't let it show. For many of the men stalking Germans in No-Man's-Land, or even in his trenches, was a welcome respite from life in our own. It bore a curious resemblance to what they'd done in everyday life, trapping or hunting, scraping out a living in the vastness of the bush. As my provisions came exclusively from the grocery store, and the last hunting I'd done was for a gasket for my father's car, I was the odd man out in more ways than one.

The battalion had prepared well, I had to grant them that. Naturally the list of things that could go wrong was endless, but then that was true of sitting in a dug-out. Thankfully it was pitch black.

Overhead the moon was obscured, the view into No-Man's-Land impenetrable 20 feet away. Dense banks of cloud rolled over in an endless procession. Right when they seemed to clear, and a fickle ray of moonlight peered through, another thick cloud moved across.

We followed the south bank of the Douve eastwards, not so much a river as a modest stream. At some stage we would need to cross it. But luckily a clever soul in Colonel Odlum's staff had foreseen this and, roughly 30 yards from the enemy lines where the Douve narrowed, two bridging ladders were awaiting us. Gingerly I followed the others onto the planks. They were no more than two feet wide. Aware that a misstep would land me in five feet of cold water and bungle the raid before it even began, I ran it, not trusting myself to keep my balance otherwise.

On the far side we reached their wire soon after and passed through without difficulty. A few men carried Traversor mats in the event there was uncut wire. As I knew the ground I went with the two scouts close to the front of the group. I had an anxious moment when I heard something, but relaxed when I saw a lone disoriented bat flutter past, flying so low it almost brushed our heads.

Once past the wire the parapet of the German line loomed up almost immediately. I could make out the long row of shell-scarred willows behind which was the ditch, now a deep trench, and then the hard pavé of the road northeast to Messines. On the opposite side of the road was another smaller trench.

Captain Thomas, who was leading the party, turned to the three of us. 'Alright, this is it. Are you ready? Pass the signal.'

'I'm ready, sir,' I said grimly. The words were no sooner out of my mouth than it began to rain heavily.

Thomas gave me no time to consider if this was a portent and took off at a sprint, followed by a couple of bayonet men and a bomber. The scouts and I tore after him.

At the trench – there fortunately being no wire in front – the captain bounded over the parapet and jumped down. An unholy crashing noise came. When I reached the same spot seconds later, I saw the cause of it. The captain had landed dead in the middle of a sheet of corrugated iron, underneath which an unsuspecting sentry had been sheltering. The sentry was pinned under the sheet when I jumped down after the captain, winding him once more.

From all around came startled shouts. A rifle cracked. A loud whistle blew, its shrill note piercing the night. Then a bomb went off nearby. To the north a machine gun began stuttering up at La Petit Douve farm, whereupon almost immediately the dull thuds of our trench mortar battery could be heard. However long before their rounds arrived, the pulsing in my head drowned out everything as I rushed down the trench in pursuit of the captain.

To call it a melee would be to overstate it. From every nook and cranny emerged a Heinie, the first bayonetted before he could move a step, the second shot as he raised his rifle, and so on it went. Our rifles were equipped with a flash-light at the muzzle end, which lit up at the flick of a switch on the stock, and this proved an ingenious device. The bombers were wearing special aprons holding twenty bombs apiece, and they were throwing them with abandon. When I reached the entrance to a dug-out, I saw that one of the bombers was standing to one side, peering down.

'Wait,' he said curtly, holding up a hand. A second later there was a soft bang, no more than that, and acrid smoke began to billow up from below. I pointed my rifle down the hole and flipped the switch forward. The flash-light went on. At the bottom of the ladder, probably twenty feet down, dense black smoke curled round and through it I could see little. As I stared down, a shot sounded from below and I recoiled. The man beside me pushed me roughly aside with one arm. With the other he pulled out a bomb from his apron and held it in his hand for a second or two, before tossing it down the hole. It went off with a bang and he grinned at me.

Above us, violent flashes from our guns lit the low-lying clouds as the artillery started to bombard the support trenches. It was from there that the enemy would send his reinforcements. Every few seconds another red flare soared into the sky from trenches nearby, the glow colouring the scene a peculiar crimson. I wondered what their commanders made of these desperate calls for help.

It was then I spotted the officer lying prone on the parapet. The trench was full of our men rushing in all directions, bombs were exploding and the sound of rifle fire was pervasive. Nowhere was there a German to be seen. Except this one officer who I now noticed had a telephone hand piece clamped to his ear. He was calmly relaying the details of our raid to his headquarters as they happened. I raised my rifle. As his head filled the sight – he wasn't twenty feet away – he spotted me. I could have fired but I didn't. Instead I let the rifle sink a notch and saw down the barrel that he was staring at me – not an uncommon reaction when someone has a loaded rifle pointed at your face. It had taken a very cool head to do what he did. In the meantime, the reality had evidently dawned on him that his war had come an end. Slowly he raised his arms into the air, the telephone still in one hand.

When I reached him I motioned that he should climb down into the trench. He did and handed me the telephone.

I looked at it, puzzled, then put it to my ear. Hearing nothing I pushed up the large toggle on the right side. 'Hello?' I said tentatively.

'*Ja. Ebeler. Was ist los?*' demanded a loud self-assured voice. This was followed by more questions I didn't understand.

'So sorry, Ebeler's somewhat indisposed at the moment. Please call back later,' I said and dropped the hand piece to one side.

Precisely twenty minutes from the moment the raid began, it ended. Two long blasts on a whistle followed by three short ones signalled it was over. We escorted the twelve German prisoners with their new-fangled gas masks across No-Man's-Land to the advanced listening post, where a support party took over and led them and the officer I'd captured back to our lines. Behind us in the trench we left a proper chaos; every dug-out was bombed and I counted some thirty of the enemy lying on their backs in the mud. It was a night Fritz would remember.

Around dawn I finally made it to Bulford Camp. It had been a long walk and a long night. There I came across the very person I was least anxious to see. He smirked when he saw me. 'Have fun did we?'

Suddenly it hit me like a bowling ball in the gut. 'Harry you...'

Partly by upbringing and partly by temperament I'm seldom profane – certainly not by the colourful standards of the trenches – but I gave it to Harry Hobson with both barrels firing. Then I threw him an extra verbal bomb or two, for good measure. A couple of company men walking past, paused and stared, their mouths agog at the early morning fireworks between superiors.

'You arranged that, didn't you, Harry?' I demanded to know.

Hobson looked bashful, or as closely approximating bashful as a cocky loudmouth can ever look. 'Honestly, I hardly said a word,' he replied. 'Stiles is sick, so Drinkwater asked me who knew the most about La Petite Douve in the company. I said you. Don't look at me like that. You know it's true. And even Drinkwater's finally figured it out that it was you and not Stiles that led that patrol. So I guess he passed your name on to the captain. And so on, and so forth. You know how it is.'

I glared at him. The "so on and so forth" was the sort of obfuscation behind which the entire 2nd Bavarian Corps could have sheltered.

'I don't know any more than that,' he pleaded. 'Really I don't.'

I grunted. If the raid hadn't been such a grandiose success I think it would have ended in fisticuffs. But I was bushed and I let it be and tailed off in search of an empty bunk. The battalion's orders were to return to the front line later in the day.

CHAPTER 26

4th of December, 1915
No-Man's-Land, Messines-Armentières road, Belgium

'Oh yes, it's a commotion, alright,' replied Captain Critchley, shaking his head. 'The enemy's built a barrier of some kind across the Messines road in No-Man's-Land, and there's no way of getting past it. As you've seen yourself it's a swamp to either side of that road so the barrier is a considerable hindrance. The motor machine guns can't get up or down it anymore. To top it off, the thing's been there for a couple of days and they only just got round to reporting it. General Currie is hopping mad.'

'Who's "they", sir?' I enquired.

'Seely's Force. They have the mounted rifle regiments in the line at the moment. Well, they're not mounted anymore, MacPhail... you understand?'

'No, sir,' I said, catching myself on the verge of a groan. Did Critchley honestly think I was so dim I expected the cavalry to parade up and down Plugstreet on horseback? 'I assume, sir, in the absence of a mounted charge they do still intend to do something about this barrier?'

Fortunately Critchley missed the irony and simply answered the question. 'That's just it, Corporal, they've tried a couple of times already. I'm not aware of the details, except that they weren't terribly

215

successful. The barrier is still there. General Lipsett suggested that seeing as we know the area and have some experience in raiding that we send over a man or two to help out. That's where you come in.'

'Me?'

'Yes, you're to accompany a lieutenant from the 7th Battalion.' I could feel myself frowning. 'What's the problem?' asked Critchley.

'I'm a little surprised, sir. I would have expected our battalion to send an officer as well.'

Critchley shrugged. 'Don't ask me why but Colonel Rattray put forth your name.'

'He did?'

Critchley nodded.

'What exactly am I to do, sir?'

'Accompany the lieutenant and help them out, naturally.' The captain made it sound terribly self-explanatory. But Critchley was no idiot. For a man who'd read as many detailed operation orders as he had, he must have known it was sheer poppycock he was feeding me. I suspect he was simply in the dark and didn't want to admit as much. Hopefully the lieutenant from the 7th would know more.

However the lieutenant from the 7th frowned intently when I broached the subject.

It was the same lieutenant who'd been out cutting wire on the Petite Douve raid. The details of which, by all accounts, were virtually legendary in the British Army. Even in the French one I'd heard. While that must have done the lieutenant's career some good he was as puzzled as I was. 'Your guess is as good as mine, Corporal,' he grunted eventually. 'They haven't told me anything.'

Neither did anyone in trench 131, where we'd been told to report, provide any clarification. Moreover, they didn't seem the least bit interested in our arrival. The two of us stood in the muddy slop, twiddling our thumbs in the cold and throwing a critical eye at the state of the trenches. They definitely hadn't improved in our brief absence.

Finally one of General Seely's staff arrived. He emerged from the narrow tunnel under the road that linked 131 with 132. Above ground the hard pavé was a straight shot to Messines to the northeast, and Armentières to the southwest. The road's foundations dated from Roman times, and in more recent times coils of wire and machine-gun posts had been built at the point where it crossed our lines. The road was terribly exposed to stray machine-gun bullets, so most everyone passing from one trench to another used the tunnel. Even the cavalry.

After a flurry of apologies for his tardiness the captain welcomed us amiably. Several minutes of polite chit-chit followed, during which I stood unspeaking like a retriever waiting patiently at the lieutenant's heel. Finally the conversation ran its course and the captain led us to the rear. The lieutenant shot me a puzzled glance as we left.

I grinned knowingly. How different it had been when I'd showed up at the 7th Battalion HQ three weeks earlier. They had fired question after question at me, everyone from the colonel to the corporals. Ahead of their raid they'd wanted to know everything I knew and much I didn't. The cavalry must have felt they had matters better in hand.

Brigadier-General Seely appeared at Fusilier Farm some time later. He was a moderately tall, lean, verging-to-downright skinny man, his clean-shaven face heavily bronzed. He had that casual sophisticated air that suggested he moved in powerful circles. The general was certainly well-turned out; a little too well-turned out to have spent any time with his boys in the trenches. Avoiding the trenches was a perquisite of the office few generals turned down. I wouldn't have been surprised if the general's horse was parked around back, ready for a quick escape.

Seely's name was vaguely familiar from the newspapers. He'd been an English cabinet minister before the war and involved in some great scandal in Ireland which had cost him his head – if not literally than figuratively. Fortuitously for Lord Kitchener who'd had the onerous task of finding the head suitable alternative employment, the Canadian Cavalry Brigade happened along; Seely was made brigadier-general and commander. Whether a similar fate would have befallen the dashing Imperial Lancers or the Hussars was an intriguing question, but then we were from the colonies and in dire need of former cabinet ministers. And I'm sure Seely was quite excellent with horses – even if, as Captain Critchley astutely pointed out, the horses were absent.

The general greeted his assembled officers and the young lieutenant from the 7th Battalion good naturedly. He studiously avoided the eyes of the grim-faced corporal peering over their shoulders. In fairness, none of the officers pointed me out, either. A discussion ensued about what to do next.

The force which bore Seely's name consisted of the cavalry brigade and the six regiments of the Canadian Mounted Rifles. The war was not exactly going the cavalry's way. Nevertheless, in late 1915 they still managed a certain swagger – there wasn't a cavalryman alive who didn't look down his nose at the infantry. I couldn't imagine that any of the fellows I'd seen stomping their feet in the mud to keep warm much liked the idea they'd become one themselves. Holding the line at Plugstreet was not the most glamorous of tasks, even for an infantryman. Glamour aside, the more I listened to Seely and his officers the more convinced I became the cavalry was out of its depth.

Brigadier Seely was speaking: 'Gentlemen, I'm afraid the heavy guns were called off; the observation and communications were found wanting. However the field guns will fire a bombardment as planned. So I propose we go ahead with the patrol.'

Tepidly the lieutenant from the 7th raised a finger. He was a brave one, the lieutenant. Seely acknowledged him with a brisk nod. 'I wondered, sir, what the results of the reconnaissance were?'

Seely gently smiled. 'Unfortunately, lieutenant, the last patrol ran into some wire, and the one before that bombs. That's precisely why I've asked for a bombardment.'

'I see, sir,' replied the lieutenant.

Even to me, a lowly corporal, the meaning of Seely's answer was clear; they hadn't undertaken any reconnaissance worth the name. That the heavy artillery had begged off because the preparations were slapdash was a worrisome sign. What was equally clear was that every show we'd gone into blind had been a complete disaster... or worse. Festubert was only a half year before. Had the general forgotten about that? Either way he seemed in complete ignorance about the German works less than 100 yards from his doorstep, hoping they'd go up in a puff of smoke after a stiff bombardment. From my experience the Germans tended to be rather more tenacious.

'A bombardment, sir?' I whispered into the lieutenant's ear. 'I thought we were to help with a raid?'

'It would seem not,' he curtly replied, over his shoulder.

'Probably just as well,' I murmured to myself.

Others asked questions of their own and as the outlines of a plan eventually crystallized, it transpired that both the lieutenant and I had misunderstood. There *was* to be a raid, though the general studiously avoided calling it that; a dozen men were to advance to the barrier and capture it under cover of the bombardment. Two other larger parties were to assemble and wait in the fire-trench. One of these would follow in the footsteps of the first ten minutes later.

At these final details I moaned.

Rather loudly apparently, for a deep silence fell. General Seely and the other officers all pivoted round to stare. Whole hours ticked away in the time it took me to draw breath. No one said a word. I could have spoken up there and then. Really I should have, as I had their undivided attention. But at the sight of the general's hard eyes boring into me, and the riding crop he was impatiently snapping against his thigh, cowardly I retreated into myself and the moment passed. When the General resumed his discourse I sighed in relief. The regret would come later.

Once the general was finished the group broke up and I quickly made for the lieutenant.

'Sir?'

He looked at me enquiringly.

'The enemy is sure to retaliate once our bombardment begins. It never takes their artillery more than a few minutes, sir. If the men from the second and third parties are standing around in a group in the front line…' I paused, wondering if there was a better way to phrase it. Then I gave up. 'Well, they're going to die, sir,' I stammered.

'Yes, I know that, dammit.'

'Of course, sir. But I thought you might consider suggesting a change of plan to the general?'

'What makes you think he'll listen to me, corporal?' he said testily. I had to admit it was not an unreasonable concern. 'You tell him.'

Cautiously I glanced over at the general. He looked harried. He was addressing a pair of captains, both of whom were listening attentively, their concentration no doubt heightened by the riding crop drumming on his left palm. I grimaced and shook my head.

'No? That's what I thought,' said the lieutenant. He strode away grumbling something about a 'bloody mess', interlaced by the lads' favourite four-letter word.

That evening when I met Lieutenant Rutter of the 4th CMR and the sergeant, corporal and ten men who were to seize the barrier, the pattering of the rain had returned and the wind was picking up. However much I hated the idea, I'd invited myself along. I couldn't see how I was to be of any use otherwise, and the lieutenant from the 7th concurred. He pluckily volunteered for the second party – presumably with the idea of spurring them ahead when the time came, to avoid the worst of the German shells. Neither of us was terribly upbeat.

I eased over to the corporal from the Mounted Rifles. He and a handful of others were huddled around a smouldering brazier, rubbing their hands above it for warmth, the collars of their great coats turned on end. It was a scene I'd witnessed a thousand times before. The corporal was inspecting the actions of their Lee-Enfields. Tired of having to watch my Ps and Qs with the officers I was looking forward to speaking with someone of more modest rank.

'I'm from the 10th Battalion.' I told him and introduced myself. 'From what they tell me I'm supposed to help you fellows out.' The corporal smiled. A smile is a favourable sign when you meet someone you don't know, so I immediately plunged into the cesspool. 'For some reason your General Seely is dead set on pushing ahead with this raid,' I said. It could have been construed as both a question and a comment. I'm not sure I knew which myself.

The corporal's smiling eyes did a barrel roll. 'He's feeling the heat from headquarters. Everyone's in a tizzy about that barrier. I'm Forsdike, by the way. Frank Forsdike.'

Forsdike was considerably older than me, well into his thirties, with penetrating grey eyes, dark eyebrows and a modest – by cavalry standards – well-groomed charger of a moustache.

We talked easily for a few minutes and he happened to mention this was his second war, having apparently fought in the Boer one as well. Thinking back to Sergeant-Major Atkins, who was positively ancient compared to Forsdike, this surprised me. I told him this was my first war but that it had lasted quite long enough. That was how the topic of the Petite Douve raid came up.

'You say they practiced for a week?' he asked, surprise lacing his voice.

'Yes, indeed. They planned everything, including for when things didn't go as planned. The written orders alone were five pages.'

'Hmm. I don't think we have any written orders. It does makes you wonder,' he said pensively.

I didn't answer. I could see in his expression that the gears were churning. There seemed little advantage in rubbing his ill-fortune in his face by telling him what I thought. Besides it was too late; we'd have to make due. Having signed up for not one but two wars, I reckoned Forsdike had ample experience.

At 9.50 p.m. we climbed the ladders and the parapet of 131, and stepped out into the full force of the gale blowing across No-Man's-Land. I pulled my cap down tight and raised my face to the driving rain. I couldn't see a thing past the lieutenant two steps ahead. He was leading us north, in the general direction of the road off to our left. It ran northeastwards and would therefore eventually cross our path.

We hadn't gone very far when our field guns began barking. The lieutenant stepped up the pace. Ahead, from the barrier I presumed, a flare went up. Buffeted by the wind it fell quickly to the ground. Before it did I caught sight of marshland in front, the swamp south of the overflowing River Douve. Underfoot the muddy grassland of No-Man's-Land had turned soft and mushy. The lieutenant halted, his tall riding boots nearly submerged in water and muck.

I picked my way over to him, one laborious foot at a time. Another flare rocketed into the sky and began its wobbling fiery descent. 'We've gone too far, sir,' I said, 'and we can't cut through. I know this area, it's all swamp. We'll have to double back and then follow the road to the barrier.' The lieutenant had intended to move through the fields and come at the barrier from the right side of the road. Only the ground in between was far too wet for that.

More flares went up. The whole area was bathed in a sterile bluish light. To the east I heard the thud of the enemy guns opening fire.

Forsdike heard them too. 'They're retaliating,' he said. As the whistles passed overhead we looked back towards the front line where a ripple of explosions followed. 'H.E.,' he added superfluously.

We retraced our steps, then cut over to the road where we once more headed northeast, this time following the ditch. In the darkness I'm certain we could have worked our way unseen all the way to the barricade. But there was no chance of that at present. Flares were going off all over the place. Approaching on the level of the road was a deathtrap. The machine guns would sweep us away in an instant. To compound matters, rounds from our own guns were falling in the vicinity of the barrier, while others – enemy rounds – fell perilously close behind. We were stuck in the middle, helpless.

Lieutenant Rutter did the only thing he could in the circumstances and told us to disperse.

I sighed at Forsdike, 'It's impossible to capture the barrier now.' Forsdike nodded. We'd have to hope the artillery somehow smashed it.

'I'm going to move up and reconnoitre,' Rutter announced after we'd gone to ground.

I offered to accompany him but Forsdike intervened. 'It's my regiment and our problem, Malcolm. I'll go.'

For nearly forty minutes I lay in the ditch, waiting and listening, soaked from the rain as the wind howled. A steady thumping concussion of shells lit their lines and ours. Black thoughts overran my mind, thoughts of what I should have said or done if I hadn't been so spineless. Thoughts about the futility of it. I'd had my fill of Plugstreet.

'And?' I asked hopefully, when Forsdike and the lieutenant reappeared. It was a few minutes past eleven. I thought they might even report the artillery had succeeded.

Forsdike shook his head. Both of them were drenched and even dirtier than I was, but every man of the patrol returned to trench 131 alive and well. I'm increasingly inclined to think that's the greatest victory of all.

Safely back in our lines, this modest triumph was swept aside. Captain MacKay of the regiment and two privates were dead. Five others including Captain Sifton were wounded. The German bombardment had hit them in the fire-trench as they waited. It was agonizingly predictable.

25th of December, 1915
Court Dreve Farm, north of Ploegsteert, Belgium

Christmas Day dawned with a sky so sullen and depressing I was tempted to return to my bunk if that had been an option the army offered. Water drip-drip-dripped from the trees and hedgerows, the clouds promised more, and a heavy cold mist hung doggedly in the air. Even here on the far slope of Hill 63 at our billets at Court Dreve Farm, the signs of war could be spotted in the holed brick walls and jury-rigged repairs to the roof of the old farmhouse. It was not a particularly difficult shot for the German gunners – no more than three miles away, and likely closer to two.

For lunch we ate plum pudding to celebrate the day and were treated to cigars and fruit afterwards. A gramophone in the corner of the old farmhouse scratchily played out a tune everyone with the exception of me seemed to know – after a few bars I recognized the tune with prompting, although the words remained a mystery – and the men lustily sang along, determined to make it a festive occasion.

Any festive sentiments I might have had were rudely dispelled when Harry Hobson presented himself in front of me after lunch. From the smell of him he'd had some good Christmas cheer: the kind that comes in a bottle and of which he'd offered me none.

'It looks pretty don't you think?' Hobson brandished his arm in my face, the sudden flap of his elbow nearly knocking my nose astray. A third chevron was prominently displayed on his sleeve.

'Finally got it sewn on, did you? Congratulations. Good for you.'

Hobson frowned, uncertain how to respond. I expect he was steeling himself for a sharp rejoinder. He knew that when Sergeant Stiles was struck off strength – word had it he was down with a severe case of pneumonia – many in the company had put their money on me being his replacement.

'Well, thanks, MacPhail,' he grumbled, once it was abundantly clear I had nothing further to say on the issue. He pottered off to share his good fortune with the others.

Dundas shook his head. 'Harry Hobson, a sergeant... If I live and breathe...'

'Oh, I don't know. He deserves it as much as the next man,' I said. Dundas looked at me incredulously.

I reddened. 'Well, he was a corporal. So sergeant's a logical next step. Besides, I told the captain I wasn't the right man for the job so he went looking for someone else.'

'You what!?'

It was a self-imposed penance of sorts. An inadequate one if I was truly honest with myself. But I didn't say this to Dundas. Nor did I tell Dundas that I'd prevailed upon the captain that he be promoted to corporal in Hobson's place – days later Roy was still completely puffed about it. That pleased me greatly, which is precisely why I didn't tell him.

'Don't tell me you're still cut up about that raid at the barrier, Mac?' I shrugged.

'It wasn't even the battalion, it was the cavalry, for Pete's sake. Without their horses to lead them they don't know what they're doing. You told me that yourself. It certainly wasn't your fault.'

'That's why I was there, to help them along.'

'Which you did. Need I remind you of the last time you spoke your mind to a general? You were demoted… And do you think Brigadier-General Seeley would have reconsidered his plan in the light of the good Corporal Malcolm MacPhail's objections? Anyhow, the 5th Battalion's already cleared it up. It's history now.' Wearily, he shook his head. 'Passing up the promotion you wanted so badly? I don't think I'll ever understand you, Mac.'

I shrugged.

That afternoon I put my name up for the night's working party. There were a lot of surprised looks when I did. I was mildly surprised myself as I'd never before done anything of the sort. I don't think anyone in the battalion ever had. For some reason spending a night digging trenches seemed a lot easier than putting up a front of good cheer.

PART FOUR

CHAPTER 27

27th of January, 1916
Trench 134, Ploegsteert trenches, Belgium

The aeroplanes came from behind, first with a drone, barely audible, then a bee-like buzzing that grew steadily louder. Initially the sight was no more imposing to the eye than a couple of flies of the kind that swarmed the trenches in summer. This being the first month of 1916, and the dead of winter, gave the first clue something else was afoot. There were two of them, one pursuing the other, both biplanes. The one being hunted twisted and turned from side to side, his wings dipping left and then right, frantically attempting to shake off his tormentor. As he neared Hill 63 he began to climb, his motor whining loudly, but his foe was climbing in close pursuit. The anti-aircraft guns had spotted them and puffs of white smoke straddled the lead plane. From afar the *rat-tat-tat* of a machine gun sounded as the hunter mercilessly strafed his prey. The lead plane seemed to waver, then it ceased climbing and fell over into a deep swooping dive heading directly towards us.

'It's a Heinie,' someone shouted. The men in the trench were raising their rifles. The machine gunners had swivelled round and were taking aim.

'Damn rights it is,' shouted Dundas, louder than I'd ever heard him. 'It's an Albatross!'

'Are you certain?' I asked. That it was an aircraft I was quite confident. Beyond that it was all conjecture; aeroplanes had always been a mystery to me.

He was headed straight at us, a sleek elongated tear-drop in dark colours sandwiched between two wings, rubber-rimmed discs of wheels hanging underneath. While I couldn't make out any insignia, I could plainly see the brown leather head of the pilot through the whirr of the propeller, with his scarf flapping incongruously behind. However I appeared to be the only one in trench 134 uncertain of the plane's provenance. No one heard my question. Every man in the trench was firing like mad. If I hadn't been the one asking I wouldn't have heard myself, either. This was an answer in itself, so I raised the Lee-Enfield to my shoulder, lined up the plane and pulled the trigger.

Afterwards I calculated that my small section of trench fired more than 1100 rounds at the plane in the minute that followed, 800 to 900 from the two machine guns, and 300 or more from the 30-plus rifles. Not everyone was a crack shot by any means, but even allowing for this the plane was flying low and an easy mark. It's anyone's guess how many rounds hit home; the propeller kept rotating, but the plane turned turtle before it passed overhead and went on to crash in No-Man's-Land.

'The pilot was dead, but we found the observer alive,' Harry Hobson was saying. 'Let me tell you fellows… he looked even worse than you do after a night at Madame Manon's.' There were laughs, hearty laughs of recognition from men whose experiences at Madame Manon's were not vicarious ones. Madame Manon ran a particularly seedy kind of estaminet at Ploegsteert, where drinks of a dubious and thoroughly alcoholic sort were always in plentiful supply; provided you had a billet fold of francs and an undemanding palate – most of the Canadian Corps in other words.

'Found some maps and photographs, as well. But you know what the damnedest thing was?' Hobson asked. Every eye in the bunkhouse at Bulford Camp was glued on him. The man had a way with a crowd; there was no denying it. 'We found a machine gun.'

'No!' cried someone. Spirits had lifted since we'd gone into relief early that evening.

Hobson smiled. 'Oh yes. We did. And you know what?'

Gamely someone took the bait, 'What?'

'It was one of ours. A Colt.'

At that revelation twenty men all began asking questions. It turned out the explanation was simple, although it stuck in my craw; the Germans had found the gun at St. Julien in April after General Turner's ill-considered and hasty order to his brigade to withdraw. The Germans, never ones to pass on an extra machine gun, mounted it in one of their aeroplanes. Through some strange twist of fate it was back with its rightful owners.

When I spotted Hobson not long after, his mood had visibly changed; the flush in his face was still there. Gone however was the healthy reddish glow and beaming eyes from having entertained the boys. In fact he appeared angry. He was standing with another man away from the camp building and in the middle of the path, one facing the other. The second man had his back to me. I slowed my pace, curious what new machinations Harry Hobson was involved in. With him it was always a question of what, not if.

Hobson was vehemently shaking his head and it turned redder than a lobster at the boil as I watched. He raised a clenched fist and waved it menacingly in the other man's face. Then both men whirled round as they discerned my approach. Hobson let his hand fall. I gasped when I saw who Harry had been threatening – it was Lieutenant Drinkwater.

Awkwardly I passed them by with an obligatory nod and a salute, giving both a wide berth, my stride lengthening as I discovered a new-found reason for haste. Drinkwater eyed me suspiciously. But neither he nor Hobson said a word. Once I was past I didn't look back. I wanted to be as far away from this quarrel as possible. With Harry's knuckles threatening to land on the lieutenant's nose I had no desire to witness what came next. Even if they didn't land, the army didn't take kindly to soldiers (sergeant or otherwise) threatening to punch out their superiors. I wasn't sure it rated a firing squad at dawn – it may have – but I wasn't going to stick around to learn the finer points of military law. *What in Heaven's name was going on?*

To my relief I didn't encounter either Hobson or Lieutenant Drinkwater for the remainder of that week at Bulford Camp. It wasn't entirely a coincidence as I'd been relieved of all other duties. Consequently I saw little of the rest of the battalion. I did know that no MPs arrived to take Harry into custody, as I half expected they would – that would have been the sort of news that spread faster than a fire in a bomb dump – the analogy springing to mind thanks to the three-day bombing course at Bailleul I'd recently completed.

I may have been relieved of other duties, but that was not nearly as restful as it sounds. I was part of a group of fifty-odd men selected to carry out a cutting-out operation, better known as a raid. Since going into relief we'd resumed practice, often from early in the morning to late in the evening. The rest of the time I slept like a log.

Since the boys from British Columbia had pulled off their stunt at La Petite Douve a rivalry of sorts had taken root as to which battalion would be next, and Lieutenant-Colonel Rattray was not immune to the competitive spirit. While the men took it to their rivals in football matches and lacrosse, the colonels occupied themselves with raids.

'Here we go again,' muttered Atwood. The sappers had built a remarkable scale replica of the enemy trenches. Rain or shine we rehearsed until we knew every inch of them. It was raining as we spoke so that likely explained Atwood's mutterings, for rehearsal or not you tended to get wet and cold. 'We've spent the whole month practicing and we're still at it,' he grumbled.

'You should be thankful,' I told him.

'Why is that?'

'First of all, hopefully you'll know what you're doing when the show really begins. And secondly, every time we've been in the trenches this month, it's been a clear night. Sneaking across No-Man's-Land is bad enough. You sure don't want to do it under the full glare of the moon. Better to rehearse than have Fritz practice his shot with your big head featuring prominently in his sights.'

'Yes, I suppose so,' he conceded.

The attack was to come at the furthest point of a 150-yard deep concave in the enemy line where two trenches intersected at an angle. The spot was probably no more than 600 yards down the ridge from the fortified village of Messines. Not that that mattered – our visit was to be limited to the fire-trench and we weren't planning on staying long enough to meet the legions quartered behind. Drop in, drop some bombs, capture some prisoners and be gone was the motto.

Similar to most of the enemy line in this sector, there were two bands of wire guarding the German trenches; a double line of wired fence posts 50-60 yards out, followed by a 30-yard gap; then a second band, much wider and denser than the first, ending virtually at the enemy parapet. Which is a lot of wire, although not quite enough to keep us out even if Fritz had taken to using tempered steel of late. Between the artillery and the wire cutters a way would be found.

It was little wonder the Germans were more vigilant in recent weeks. There is nothing quite like the clunk of a bomb landing in a cozily furnished dug-out to permanently wreck a man's rest, along with the morale of every mate who survived him.

'You've been on raids before, Corporal. Do you figure we can do it?' Atwood was eyeing me with obvious curiosity. He was from one of the recent drafts, a quick learner, athletic, and one of the best shots in the company, which is why I put his name forward – I didn't tell him that.

Thoughtfully I rubbed my chin. The very thought filled me with terror; of sneaking across No-Man's-Land again, creeping through the wire in the dark, anxious lest anyone make a noise, then springing into the unknown of an enemy trench.

'Ah, keep your head about you, Atwood, and we'll be fine,' I said. 'You'll see. It won't be long now.'

We returned to the trenches a couple of days later on the evening of February 1st. The next day word arrived that the attack was imminent and we should be prepared.

On the 3rd the gas alert was removed and the orders came. We stood-to in nervous anticipation for what seemed like half the night, but the attack was called off very late – German patrols had discovered the newly-cut holes in their wire. Not only had they repaired them, they'd added a new line. I was pretty tired when I got back to the dug-out and fell asleep almost immediately. I would have slept much longer but for an interruption around 5 a.m.

'Mac! You'd better wake up. The captain sent me.'

Drearily I blinked, and with an effort forced open my eyes, focusing on the shadowy wraith bent over me. I could hear the wraith breathing heavily. Around me the others were beginning to stir.

'Who are you?' I mumbled incoherently.

'It's me,' said the voice. 'Wake up, Mac.'

I blinked a third time, and rubbed at both eyes, and his features came into focus. 'Oh. Roy. Listen, it was a long night. Can we talk tomorrow?'

Dundas drew his lips together, his face uncharacteristically serious. He shook his head.

'Lieutenant Drinkwater has gone missing!'

CHAPTER 28

4th and 5th of February, 1916
German lines, 600 yards southwest of Messines, Belgium

When I arrived in the trench no one knew anything, or at least any-thing worth knowing. It shouldn't have surprised me. But I muttered a few choice expletives under my breath after meeting a wall of blank faces and even emptier responses. I can be a little cantankerous when roused out of bed before dawn on a winter morning. And on the face of it for no good reason.

Following Dundas from the dug-out my first thought was that it was flattering that the captain required my personal assistance. However, it soon became obvious this bore no resemblance whatsoever to reality. The captain was nowhere to be seen. I think he just wanted to have all hands on deck; for several moments I thought longingly of the attractions of shovelling coal in a cruiser's sweltering engine room, stripped to the waist with a bandana around my head. The only thing the army could offer in the way of warmth was an old oil drum with a bottom of smouldering coal, close to where Currie Avenue met trench 135. It was modestly warm and I huddled round it with Dundas and a few others, stomping our feet, rubbing our hands and blowing clouds of white vapour into the air.

'Well, one of you must know something?' I demanded.

'An officers' patrol is out as we speak, looking for him,' said Dundas.

'There was another patrol out before that,' offered someone else.

I waited for the denouement but if it was coming it was taking the scenic route, and my impatience got the better of me. 'And?' I finally asked.

'No. Nothing. Not a sign,' said the man.

'Strange,' I said. 'Drinkwater out on patrol and he just disappears?' I snapped my fingers. 'Like that?'

There were nods.

'What about his patrol, then? Surely they must have heard or seen what happened?'

'Apparently not,' said Dundas, 'I think the battalion staff are questioning them.'

'So the lieutenant takes a dozen men out into No-Man's-Land, doesn't even run into the enemy and manages to get himself lost?'

'There were ten of them and an NCO,' said a man, as if this small correction explained all.

'They never did find that fellow who got lost in January, the one they think drowned in the Douve,' I mused. 'Perhaps something similar happened?'

Dundas shook his head. 'Not likely. They were nowhere near the river.'

'Very strange,' I said, a curious notion coming to me. 'Who was the NCO?'

'Sergeant Hobson.'

'Harry Hobson. Was it now? Hmm, isn't that something?' I murmured.

There must have been an edge to my tone for Dundas said, 'What do you mean by that, Mac? I know what you think of him, but Hobson is as much in the dark as the others.'

'Oh, just thinking,' I said distractedly, recalling the dramatic scene of an angry Harry Hobson waving his clenched fist in Lieutenant Drinkwater's face. 'Just thinking.'

As evening fell there was still no sign of the lieutenant, despite a half dozen patrols that went out looking for him along a 2000-yard swath of No-Man's-Land. Of course, if he'd wandered accidently into the German lines we would only hear about that in due course. I didn't think there was any chance he'd slipped back through our lines and disappeared – you sometimes heard the wildest tales in the trenches. Drinkwater's whole being was defined by the army, so desertion was out of the question. Someone did joke that he was probably heading for the Spanish beaches to pick up some colour – the lieutenant was neither the most popular, nor the most tanned, officer in the battalion.

The only real news, and I heard it second-hand, was that Drinkwater and Hobson had gone on ahead to reconnoitre when one of the men thought he heard an enemy patrol approaching. In the early morning mist – so said Hobson – they'd lost sight of each other. When Hobson brought up the others to help they searched extensively but couldn't find him.

However, the mystery of the lieutenant's disappearance was quickly overshadowed by the announcement that the cutting-out operation was to take place that very night. Preparations began immediately.

By 7 p.m. when the wire cutting party departed it was very dark and drizzling. Fortunately it wasn't snowing. Still I was relieved I wasn't to accompany them. Lying on one side on the cold ground with a mere handful of others clipping at strands of wire above your head, each sharp snap of the cutters potentially alerting the enemy, and fearful all the while that a patrol might loom up out of nowhere, was a nerve-wracking and exhausting business. But it was critical if the raid was to be a success.

The rain ceased around 10 p.m., a small if belated comfort to the wire cutters. However, five-and-a-half cold hours passed before Sergeant Milne arrived back at the trench to guide the attack party forward. The wire had been cut.

Faces blackened with burnt cork we followed Milne across No-Man's-Land and up the slope of the Messines Ridge – the incline quite pronounced at this point – towards the spot marked on the maps as U.2.d.2.5. Anything sounded innocuous when translated into map coordinates, explaining perhaps why headquarters used them so prolifically, and the average soldier not at all.

The wind had died down and it was very quiet, quiet that is except for the Colt machine guns from an armoured car on the road to the north that were stuttering away periodically. They'd been at it all night. While I don't expect they hit much, it did give the Fritzs an added incentive to keep their heads down, as well as masking the sound of the wire cutting.

Before long we reached the line of willows. The trees extended on through the German lines and up towards Messines. Where the trees began the officers formed us into two parties, one in front of the other. With the pollarded willows on our left we edged forward in well-spaced single file. It was overcast and dark, but if a sentry spotted anything or heard so much as the snap of a branch underfoot, a well-sited machine gun might wipe out half the party with a single burst. I clenched the rifle tighter and tried not to think of that or all the other myriad ways this could end in disaster.

At the outer belt of wire I found myself holding my breath. In the silence that echoed off into the night it had sounded so painfully la-boured and loud. I was only too conscious of the crunching that came from my boots at every step, no matter the care I took. We entered the wire.

The wire cutters had done their job admirably and there was a clear, albeit narrow path. Only once did I feel a loose strand of barbs tear at my sleeve, before yanking it brusquely away. Through the first belt we came upon the wide buffer zone, exactly as it had been at Bulford Camp. In the pitch black, and moving at a deliberate pace, the gap between the two lines of wire seemed much larger and more ominous than it had then. That was the real value of practice; when the time came you did unthinking what you'd done before, having effectively lost the ability to think much at all. After a minute or two I made out the second belt of wire looming.

Ten paces from the fence post and its looping coils, the file came to a shuffling halt. I was at the end of the lead party. There were maybe fifteen men already into the wire ahead of me. Anxiously I cocked an ear, but close to hand there was only the thumping in my head to break the cloying stillness.

We stood there uneasily for a minute, looking round and at each other, not daring to say a word. *Why had we stopped?* The minute became two. By the time that had expired I'd lost all sense of time. After what seemed like an eternity passed, but was likely only five minutes, I wondered whether I should move forward to Lieutenant Kent and Lieutenant Younger at the head of the column. I decided

236

not to; they'd send for me should they desire, and Kent had explicitly said I was to bring up the rear. As the second party was immediately behind us I didn't see the point of this order. However, Kent was the lieutenant and as a general rule officers prefer their orders to be obeyed not questioned. I didn't anticipate that this would put me in the front of the action.

There was a flash, then a *BANG* as a bomb went off. I swung around to my left.

All the carefully thought-out plans and weeks of preparations vanished in that muffled bang and puff of smoke; the war had taken its own course, and it was sheer chaos.

'A Heinie patrol,' someone shouted. Rifles began firing. Another bomb went off. It was only then that I spotted what the trouble was – there were twenty of them, maybe more. They'd been moving down the gap between the inner and outer lines of wire, checking it for gaps, patrolling on the off-chance they might encounter one of ours. By sheer dumb luck they'd passed through the row of willows and stumbled almost immediately into the left of the waiting file of men preparing to attack.

I went to bring the rifle to my shoulder, but realized half-way that it was pointless – there was barely 20 feet between us. Both the Germans and our own men were closing the distance rapidly. It was impossible to make out a target.

'Atwood, Wannacot,' I shouted to the two men directly in front. They hadn't yet entered the second belt of wire. 'On me!'

There was no time to think. The Germans had to be prevented from cutting through. Otherwise they'd catch our lead party from the rear and seal off any chance of escape. Most of the attack party were somewhere in the wire, with nowhere to go to either side, facing an enemy in the trench ahead, now forewarned.

I didn't await a response from Atwood and Wannacot and rushed for the brawling melee of men. As I ran Atwood appeared at my side, his rifle bouncing up and down, grasped with two hands in front. Wannacot was on my heels.

Men were shouting, more bombs were going off. There were revolver shots. There was no order or strategy to it; it was a mad, scrambling free-for-all in the dark. Ahead of me a soldier brought down a knobkerrie on the head of a German. Two other men, one from the battalion and the other a Fritz, were locked in a furious fencing duel with the stocks of their rifles, neither able to bring one to bear.

I lunged at the first German I saw, intending to stick a bayonet in his side. He spotted me though, and in a desperate arching swing of his arm brought an entrenching tool down on the barrel with a hard clang. The blow reverberated through the rifle and nearly led me to drop it. I didn't, but the muzzle end was pushed down and away. I was on him by then, close enough to see his face contorted in exertion, his eyes flashing. I tried to recover the initiative by giving him a stiff cross-check, pushing with the rifle held in both hands. But he spun to one side and it glanced off his shoulder.

He began lifting the entrenching tool again. Quickly I let go of the rifle with my right hand and threw him a hurried punch. It connected with his jaw. He took a step back, dazed. I rewound for a second attempt, this time bringing my arm well back and I slogged him with everything I had. It hit him again on the side of his head. There was a cracking noise and my fist felt like it had run up against a brick wall. But he went down.

I glanced at him briefly, long enough to know he was out of it for the time being. And we needed some prisoners. Nursing my hand I hastily scanned the scene. Everywhere men were fighting. From the uniform count it appeared we had them on the run, although none were running. The ones that weren't lying on the ground were fighting desperately for their lives.

From the south, off near La Petite Douve Farm, a red flare curled into the sky, followed by a white one.

Almost immediately a machine gun began to fire from the German trench. A long staccato. There were a few bangs from that direction and our men began rushing out of the second wire entanglement.

'Retire! Retire!'

Another enemy machine gun started up, and there were rifles as well. They were firing indiscriminately, in near panic it seemed for I saw two of their own men fall in the spray of bullets.

I hadn't noticed him earlier, but on the ground a few steps away lay Atwood, holding his leg. He was the same man who at Bulford Camp I'd breezily assured that it would be "fine". Only he wasn't fine. Other than his leg, which had been pierced by a bullet, there was a nasty gash in his tunic sleeve and I knew it was more than a scratch as a dark patch had formed.

'You, okay?' I said as I knelt beside him. The last of the German patrol had their hands in the air.

He gritted his teeth and grimaced. 'I think so.'

'We're pulling back,' I said to him. 'We've got to get going. Here, I'll help.'

I slung the Lee-Enfield over a shoulder, and with both arms helped him to his feet, whereupon we began an awkward limping shuffle towards the outer wire. Bullets were whizzing everywhere. The thought came to me that we might not make it to the wire when, from the direction of our lines, sounded the retort of a field gun. Seconds later there were more thuds. Along the length of the enemy trench a series of explosions boiled. They were giving them everything they had. The two of us huddled low, waiting it out. This went on for a couple of minutes before the gunfire died down, then ceased completely.

'We'll make a run for it while we can,' I told Atwood. 'Don't worry, I'll get you back.'

Half dragging him – he groaned several times but remorselessly I kept going – we crossed through the gap in the outer wire. Ahead and behind us others were pulling back too. A fair number of them were wounded. Entering No-Man's-Land I spotted the row of willows and turned towards them. I couldn't carry Atwood, he was too heavy for that, and both he and I needed to pause. There'd be some shelter at the trees. I wasn't certain if the Germans merely had their heads down, or whether the artillery had dealt with them decisively, but after a year at the front I wasn't about to assume the best.

Upon reaching the trees I saw a ditch that ran alongside and Atwood and I climbed down into it and collapsed in a heap. 'Thanks,' he mumbled.

'Don't thank me, yet,' I replied.

Something beside me in the ditch suddenly caught my attention and I reached out to grab it. When I did my heart did a somersault. Violently I thrust it aside. 'Holy shit,' I murmured.

'What's wrong?' asked Atwood in alarm.

I didn't respond, instead I looked closer. It was a hand all right.

And the hand was attached to an arm, and the arm was attached to…
I pulled at some of the branches strewn on top and groaned.

'What is it?' demanded Atwood.

'It's a dead body,' I replied. 'One of ours, too, by the looks of him.'

'Maybe it's someone from the battalion.'

I got on to my knees so I could work better. The body was at the bottom of the ditch lying face down, almost completely covered by the bough of a tree which had been brought down by a shell splinter. If I hadn't sat next to it, I'm certain I never would have seen it. With a grunt I pushed the bough aside and wrestled the body onto its back.

'Damn,' I whispered, taken aback by what I saw.

'Who is it?' asked Atwood. 'Is it someone we know?'

'Look for yourself.'

He leaned onto one side, craning his neck and wincing at the effort. Then he saw what I saw and whistled softly. 'Damn…'

Thoughtfully I looked down at the body. There didn't seem to be any alternative. 'I'll have to bring him along,' I said.

'Are you sure? I'm not going to be much help, corporal. I wouldn't have made it this far without you.'

'Yes, I know that. But we can't very well leave him. Do your best, Atwood. We need to move. I don't want to be out here at dawn, not with the Fritzs in a foul temper. They didn't have a good night.'

With that I set to work and dragged the soldier's body out of the ditch. Then I helped Atwood to his feet. After he assured me he could stand for a moment without help, I bent down and with difficulty lifted the body over one shoulder. Then I put my other arm around Atwood.

The firing had ceased and No-Man's-Land was again cloaked in darkness.

We hadn't gone more than a few steps when an officer with revolver in hand overtook us. It was Lieutenant Kent bringing up the rear of the attack party.

'MacPhail, is that you?' he said.

'Yes, sir,' I replied.

I stood there swaying on my feet, barely able to hold the body folded over my right shoulder. Atwood could hardly move his wounded leg and just out of the ditch he'd stumbled and almost brought us crashing to the ground. 600 yards to our lines seemed an impossibility.

Kent looked at me keenly. Then he motioned at the body. 'He's dead, I presume. Who is it?

'Oh, yes he's quite dead,' I replied. 'This, sir, is Lieutenant Drinkwater.'

'Drinkwater!?' Kent helped me lower him to the ground. After a moment studying his face he nodded. To my surprise he began rifling through Drinkwater's pockets. 'Take the insignia off, would you, MacPhail?'

Lieutenant Kent was a sharp one. He'd been out with the wire-cutters half the night, led the attack party in, and been in the midst of the action ever since. Still he had the wits to remember to remove any identifying marks.

'I'm sorry, we'll have to leave him,' he said when we were done. 'We've got too many wounded to carry as is. You look after Atwood. We'll come back for the lieutenant tomorrow.'

'Yes, sir,' I said, and paused. 'If I may, sir, why did we wait so long before going through the wire?'

Gruffly Kent responded. 'There was an enemy working party up on the parapet. We were hoping they'd move off, but then... well, you know the rest.'

'Yes, sir,' I replied. Not for the first time in this war the plan proved no match for events. In any case we'd given Fritz a bloody nose for our trouble.

'Here I'll help. We'll lay him back in the ditch. He should be safe there until we come back for him.'

CHAPTER 29

7th of February, 1916
No-Man's-Land, southwest of Messines, Belgium

The tops of the willows swayed gently to-and-fro in the breeze, dark spindly forms silhouetted against the clear night sky. Up on the ridge towards Messines other shapes could be seen, the copse of a small wood, a line of wired fence posts that the Germans had placed so liberally everywhere on the slope, and at the peak of the ridge the crenellated outline of the shattered village itself. Lower down, the enemy trenches were lost to sight. I knew they lay straight ahead where darkness reigned, a few minutes distant by foot, less than a second by the round from a rifle or machine gun.

This afternoon the German howitzers and field guns had been at it again. They were quiet now and No-Man's-Land had an almost pastoral serenity to it, if one ignored the steady pop and crackle of shooting off in the distance. The night after the raid Lieutenant Younger took a patrol to look for the bodies of those who had been killed, but returned empty handed; German working parties were out in force, covered by strong patrols. Tonight we were to try again.

Normally I would have accepted another summons for a night-time stroll in No-Man's-Land with weary reluctance (there being no question of turning it down), but I was uncharacteristically eager. We were to recover the remains of our men. One of them in particular interested me a great deal. If we could locate Drinkwater's body, the mystery of his disappearance might become clearer. I had developed an entire theory about it, and while I never much liked the lieutenant, he was a loyal soldier and a comrade, and it seemed only proper that the reasons for his death be known. I hadn't yet told anyone of my suspicions, not even Dundas, but after tonight I hoped to know one way or the other. On top of which, Lieutenant Kent had approached me as I was preparing to inspect the platoon's kit and feet – the latter never one of my favourite chores.

A Frenchman was accompanying us, a Lieutenant Dallennes of the 26th Battalion Chasseurs à Pied, come to learn the tricks of night-time raiding. That was another reason Kent had asked me along, to help translate. The French lieutenant spoke some English, Kent barely a word of French, and I think he wanted to ensure things went smoothly. Out in No-Man's-Land there was typically little talking and consequently little danger my questionable translation skills would land us in a fix.

We walked in file, following almost the exact route from two nights earlier. Approaching the gap in the first line of wire, Kent drew us to a halt. With a couple of men he crept off in the direction of the wire. It was understood that we were to cover them.

'*Il faut attendre ici, monsieur*,' I whispered to the French lieutenant. He drew his revolver and we sat on the ground to await the results of Kent's investigation – no sense providing Fritz with a target.

Time has a tendency to pass very slowly in No-Man's-Land and it was therefore a surprise when I saw the figures moving towards us. Alarmed I raised my rifle. My first thought was of a German patrol, the memory of how they'd blundered into us during the raid all too recent. My finger was on the trigger guard, only a hair twitch from the trigger should the need arise. Dallennes shot me an anxious glance and followed my example. He had a Modèle 1892 in hand, the standard French service revolver. Behind him the men were prepared.

I peered down the steel barrel of the Lee-Enfield, watching intently. Fortunately there weren't many of them. Then I recognized the gait of the man in front. Though his features were obscured by the gloom there was no mistaking who it was.

Lieutenant Kent shook his head from side to side when he reached us.

'*Non, c'est impossible de continuer, monsieur,*' I informed the French lieutenant, by which I meant the first line of wire had been repaired and we'd gone as far as we could. I hoped he'd understand the mangle I made of his mother tongue.

He looked me in the eye and nodded solemnly. After the mangle the Germans had made of their country the French were remarkably good-natured about such matters.

'Sir,' I whispered to Kent, 'May I go and look for Lieutenant Drinkwater?'

Kent nodded his assent, signalling with a finger that I should take a man along.

The route to the willows and the ditch was a short one. I found the spot where Atwood and I had sheltered with surprising ease, at least I thought I had. However, of the body there was no sign and that made me think I'd made a mistake. I sent the private off one way down the ditch and I went the other, a venture that proved as fruitless as the attack at Festubert, although thankfully less sanguinary. There was no mistake about it, Drinkwater's body was gone. Here too the Germans had tidied house. Which was very unfortunate.

It was closing on 2.30 a.m. when I reached La Grande Munque Farm where the company was bedded down, a walk of close to two miles from our front lines. Only with difficulty did I eventually find a corner with a little hay where I could sleep – not a bunk, they were all taken. I don't recall much after that. As a result I didn't see Dundas until the next morning.

'What's all the hush-hush for, Mac?' he asked, after I found him and furtively motioned that I needed to talk.

I didn't respond but led him by his free arm – the other was cradling a mug of coffee – into the courtyard. There, standing in the mud amongst a handful of horses, an ammunition limber in sore need of a new wheel, and men moving back and forth between the farm buildings, I explained. I told him first about the exchange I'd witnessed between Drinkwater and Harry Hobson. Then I told him

244

about having stumbled upon Drinkwater's body on the way back from the raid. I told him all the details I hadn't told anyone else.

'The strangest part of it all was that I didn't see any sign of a wound on Drinkwater. Admittedly it was dark, but I had a fair look when Lieutenant Kent and I were removing his identification. No bullet wounds, no stab wounds. He was lying all crumpled up, his head face down in the dirt.'

Dundas whistled, then drank from his mug. 'I know what you're thinking. You think Hobson killed him, don't you?'

I nodded. 'Why or how, I don't know. But it's the only explanation that makes any sense. Drinkwater couldn't have just ended up in a ditch of his own accord.'

Dundas scratched at his chin. 'You realize you've no proof,' he said finally.

'Of course I realize that. I was a lawyer, remember?' I responded, a trifle irritably.

'So what are you planning on doing about it?'

'I don't know, that's why I wanted to talk to you.'

'Do nothing,' he said. He didn't even pause to think about it. He just said it.

'Nothing!?'

'Yes, nothing. You can't go around accusing one of the battalion of killing a mate, particularly an officer. Not without proof and you have absolutely none. Thanks to you Hobson's a sergeant, so there's a considerable chance you'd end up on charges yourself. Undermining authority or some such thing. You know the rules better than I do.'

'Yeah,' I said glumly. He was absolutely right. In the absence of an open and shut case there was every possibility they would throw the book at me and Hobson would emerge scot-free. That was where the army differed from civilian life. One's superiors were on a pedestal and no one from the field-marshal on down took kindly to subordinates kicking at the supports underneath. With good reason, I suppose. That was the reason why the army was an army and not a mob.

'Mac, I know you want to do what's right. But there's nothing that says Hobson had anything to do with this. Sure, you saw an argument. So what? And Hobson was along when Drinkwater disappeared. So were ten others. Plus several hundred Fritzs in the immediate vicinity.

You've been out there yourself more than once; strange things happen in No-Man's-Land. All I'm saying is I wouldn't be so quick to jump to conclusions. More than likely it's all a terrible coincidence. Hell, you told me yourself on more than a few occasions that you'd like to throttle Drinkwater.'

I smiled weakly. 'I was joking.'

Dundas drank some more coffee. 'Well. To put it in perspective.... how a little thing might be misconstrued.'

I'd been so certain, the scenario so clear and vivid in my head. Facing Dundas's scepticism a dense smokescreen moved across. I wasn't so sure anymore.

'Let's go, Mac,' he said after a bit, noticing my quietness. 'I've got a sick parade to look after.'

13th of March, 1916

I awoke to brilliant sunshine, a freak of nature in the succession of bitterly cold, wet and gloomy days that constituted winter in Belgian Flanders. Stepping out from the covered bay in the appropriate-ly-named Winter Trench, where I'd spent the hours from dawn till well past noon, I could see that the snow was melting once more. A week ago it was all but gone and then on Wednesday (today being a Monday I was fairly sure), it had come drifting down in thick heavy flakes that filled the air, turning the visibility to nothing, and grown men into little boys for a few precious hours. The mood was even better after the announcement that the night time working parties were cancelled. Folds of white still blanketed the parapets, the fields and the fence posts, and coated the Messines Ridge, and the war and the sun were vying to sweep them away.

There were many who were happy about this. The snow for all its charms made an excursion into No-Man's-Land all the more harrow-ing; the Germans had sighted their rifles and machine guns on some of the little trails we made, now highly visible. Furthermore, even at night, the form of a man in khaki was in vivid contrast to the land about and I'd been on edge when it was my turn to head out to man a listening post. I'd seldom moved quicker.

The listening post went well, apart from the biting cold, and I was returning to trench 134-135 where the platoon was relieving another. It was a state of affairs I was anything but happy with. Admittedly the north end of 134, abutting 135, was a lot drier than the southern sector where the Douve flowed through, but it was one of the spots where the enemy lines were nearest ours. Nor did it help that directly opposite was the local citadel of La Petite Douve Farm. Later tonight large salvoes of rifle grenades were expected to arrive. One wearied of German punctuality.

Hobson had taken the sector further north, and slightly further away, assigning this one to me. 'Your own damn fault,' snapped Dundas when I mentioned it to him. At intervals he still remonstrated me for turning down the sergeant's stripe – a point of view I was increasingly inclined to share as the weeks passed and Sergeant Hobson found new and creative ways to remind me of our respective positions.

'Oh, you're just sore because you're going to be up to your knees in water all night, Roy,' I responded. Which was probably accurate. Dundas had drawn the section beside the river. He snorted.

'Be thankful for the pioneers,' I called after him. 'They're good at pumping.' The small group from the 1st Pioneer Battalion, who I was to tutor in the intricacies of the trenches this night, glanced at me apprehensively.

'Cheer up fellas. You should be plenty dry tonight,' I reassured them. 'You'll want to prepare for when the pineapples start to fall from the sky, though.'

I might have mentioned that they should be thankful we didn't have any such plans ourselves. The last time we'd been showing off, we fired 42 rifle grenades and got almost exactly the same number by return messenger. It was the sort of tit-for-tat that kept both sides on their toes.

That I knew the exact number was because we had instructions to count them – theirs and ours – although for what purpose was beyond me. I imagine it made for titilating reading for some under-employed soul at army headquarters. When the bombardments began I usually found I was too busy running one way or the other to count much of anything, so the statistical accuracy was questionable.

The only statistic that mattered to me this night was that my section of twelve, and the pioneers, survived. As objectives go it wouldn't go down in the annals of military history, but then few days in the trenches would. I had the men well spread out, each of the pioneers instructed and paired with a reliable man. The NCO I'd relieved told me that midnight was when we should expect fireworks.

I was standing at the look hole when I first heard them. A succession of soft pops due east.

'Heads up!' I yelled. Men went scurrying.

Like arrows of old, a flight appeared in mid-air for an instant before descending toward the trench, straddling it in a flurry of small bangs. One landed several feet behind and exploded with the sound of a large firecracker. Had I not been up on the fire step I would have had a leg full of metal shards.

They were rifle grenades. Deeper thuds followed and I knew without even seeing them that they were large aerial torpedoes, fired from a trench mortar. As with the rifle grenades they appeared similar to a medieval mace, a length of rod sticking from a metal ball, but considerably larger. Unlike a mace the punch came from the explosive within, not the steel. If one landed beside you the chances were quite high you were heading west. A second or two later three large bangs went off near 135. Our artillery began shooting in response.

Too late I noticed another salvo of rifle grenades. They rained down in a cluster in the sector where I stood, a half dozen of them, exploding around us.

To my right there was a clatter, as of a stone falling on the plank we were standing on. I wrenched my head round and saw it lying there, halfway between Partridge and me. A wave of cold sweat rushed over, the thought that this time I was truly done for flashing through my head. However it didn't explode. It just lay there. A steel rod attached to a small steel pineapple. Innocuous.

'A dud,' said Partridge weakly.

I exhaled. 'Thank God for duds,' I breathed.

Then from the traverse to the north came a man running. It was

Harry Hobson and he was going full tilt. Of his rifle there was no sign, and my first impression was that he was in panic.

When he was close enough that I could see his face my second impression confirmed it. Hobson's eyes stared ahead, unseeing, a look which I'd seen before in men who'd lost their senses amidst the crash of a bombardment. I could guess what had happened; one or more of the aerial torpedoes had landed close to him. 'Whoa,' I called out and stepped down from the fire-step, extending an arm in warning. He brushed past it and me. I swivelled and grabbed for his arm, was towed along for a couple of feet, and finally was able to steer him with a rough push into the wall of sandbags.

He was breathing heavily. 'Calm down,' I said firmly, 'Get a hold of yourself, Hobson.' I kept a tight grasp on his arm until I felt the tension ease away, then released it. 'It's a lucky thing an officer didn't see you. This is not the behaviour expected of an NCO. What will the men think, you running away like a chicken with your head cut off?' A corporal dressing down a sergeant was not foreseen in the army regulations. There were, however, several paragraphs in those same regulations which would have been of far greater concern if I hadn't stopped him – I was quite certain the penalty for cowardice was death. It didn't end well for NCOs fleeing their posts and their men. And I was angry with him, too; he was letting down his men, not to mention the rest of us. As his breathing slowed and the fog in his head cleared, he became as docile as a lamb. He knew the penalties for cowardice.

'I'm sorry,' he mumbled. 'I… I just sort of lost my mind. Those torpedoes went off and…'

At the last sentence I looked skyward, conscious the barrage was finished. It had ended as suddenly as it began.

Then I noticed Partridge up on the fire-step. He had turned and was observing us. I barked at him: 'Damn it all, Partridge. You're supposed to be standing watch. Do you see anything in front?'

He turned to the slit in the metal plate and his head made a slow pass from left to right. 'No, Corporal,' he replied.

'All right. Get down the trench, then. See if there's anyone hurt. Jesus… I didn't think I'd have to wet-nurse you, as well.'

With that I addressed myself to Hobson once more. He looked as contrite as a schoolboy with his hands in the jellybean jar. It was not a look I'd ever seen on him before.

'Feeling better?' I asked. I said nothing about shirking or cowardice. We'd all had our moments of weakness. Even if few let it show as Hobson had. At the sternness in my tone Harry nodded meekly, his eyes downcast.

'What are you going to do?' he asked. It was barely a whisper.

I hadn't thought about this. There was little question I *should* report him. The army would have demanded as much. I stared at him; the flat cliff of a forehead, the little clam-sized ears, and that whopper of a nose which I'd wanted to take a baseball bat to for the better part of a year. Hobson and I had been at loggerheads since he'd arrived. Nor had I forgotten about Lieutenant Drinkwater. Even though my silence these past weeks suggested otherwise. I looked at him intensely. He just looked back, all the guile and pretences gone, unconsciously baring his soul through abject eyes.

I considered what I saw then shook my head – had his attitude not changed it would have been different, I told myself. 'Nothing,' I replied.

His eyes widened.

'Don't ask me why. But I think there's a better man and a better soldier hidden somewhere in you, Harry.'

'You won't regret this, Mac.' In all the time I'd been acquainted with Harry Hobson this was the first he'd ever called me anything other than "MacPhail".

'I hope not.' I hesitated. Then figuring there might never be a better time, said, 'I've been meaning to tell you this, Harry. I really am sorry about hitting your old man,' and began to relate the events which had led me to knock him on his behind.

Hobson waved me still. 'I'm sure he deserved it.'

I could feel my mouth hanging open. It was my turn to stare in disbelief.

'He can be a prickly old geezer at times. I'd have liked to have done that myself more than once.'

All of which left me completely puzzled.

'I thought you were sore. You've been bruising for a fight ever since you arrived?' I said.

'No,' he said, his face expressionless, '*much* longer than that.' Then he smiled.

'Then why? –'

'Because you're the one that got me here.' I was at a loss for words, but Harry continued. 'You probably don't know this, but Pa was your biggest fan. Whenever you and he met, he couldn't talk about anything else at the dinner table that evening. It was Malcolm this, and Malcolm that. And I never measured up to you in any of the ways that mattered… You must have heard the stories about me.'

'Sure,' I said, nodding. 'But I nearly knocked his jaw off. That must have changed things?'

'Not really. He soon heard about your wife. Before he had the chance to speak with you, you joined up and shipped off. After that it was as if I didn't exist, except to berate me for this, that and anything else that came to mind.'

'So you enlisted as well?'

He nodded. 'Seemed like the only way to get him off my back. Worked, too. In the week before I left, he was actually proud of me. For the first time in my life.' At the thought Harry's eyes watered over and he blinked rapidly a couple of times.

'I see,' I said. 'I'm sorry, Harry, I never realized any of this.'

'No, you wouldn't. But that's how it was.'

'I'm glad you told me,' I said. Out of the corner of my eye I could see Partridge rushing back to report. 'You'd better get back to your section. They're going to wonder where you are.'

Hobson went to leave, but before he did I said, 'Good luck, Harry.' Then he was off, leaving me to marvel at this unexpected turn of events. I still had some pressing questions that needed answering, but perhaps things were not entirely as I'd thought.

Then Partridge reported that a man was down and there was a hole in the parapet, and the business of war resumed.

CHAPTER 30

9th of April, 1916
Hill 60, Belgium

The city loomed in the distance only a few miles off, a beacon that kept summoning us back like moths drawn to the flame that would eventually consume them. The broad tower of the Cloth Hall, and its slightly taller and thinner cousin, the Cathedral, were unmistakeable. So too was the shell damage. It had been a few miles west of here in April, a year to the day almost exactly, when I discovered what war truly meant. In the gaping holes of the ancient stone buildings I could see that the war had soldiered on in the interim. Walking to Hill 60 last night from the city outskirts, passing the small farms and shell-furrowed fields, the air was heavy with smells of manure and things rotting. We dodged shells at Shrapnel Corner and old memories were awoken. Memories I'd hoped never to revisit. For better or for worse I was back in the Salient. Even if the sun was shining.

'I thought I might never see it,' mused Partridge. 'The famous Ypres.' He was beside me, gazing in obvious fascination down the slope of the hill.

'In a few days you're going to wish you never had,' I grumbled.

Partridge glanced at me, in surprise. He probably thought I felt the same. The battles in the Artois, and the many months in the Plugstreet trenches aside, Bill Partridge had somehow retained his insatiable curiosity. He had an enthusiasm I once would have described as infectious. Having been at it for longer than Partridge I was immune to those sorts of emotions – more so every day it seemed.

I had to smile, however, when I saw his helmet. 'I wondered how you'd manage that,' I said.

Partridge grinned. He removed the helmet with both hands and held it out for presentation. His trademark flower (it was red today from which I deduced it was most likely a poppy – roses, the flower of love, not being thick on the ground near Ypres) was skillfully fastened with a length of thin twine, tied around the metal bowl where it met the broad saucer rim.

'Let's hope it can stand up to some real punishment,' I said, referring to the helmet. With my knuckle I beat out a drumbeat on top and a reassuring *clang, clang, clang* sounded back. The poppy also looked fine. After a few days I wasn't yet accustomed to having 1 ½ pounds of extra weight on what was already a heavy ballast atop my shoulders, and I seemed to sweat more than with my cap. However, having seen numerous French soldiers, all of whom were sporting metal helmets by late 1915, it struck me as a fine idea – what with all the falling shrapnel around. Allies or not, the helmet was French and therein I surmised was the explanation why it had taken so long before we had one on our heads – the British Army being rather coy about anything French since roughly the time of the Peninsular War.

To the south a clap of thunder resounded. This being the Ypres Salient it naturally wasn't thunder but a salvo of shells, probably from the 5.9s. The helmet was fitting better by the minute.

Dundas had joined us in Fort R7, a fort quite unlike any other of my acquaintance, consisting of a circular trench with none of the usual accoutrements such as stone walls, or even wooden ones, that one might typically associate with a fort. I don't think the Germans were fooled by the nomenclature either; their lines further up Hill 60 were in plain view only 100 yards away.

'Look,' Dundas said, pointing south – our nonchalance owing much to the fact that we were in the half of the trench circle facing west, not east. 'Isn't that down Plugstreet way?' A plume of smoke could be seen erupting three miles distant as another shell landed in a moonscape of craters and holes.

'No, Plugstreet's even further. That's St. Eloi,' I said. 'There's a big fight going on. Apparently 2nd Division is in the midst of it.'

'We have a real grandstand seat,' said Dundas, appreciatively. No one replied as three more shells landed, one after another in a neat row – an effect best appreciated at a distance.

Partridge sighed. 'Boy, I'm glad it's not us.'

'Yeah,' I replied, 'count your blessings. I have a feeling our turn will come soon enough.'

Dundas and Partridge looked at me in alarm.

'Oh, nothing definite,' I said. 'Just a feeling. Look around.'

Manning the Plugstreet trenches was no sinecure, but on the evidence of this morning's sniping I wasn't convinced our lot in life had improved much. After weeks of vague rumours the division had finally been pulled away from Ploegsteert and Messines at the end of March, given a week or two to recuperate in the rear, and now we were here: at Hill 60.

Hill 60 was a 60-metre high hillock astride the Ypres-Menin railway that ran southeast. The rail line was concealed in a cutting 50 feet deep, the excavation of which was how the hill had come to be. There'd been a lot of fighting at Hill 60. From what I could see the Germans had come out on top, literally and figuratively – their trenches ran all over the peak and down the eastern slope. Whatever part of the line we were in, Fritz had unfailingly inveigled the choicest spots for himself. And getting them back was a priority for our generals, which was why I worried. The offensives this year and last hadn't been resounding successes. There were worrisome signs of new preparations being made.

As if he'd been reading my mind, Dundas piped up: 'Did you see the tunnellers down near the railway cutting? Apparently they're mining all the way into the hill.'

Seeing my face deepen into a frown he went on, 'At least they didn't send us to Verdun, Mac.'

'No,' I allowed, 'at least they didn't send us to Verdun.' According to the papers, the Germans and French were locked in a battle of titans the past month. 'But keep that under your hat, Roy. You don't want to be giving anyone any ideas.'

12th of April, 1916

'What's it all about?' I asked Hobson.

It was well past dawn and the battalion was racing to stand-to. It was not an hour anyone ever chose to begin an attack. There hadn't even been a gas alarm.

'They're setting off a mine,' he said hurriedly. He had things on his mind and he was trying to get the platoon together. His impatience showed.

'A mine? So we're attacking, is that it?' I asked. I hurried to catch up with him.

'No, it's a camouflet,' he said.

'A what?'

Hobson shrugged irritably. 'I don't know and I don't want to know. The captain told me to get the platoon assembled and that's what I'm trying to do… Corporal, can you…'

'Yes, of course, Sergeant' I said, reverting to the respective roles the army in its wisdom had assigned us. 'I'll get at it.'

The platoon – two entire companies in fact – were soon lined up in the trenches, all accounted for, bayonets fixed, awaiting what might come. Whatever that was.

Just before eleven word was passed along that we should get ready. No more than that, although it took no fantastic leap of imagination to conclude that the mine was to be blown. I found it very strange there'd been no preparations to speak of, if we were indeed to attack. But there was no one to ask, no orders to be had, all the officers were elsewhere.

I didn't have long to ponder the implications of this. At precisely 11 a.m. a throaty muffled boom went off, not especially loud by the standards of the front, but more than loud enough to hint at the enormous power of the mine somewhere under the hill in front. The ground trembled and shook. Even the sturdy wooden posts that stood every few feet wobbled back and forth, something I'd never seen in the heaviest of bombardments. Men were darting nervous glances at one another. I reached out to the parapet to steady myself and others were doing the same, only to realize the parapet was shaking too. Lines of sand from the sandbags and clumps of dirt spilled downwards. After a second or two it was quiet. The shaking ended. Broad grins emerged on the faces around me, like the sun after a heavy downpour, quickly followed by a buzzing chatter.

'Quiet!' I roared, fearful the attack could start at any moment.

No whistles blew. I probably wouldn't have known what to do if they had. The enemy lines were east so that was a fair bet. Nor did any orders arrive. Most puzzling of all there was nothing to see of the explosion. The surface of the ground was untouched. After two or three minutes, peering anxiously towards the German trenches for the sign of a reaction, Lieutenant Powers arrived.

'Stand-down,' he said without ado.

'One question, sir,' I said, springing in front of him before he could leave. 'What was this all about?'

Powers looked preoccupied, but he replied. 'To blow an underground German gallery. The tunnellers were concerned the charge they'd set might be too heavy, in which case there would have been a crater. We were to occupy it if there was. But it all worked out as you can see. Now, if you'll excuse me, I have other things to attend to, MacPhail. And so do you.'

Partridge appeared at my side the instant the lieutenant left. 'What did he say? What was that?' he asked.

'A camouflet,' I said tersely.

I was irritated by the summary way the lieutenant had dismissed me, although he hadn't been harsh, nor had he said anything I hadn't heard a thousand times before. Ignoring the questions in Partridge's eyes I began directing the men. If Powers wanted us out of the trench, then so be it.

When Hobson turned up I was still thinking about the young lieutenant; he was no older than I was and considerably less experienced, having arrived only a month previous with the latest draft. And yet he was an officer and I was a mere corporal; he had responsibility and knew what was going on; I didn't and had to follow orders from every Tom, Dick and Harry, the latter being particularly frustrating. It was time I did as Dundas suggested and apply for a commission. Though he'd had two warnings for me: 'It can take a year, and even if you are accepted you must realize, Mac, you don't begin as general.' I'd groaned and assured him I had no interest in such things. In the meantime I'd reconsidered.

Now I looked at Harry who was grinning from ear to ear. 'Did you feel that? Quite something, eh?'

By then only Partridge, two other men, and Hobson and I remained in the trench. Which proved fortunate as at that instant the German artillery opened up. There was a short whistle, then a bang.

The shell burst to the rear of us, twenty feet in the air, a white puff followed by a rippling in the ground as a hundred pieces of steel bore into the earth. Something tore at my cheek. Shrapnel!

Then I was pushed and I felt myself tumbling to the ground. I landed heavily on my side on the bathmat. My helmet lay upside down in the dirt beside me. Hobson lay almost on top of me.

'What the...' I began. Only then did I see Partridge. I knew it was him before I could really see him. He sat in a crumpled heap, leaning against the parapet wall, a tin helmet adorned by a red flower tilted down over his face. Madly I scrambled towards him on my hands and knees. He was moaning terribly. I called out his name but he didn't respond. When I saw what had become of his stomach I winced, a lump in my throat. Hobson appeared.

'And?'

I glanced at him over a shoulder and shook my head.

Hobson recoiled visibly when he went to look closer. The other two men were with us now.

'See if you can find a stretcher bearer, will you?' I said to one. 'And get some morphine. Hurry!'

It was obvious what had happened. We'd been straddled by a salvo from the whizz-bangs. Partridge was on the fire-step and must have turned to face the rear in order to see the shell that had burst when a second fell. It had been a matter of a second, or perhaps less. I would have caught the full effect from the shoulders on up.

'Thanks, Harry,' I mumbled. I'm not sure he noticed but my voice was trembling. 'You saved my life.'

'You're bleeding,' he said. I touched at my cheek. It was sore to the touch and my fingertips returned coated in blood.

'So are you,' I said. 'Just off your shoulder.'

Startled, he examined his arm, apparently conscious of it for the first time. 'Wounded. Isn't that something? With any luck they'll send me to Blighty.'

A stretcher bearer appeared. He glanced briefly at Partridge and I knew from his expression that I wasn't mistaken. Kneeling down on both knees he rapidly and expertly gave him a shot in the arm. Partridge's eyelids fluttered momentarily. His eyes closed and the tension seemed to ease out of him. The moaning ceased. I think we were all relieved when it did.

'I'll look after him,' said the stretcher bearer. Then in a whisper, 'There's not much I can do, you understand.'

There was certainly nothing more we could do, and the bombardment appeared to have ceased, so Hobson and I walked down to the railway cutting and followed the tracks in the direction of the Railway dug-out. There was a dressing station there.

'He was a good fellow,' I said once we were underway. '*Is* a good fellow,' I corrected myself.

'Partridge? I hardly knew him.'

'No. I suppose you wouldn't. You were in a different platoon most of the time. Rough luck though. I liked him.'

Hobson grunted but said nothing. In a way there wasn't much else to say. Another day another man from the battalion dead or wounded. Soon a draft would arrive to replace those lost, and life would go on – or not. Either way, its ranks replenished, the 10th Battalion would carry on as long as the war did.

We were walking together, stepping from railway tie to railway tie. 'Harry, I have to ask you something.'

'About Drinkwater, right? Oh, don't look so surprised. I knew you were going to ask. I'm only surprised it took you this long.'

'Well?'

'Yeah, well we had a falling out, you might say.'

'That much I saw. What was it about?'

Hobson walked a few steps before replying. 'You were right. I did give him some money, and before you ask – no, it was not from any diamond heist. Before I left home my father gave me a whole wad of cash, some gold, too. Pa was prouder than a peacock, but I think he was worried as well. I never saw him part with so much money so easily. Anyhow, when I heard about Drinkwater's money problems

I figured I could buy off a lot of trouble by helping him out. A few hundred dollars goes a long way. What else was I to do with it?'

'That worked well,' I mused.

Hobson gave a curt nod. 'For a while, sure. It went splendidly actually. I was a corporal. Drinkwater made certain I never got assigned any of the worst tasks. It worked like a charm.'

'And then?'

'Then? Then he wanted more. Threatened to have me reverted if I didn't pay up. Worse, he said he'd have me up on cowardice charges. He'd caught me hiding away in a dug-out at Plugstreet one night when I should have been out on patrol.

'I refused. Of course I was afraid of what he might do, but I mean, where would it have ended? That's why I was so angry.'

'What about the patrol?' I asked. 'The one where Drinkwater went missing. Surely you must know what happened to him?'

'Nope. I don't. All I know is he and I went off to scout out ahead. Someone said they heard a German patrol and he wanted to investigate before we moved on. Shortly after, he went right and I went left, and I never saw him again. Searched everywhere, but I think now he must have tripped over some of that old wire. Maybe he hit his head on a fence post, or a stone, and fell on his face in that ditch. I don't know. I was surprised when I heard you found him, though. I was certain the Hun had him.'

'They do now,' I said. 'Although he's quite dead.'

Harry seemed pleased at this last revelation. I suppose I couldn't blame him.

Regarding his story, it was all too believable – even though I was mildly incredulous thinking of the Dickensian Mr. Hobson handing over an envelope stuffed with cash to his errant son. I didn't know Drinkwater well, but from my previous occupation I knew people; well enough to know that they were capable of pretty much anything, especially when it came to money. A couple of hundred dollars was a tidy bounty. Harry told the story with aplomb and I was convinced he'd spoken truthfully, though the lawyerly part of me plugged valiantly away for a short while, trying to knock holes in it. In hindsight I might have better listened to the lawyer.

At the dressing station we loitered around, waiting for a short while. However the casualties weren't heavy and someone was soon examining my cheek and Hobson's shoulder.

'You'll live,' he said dryly when he was finished.

'No Blighty?' I asked wistfully.

He laughed. 'No Blighty. It's a scratch, so you should be happy. The ladies will think you're a proper hero. And stop fidgeting.' He preceded to paint my cheek with iodine in ever wider concentric circles, much as I'd done as a boy with crayons on the kitchen walls. I didn't shriek nearly as loudly as my mother had then, that only came afterwards when the mirror divulged the humungous white plaster patch he'd applied.

Hobson got roughly the same treatment, plus a tetanus shot. The shot left quite an impression on him for he told me about it in excruciating detail all the way back.

It was therefore with some degree of relief that I arrived at my dug-out. It had been a tough day and I wondered if I should volunteer to write the letters for Bill Partridge. I hadn't heard anything, but I hoped for his sake it was over. However, a message was awaiting me; I should report immediately to the quartermaster.

'I have a stores sheet signed by you, Corporal,' he began weightily, 'attesting to the fact that there were two pumps in trench 134 when you vacated it. Yet I have a quartermaster from the 12th Royal Fusiliers who swears there's only one.' I groaned. The quartermaster's bushy eyebrows came together in a frown and he drew himself up in his chair. I realize you're a young chap, but you're a corporal and you have responsibilities. And this is a serious matter. Promise me you'll do better.' He paused, and I bit down hard on my lip, determined not to let fly with all I was thinking. Then he winked conspiratorially. 'I don't think there's any need to bring this up with your superiors.'

CHAPTER 31

30th of April, 1916
Scottish Lines, near Poperinghe, Belgium

'MacPhail, wasn't it?' asked the general, leaning on his cane and staring intently. I stood rigidly at attention, resisting the temptation to stare back.

Late night gas alarm or not, and I was still a little sleepy, there was little doubt who it was. I hadn't a great deal of experience with generals – although as it happened the Commander-in-Chief, General Sir Douglas Haig, had popped in for a hurried inspection two days earlier – but it was most definitely General Lipsett. The searching quizzical eyes, polished broad forehead, and sandy-coloured moustache and eyebrows all belonged to our brigade commander. Accompanying him were several senior officers, of whom Lieutenant-Colonel Rattray was the most prominent. Quite by chance I'd bumped into the party walking through Scottish Lines in search of some lunch. I was feeling rather chipper away from the shells, and having been spared a day laying cable near the Advanced Divisional Headquarters in the company of Sergeant Hobson, Corporal Dundas and several other worthy souls of my acquaintance.

'Yes, sir. MacPhail it is,' I replied and flapped the general a decent rendition of a salute.

'The Petite Douve raid,' he said slowly. 'You were along, I believe?'

261

'Yes, sir, I was.'

'Well, enjoy your relief,' said the general. 'Who knows what the future will bring.'

'Yes, sir, that's precisely what worries me as well.'

Lipsett looked at me oddly. Then the colonel hurried him away in the direction of Gant Road and the Officers' Mess.

'He was rather helpful at the time, I seem to recall,' I heard Lipsett say.

Colonel Rattray responded with something I couldn't hear and Lipsett laughed. It made me wonder whether I'd heard him correctly the first time. The group of them rounded the corner by the washing benches and disappeared from sight behind one of the camp's timber huts.

Two generals in two days. It might have been a coincidence, only I didn't think it was. There was no mistaking that the Germans had their wind up this past week. The bombardments on our front were heavier and more regular, hardly a day passed without the clanging of another gas alarm; they even launched a small attack recently. And I don't imagine I was the only one who'd noticed that the calibre of the German shells had markedly increased – big howitzers on top of the field guns, and heavy trench mortars to supplement the smaller ones and the rifle grenades. I bet some of those officers accompanying Lipsett knew more…

5th of May, 1916
Hill 60, Belgium

The month of May began with the most glorious weather. Day after day clear blue skies and bright sun held sway, barely a fluff of cumulous cloud to break the monotony. The stands of trees and hedgerows that survived wore shades of green, vibrant against the lighter tapestry of the rolling fields where the grass had already grown to past the knee. Even the grey stone shards of Ypres's distant towers had a statuesque beauty to them. At dawn and in the soft light of the warm evenings the birds could be heard, chirping incessantly, songs of goodwill and cheer – sentiments utterly lost upon our foe. I checked my watch. It was approaching 6 p.m.

The thump of a trench mortar signalled that it was beginning: the evening bombardment.

'Get ready, fellows,' I warned. There couldn't have been anyone in the trench who hadn't heard it for themselves, but such things warranted repetition.

Thirteen heads peered skywards.

'A pig,' said someone.

'Must be,' agreed another. 'Look how high it is.'

'Forget how high it is, look how bloody big it is.'

The huge round was far above our heads, easily visible, to all appearances bracing itself before making the hurtling descent towards earth.

'We're much too close. They can't hit us here with those things,' said Dundas. He spoke with a laidback casualness I didn't share. The others didn't share it either, for they warily tracked the shell with their eyes as it plummeted downwards, preparing to bolt at an instant.

It did miss us, but not because we were too close; they were simply aiming elsewhere.

A deafening explosion came from a couple of hundred yards to our right where the 7th Battalion manned the trenches. The ground shook and a cloud of dust lazed in the air marking out the point of impact. It was too far away to gauge the damage without poking my head up and it had been a long while since I'd been dumb enough to do that.

But I realized Dundas was correct when I thought about it. The mortars would have to fire their rounds almost vertically if they wished to hit us, only 100 yards from their own lines, and mortars weren't built like that. Not even these two-ton monstrosities lobbing a shell roughly the weight of me. So we were in little immediate danger. The same couldn't be said of the 7th whose position must have been exactly right for the mortars's trajectory. The dust from that first chest-pounding explosion had barely settled when the next shell fell with an even louder bang. Not only had the Germans brought in heavier guns, there were an unhealthy number of them.

'God, help them,' said Dundas. 'The poor bastards will be shelled to pieces.'

'They'll have pulled back,' I said assuredly. 'They must have seen it coming.'

Dundas looked sceptical. 'I hope so,' he replied. 'There's sure as hell not going to be much to return to once Fritz is finished.'

'No. It'll be messed up awfully bad.'

A little less than an hour later I learned more. It was worse than I feared.

'The trench is completely blown in: the entire section. I met a 7th Battalion man in the rear. He said it's as if the trench was never there. Gone. And the snipers are taking a real toll. All told they have a dozen dead and three times that many wounded.'

I whistled.

'Get your section together,' said Dundas, who'd just returned. 'You're to pull back without delay.'

I recoiled in surprise. 'Pull back?'

'That's right. Brigade is concerned that the enemy are going to make a night attack, so we're to concentrate in the support line.'

I thought about this. 'Makes sense, I suppose. What with this gap in our front line. And it'll give the 7th a chance to get some shelter.'

'The brigade major will be delighted to hear that you approve,' Dundas said, a brief grin appearing. 'But I'm afraid they didn't send me to ask your opinion, Mac. Only to get you moving.'

Dundas left me to it and scurried off to warn the others in the company. In no time I had the men assembled, hissing at them to keep their heads low and their mouths shut as we filed off to the support trenches. The last thing I wanted was for the Germans to get wind of what we were up to; at 100 yards a couple of rifle barrels moving in file along the trench, or the blather of some comedian from Red Deer would be sufficient to alert them we were up to something. Furthermore, it was still light. As the sun set behind us we would be silhouetted for some time to come for the observer to the east.

Events were moving quickly. By my reckoning it had taken the Germans a mere twenty-five minutes to level a long length of well-constructed trench and everything in it. I half expected to hear a gas alarm. At the thought my head sprang up. Then I rushed off to warn each of the men individually to watch for the signs. Whatever the Germans had planned, our position in the line ensured that we would be the first to face it.

Initially I was conscious of every passing minute, certain that when the enemy came they would come quickly. However, no one did, and as the first hour ticked slowly by I began to think about other things, like whether the men had sensed my nervousness. This was my fifteenth month at the front. Where I once thought I'd grow out of the fear with experience, I found myself worrying more than I had as a new private arriving at Ploegsteert. Perhaps I wasn't cut out for the worries and responsibilities of being sergeant. The blissful ignorance of the lower ranks did have its advantages. Then I thought of Hobson, who had my stripe, and his unseemly panic near the Winter Trench, and I didn't know what to think.

By now it was very dark, the moon all but invisible.

'Who's there?' asked one of the men suddenly.

There was a clatter and the sound of rifles being brought to bear.

'It's me, Corporal Dundas,' said a voice.

'Jesus, Roy,' I mumbled as he stepped into view. 'This is not an ideal night for dramatic entrances.'

'Sorry,' he said. 'I didn't realize you were all so on edge.'

'You were the one that got us there so it can't be that much of a surprise,' I grumbled.

'Sorry,' he repeated. 'You'll be happy to hear they believe it's all right to return to the front line.'

'What happened?'

'Nothing. I think it's probably far too dark, that's all,' he said. 'I don't think Fritz would dare mount an attack under these conditions. They wouldn't see a thing on a night like this.'

'So, if not tonight, when?' I asked.

'You really think an attack is coming?'

'Don't you? Look I'm only a mere corporal like you, Roy, and I'm not sure we're encouraged to think. But only a few short weeks ago these boys from Württemberg opposite were cowering in their trenches. Now they're blowing us to bits with heavy artillery three times a day. Need I remind you that the only high ground around Ypres not already in German hands is held by us?'

'Yes, I see your point,' he said.

22nd of May, 1916
Connaught Lines, near Poperinghe, Belgium

Major-General Arthur Currie navigated the rigid rows of equally rigid faces of the 10th Battalion with a practised ease, and a word to several. I thought briefly he might share one with me but he passed me by without as much as a blink. I was only one of many hundreds he would see today, and likely again tomorrow, I told myself. At the end of our row, anchored by the sergeant as was traditional, the general checked his step and paused in front of Hobson. They exchanged a few words. Out of the corner of my eye I could see Harry glowing as the general moved on.

Our divisional commander was not a man for great flights of oratory. However, he addressed us for a few minutes, complimenting all on our turnout and our "steadiness". He said nothing of battles to come.

'Did you see Harry?' asked Dundas, after we were dismissed. 'I've seen Very flares light up less brilliantly than him.'

I chuckled politely. 'I told you, he's turned over a new leaf, our Harry has.'

'Yes. Yes, you did tell me that.' From his expression he looked like I was trying to pass off second-hand socks as new.

Most of my life I've felt I was reasonably good at reading people. But after hearing Hobson's side of the story I had to admit I'd walked off the duckboards. I decided this was finally the moment to tell Dundas about it and how wrong I'd been. He wasn't immediately convinced, and that likely explains why I hadn't told him earlier.

'You're raving mad, you know that?'

I frowned. 'I thought you'd find it a great lark, me admitting I was wrong. Now that I think about it, weren't you the one that told me I should let Harry be?'

'Yeah, but not because I didn't believe you. Nor because I thought you were wrong about Hobson. He's not to be trusted, that fellow,' he growled.

'He saved my life,' I said tetchily, at which point Dundas shook his head and changed the subject.

'Currie didn't say a lot.'

'He rarely does,' I replied. 'Surely you noticed how he commended us on our "steadiness"? I think that was a hint. He knows something's coming.'

Dundas's eyes twinkled. 'Festubert was a year ago, Mac. I think General Currie was probably referring to the battalion's actions during that battle.'

'Yes, well…'

'And don't you suppose that if the general knew more he might warn his own division, not just hint about it? You've been going on about an attack all month, Mac, and yet nothing has happened. Perhaps you're reading too much into things?'

'Just wait and see,' I said gruffly.

'There is one thing in your favour,' said Dundas calmly. 'There's a war going on, so eventually you'll be right.'

CHAPTER 32

2nd of June, 1916
Swan Château, south of Ypres, Belgium

When it came, the thunder sounded from the direction of the ridgeline to the east. This in itself was entirely predictable as that was usually where the trouble began, Fritz having already moved in everywhere else worthy of the effort. The ridgeline circled around to the north and east of Ypres like the rim of a saucer with the city in its centre. The village of Hooge and four minor hills protruded from the rim – Hill 60, Hill 61, Hill 62 and Mount Sorrel, not peaks, more like bobbles, but crucial all the same.

It was a fierce bombardment; I dare say as fierce as any these past weeks. From my listening post at the Swan Château, a mile to the south of the city's Lille Gate, the heights that ringed Ypres were a walk of 4 miles or longer. Consequently, one wasn't inclined to pay a great deal of attention and I didn't – a bombardment four miles distant was not of any particular significance and certainly no danger. It seemed a morning like any other. However, by 9.30 a.m. when the shellfire showed no signs of abating after nearly an hour of steady rumbling – in fact I swore it had intensified – I was not the only one taking curious glances eastward. There was nothing to see however.

By the time it reached 10.30 a.m., the glances were longer, more wary. I saw a group of battalion officers congregate, evidently speculating what it was all about. This was not the typical morning wakeup call. However, they quickly dispersed when the crump of shells falling in the immediate vicinity began. I raced back to the rows of little huts where the company was billeted.

There was an explosion to the east of the château grounds. Others could be heard at various points not far away. As Shrapnel Corner was only 1000 yards distant, and there were a profusion of billets, headquarters and artillery positions in the area – all of them within easy reach of the German howitzers from almost any point surrounding the Salient – sporadic shellfire was a fact of life. Private Dodd had been wounded only yesterday. The tempo was increasing. A loud boom went off in the grounds.

I scanned round searching for an officer or NCO of the company. Just as I was preparing to head over to the officers' quarters at the château to find one, I spotted Hobson.

He looked grim but waved an arm when he saw me approaching.

'Another bloody bombardment,' he said when I was within earshot. 'But they haven't got our number yet.'

'They soon will. Shouldn't we move the men into the woods as a precaution?'

Hobson looked around uneasily. I'm not sure what he hoped to see. An officer to tell him what to do, most likely.

The lone bell near the mess began to clang urgently.

'That settles it I would think,' I said. With any other NCO or officer I wouldn't have been so presumptuous, but Hobson required a nudge now and again.

He nodded, but was spared the exertion of exercising any independent thought or responsibility by the timely appearance of a lieutenant.

'Tear gas!' shouted the lieutenant. 'Get your men assembled, sergeant, and take them into the woods.'

'Yes, sir,' replied Hobson. We both started to don a smoke helmet.

There were few things I hated more than a smoke helmet. Gas was one of them, so I hastened to pull mine over my head. The helmet was a simple enough construction, a thick flannel hood with goggled eyes that typically fogged up and left you feeling like someone had wrapped your head prior to mummification. Every few months we'd been issued with new and improved variants, yet the latest style still resulted in my head being bathed in sweat within minutes, and wheezing for breath through the rubber mouthpiece clamped between my teeth, like any 90-year old asthmatic.

As we formed up, my eye caught sight of a marching column down on the road. Judging by their numbers it was company strength. They too had their PH helmets on and their tin ones on top of that, a ridiculous looking sight, which if it hadn't been so deadly serious would have been comical. The first column had barely passed when a second appeared, also heading towards the front.

I was very curious who they were but resisted the temptation to run down the lane to the road to read their insignia. The shells were landing at intervals and we needed to seek shelter.

Fortunately only a couple landed nearby. By then the battalion was milling around in the relative safety of the woods behind the main buildings. The shelling ended not long after, though it took forty minutes before the all-clear signal finally sounded. With relief I peeled off the helmet. No one was hit and the camp appeared to have escaped without serious damage, although the château was already so well ventilated I'm not sure a new hole in the walls would have caught my attention. To the east the bombardment crashed on, each thud, each explosion, following closely in sequence so that the sounds merged into one; a menacing deep rumble that echoed in the distance.

Dundas was rubbing furiously at one eye – the solution in which the helmets were treated had a tendency to run and burned the eyes terribly when you sweated. When he saw me looking at him, he grinned self-consciously.

'Did you see those troops moving through, Roy? There's something going on.'

'As a matter of fact I did see them,' he said. 'It was one of the CMR battalions. I couldn't see which.'

'Hmm… the Mounted Rifles…' I said pensively. It came to me in a flash. 'Oh, yes. Of course.'

Dundas frowned. 'Why "of course"?' When I didn't immediately respond he tried again. 'Mac?'

'Think about it. They're 3rd Division, aren't they?'

Dundas's face was twisted in puzzlement. It was common knowledge that the Mounted Rifle battalions were now permanently dismounted and formed one of the three brigades of the new 3rd Canadian Division. He also knew perfectly well I wasn't the sort to pose pointless rhetorical questions. It took him only a moment. When I heard his pent-up breath being expelled in a sudden rush I knew he'd made the sum for himself.

'Ah, yes, *of course,*' he said. Then: 'Jesus, something *is* happening.'

The army was not in the habit of briefing the other ranks on the latest dispositions and strategy, but even the new drafts saw that the bombardment was coming down square on our newly formed and fielded 3rd Division – knowing that from Hill 60 all the way north to Hooge they were the ones holding the line. And no general would send for reinforcements in the midst of a bombardment. Not unless there were other concerns – such as an imminent attack.

At 1 p.m., four-and-a-half hours after it began and timed to the very minute, the background thunder ceased. In a moment. An uneasy quiet settled over the Salient. The smoke and dust had long since dissipated in the château grounds, but I imagined things were very different four miles east.

'Now it's really beginning,' muttered Dundas. He spoke with the weary wisdom of a man who'd seen this many times before and knew precisely what followed the end of a long and harrowing bombard-ment. We all did. Yet none of the old hands among us, not even the officers – I cautiously broached the subject with a couple of the more talkative types – could add anything useful.

The afternoon was devoted to the customary diversions of cards and sleep, as it always was when we were in reserve. But a current coursed underneath this patina of rest and relaxation. I think I felt it more than most for neither sleep nor games of chance held the slightest attraction. Instead I read a few of the London papers. They were full of news about the great battle at Verdun, now entering its fourth month, and a French counter-attack at Fort Douamont which had been – reading between the lines – bloodily inconclusive. Predictably there was nothing in the newspaper about the "Big Push", neither in the lines, nor in between. I suspect the average German POW could have told me more than the *Daily Mail*. The rumoured offensive wouldn't be long off, though – some of our own artillery was already moving south into France. The railheads and roads behind the lines were teeming with Imperial regiments and artillery on the move. It was no secret why. Naturally I'd wondered several times if our turn would come. However events closer to hand were what concerned me most.

I paced the camp, thinking and chatting with those I encountered. That's how I bumped into one of the signallers, Corporal Weatherstone. In point of fact I ambushed him after seeing him exit a side door of the battered farmhouse they called Swan Château. That was where Colonel Rattray and his staff bivouacked. Cooks, clerks and signallers; those were the men who knew things.

At the last moment he saw me hurtling down upon him and began furiously shaking his head.

'No. Not now, MacPhail. I'm busy. If you want to know something ask the colonel.'

'Ah, be a sport, Gary. It's not going to kill you. I'll walk with you.'

A sound emerged that resembled a moan, and I took that to be agreement.

I broke into step beside him. 'So, what's happening?'

'Look, all I know is there are Germans reported all over Mount Sorrel and Observatory Ridge. They've run over the Mounted Rifles.'

I gulped. 'And Hill 60?' I asked. Hill 60 was immediately to the right of both Mount Sorrel and Observatory Ridge, the latter a spur of the main ridge. One of our battalions was holding the line at Hill 60 so it was a sure bet we'd be sent back if reinforcements were needed.

He shook his head. 'Nothing I know of. But it's chaos at the moment. Look, Mac, I have to go.' Without awaiting a reply he dashed off, leaving me abandoned to my thoughts, pondering my own unanswered questions and trying not to succumb to the gnawing fear of impending action.

A little after 4.40 p.m. I spotted Weatherstone again. He was hurrying in the direction of the farmhouse, a sheet of paper flapping in his hand. Given his haste the news was clearly urgent.

Fifteen minutes later a flush-faced Captain Fisher strode into our midst with three lieutenants of the company in tow. I'd been sitting around with some of the men and the NCOs, speculating what it all meant. We jumped to our feet.

'Assemble the men,' Fisher snapped.

'Sir?' a voice interposed.

'You heard me. The battalion is to man the GHQ Line. So let's get a move on. There's no time to waste.' He glanced around at the assembled faces, nodding slowly as he counted heads. Then in a tone of exasperation said, 'Where's Sergeant Hobson? Find him!'

With that the calm of the afternoon was swept away, replaced by a bedlam of activity, orders being shouted and men rushing to and fro.

A breathless Dundas caught up with me as I went in search of Hobson. 'What do you think, Mac? Have the Germans broken through?'

'It's quite possible,' I replied. 'If they have, the GHQ Line is the only thing keeping them from Ypres. It doesn't sound good, I'm afraid. But I have to find Harry.'

I found Hobson where he was often to be found: fully clothed, in his bunk, snoring.

'Harry,' I called out to him, as I walked over. But Harry didn't as much as move. His snoring was loud enough to drown out several batteries of *minenwerfers* so this was not exactly a wonder.

I reached out to shake his shoulder and at that moment he rolled over onto one side. As he did, my hand brushed up against the breast pocket of his tunic and I gasped. My heart was beating. Warily I looked down at him, wondering if I should take the chance. He was still fast asleep. Holding my breath I reached round to his pocket again. Cautiously I touched the small bulge with my fingertips. Then I squeezed it gently, trying to make out what it was.

'Hey, what the devil are doing you, MacPhail?' Hobson's eyes were open, blinking and focused on me. Quickly I retrieved my hand.

'Captain Fisher sent me,' I blustered. 'The battalion is moving out and there's no time to waste. The Germans are attacking.' I said it one breathless rush.

Hobson merely grunted. 'Why didn't you just say that, then?'

It was almost six by the time we were on the road, marching south towards our assigned positions near Bellegoed Farm, when an officer on a horse galloped past at speed. He drew to a halt at the head of the column, but was lost to my sight when he sprang off.

'Company, Halt!' bellowed the Company Sergeant Major. In an awkward accordion of shuffling feet the file obeyed. The men were looking around in confusion. Captain Fisher marched purposely forward.

A few minutes later came the shouted order, 'About face!' and we were marching again, this time north retracing our steps. Once past Swan Chateau we crossed over the Ypres-Comines Canal, where twenty soldiers stood guard at the bridge, and made a hasty passage of Shrapnel Corner at the quick march. At the crossroads, Captain Fisher led C Company south once more, along on the eastern bank of the canal until we reached Woodcote Farm.

It seemed a lot of marching, burdened down by rifles, overcoats and full packs, to arrive nowhere in particular. We were barely 1000 yards east of Swan Château and long miles from the front. The only explanation I could think of was that we were to guard this bank of the canal. That would mean the Germans were through our lines on the ridge at Mount Sorrel and converging on Ypres. For the second time in little more than a year the Salient was in danger of total collapse. And for the second time I somehow found myself in the midst of it.

The men, unburdened by such concerns, immediately took to the ditch, with the intention of bedding down for the night. It was the sensible thing to do – sleep when you can – and while I'm as fond of a good night's sleep as the next man (perhaps even fonder), my head has an irritating tendency to get in the way, especially when it was as preoccupied as it was at the moment. Off I went looking for an officer and answers, and found the former in the shape of our platoon commander, Lieutenant Powers.

As to the latter, Powers didn't know much. He stared at me curiously when I asked however. He was still unaccustomed to briefing lowly corporals – I really would have to fill in those commission papers sometime I reminded myself – although he seemed plenty eager to talk. He obliged me with what little he'd heard. 'I wish I knew more,' he concluded. 'Oh, and General Mercer and General Williams are missing.'

The bombshell he'd saved for last.

'Really?' I stuttered.

'Oh, they'll turn up, I expect. Communications are a bit of a mess.

If I were you, Corporal, I'd try to get some rest. It may be a long day tomorrow.' Powers yawned in emphasis.

Fritz was running amok over the 3rd Division and the Mounted Rifle Brigade, the commanders of both were missing, and Ypres lay only an hour's march to the west. Powers was right about one thing; it was going to be a long day. 'Yes, sir,' I said.

The lieutenant departed in the direction of the farmhouse and I took the short route to the ditch.

Eventually I must have dozed off. The next thing I knew I felt a boot prodding me in my side, gently at first, then with a pronounced kick to it. With a start I awoke, half expecting to see a Württemberger clothed in field grey and *Pickelhaube* holding a Mauser a foot from my head. It was as dark as the soles of my boots. I relaxed when I saw he was clad in olive green and wearing a tin hat. When I recognized who it was I closed my eyes again. I could still hardly believe it.

'Rise and shine, MacPhail,' growled platoon Sergeant Harry Hobson. 'It's one-thirty and we've got quite a march ahead of us.'

'Just a march?' I mumbled.

'No,' he said. 'They're sending us in.'

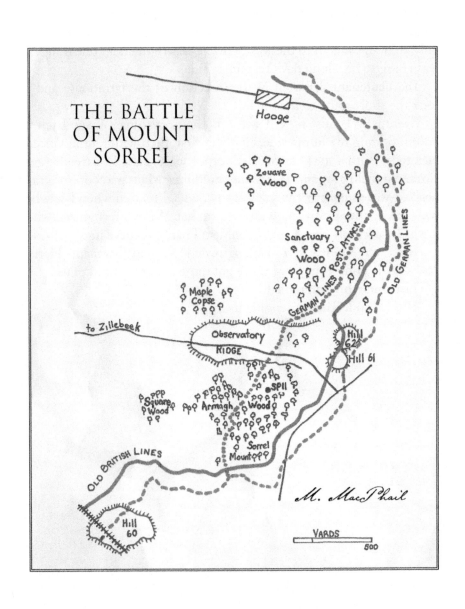

THE BATTLE
OF MOUNT
SORREL

Hooge

Zouave
Wood

Sanctuary
Wood

GERMAN LINES POST-ATTACK

OLD GERMAN LINES

Maple
Copse

to Zillebeek

Observatory
RIDGE

Hill
62

Hill 61

SP11

Square
Wood

Armagh Wood

Sorrel
Mount

OLD BRITISH LINES

M. MacPhail

Hill
60

YARDS
500

CHAPTER 33

3rd of June, 1916
Armagh Wood, Belgium

It is the endless waiting and that first minute of an attack that can break a man; when the enemy is yourself, and doubt and uncertainty festers and weighs heavy on the soul. This night there was no need for leaps of imagination to enlighten the mind about what lay ahead, and that made it worse. We encountered small parties of survivors from the Mounted Rifles as we marched, all of them wounded, many terribly, their heads downcast, struggling at every step.

The sight of them reminded me of someone. After I saw the three, standing in the ditch and gathering their strength, I looked closer. Then when I spotted the brass moose of the battalion emblem, I nudged at Dundas to cover for me and fell out. Against all regulation. But it was dark and rainy, and most including the officers and sergeants had their heads bowed forward.

At the sight of me appearing before them these three heads looked up.

'You fellows are 4th CMR, aren't you?'

One of them nodded.

'I'm looking for a fellow I know. Met him at Plugstreet. Forsdike? Corporal Frank Forsdike. Maybe you've seen him?'

The soldier who'd nodded, shook his head. He looked enquiringly

at the other two but they too shook their heads. 'You have to understand, the battalion is gone,' said the first.

'Gone?'

'Obliterated. There's no one left. The bombardment...' His voice
cracked. 'Well, it was like nothing you've ever seen. The few of us who
were left held them back as best we could...' He looked away, his eyes
glistening.

'You did well,' I said, embarrassed that I had no time and no better
words than these. The last rank of the battalion was almost past. 'I'm
sorry I have to leave. Duty calls.' I jerked a thumb to the east where
flashes lit the sky and white flares momentarily illuminated the ridge,
while the guns bellowed. 'Good luck, fellows.'

'Good luck to you, Corporal,' said the soldier. A long pause. 'You'll
need it.'

We arrived at the Leicester Square dug-outs, less than a mile to
the northwest of the flat crest known as Mount Sorrel, expecting to
move forward immediately. The counter-attack was to be at dawn. The
situation was not as disastrous as I first thought, but I understood the
need for haste. There was still hope if we moved quickly. The Germans
had seized Mount Sorrel and the entire ridge northwards, almost
as far as Hooge. But whether through hesitation or because of the
stubborn and unexpected resistance they'd met – or a combination
of both – they hadn't advanced further than the woods that lined the
ridge's western slopes. All was not yet lost.

Colonel Rattray arrived shortly after we did. For a brief while it
appeared as if it was "on". But then it was "off". There was a lot of
bustling around. I saw the colonel conferring with the company OC
Major Stewart and generally looking like he'd singlehandedly man-
handled a field gun into position. That was clearly not the case; the
uncertainty about a bombardment was one of the things vexing him.
Nor, aside from three machine guns and some Stokes mortars, was
there any sign of the 7th Battalion who were to lead the counter-attack.

We were told to dig in behind X Trench. The trench, for all its
significance as the new front line facing the mustering regiments of
Württembergers, was little more than a furrow in the ground. Maple
Copse was off to the left, Square Wood to the right, and Sanctuary

Wood ahead. The digging proved to be no futile exercise as shells began to fall almost as soon as we began.

'Dig like your lives depend on it,' I advised the three soldiers. I barely reached the next hole when I heard the crash in my wake and felt the concussion. In the darkness there was nothing to see. A few minutes later the report came that a shell had wiped them out. They were not the only ones that first half hour. Nor were the Germans content to hold us at bay with shells alone.

Despite the darkness the gas was easily visible, a dense pale mist hung virtually unmoving over the fields, the very ones we would soon have to cross, the black silhouette of trees and Observatory Ridge jutting out behind. There was the thump of more shells with more gas. Reluctantly we pulled the flannel masks down over our heads and sank our spades into the clayey ground with renewed urgency.

It was a reprieve when several hours later I was summoned by Captain Fisher to an NCO conference in the comparative safety of the Leicester Square dug-outs. There were roughly a dozen of us plus a couple of lieutenants, one of whom was Powers, and we clustered around the captain. He was a very tall, imposing-looking man who I had no difficulty picturing as the broker he'd once been. We were an odd crew he'd summoned, helmets askew, faces smeared and sweaty, most still wearing masks but rolled up like one might do with a bala- clava in order to speak. Fisher however was the only one speaking.

'C Company is to follow 7th Battalion and consolidate the positions on the ridge,' he began. 'They're to recapture the trenches on Mount Sorrel from 47 through 52. Lieutenant Powers and Sergeant Hobson, you'll be in the van with me. We'll form up in Square Wood.'

I stole a glance at Hobson. He looked like he'd seen a ghost, so white was his face. He was fidgeting and shifting nervously from foot to foot. Fisher was looking none too certain, either, though he put on a valiant show.

Hobson appeared at my side breathing heavily, as I headed back to the platoon. I would have preferred Dundas for company but Hobson beat him to it. 'Mac, I'm not sure I can do this,' he said. There was a pleading tone to his voice. In his eyes was what I felt in my gut, a sensation for which words are hopelessly inadequate.

Two days earlier I might have consoled him. I might have grabbed his arm and looked him sternly in the eye and told him he'd do fine and that he had nothing to worry about. I'd have told him to think of his men, and perhaps even his parents, who would be proud. Instead I said coldly, 'I'm sorry, Sergeant. You'll have to do your best. Orders are orders.' And I quickened my pace, leaving him bedraggled and alone in my tracks. Another dash of rain came driving down. Our artillery started to bark.

A grey and stormy dawn was already long upon us, but of the six green rockets that were to signal the attack I saw none. Neither did Major Stewart who'd come to observe. I heard him curse as he turned and left posthaste to the rear. It was some time – past 7.30 a.m. and well past dawn – before he returned. When he did he signalled that the attack should begin forthwith.

Ominously the major took a machine gun bullet almost immediately after climbing up onto the parapet to cheer us on our way.

The 7ᵗʰ Battalion's four companies led. The right fork consisting of A and C companies headed in a straight line towards the slopes, through the woodland, and up to the modest summit of Mount Sorrel. The left fork under Captain Holmes made for Armagh Wood in the lee of the ridge. We were to follow Holmes and his party. I had anticipated this would be at some distance. However Captain Fisher was anxious and we piled out virtually in the footsteps of the 7ᵗʰ. Through some unforeseen and almost divine roll of the dice we trod unknowingly through the eye of the hurricane. Scant minutes later the German barrage descended.

Interspersed with the loud blasts was the tell-tale *rat-tat-tat* of machine guns. Long bursts zipped over the open ground. Dust and debris flew. Men fell. A mere 500 yards off to our right were the German positions on Hill 60, with an unimpeded view downslope to the fields where I and a thousand others were rushing, closing with the enemy ahead in positions we knew not where. Bursts of fire swept the running lines from in front and from the right. Some succumbed, the others ran on.

Captain Holmes and his two companies were racing left to the shelter of Armagh Wood, thankfully a sprint of only 50 yards, the gas having dissipated with the dawn winds and the rain. As the machine-gun fire intensified Captain Fisher and our lead platoon broke in to a run, and in desperate pursuit I followed, my heart thumping, my fear forgotten for the excitement.

'Run,' I shouted to those around me. Not that encouragement was needed.

Armagh Wood was unlike any wood I had ever seen. Ugly pointed stumps, shorn of every branch and even bark, protruded from the earth at ungainly angles. Only days before, from Hill 60, I had viewed the verdant greenery from afar, now vanished without a trace. The ground underneath was uneven and discoloured, pocked by shell holes invisible to the eye for the tangle of underbrush and fallen branches. Images of a forest in the Rockies ravaged by fire came to mind, though this was no fire that had raged. Modern artillery from the Krupp factories, massed and concentrated, and put to use with the consummate skill of our enemy had reduced a forest to kindling in less than five hours. Only then did I think of the young soldiers from the 4th CMR; they and the other survivors had held the line in this unholy wasteland against all odds. It was a miracle the Germans were not further.

There was a harsh zipping noise. The machine-gun fire came from ahead. Captain Holmes' companies were encountering resistance.

300 yards in on our right, just beyond the treeline, was Armagh House. Captain Fisher had said it was quite likely in German hands. We paid it no attention; the objective was further and we had yet to encounter the enemy. We moved eastwards through the tangles of underbrush and up the slope, now more pronounced, towards our old line on the crest of the ridge. Without those crucial heights Ypres would – must? – surely fall.

The rattle of machine guns sounded close by.

'Wire!' someone shouted. I saw it stretched across our path 100 yards away. Lines of it, new, coiled, glistening; fastened to the earth by the formed iron stakes designed with no other purpose than to anchor the barbs in rows so as to allow no man to pass. Behind the wire was the outline of an enemy trench where according to the map none existed, which meant they had been dug recently and in haste. As our battalions marched forward last night in the rain and confusion, the Germans had dug trenches and lain wire. As only Germans can.

And now manned by machine guns it was going to be a devil's work to roust them. That much I could see.

The men of the 7th Battalion were spread out and firing. Some of them had made it through the wire and were attempting to close with the Boche in the trench. But that it was not easy was testified to by the bodies that lay strewn about.

'Come on, boys,' yelled Captain Fisher in the lead, whereupon he broke into a run, waving his revolver high in the air to rally those following. I don't know why he did it; the wire was uncut and the air whined from the bullets; a charge was pointless and he should have known it – but for his fear and the stupid pointless fear that others might see it.

I saw Hobson take up the charge, screaming wildly like the others, afflicted by the same madness as Fisher. Then after a few paces he suddenly dove for the ground. The men on his heels rushed past.

Fisher went down. The men behind him went down. Lieutenant Powers went down. The only thing I could hear was *TUF-TUF-TUF*.

Like that the rush came to an inglorious end. Captain Holmes of the 7th was shouting at the remnants of C Company to take cover.

Dundas appeared at my side. 'Do you think many made it?'

Glumly I shook my head. Something in Dundas's voice made me take a closer look. His face was drawn and serious, but he was in command of himself, clearly thinking about what should be done next. It was strange how people weren't always as you expected; Roy, quiet and unassuming in the mess, even timid – hardly anyone's idea of a soldier; Harry brash and full of bravado, yet it was Harry who'd gone bugs from the fear while Roy was readying himself to get on with whatever had to be done.

'Let's go, Mac.'

I stared at Hobson, who was obviously unscathed, now pulling himself to his feet. He saw me and looked away.

'Mac, let's go,' urged Dundas, more loudly. 'We have to find a way around this wire.'

'Alright.'

'Let's try their left,' he said. 'We may find an opening. See if you can find an officer.'

There wasn't a single one from our company to be seen. I'd think they'd all been hit. The only one I could spot at all was Captain Holmes, who was attempting to consolidate what remained of his two companies in a ditch 40 yards from the German trench. Distractedly he heard me out and waved me promptly on my way with a 'good thinking' and 'good luck'.

In the meantime Dundas had rounded up some men from 10 and 12 platoons who'd survived the charge, together with a few from the 7th Battalion. Roughly twenty strong our motley band skirted along the trench heading north. There was no need to remind anyone to keep low and out of sight. It was one of the men who spotted the hole.

'Corporal!' he hissed. 'Look.'

There was no mistaking it. Near a couple of particularly large tree stumps was a gap several feet wide in the line of wire entanglements. Someone hadn't completed his work. Perhaps they'd had trouble because of the trees and the fallen foliage, or they may have intentionally left a hole to allow their own patrols to pass. It certainly wasn't the artillery's doing; they'd only warned the Germans we were coming. Regardless, the gap was precisely what we needed most.

Dundas led the way. We stepped through the gap and around the trees, and rushed the trench behind in a fearsome crackling of branches. It took no more than a minute at most. There was a hurried shot fired in our direction but only the one; we surprised them. The handful of defenders were bayonetted in short order as we swept over.

When it was done I approached Dundas. 'By my reckoning trench 52 is straight up the slope,' I said.

'What are we waiting for, then?' He was raring to go.

Almost immediately, however, we came upon the fortified post marked as S.P. 11 on the maps. A day ago it had belonged to the 4th CMR, one of the strong points behind the front line. Today it was in German hands; rebuilt and bristling with guns. And I had completely forgotten about it. Not that I'd had more than a couple of minutes with a map before the assault. But I should have known, and known that Kaiser Bill's boys would have it manned to the brim.

Dundas was in the lead once again. I don't think we'd gone twenty yards. Off to our left was a clearing of furrowed earth, and even in the wood itself the ground was upturned and uneven. The scattered white stumps on the wood's fringes offered precious little shelter to a man walking upright – not in broad daylight.

TUF-TUF-TUF.

Damn it. The realization hit me like a hammer in the chest. But then it was too late. Loud and brutally insistent the machine-gun rattle came out of nowhere. Only it wasn't nowhere. I knew that as I dived for cover. It emanated from the barricaded strong point 80 yards away. Two machine guns, maybe more, and rifles as well. The air zinged from the bullets.

The whole row of men from Dundas back to number eleven went down like bowling pins. Every last one of them. If we hadn't been further back, and well-spaced – that was one thing I *had* made certain of – none of us would have survived.

To either side the men were valiantly firing, in fear and in anger and because an ingrained sense of duty directed their actions, and for a short spell I joined in. Until I concluded it was hopeless. We were too few and too far away. There was no cover to mount an assault on a barricaded dug-out filled with defenders aplenty and two machine guns or more.

'We have to pull back,' I yelled. 'But first the wounded. Cover me.'

'Thank God,' I murmured, when I reached Dundas on my belly and saw that he was still alive. Six of the others were as well. It took some time before we were able to collect them all and stumble our way through the German lines back to Captain Holmes. In the process we lost another man.

A couple of stretcher bearers had come up and they took the worst cases, a process of elimination whereby the others automatically became walking wounded, consigned to finding their own way to a dressing station.

Dundas was clamping his side – it obviously pained him – his face streaked with long fingers of blood where he'd put a hand to it earlier. One of the stretcher bearers had bandaged him provisionally and with his tunic off I could see where he'd been hit. He had his other arm outstretched, urging on the last man being gingerly brought forward by two of his buddies. Then the little group would depart.

'I'm really sorry it came to this, Roy,' I said. 'I should have remembered about that position.'

'Don't be silly, Mac. I know you think you're the only one looking out for us. But we're all big boys and we look out for each other, and ourselves. It's my own damned fault.'

'Take care,' I said softly, a lump in my throat. 'With any luck you'll be in a starched white bed with a pretty nurse attending to you in a day or two. I almost envy you.'

He grunted and the flicker of a smile passed over his face. 'We'll see,' he said. 'But don't think for a minute I'm going to leave the war in your hands, Mac. There's too much at stake.'

I watched them leave, feeling an upwelling of relief that he'd be okay, but bitterly conscious that I was losing my only real friend.

When Captain Holmes returned from battalion headquarters later that afternoon he relayed the news that Colonel Rattray had ordered us back. Back almost to where we'd begun at 7.37 a.m., many hours and countless men before. The heavies were preparing to fire and they wanted us out of the way.

'Aren't they a touch on the late side, sir?' I asked. 'They might have been helpful if they'd fired before we went in.'

An acerbic expression appeared on his face but Holmes said nothing.

The counter-attack had been left far too long. It had been only hours, eighteen at most, but it was plenty long enough for the Germans to entrench, and not nearly long enough for us to plan for the fact they'd done so. To me it seemed simple. Either you hit back while the fog of battle hung thick, or you waited until your little lead soldiers were all lined up to do it properly. We'd done neither. And we'd paid the price.

Those were lessons we hadn't yet learned from the French. Our allies had mastered the art of the counter-attack much better. Dash and gallantry were in ample supply this day, but once more they had proven themselves no match for dug-in rifles and machine guns, ensconced behind wire and protected by artillery.

The 7th Battalion was shattered. Two-thirds of my company were casualties, including most of the officers and senior NCOs. Dundas was wounded. Captain Fisher was dead. And Mount Sorrel was lost.

Worst of all I was quite certain High Command would not let

things rest. This would not be the end of the matter, I worried. Not by a long stretch.

CHAPTER 34

4th and 5th of June, 1916
Dickebusch Huts, 4 miles southwest of Ypres, Belgium

I cannot begin to describe the joy I felt when finally we arrived. It had been a three-hour hike in the dead of night. While the Dickebusch camp of little huts in a sea of half-dried muck was not especially inviting to the eye, to mine – weary beyond belief – it was a godsend. It was 6 a.m., past dawn on the 4th, and I'd been on my feet for longer than an entire day. Precisely 36 hours had passed since the battalion departed Swan Château on our bold and costly adventure in the Salient. They let us sleep that first day in camp, away from the sudden, angry storms of German shells that swept down without warning, although here too their big guns whistled one over at intervals. When we were finished sleeping we slept some more. The next day the rest and relaxation ended. In my case at 8 a.m.

'MacPhail!'

At the sound of his voice I straightened up, hastily shedding my habitual morning slouch. The Regimental Sergeant-Major had once commented upon it in less than favourable terms.

'Yes, Sergeant-Major?'

'You're to report immediately to Colonel Rattray. He's expecting you in his hut.'

I returned his look with one normally reserved for momentous and daunting events in one's life such as being invited to meet the King, and said, 'Right away, Sergeant-Major.' Any other answer was unacceptable, even foolhardy.

I had expected I might be called to account for the debacle in Armagh Wood. I hadn't anticipated that the colonel himself would be involved. Therefore I wasted no time. In common with other unpleasant events like swallowing a spoonful of cod liver oil, or going over the top, it was best not to think overly much and get it over with as soon as possible. Nevertheless, it was curious the colonel wished to receive me in his personal hut. One advantage was that he'd probably be alone, sparing me the ignominy of being dressed down in front of half the staff; on the other hand that might well make it worse as there was no reason for him to watch his words. With trepidation I knocked.

'Come in, MacPhail,' said the colonel. He looked weary. He was standing, his tunic over the back of a chair and his cap on the table. Deep lines marked his face, in addition to a dab of shaving cream – he'd clearly just finished.

'Sir?'

He drew out the chair and sat down. 'Yes, thank you for coming. I've read your report and that of Corporal Dundas,' he said slowly. Then he preoccupied himself with refilling his cup from a small pot on the table. He didn't offer me any, but that was no surprise. I stood at attention and concentrated on keeping my breathing steady.

Finally the colonel spoke again. 'It was terrible luck that you ran into that strong point when you did. Though I dare say it wouldn't have changed much even if you hadn't. You and Dundas are to be commended on your initiative. You probably heard that Lieutenant Elliot's party on the right made it all the way to the ridge, but they were beaten back in the end by the machine-gun fire.'

The interview was taking a surprising turn. 'And the rest of the attack, sir?' I asked, anxious it not suddenly veer in other directions.

Rattray shook his head. He sipped at his tea before responding. 'No. None of the battalions made their objectives. The positive thing is that we fired a shot across the enemy's bows at an important moment. Pushed them back in a few spots, too. The Boche are in an unenviable position.' Before I could ask what on earth he meant by that – to me the Germans held all the cards – he continued. 'However, that's not why I wanted to see you.'

'No, sir?' I said, sensing that the wind had shifted.

'No. Actually it concerns your missing stripe.' I frowned. But the colonel was too preoccupied with his own discourse to notice or to comment. 'It appears that the paperwork concerning your "reversion" to corporal is missing,' he added. 'I'm told it may have been lost in that flooding we had at Ploegsteert.'

To this I smiled. It was truly astonishing how many (inconvenient) pieces of papers had been washed away when the Douve overflowed its banks last November. Whole libraries full.

The colonel's eyes fixed me in a stare, but a good-natured one.

'Does any of this this mean anything to you?' he asked.

'I can't say that it does, sir... unless...'

The colonel's mouth curled into a smile. 'Yes, I can see it might now. For the life of me I can't recall how you lost your stripe. As the army records plainly indicate your rank is sergeant, I feel I should apologize. I've decided it would be best if you had a replacement sewn on as quickly as possible. And obviously you'll be up for any back pay you've missed.'

'Sir?' I managed to stutter.

'See the quartermaster about a replacement. Under the circumstances I think it's quite fortunate we can rectify this. C Company will need to be rebuilt and I'm counting on your help, MacPhail.'

'Of course, sir. Thank you, sir.'

'No need to thank me,' he said.

I didn't say anything. I just stood there with a goofy smile on my face, like a half-wit who'd been told dinner was to henceforth consist of chocolate cake.

'That will be all, Sergeant,' said the colonel.

6th of June, 1916
Hill 60, Belgium

Ultimately the sweet afterglow of the moment disappeared almost as soon as the quartermaster's assistant had affixed a new chevron. A flood of tasks reared its head. And from then on my head was fuller than ever. We moved to D Camp that afternoon and to the Hill 60 trenches the next. All the while I was juggling problems of missing kit, missing men and dealing with an influx of reinforcements who while most welcome, were clearly untrained and of a very soft condition. There were a thousand things to do; the trenches we'd assumed were in many places completely obliterated by shellfire and required urgent work.

Early one morning I came across Hobson sprawled alone in a dug-out to the rear, his tunic thrown over a chair, snoring heavily.

I debated the matter for the better part of a second.

I stole over to the chair and addressed my attentions to his tunic. All the pockets were buttoned. I poked around at a few letters, a pay book and other papers, rolled my eyes when I discovered his well-padded billfold, and nearly choked when my fingertips touched something else.

Hobson groaned and began to twitch uneasily. I stood there not daring to breathe. The snoring began again. I snatched out the soft small bag and stuffed it in a trouser pocket. Then I made my escape, as quietly as I could. Behind me I heard coughing.

It wasn't until later, in a support trench, that I tentatively I pulled out the purple velvet sack. Untying the draw cord I prised it open with my fingers and upended it. The contents spilled out on to one hand. They lay there in a small heap, barely enough to fill the cup of my palm, glittering. Diamonds.

'Harry, you bugger,' I murmured to myself, then – louder – 'you lying bugger.'

Several feet away a soldier shifted his attention from a mess tin to me and glanced curiously. Hastily I poured the little stones into the bag and stuffed the bag deep into a breast pocket, buttoning it tightly.

With an unwavering gaze Harry had met mine and swore he had

nothing to do with the Doll Block. The worst of it was I'd believed him. I think it was all too easy to suspect Harry before I really knew him – apart from his reputation – and equally easy to dismiss my suspicions when I thought I did. Like any accomplished and inveterate liar he'd assuaged my doubts with half-truths and convinced me by selling me the story I wanted to hear. That much of what he'd said rang true made me swallow the rest like it was sugar coated. Dundas had been a better judge of character than me. I felt like kicking myself.

I took a bite of cold, fried bully beef. Normally I'm rather fond of the stuff. Now it might as well have been sawdust for all I tasted.

There was a nasty corollary to this I realized, the figurative mine under the parapet – an expression that sprang to mind because the Germans blew four of them under our positions at Hooge that afternoon. If Harry had fibbed about the diamond heist, what else had he fibbed about? There was one thing that mattered above all else: Lieutenant Drinkwater and his mysterious death.

But that was what puzzled me. Harry's story about Drinkwater was what had won me over. The lieutenant weighed under by debts and suddenly relieved of them. Tasting the good life on leave and determined to continue it. Not only was it plausible, I'd seen most of it with my own two eyes. Harry had admitted he'd been the lieutenant's benevolent financier. There was little imagination necessary – not anymore – to figure out where the funds came from. As to his death it still seemed too fantastic to think Harry had somehow contrived to bring that about. There'd been barely a scratch on Drinkwater.

I was perplexed.

'Well, Mac, even Greek gods fall flat on their faces from time to time,' Dundas would drolly say when he heard the latest, referring to me. Assuming I ever saw Dundas again.

Then with a clatter I dropped my half-full mess tin, something that had never happened in all my time on the Western Front. Not even in the midst of a bombardment. I repeated Dundas's words in my head – slowly – word for word.

'That's it, Roy,' I murmured, as the revelation hit. 'By golly, that's it!'

The soldier a few feet away was hurriedly packing his mess tin, eyeing me warily out of the corner of one eye while trying to make as if he wasn't, preparing to leave. No soldier was keen on spending time with the clean crazy if he didn't have to – it was hard enough staying sane at the front.

'Maybe he hit his head on a fence post, or a stone, and fell on his face in that ditch,' Hobson had said. 'Fell on his face', '...that ditch'. The only soul to whom I'd told those details was Dundas. Private Atwood knew it too, but he was shipped off immediately afterwards to a casualty station. There were too many coincidences, the motive too strong. That Harry was a thief I could reconcile myself with, but a murderer? Worse he'd murdered an officer and a comrade in arms. Whatever I thought of Drinkwater he didn't deserve that.

10th of June, 1916

Days later Hobson was still stalking around, his face a thundercloud of displeasure.

What to do, whether to report the facts I knew and those I suspected to the proper authorities, those were questions for which I had no answers. So I resolved to do nothing... not yet at least.

Furthermore, there were plenty of things to occupy myself. There's seldom a shortage of worries or work in the front line, and these past days had been tougher than many.

There was a prevailing wind from the southwest, from the direction of the Channel. As in days previous it brought with it frequent showers and low-hanging grey cloud. It didn't bring the bombardments; we had the Württembergers to thank for those. All the guns assembled ahead of their attack on the ridge were still here, perhaps for the final push to take Ypres. The terrifying whoosh and whistle of the approaching shells came in sudden violent bursts. The detonations that followed laying waste to the trenches and to anyone in them, testing the fortitude of even the veterans who knew very well what it was to be tested.

The Germans had taken the last high ground on the ridge at Hooge, 500 yards north of Sanctuary Wood. For seven long hours their guns pummeled the lines without pause. Then they detonated the mines underneath our front-line trenches. An entire company of the 28th Battalion disappeared. In the end a breakthrough was prevented but the Hooge knoll was theirs, and with it the entire ridge. Now the city beckoned.

We were at work again, shovelling away the earth and debris from another section of the line that had collapsed.

The distant thuds had presaged the latest bombardment. Barely time to scurry for shelter in a deeper section with a proper parapet, hoping it would be spared a direct hit. Then the deafening bang, a shower of earth twenty feet into the air, and the sensation of someone shaking you violently.

Our own artillery was quick to reciprocate – there seemed to be many more guns available – heavier ones, too. If the Germans wanted Ypres, they weren't going to get it without a fight, was the message. The air overhead filled with arching shells and shifting clouds of smoke. Eventually it ended.

To me fell the task of sorting out the remains. One of the men of the company was dead, three were wounded and the trenches were once more a mess. We continued our digging and a few hours later I heard we were to be relieved.

Under the waning light of a June evening we began the dangerous balancing act. A 7th Battalion company filed into position and we filed out. Reliefs were always tricky with the enemy so close. I was pleased when it was concluded without incident and to the satisfaction of myself and my superiors.

'Sergeant MacPhail?'

Suspiciously I stared at the young soldier. He'd somehow found me amongst the throng on Knoll Road. I was assembling with the rest of the company before marching towards Zillebeke and on to our billets at the Dominion Lines. I grunted in response.

'You're requested to report at the Railway dug-outs, Sergeant.'

As they were on the way this was not inconvenient. Curious but not inconvenient.

What was considerably more curious was that when I reached the dug-outs, a few other men fell out as well. Two were sergeants, the rest corporals. One was Hobson. We reported and were sent off to a hut. To a man we'd been in the failed counter-attack. We were what was left of the old C Company.

Lieutenant-Colonel Rattray appeared shortly after our arrival.

'Thank you for coming,' he said. Rattray in my experience was always polite. Not that politeness is required when a commanding officer makes a request, but I appreciated it. 'What I'm about to tell you is under the strictest confidence. I trust I can rely upon each of you?'

There were nods and murmurs of assent.

'In little more than two days, early on the 13th, the Canadian Corps will make an assault on the ridge from Hill 62 to Mount Sorrel with an objective of retaking our old lines.'

A loud buzz of approval swept over the group. 'Give them some of their own back,' muttered someone darkly. For me it had been a toss-up who would attack first, us or the Germans. I'd put my money on the Germans; it appeared I was wrong. From the determined faces surrounding me I could see they were glad at this turn of events. Ypres and the entire Salient were at stake, plus doubtless other matters of strategic import at which I could only guess. But the fight was much more important than that. It was personal.

The Württembergers had killed and wounded us by the thousands. We'd all lost friends. They'd literally blown us out of the line. Unfairly or not they'd made us a laughing stock in the eyes of the Imperials some of whom, in the rear, were openly mocking, questioning whether we had what it took. No one was content to let it rest until we'd had our revenge. I hadn't realized the feelings ran so deep.

Lieutenant-Colonel Rattray cleared his throat and the whisperings died down. 'The 10th will be in reserve and won't be involved in the attack. However General Lipsett has asked whether we could provide guides. He's sending the 3rd Battalion into Armagh Wood and he thinks it would be helpful if there were men who knew the ground. I agree with him.' The colonel paused and briefly glanced at each of us in turn. 'This is purely voluntary, gentlemen. But are there any volunteers?'

Silence fell.

I glanced over at Hobson who was carefully studying his toes. A wave of anger passed through me.

'I'll go, sir,' said a voice.

To my surprise I recognized it as mine.

CHAPTER 35

13th of June, 1916
Armagh Wood and Mount Sorrel, Belgium

Anxiously I checked my pocket watch. It was a cheap thing I'd found second hand in Poperinghe, but synchronized at seven this very evening. It read 44 minutes past midnight. In a minute it would begin.

The rain drove down in unrelenting torrents. Water splashing off the helmets and the corrugated roofs of the trench dug-outs, off anything hard and unyielding and even things that weren't, like our shoulders. Most of the company, among whom I now included myself – rather appropriately I was assigned to C Company – were soaked to the skin in the first few minutes of the deluge. Underneath the duckboards the trench floor was already a bubbling porridge and rising fast.

'Damn, it's cold,' muttered the man beside me, shivering. Even the warm glow from a double tot of rum had dissipated under the cold lashings of rain and wind. The platoon lieutenant had given me the honours and I'd poured generously. Rum wasn't particularly conducive to fine marksmanship, however, in my experience, fine marksmanship was seldom a major concern – not like willing yourself over a bullet-swept parapet.

'Won't be long now,' I assured him, at which moment the sky lit up and with a roar that could have awakened the dead, the bombardment commenced.

'Every field gun and howitzer in the Corps will be in action,' Captain MacNamara, the company adjutant, had explained. To left and right, guns big and small had been begged, borrowed and offered freely by the Imperial brigades. Even the Belgians had lent field guns for the purpose. According to the captain there were more than 200 pieces, an astonishing number for a frontage of only 2000 yards.

Pedersen, the man beside me, was grinning broadly. 'Finally a taste of their own medicine,' he said exuberantly, when he caught me observing him. I wiped the water from my face and grinned back. We'd been at the receiving end of the German guns so many times in recent weeks I'd lost count, so there was a morbid satisfaction in viewing volley after volley of high explosive and shrapnel break over their lines. The flashes lit up the ridge behind. These past days our artillery had punished them mercilessly. Barely an hour had gone by without another shoot and, every so often – the last one was only three hours ago – came a hurricane bombardment of terrific intensity, advertising an attack that never came. The Württembergers would be so antsy they'd barely notice when we actually did come. That was the hope.

I moved over to Hobson. After the others had all volunteered he'd had no other choice. I could see he was not pleased where he presently found himself.

He glanced at me dolefully, his face ashen.

'I hope you're not going to hide out under a rock this time, Hobson,' I said.

Startled he looked at me.

I stared at him, contempt flashing in my eyes. 'You were man enough to deal with Drinkwater. Maybe you'll be man enough to kill some Fritzs for a change.'

His eyes widened. 'I told you, it wasn't like that,' he mumbled.

I shook my head. 'Don't even begin, Hobson. I know all about it. Just wait till your buddies hear.'

CRUMP! The parapet fifty feet away disappeared in a geyser of dirt and the ground shook. The shell was short, but not by much. We scrambled away. I went right. Hobson went left.

Fritz was not reconciled to taking his punishment lying down. Somewhat belatedly the waiting lines of men crouched low, to hug the front wall of the trench. Barring a direct hit that was the safest place.

I sank down with them. A moment later I heard the unmistakeable *whirr* as a hundred pieces of steel shrapnel flew past in a burst, burying themselves in the parados opposite and releasing clods of dirt and splinters of wood. Any earlier and the shell would have taken me and half the platoon with it.

After the initial excitement things settled down and we squatted uncomfortably, resigned to the rain and the shells, awaiting the signal.

Forty-five minutes later it came. At 1.30 a.m. Through the gusts of another squall the whistles blew shrilly. By then we were prepared, already on our feet, holding our rifles up and our fears down where they could do no harm, ready to follow Captain MacNamara forward. As MacNamara had his whistle going two feet from my head, I was actually relieved when his breath gave out and we could vault over the parapet and in to a frenzied charge.

The platoon and the company exited the trench on the very edge of Armagh Wood. We pushed forward rapidly, anxious to get ahead of the German barrage, which showed no signs of diminishing. In a bombardment there is little point in trying to predict where the next shell will fall; you spread out and you move as fast as you can.

Once into the wood, the captain turned to me with a similar message. 'MacPhail, you're in the lead. Whatever you do, keep moving forward.' Without awaiting a reply he left to the rear; to spur on the rest, I presumed. Our pace had slowed markedly; in the thick underbrush each footstep required thought and effort.

I'd last seen Armagh Wood by daylight and that was how I remembered it. It was not how I saw it now and I worried that I would lead the company astray.

Ten more days of intense shelling had reduced the forest to a true ghost wood. The landmarks of large trees were little more than spindly skeletons. Against a gloomy and rain-streaked night sky, lit by the burst of a flare falling somewhere and the orange flashes of the shells exploding, you could make out the form of the trees when you looked skywards. But that was inadvisable, for at eye level the visibility was wretched and I found it took all my concentration simply to find a path. Behind me and to both sides there was the sound of cussing and branches being snapped – a herd of elephants on the forage, with me in the lead. That wouldn't have concerned me in the slightest were it not that the Württemberg Corps with its sighted machine guns were dug in ahead.

Through some combination of an in-bred homing beacon and sheer perseverance, Captain MacNamara quickly found his way back to the head of the company. I accosted him immediately.

'Sir, I'm afraid we're going to get all muddled up like this,' I said, as he stood there puffing.

The captain's helmet was impossibly large on his smallish head. His ears were close cropped and he had barely a chin to speak of, yet his eyes exhibited a flashing boldness the rest of him lacked.

'With all the underbrush it's impossible to make any speed, sir,' I continued, 'Let alone keep abreast. The Germans can hear us at a thousand paces, the noise we're making.'

'What do you suggest, Sergeant?'

'Everybody in file. We can spread out when we need to.'

'You realize what a straight shot with a machine gun would do?'

I'd thought about this so I had a ready answer. 'Of course, sir. But the path is hardly a straight one. This way we may have a chance at surprise and less chance of blundering into them. As far as I can recollect we've a ways to go before we hit their lines. Besides, we'll be much faster.'

A shell tumbled down through the trees and went off in a flash of light and sound. That apparently decided it for the captain. 'Alright, section in file, it is,' he said. 'You're the guide, MacPhail, so guide on.'

I hadn't exaggerated the difficulty. In places the underbrush and the piles of fallen branches were waist high and it was impossible to expect a platoon of 50 men, let alone the entire company, to move through that tangle on a wide front. We needed to take some risks. If we could get ahead of the German barrage that would be one worry less. I stepped up the pace.

The captain had a compass out, which was sensible, even if reading a compass in the dark and the rain while walking quickly through a forest was a skill I hadn't yet acquired. Without a compass, I paid close attention to the surroundings and even the sounds. I was searching for small hints that might confirm I'd chosen the correct direction. The captain, I think, thought I knew the ground like an Indian trapper.

Fearing his good opinion of me I hadn't the inclination to inform him otherwise.

'I believe we've made it out of the barrage, sir,' I said over my shoulder. Barely ten minutes had passed since we exited the trench.

Behind me the captain grunted.

Our immediate objective was S.P. 11, the 4th Mounted Rifles' old strong point, the very spot where we'd been swept away earlier by the German machine gunners. It was critical that it be taken as soon as possible. After listening to my description, the battalion commander, Lieutenant-Colonel Allan, had gone so far as to call it the crux of the assault. We were on the far left of the 3rd Battalion. To the battalion's immediate left was the centre battalion, the 16th. If S.P. 11 held out there would be a 100-yard gap between the two and the flank of the all-important central thrust would be dangerously exposed. The night's attack might very well fail in that event.

'That must be Observatory Ridge,' said MacNamara, coming alongside. He pointed left.

Another shell detonated in a flash of orange. In the flash I saw it, a momentary picture forming in my mind. It was Observatory Ridge. But the flash had revealed something else. We were precisely where I'd hoped we'd be. As important, the Germans hadn't extended their new trench this far north.

'Yes, sir,' I replied. 'That would be it alright. This is where we should split the company, sir. The clearing is off our left. As I told you, the enemy have a clean shot from the fort but it's a very narrow one. If we cross the clearing at this point I don't think they'll see us.'

Fortunately I'd been able to sketch it for him in advance. The clearing extended towards us from the east, a 100-yard wide tree-less cutting, the spur of Observatory Ridge paralleling it scant yards to the north. Near the far, eastern end of the clearing, in the direction of the main ridgeline and our former trenches, the trees on one side made a small bulge southwards. As it happened this outgrowth was 30 yards in front of the strong point. It was those trees, or what was left of them, that limited the view of a Württemberger peering over his sights in our direction. Which was undoubtedly all rather irritating if you were a Württemberger, but then the strong point hadn't been intended for Württembergers.

Captain MacNamara nodded. He called a halt and went back to confer with Major Mason. I didn't need to explain that if I was wrong, a flare or a shell would dangerously illuminate the fifty-man platoon in the open. When he returned the decision had been made.

I went with the captain and one platoon, cutting across the clearing at a brisk trot. The major took the other three platoons. The plan was that they were to go roughly east, following the crescent-shaped treeline of Armagh Wood to the point where our advance on the 3rd had come to such a sorry end. There, the main body would engage the fort from the south, while we crept forward and assaulted it from the other flank.

In no time we crossed the clearing and turned due east. 500 yards further east, on the ridgetop, explosions from our artillery could be seen. To the rear the Germans were still pounding the trenches and the approaches to the wood, seemingly unaware the troops were elsewhere. Once amongst the trees those sounds lessened; the crackle underfoot and the drizzle of the rain absurdly loud.

'Hold up,' I whispered to the captain. With a hand he signalled a halt.

'Is that it?' came the whispered reply. Past the trunks of a few trees, maybe 30 yards distant and in the open, was a dark low-slung structure.

A crackling of rifle fire came from the far side of the clearing. If there'd been any doubt as to whether this was the strong point it was dispelled at that moment. From the structure sounded shots, followed by a rattling burst that lasted a few seconds.

I frowned. Someone had been too eager.

MacNamara and the platoon lieutenant were shouting instructions, assembling the men into attack formation. There was no need to be quiet any longer. The first wave of twenty took up a run, led by the captain. Hobson glanced over in my direction. He seemed to steel himself, then he stormed after the others. A white flare shot up from the fort, bathing the whole scene in a light so bright it might have been the midday sun.

The second machine gun opened up as they moved into the open. Rifles forward, bayonets flashing in the rain that still fell, they charged recklessly, screaming bloody murder as they went.

One moment Hobson was running. The next he was not. His head jerked, his rifle fell, and his body gave way – all in one breath.

The captain was the next to go down. He sort of crumpled and fell. To his left and right the two men beside him were hit. Undaunted, the second wave led by the lieutenant and a sergeant was already racing forward, barely ten yards behind.

I went in pursuit. Reaching Harry I glanced down. He was done for; a round had caught him square in the head. At that instant, all I could think about was poor old Mr. Hobson and his wife. I was running again.

Everywhere bullets were zipping. Thankfully the flare was extinguished.

Captain MacNamara, prone, had lifted himself up on a side with one elbow and was waving the men onward. *The fool! He was going to get himself killed!* I ran towards him, stumbling, nearly falling when a foot slipped off into a shell-hole – recovered – and ran on.

When I reached him, I slung my rifle over a shoulder and grabbed with both hands from behind. 'Hang on, I'm going to get you out,' I yelled. I went to lift him to his feet and he buckled. Only then did I notice he'd been hit in both legs. They were bleeding profusely. The machine-gun bursts followed one upon the other. Around me I sensed the attack was wavering. The men were hesitating, going to ground. The fire was too intense.

'Leave me,' protested MacNamara.

'Not a chance,' I replied and began dragging him back to the treeline, to shelter. It took longer than I expected but somehow we escaped their fire – the garrison had more pressing targets, I expect. At the first tree I came to I propped him up against it with his back to the trunk. 'Have a drink, sir,' I said, thrusting my canteen at him. He drank briefly but then put it down, wincing. A brief moment of silence passed between us in which our eyes met. Until I said, awkwardly, 'I'm sorry, sir.' I looked anxiously back over my shoulder. 'They need me. I have to go.'

'Go,' he replied.

'You'll be fine, sir.' And with that I was gone, my rifle already in both hands.

There were numerous little groups still fighting, but dispersed and uncoordinated. Some were prone, firing futilely at the strong point's walls. I watched as a half-dozen soldiers made a brave game of it and attempted a renewed charge, only to meet a hail of bullets. The lieutenant was nowhere to be seen. Behind some fallen trees I spotted a sergeant with a substantial party who were pinned down.

The strong point was little more than a large dug-out, earthen embankments to either side, a roof of thick timbers and sandbags. Where the exit had once been, facing west, the Germans had erected a wall of tree trunks, debris and sandbags with narrow slits for their guns. It was as good as impenetrable to rifle fire. Nor did the Lewis gun, whose distinctive chatter I heard to the south, have a chance. The only chance was at close quarters. That thought led to a plan, if something so paper thin deserved the name.

I sprinted left, on the assumption that a lone man on the far end of the machine gun's traverse might escape attention with a bit of luck. In that I was proved correct. However a round from a rifle is every bit as lethal as a round from a machine gun – in fact the Mauser and the MG-08 shared the same 7.92mm cartridge – so when I heard one whistle by my ear, I dove for the ground. Then I picked myself up and did it again. Running, weaving. Short sprints before crashing to the ground.

For the first time I could ever recall – and it wasn't because of the rum – I didn't feel the pulsing knot of fear in my gut, gnawing at me, dragging me down as surely as soles of lead might have done. My body had taken command and mercifully left my mind flailing to catch up.

I landed beside two soldiers in a furrow in the field. The strong point was not 10 yards away – so close you couldn't even call it a sprint.

'Are you two planning on sitting here the whole bloody war?' I growled at them. Before they could reply I heard the second machine gun open up – it was the one closest to us – and I jumped to my feet and ran like the dickens. If Fritz was shooting elsewhere he couldn't shoot at me was the theory.

I reached the side of the strong point and backed up against it. A quick glance around, then I grabbed for my satchel. *Jesus! Where were the Mills bombs?* There'd been explicit orders that each man should carry two, and a Mills bomb was precisely what I was intending to lob through the slit to my left. Then the memory of me placing the haversack beside Captain MacNamara as I gave him the canteen began playing in my head.

I mulled it over. There would be an entrance. There had to be. When I saw the two soldiers making a run for it in my direction, I took a deep breath, gripped the rifle and stepped around to the rear.

The entryway was nothing but a dark hole in the wall, easily big enough for me and a short Lee-Enfield. I stepped through it and fired at the first man I saw. Then another appeared out of nowhere. Flustered, I tried to work the bolt but was too slow, so I clenched my teeth and put my back and a foot of Sheffield steel into it. He sagged away. Behind him I glimpsed a sizeable room. At the far wall a row of soldiers was bent over with rifles to their shoulders. A little off centre, three men were tending to a machine gun that was thumping away, one firing, another nursing a long belt of ammunition out of a steel box, the last helping.

With a roar of anger I leapt at the machine-gun crew, stabbing with my rifle, first at one then the next. The man at the gun turned his head at the commotion behind, but too late. The look of sheer terror as I thrust the bayonet into his side is one I shall never forget.

Suddenly there were shouts of a tone and a vocabulary I recognized and I saw the familiar olive green rush past, his tin hat down low, bayonet extended. Like that the strong point was full of men. And like that the battle was over – abruptly – without a word. Twenty corpses, all clad in field grey, lay sprawled on the ground. The air in the dugout was hazy, the sharp sulfurous odour of gunpowder and cordite overpowering. The smell of battle. Battle won.

Planting the butt of my rifle on the ground I leaned on it for a moment. My head was swimming. When I lifted it again I became aware that the soldiers were observing me. One with a furtive glance to the left, another with a casual sweeping gaze that lingered that tiny instant too long. The whispered words spoken casually man-to-man were lost to my ears, but the looks they shot me revealed them. Self-conscious I turned away and left the strong point.

This battle was over, but the next awaited on the ridge. There was little time. The need for haste had been drilled into us too often to forget that.

The platoon lieutenant came charging up at the head of ten men.

'We've taken it, sir,' I reported.

The lines in his face softened as the relief hit, then hardened again with the recollection of his orders. 'Very well,' he coolly replied. 'Help me get the men assembled.'

It was the work of minutes before the platoon was once more on the move, this time spread out, heading east-southeast up the shallow incline of the ridge towards the scene of our old lines, less than 300 yards further. The savage devastation of Armagh Wood even more pronounced than it had been lower down. Underway, we soon encountered the three other platoons and joining them we strode on. The faces told the story: grim, determined, resolute. Behind we left the dead and the wounded where they had fallen. It couldn't be helped – the stretcher bearers would arrive shortly.

In the battalion orders the company objectives had taken no more than a single terse sentence to describe. Despite the paucity of words their intent was clear; retake trenches 51 and 52. The trenches in question were 600 yards northeast from Mount Sorrel, roughly the same distance again to Hill 62, and a little shy of the north-south road that had once marked the centre line of the ridgetop. On the other side of that road – now all but invisible for the sea of craters, old wire, and debris – were the former German trenches. I was quite certain the Württembergers had moved into ours in the interim.

'Look, the barrage is lifting,' said the major to the platoon lieutenant. 'Right on schedule. Get your men moving.'

We had reached the fringes of the wood, at the very crest of the ridgeline. From that point, the ground flattens to the east at some 50 to 60 metres above sea-level forming a plateau. On the edge of it, in daylight, grand views of Ypres and the Salient can be had – the enemy knew all too well what they were after. However, the bombardment was indeed lifting from our old trenches to the old German ones, presumably now their support lines. That was the signal for the final charge.

The company took it in a dash. A silent run of sixty seconds across open, shell-torn ground hoping not to sprain an ankle or awaken the devil. Gear clattering but boots muffled in the soft wet earth. The rain still falling, though not with the fury of earlier. We hit them in the flank, the stunned defenders still picking themselves up from the horror of the bombardment, nervous and unhinged and unprepared for the waves of cold steel that crashed down upon them. Three parties, including mine, swept past and on down a communication trench toward the trenches behind and threw up a block. When we returned to trench 52 it was over.

White Asteroid rockets were to be fired if a counter-attack was forming. Instead a single red flare went up. As it soared gracefully into the sky before arching over and flaming into a crimson ball, I took out my pocket watch and flipped open the tarnished cover. High above the flare glowed. It was 10 minutes past 2 a.m.; 40 minutes had elapsed since the attack began. For C Company the objective was attained.

Mount Sorrel. Hill 62. We carried them both. We got our own back. And as the breathless engineers arrived, almost in our wake to begin the pressing task of consolidation, I knew that the day to follow would sorely test us all. Equally I knew that we would not be budged. Not for anything. Not here.

CHAPTER 36

17th of June, 1916
E Camp, between Poperinghe and Elverdinghe, Belgium

In between the plywood huts on the muddy grass, the long wooden trestle tables and benches were laid out with military precision; the only jarring note the vase of flowers perched in the centre of each. It was something Bill Partridge would have appreciated. Something from home. The cooks and the assistant cooks, and a whole crew who had been pressed into urgent service were up early and long at work. Nothing had been left to chance. That was a lesson hard won this past year.

Today our brigadier, General Lipsett, was visiting – visiting and saying farewell in one fell swoop. Lipsett had been promoted to major-general and commander of the 3rd Division. His predecessor, General Mercer, once thought missing, was not missing for long as he was found in Armagh Wood late on the 3rd, a day after the German attack, a casualty of the same savage bombardment that had decimated his division. And so two weeks later, once the immediate threat to the Salient had been put to rest, a replacement was found.

Most of us who'd served under Lipsett thought him an inspired choice. He was a popular general and the mood in the camp had a certain festivity to it. Not least because only two days earlier the battalion had been in the trenches, between Mount Sorrel and Hill 62, rushed up after the attack to consolidate the line. A task to which no glory accrued even if the casualty toll might have suggested otherwise.

One of the men caught me staring at the tables. 'Should be a swell feed, Sergeant,' he said gleefully, not quite licking his lips.

Inwardly I grinned. But conscious my rank dictated I should maintain a certain distance, I threw up a smoke screen and suggested that there were plenty of tasks awaiting those who had none. With that he was gone and I was a step closer to becoming Sergeant-Major Atkins.

Back on Salisbury Plain eighteen months earlier I hadn't known the answer to Atkins's question – the one about why I was here. It was a perceptive question and it had taken me all of these 18 months to figure it out. But the answer was all around me; in the men who two days earlier had gritted their teeth and clenched their rifles as the German artillery tried to blast them to kingdom come, and who were now setting little plates on the table, arranging them exactly so; men joking with their buddies, having not long before helped one to a dressing post as he grimaced in pain from a piece of shrapnel or a bullet lodged within him; men strangely nervous that the general would be amongst us soon, but veterans of perilous hours marked by whistling steel fragments and concussions of high explosive. It had nothing to do with King and Empire. The King seemed a kindly soul but the empire was a concept far removed from my life; one I still hadn't wrapped my head around.

There was certainly no glory in what we were doing, only a fierce determination to get the job done, here in the mud and the blood-stained trenches of the Old World. But it could not have been a more glorious group of men.

It was for that reason that I felt justice was served. Without scandal or shame to Hobson's family, his unit or his comrades. An honourable death for a man who didn't deserve it. But those around him sure did.

I volunteered to write to Hobson's family. Naturally I didn't send the diamonds along to accompany his other effects. My letter was one of condolences, gentle words, and lofty praise; one I would have wished my parents to receive. Mr. and Mrs. Hobson would be devastated at the loss of their youngest son – black sheep or not.

'Sergeant?'

The soldier said it a second time, louder. Startled I turned to face him.

'Captain Critchley is looking for you.'

'Thank you,' I said, wondering what he could possibly want. That it would involve work was a given; the first person an officer turns to when there is something to be done is an NCO. And the general was to arrive within the hour. I left at a fast gait.

On this occasion the problems were solved easily enough and I felt confident the platoon and the company would pass muster. A week's mud and grime had been scrubbed away in the hot baths this morning, the uniforms were sharp; even the buttons were polished, of a sort. The smiles couldn't be bigger as the men had mustered for pay parade this morning.

First would come the inspection. Then the general would undoubtedly say a few words, a compliment or two amongst them if he was so inclined. Then when all was said and done, the battalion would sit down for the farewell dinner which I too expected to be pleasant. I was hungry already.

All went according to expectation until I saw the colonel whispering long and furtively into the general's ear. They were walking along the ranks. Within a stride or two they'd be at C Company.

Uneasily I sensed that it concerned me for the general suddenly glanced over in my direction, still attentively listening. Lipsett's reply when it came was brief and Colonel Rattray nodded. They made their way towards me. Their faces seemed more impassive than normal, even stern – or was I imagining it? I sucked in my gut and tried to look soldierly.

'Well, well. Sergeant MacPhail,' said Lipsett at length. Colonel Rattray stood a foot length behind, observing.

'Yes, sir.'

'Colonel Rattray informs me you were one of the guides sent to assist the 3rd Battalion during the attack.' He paused and glanced back at the colonel. 'I seem to recall your name coming up in another regard.'

I swallowed. 'Yes, sir.' *Wherever could this be going?* The only thing I could think of was the business with Hobson and Drinkwater, but it was impossible that they knew about that.

'Oh yes,' said the general, the recollection apparently coming back to him. 'I received a full and detailed report from Colonel Allan. In it he suggests you did precious little guiding in your time with his battalion.'

My eyes widened. 'Well, sir,' I stammered. This was the last thing I'd expected.

Colonel Rattray and General Lipsett were staring at me.

'However the colonel did write extensively about the events at S.P. 11. He told me you're the talk of his battalion. He also told me he's put your name up for a medal.'

What might have been a sparkle appeared in Lipsett's eye. Colonel Rattray was beaming.

'It's quite fortunate I'm visiting today for the colonel has asked a small favour of me. One which I'm only too happy to oblige him in.' There was no doubt now about the sparkle in Lipsett's eyes. 'Sergeant MacPhail, I have the honour to inform you that you are hereby promoted to lieutenant. Congratulations.'

'Sir?' The word croaked from my mouth. If he hadn't been a major-general it's doubtful if I would have managed that; most major-generals expect an answer rather than a mouthful of air.

General Lipsett offered his hand, followed by Colonel Rattray. In a haze I saluted them both.

'Thank you, sir,' I said to the colonel.

'You did it yourself,' Rattray replied. 'And the 10th Battalion needs some good officers, Malcolm.'

'By all accounts you've got yourself a very good one, Colonel,' added General Lipsett.

Dinner was a swell feed indeed, served up on china plates, with baskets of bread rolls and knobs of real butter. A half pint of dark beer was for many the highlight. I noticed little but enjoyed it all.

'Let me be the first to congratulate you, sir,' said the voice from behind.

He had it wrong if he thought he was the first. I'd already shaken hands and exchanged words with half the battalion. But I knew the voice out of thousands.

'Roy Dundas! What in heaven's name are you doing here?' The incredulity in my voice was nothing compared to what I felt. 'You're supposed to be in a hospital!?'

He stood rigidly at attention, saluting as I'd never quite managed to, a bandage on his forehead, another protruding from under his tunic, and a huge grin lighting his face.

'You really didn't think that just because you're a lieutenant I'd let you fight this war by yourself, did you? Not right when we're finally winning some battles.'

I hemmed and hawed. 'No. I see what you mean,' I said. Then I laughed.

For a few precious moments the war seemed a very long way off. It wouldn't remain that way. But if nothing else war teaches you to appreciate the small things in life.

Apparently Dundas thought similarly. 'Hey, I thought I saw some beer around here,' he said. 'Or, don't tell me you drank it all... sir?'

AUTHOR'S NOTE AND ACKNOWLEDGEMENTS

As 1915 dawned, the war on the Western Front had already solidified into the fixed lines of trenches and wire which we associate with it today. For much of the war the outlines of the front would change remarkably little, and it was in 1915 that this process of digging in for the long haul began in earnest.

The Canadian contingent, raised as a volunteer force from across the dominion, came from a far-flung corner of the Empire but arrived as one of the first British Army divisions outside the regular forces – a remarkable feat. Landing on Europe's shores in February of 1915, within short months they would be sorely tested, and from that time forth would play an important role in many of the war's pivotal moments.

Malcolm's story in *A War for King and Empire* is above all a story of the ordinary Allied soldier as both sides struggled to adapt to a new era of warfare. It was a time when the will to achieve victory proved greater than the means to do so. The cemeteries of Belgium and northern France attest to how the foot soldier paid the price in the pursuit of breakthroughs that never came, painful lessons that would need to be learned and relearned. All through this second year of the Great War, and on into the next, no battle was decisive, no strategy a solution. More often than not victory meant to stave off defeat. And to hope next time would be better. Two such battles begin and end the book. The first, Second Ypres, with its dramatic and horrifying use of poison gas, is well known to many. The other, Mount Sorrel, sadly less so.

While this is unapologetically a novel, not a history book, it is fiction firmly rooted in history. Though few will mourn the absence of footnotes or bibliography, rest assured they are there behind the scenes. I spent countless hours scouring war diaries and maps, histories and memoirs, letters, photos and more, anxious both to accurately convey the history as well as the myriad tiny details. I felt, and still feel, that the historical novelist must take good care with such things.

At crucial moments I allowed Malcolm glimpses of the broader war, but as a young private his story necessarily revolves around his own little world, that of the 10th Battalion. In my opinion what happened in the trenches best summarizes this period of the war. I hope in some small way to have opened a window into what it was like on the battlefields of Belgium and France more than 100 years ago.

All the senior officers described, and many others, were real people. While much of what I have them saying and doing is informed by history, the details and dialogue are almost always invented. The main characters, however, are my own creations. Malcolm himself, Roy Dundas, Bill Partridge and many others in Malcolm's circle of acquaintances, including his adversary Harry Hobson, fall into this category.

A great many of the incidents in which Malcolm is involved (not just the battles) are based on real events. One such event was the Doll Block robbery described in Chapter 10. Searching for something completely unrelated I stumbled across the story of this then-famous diamond heist. It became the cornerstone of the subplot involving Harry Hobson, who was an easy mark to pin it on, not least because the real culprits were never caught.

Learning about the German spy behind the lines at Plugstreet I was immediately intrigued. That became Chapter 20. The "spy" in question was eventually hunted down and shot, not by Malcolm and Roy Dundas, but by an unnamed soldier of the 7th Battalion. The details of this sniper in farmers' clothing and the setting where he was found were much as I described. The history neglects to mention whether a wine collection was involved.

Chapter 27 begins with the scene of a German plane being chased over the front lines. It is soon shot down and the Colt machine gun aboard reclaimed by the battalion which had lost it in the battles of April 1915. Ironically I think I would have felt uneasy inventing such things. Fortunately I didn't need to.

I have been very lucky to have had a number of wonderful people contribute to this book. Contrary to what you may have heard, books *are* judged by their cover, which makes me very fortunate to have had the extraordinarily-talented Jane Smith on my side. Diann Duthie had the dubious honour of reading my very first draft and was adept in steering me from my worst mistakes. Likewise, Dr. Gary Grothman did much to improve the manuscript and was a critical reader of the best kind, diving into the technical details and spotting the embarrassing inconsistencies and errors. The other key mate with me in the trenches was my editor, Dexter Petley. I couldn't have asked for anyone better. From his thoughts on the big picture to rooting out that one word too many, his input and support was tremendous. Finally, I owe a big thanks to Ian Forsdike for carefully and thoughtfully proofing the final product and catching all the things that somehow made it through. For those who may wonder, Corporal Frank Forsdike, who Malcolm had the privilege of meeting in the Plugstreet trenches, is Ian's great uncle. Frank Forsdike died in defence of Mount Sorrel and the Ypres Salient on that fateful second day in June 1916, his body never to be found. Today his name can be seen engraved on the Menin Gate in Ieper (Ypres).

If you enjoyed reading *A War for King and Empire* I would be very grateful if you left a review online.

For more about Malcolm MacPhail, the other books in the series, and the Great War, please visit my author site at www.darrellduthie.com.

Thanks very much for reading.

Darrell Duthie
Amersfoort

BOOKS IN THE
MALCOLM MACPHAIL WW1 SERIES

The books are most often numbered in the order in which they were written. Each can also be read on its own. Many readers prefer the chronological order.

WRITING ORDER

Malcolm MacPhail's Great War – (1917-1918)

My Hundred Days of War – (1918)

A War for King and Empire – (1915-1916)

Vicissitudes of War – (1916-1917)

A Summer for War – (1917)

CHRONOLOGICAL ORDER

A War for King and Empire – (1915-1916)

Vicissitudes of War – (1916-1917)

A Summer for War – (1917)

Malcolm MacPhail's Great War – (1917-1918)

My Hundred Days of War – (1918)

Printed in Great Britain
by Amazon

15007287R00185